CW00456196

MIM AND WIGGY'S
GRAND ADVENTURE

JAY MCKENZIE

Copyright © 2023 by Jay Mckenzie

All rights reserved. No part of this publication may be reproduced, distributed or transmitted in any form or by any means, without prior written permission.

Publisher's Note: This is a work of fiction. Names, characters, places, and incidents are a product of the author's imagination. Locales and public names are sometimes used for atmospheric purposes. Any resemblance to actual people, living or dead, or to businesses, companies, events, institutions, or locales is completely coincidental.

Serenade Publishing

www.serenadepublishing.com

For my beautiful niece Jennifer Donnelly. May all your adventures be grand.

MORE FROM SERENADE PUBLISHING

Brigadier Station Series

By Sarah Williams:

The Brothers of Brigadier Station

The Sky over Brigadier Station

The Legacies of Brigadier Station

Christmas at Brigadier Station (An Outback Christmas Novella)

The Outback Governess (A Sweet Outback Novella)

Heart of the Hinterland Series

By Sarah Williams:

The Dairy Farmer's Daughter

Their Perfect Blend

Beyond the Barre

A Dying Second Sun

by Peter A. Dowse

Winner Winner Chicken Dinner

by Sarah Jackson

A New Page

by Aimee MacRae

Middle Women

By Jack Garrety

For more information visit:

www.serenadepublishing.com

PART I

1

A GREEN THING

It was an uncharacteristically warm day for October. The sky was a pleasant shade of blue and there was even a suggestion of the big yellow ball they had heard stories about. Of course, none of this was at all appropriate for a British funeral. Drizzle and grey skies and whatnot were much more appropriate for a burial in a small corner of County Durham.

Mim pulled a rabbitty face at herself in the mirror. A lone green something snuggled between two of her teeth. When had she last eaten something green? She frowned, propping up her top lip so she could fish it out. Jamming a nail between the teeth, she seemed to push the green thing further in. It nestled between its toothy protectors, taunting her to come for it.

"Damn you, green thing".

She went in again, but the green thing backed further into its safe enclave.

"Mim!" Geraldine's shrill roar rattled up the stairs. Mim sighed, hoisting her lip up once more. It wasn't too obvious, the green thing. It could stay there for now.

Mim regarded herself critically. She looked a little like someone who had escaped from Monkwood Hall. *Monkey Dooly Home* they had called it when they were kids. She flushed shamefully and rumpled her face. The white bits of her eyes were a reddish-pink and her nose, moist at last check, was a similar shade. Her skin had given up the last of the summer freckles and she looked dramatically wan, like a Victorian painting of a sick woman. Maybe sunglasses were needed. They would of course have to come off in the church, but she thought that she might just get away with them for the hearse journey.

"Miiiimmmm!"

She pushed the sunglasses on and trudged headlong into a predictably horrible day.

Geraldine gripped her tightly at the bottom of the stairs, pushing her damp nose into Mim's ear. She smelled like Anais Anais; all flowers and the eighties. Mim opened her mouth so that she could block off her nose, glancing at the funeral assistants hovering politely by the front door. Geraldine let out a sob which sounded like a barking frog and Mim felt a dribble of snot trickle down her earlobe.

"Ahem."

A polite cough from one of the funeral assistants.

"Of course, of course."

Geraldine swiped a tissue across her face, held Mim by the shoulders for a second, then dragged her by the hand and to the awaiting car.

So shiny, thought Mim, the sun all bouncy and light on the obsidian surface of the vehicle. She kept her eyes firmly on the car they would be riding in, pointedly not looking at the one in front. She could not. It just was not possible that he was in there. Except that he was. Or at least his body was. She swallowed hard, a welcome tingle flushing through her body.

Geraldine cried the whole way. Mim stared at the floor of the car. A stowaway leaf peeked out from under her seat. She wanted to pick it up, but could not have broken free from Geraldine's clutch without some kind of tussle.

The church was only down the road - it would have taken ten minutes to walk to it - but they dawdled along instead. Mim wasn't sure why they had to drive so slowly. She pictured the hearse racing the short distance to the church, arriving with a cartoonish halt and twanging the coffin out. A chuckle wriggled up her throat. She success-fully turned it into a sob, causing Geraldine to squeeze her fingers a bit too hard.

They pulled up to the church slowly. Mim let her dark-ened eyes lose focus, so that the sombre faces of the strag-gling mourners became blobby. If she couldn't see them, maybe they wouldn't see her. She slipped ghostily from the car, successfully disentangling herself from Geraldine.

The latecomers hastened inside while smart pall-bearers hoisted the coffin onto their shoulders - stiff jackets restricting the grace of the hoist - and paused at the yawning door of the church.

"Oh Mim!"

Mim took Geraldine's arm, who gripped it like a wood-working clamp, and the pair followed the coffin onto the wet red carpet that split the smelly church in half.

Eyes turned. Heads swivelled. Tissues dabbed leaky noses. Mim could barely make out faces through the combined darkness of the sunglasses and the lack of light in the church. She reached for the glasses. Geraldine leapt in front of her.

"No Mim! We have to let him go."

Her face was contorted, features sloping like the victim of a recent stroke. Mim, startled, supposed she must have looked as though she was reaching for the coffin bobbing just ahead. She fixed her mouth into a grim line. She would have to wait until she got to her seat to take off the blasted sunglasses.

The two women shuffled sideways into the aisle at the front. Mim discreetly reached for her shades once more. Geraldine thrust a mansize Kleenex between her fingers, nodding knowingly. Unsure of what to do with it, the tissue hung between her fingers, wafting in the draught; a little flag of surrender to the horror that was this day. The dirgey organ music plodding about the church dwindled to a stop, and Mim lowered her buttocks to the pew, the only body in the room that moved. Geraldine yanked her back to standing.

"We come, each one of us, to pay our respects for a life lived." The minister was all doughy-faced concern and pudgy waving fingers. "We come to give thanks for that life, and for the love and memories that you shared with…"

A loud groan, like a dying cow bounced from the rear of the church. Mim twisted in the pew, taking the opportunity to pull the sunglasses off. A woman staggered to her feet and into the aisle, where she promptly fell flat on her face. Whispers leapfrogged the church.

"Who's that?"

"Not very polite."

"Think I heard her nose crack."

Someone - it looked a bit like their old neighbour Mabel - scooped the crumpled woman up and gussied her out of the church. The minister cleared his throat.

Mim sighed and turned back to the altar. Time to say goodbye.

2

FUCKING CHICKEN

Before...

"I don't want fucking chicken."

Steven did not want fucking chicken. Steven had however asked for fucking chicken yesterday when they had been watching Countdown. Mim remembered very clearly, because he had been celebrating a seven letter word. He had spelled *gargoyle 'gargoil'* and was so pleased with his brilliance that he awarded himself a two-stroke hand clap, before folding his arms smugly across his chest. He nodded.

"Let's have that weird chicken thing you do for dinner tomorrow."

Mim had clenched a fist. Not about the chicken, or the fact that he had called it weird, but about *gargoil. Gargoil!*

And now Steven did not want the fucking chicken. Mim did want the fucking chicken, but she wanted to be eating the fucking chicken up a mountain on the other side of the globe.

She placed her knife and fork on her plate, taking care not to clatter. "What *do* you want?"

"A divorce."

Mim looked at her husband of four years, then at the chicken on her plate. A blob of congealed grease perched awkwardly on the protruding bone. She was honestly just going to flick the blob of grease off when she reached for it, but the chicken found itself in her hand and she hurled it. The chicken slapped wetly on Steven's cheek.

"Did you just...did you?...You see?"

The blob of grease was clinging to Steven's eyelashes. She wanted to remove it. It didn't go with Steven's immaculate appearance and it was her job to make sure this was upheld. Except it wouldn't be anymore, would it? If they got a divorce.

Steven was standing now, shouting, arms waving. Something about her being 'straight-up mental'. Mim watched him calmly, feeling like she was floating about somewhere else. In the television maybe, which Steven liked to keep on permanently, though he had the good grace to switch it to silent when they were eating dinner. Except they were not eating dinner. Steven was wearing hers on his cheek and shirt, while his grew cold and sad on the plates her dad had given them as a wedding present. Steven swiped a napkin across his face, though failed to round up the grease-blob.

Apart from the eyelash intruder, he was looking particularly smart that day. Some presentation at work, she recalled. He was wearing the navy blue tie her dad had bought for him last Christmas. It was a smart tie, and Steven had put it on immediately, which had made her dad chuckle. Only later, he confessed, the word 'knob' was embroidered subtly into the fabric, over and over again. Steven had never noticed and Mim had never told.

Steven was still shouting. Mim was still sitting.

He pulled his seat around the table so that it was beside hers and parked his rear on it. He leaned to her, scooping one of her hands into his.

"I know you didn't mean that Mim. I know you're just upset. Believe me, this is hard for me too. But you and me, we're different people now. We were so young when we met. So young and unformed. We're not who we were when we met." He dropped his forehead to her hand. "You've got to let me go. I have to spread my wings and fly."

Mim cocked her head, wondering where he had found the speech. Those were certainly not his words. It wouldn't have been out of place in a Christmas Day episode of EastEnders, though his performance wasn't as good as the actors in the soap. Not enough sincerity. Everything felt very surreal. She glanced at the television. A rerun of a Russ Abbot show was playing with Russ dressed as Basildon Bond silently mouthing mean things to Bella Emberg.

She swallowed. "You want to divorce me?"

"Correct."

"Because of the chicken?"

Steven squinted. "No! Weren't you listening? It's us. Me, you. We aren't who we were. And I need to be me. And I suppose you need to be you."

"I am me."

Steven pinched the bridge of his nose. *That's what he does when he doesn't get his own way*, mused Mim. She had seen it at a stupid corporate dinner once when he had been - pathetically in Mim's opinion - begging for a promotion. He had used it on Dennis too, before he had packed up for America and never returned.

"You'll never get it, will you? You are the problem,

Mim. You are boring, stuck in your ways. Your social life consists of hanging out with your dad and psycho Trisha. I resent you Mim. I'm ashamed to be seen with you." He hopped back to his feet and took a glug of Mim's Ribena. "I'm going places Mim. I'm going places, and you are not."

Mim stared at him. He sat back down beside her. She licked her lips, wishing he hadn't touched her Ribena, and slapped her hands down on the table.

"Right. Where will you go?"

Steven blinked. "What?"

"Where will you go? You're going places, remember? I'm not. I would like to know where you will go."

"Nowhere." The grease was no longer on his eyelash. "I pay most of the mortgage. It's only fair that you go."

The blob of grease was now on Mim's finger. She felt strangely protective over it.

"What if I don't want to go."

And then Steven was on his feet shouting again, pinching his nose, pacing. Mim picked the grease from her finger, wiping it gently onto the rim of the plate. Happy that it was safe, she pushed back her chair.

He hovered all the while Mim packed the big orange suitcase that she didn't really like, but had bought because Steven particularly hated it. The hovering continued as she slowly folded some jeans, cardigans and jumpers and tucked them neatly into the case. Steven hovered still as she struggled to heave the luggage down the stairs and did not, Mim noted with irritation, offer to help.

In the kitchen, Shubert watched her mournfully, heavy head resting on oversized paws. She filled a Tesco bag with a bowl, tin of Mr Dog and a squeaky pig, before hitching him up to his lead.

"You're not taking the dog!"

Mim ignored him. "Come on Shubert."

The shaggy hound pushed himself to his feet, gave his grey locks a shake and trotted after Mim.

Getting out of the door with a fully grown Irish Wolfhound, a Tesco carrier bag full of dog paraphernalia and a massive orange suitcase was not particularly easy, and it certainly was not a dignified exit, but Mim kept her head high anyway.

"Shubert! Come back!" Steven made a valiant attempt to drag Schubert back inside, grabbing at his silver haunches. Schubert, with a swift waggle of his rear end, dislodged his erstwhile owner. Steven wept as the wolfhound made the executive decision to head into the night with Mim and her orange case. A small Mim and a massive dog made their exit under the carrotty glow of the streetlamps, Steven dropped to his knees, silhouetted in the doorway.

"Shubert! No!"

Mim bit her lip and marched as swiftly as one can march with such cumbersome adornments. She marched to the end of the street, rounding the corner before it occurred to her that she had no idea where she was going. She fished in her coat pocket for her phone.

"Damnit!"

The pocket was empty, save for a bobby pin and a bus ticket. She dug in her handbag. Not there either. She sighed.

It was a tight fit. BT phone boxes had not been designed with wolfhounds and suitcases in mind. It smelled of wee, and the plastic-covered instruction notice had been half melted, the surface mottled and bubbly. It was probably scorched by a bored teenager or two, lamenting the lack of things to see or do on the bland housing estate that covered the dandelion-carpeted paddocks where Mim used to play as a child.

She listened to the flat drone of the rings.

"Dad?"

Dad started his grumbly pre-amble, but Mim cut him off quickly.

"Dad, can you come and pick me up?...No, I can't get the bus...I've got Shubert...No, not at home...I'm on Cornwall Street...Yes, the phone box...Thanks dad."

Mim perched on the orange suitcase, Shubert's heavy head resting on her lap and waited, like she had countless times as a teenager, for her dad. And like she had done countless times as a teenager while waiting for her dad, Mim cried fat sticky tears.

———

She sank gratefully into her dad's lumpy sofa and took the mug of steamy sweet tea he proffered, inhaling the tang of the creamy silver top that he had delivered twice a week. The fire was crackling gently in the grate.

"I hope you don't mind Mim, but I called Sandra." Mim nodded, cheeks tight from the drying tears. Her dad continued. "She's good with this stuff. Hearts and whatnot."

He tucked his fingers into his belt, hesitated, and then plopped to Mim's side on the sofa. Looping one hand around to her shoulder, he rubbed a gristly chin with the other. Mim squeezed her eyes shut and let the salty tears leak out.

"Oh Mim!"

He pressed his forehead gently to her temple and patted her back. Mim leaned into him, succumbing to the sobs.

"Whatever it is, you're going to be just fine." Shubert regarded him doubtfully. "She will! She's my little Mimsy."

Mim sobbed harder, body shuddering with every breath and wrapped an arm around her solid lovely dad. He smelled faintly dusty and of own-brand laundry detergent and she breathed him in.

Bong.

Dad's archaic doorbell sent Schubert into a frenzy, barking wildly at the foreign noise.

"Shush, Schubes."

Her dad leapt from her side gratefully. Mim heard the door open, shut and a low murmuring out in the hall.

"Hello Mim!" Sandra's eyes and cheeks gleamed, her voice ringing with an unnatural brightness. "Terry said that you were feeling a bit blue."

Mim bit her lip as Sandra started pulling items out of the tartan shopper she pulled behind her. A ten pack of flower-patterned Kleenex, a pink, fluffy-jacketed hot water bottle, a travel Scrabble set and - the piece de resistance - two hip flask-sized bottles of Tesco Napoleon Brandy.

"I got two because these were on special in Tescos. Such good value."

Terry clinked three glasses onto the coffee table, pouring a gleaming glug into each. Mim, tea thoroughly discarded, knocked hers back in one. She winced at the delicious burn in her throat then licked a stray droplet from her lip. Terry and Sandra sipped theirs, watching her carefully.

"What's he done?"

"Sandra!"

"Oh come on Terry. It is him, isn't it love?"

Mim nodded.

Terry ran a hand through his thinning hair. "You don't have to tell us. But if he's hurt you, I'll have to kill him."

"Dad!"

"Sorry. But I will. No-one hurts my little Mimsy-pie."

A grin tugged at Mim's lips. "Dad, I'm thirty four. I can look after myself." She snorted. "Well, obviously not, because I'm here."

Both Terry and Sandra rubbed an arm each. Sandra took Mim's glass from the cradle of her hands and topped it up for her. She sipped this one delicately. Mim stared into her drink, Sandra and Terry stared at Mim and Schubert stared at a moth fluttering around the lamp in the corner. The fire crackled.

"Right. Well let's have a nice game of Scrabble, shall we?"

3

THE EYE OF THE KITTEN

A leathery black lump swung towards her face.

"Trisha, be careful!"

"Buckets of soz. They just make me feel ready for action."

Mim had never been to boxercise before, but Trisha swore by it, even having purchased her own boxing gloves. Mim had to make do with a slightly damp mismatched pair fished out of a plastic box by the door.

"You'll get rid of your anger towards Steven and you get fit to boot!"

"I'm not angry towards Steven," grumbled Mim.

"You should be."

The community centre hall was packed with women. Mim and Trisha were the youngest by about fourteen years. Mim waved a fat gloved hand at her old primary school dinner lady, who stopped grappling with a punching bag long enough to give a cheerful waggle back, before pummelling it with renewed vigor.

A brightly clad blonde woman who could have been

anywhere between forty and eighty clapped her hands, before pulling on bright red boxing gloves. Trisha nudged her.

"That's Linda."

"Right ladies. Into lines. Are. We. Ready?"

An enthusiastic cheer almost lifted the roof. "Woo," contributed Mim lamely. The women arranged themselves into ranks, the bounciest of them jostling for the front spot by Linda. Trisha pulled Mim towards the middle.

Linda crowned herself with a headset and mic that reminded Mim of Madonna. Though her lycra was all Jane Fonda. She bent from the waist to press a button on the CD player and they were off.

Doof. Doof doof doof. Doof doof doof. Doof doof doof.

The unmistakable pump of *Eye of the Tiger* blasted, filling the space, pounding their ears.

"Really?"

Trisha shushed her, eyes narrowing, gloves raising to her face. Mim noticed that she was the only person in the room not to have raised her hands, so she did, feeling self-conscious.

They waited. Mim's eyes danced, wondering what she was supposed to do. The second round of doofs finished, and some of the women crouched a little, anchoring themselves to the ground.

Doof!

Arms and boxing gloves shot forward, one arm, then the next, marking out a steady but ferocious rhythm with the music. Tendons strained, bingo wings wobbled and all eyes glared at invisible opponents.

Mim pushed her gloves forward, trying to keep in rhythm with the other boxers, feeling very silly indeed.

"Uppercut!"

The boxers changed their punch. Mim had just started getting the rhythm of the first type when she realised that everyone was doing something else. "Oh balls."

"Imagine it's Steven's receding chin!"

Mim pushed her arms upwards feeling like a bad parody of Rocky. A couple of the women near the front were making growly panting noises.

"Hooks!"

They changed punch again and Mim was completely lost.

"Twist the balls of your feet!" Linda hollered, even though she was wearing a mic. Mim tried watching Trisha's feet - how was she getting them to twist that quickly?- but then fell completely out of synch with her arms.

"Wah!"

"That's it! Let it out Mim!"

Mim tried to pummel and twist with the others. Some of the women near the front added grunts and roars to their growly-panty repertoire.

"In the face ladies! Get that bastard in the face!" Linda's eyes gleamed with mania. Glancing sideways, Mim spotted the same ferocity in Trisha's face, and in fact, on the faces of all of the other women. "Who you punching, Trish?"

"Steven."

"Oh." Mim dug deep to find some anger, but the digging and punching just made her feel tired. She flapped her arms around and made a concerted effort to become invisible.

"Break his face girls!"

"Raaaaahhhhhhh!" The women screamed.

"Rah," squeaked Mim.

Trisha was punching a punching bag. Mim was supposed to be holding it steady, but the gloves were making it really hard and it kept hitting her in the face.

"I forgot to tell you Mim, I've got a book you've got to read."

"Is it like that weird space robot sex one you loaned me last year?"

"No! This is brilliant. It's this woman right, who goes off to find love. Travels the world, she does. You should do that."

Mim chewed her lip, stopping only when the bag hit her in the face again. Mercifully, Trisha had a kittenish punch when it came to the bag. "Where would I go? And who with? I can't go on my own."

Trisha stopped punching, gloved hands dropping to her side. "You have to go on your own. It's like a spiritual journey or some shit, find yourself. That sort of thing." She stroked Mim's head with her glove. "I'm worried about you."

"You should be. I'm barking."

Trisha hugged her. Mim angled her head away from the sweat puddle pooling in her best friend's collar bone hollow. She blinked a fat tear out, tried to wipe it, thumped herself in the eye with the glove.

"Look, read the book. Let's have a think about ways to make this all better."

"I reckon it'll take more than a book to make this better."

Trisha nodded. "Of course it will. But it's a start." She bashed the bag.

"Ladies! Time to tidy up."

Mim and Trisha joined the throng of degloving women tidying up the community centre, and for a small moment, Mim felt both wretched and elated.

4

THE UNRIVALLED SEASIDE RESORT
FOR HEALTH AND PLEASURE

"Surprise!" Trisha flung open her arms like a hostess on The Price is Right presenting a lovely caravan or a set of golf clubs. Except this was just her usual rusty Ford Fiesta with it's boot gaping open.

Mim looked at Terry and Sandra, standing beside her on the garden path. They nodded encouragingly.

"Are you giving me your car?"

"No!" Trisha jogged up the path. "I'm taking you away for the weekend. Let's call it a recovery jaunt."

Sandra proffered Mim's old Head bag that she used to carry her PE kit to school in. The artificial lilac leather bulged. "I packed you some nice clothes, although I really should take you shopping when you get back."

Mim shook her head. "I'm just not really in the mood."

"Don't be silly, Mim. You'll have a lovely time." Her dad took the bag from Sandra and plonked it into Trisha's boot.

"But what about work? I've got an extra shift tomorrow."

"Work, shmirk. You work in a friggin call centre Mim. I

think they'll manage." Trisha hugged Terry. "It'll cheer you up." Trisha was all authority and village-woman wisdom. She jostled Mim to the car, plopping her in the passenger seat. "I'll look after her!"

Terry and Sandra waved from the doorstep. Mim pulled a face like a stray dog being shipped off to the pound.

"Road trip!" Trisha ground into first gear, flipping a double cassette of *Now That's What I Call Music Volume 22* at Mim. "Chuck that on will you? It's brilliant for driving to."

"Where are we going?"

"You'll see."

Mim popped the tape out of the cracked box and wedged it in the player. "You are the only person left in the world with a tape player in your car." She turned the tape box over in her hands. "How old is this thing?"

"It's from ninety two! What were we up to in ninety two?" Trisha slapped Mim's leg.

"Geography homework, I should imagine. Can I sleep?"

"You can try!" Trisha cranked the volume on the synthetic beat of Erasure's *Take a Chance On Me*.

"Really?"

Trisha nodded. Mim shook her head, but felt a smile stretch across her mouth. "You're a numpty."

"Yes! But I'm the best numpty you'll ever have." She cranked the volume up to drum-shattering level. Trisha belted out the first line about changing your mind and still being free.

It was hard not to join in on the taking a chance bit.

Mim grinned. Trisha was the least cool person she had ever met. And that made her cool.

The Sunrise Guest House, Blackpool was a bit of a misnomer. For a start, they were on the west coast. Clouds lurched overhead and the breeze suggested that it had never even heard of the sun, let alone had ever made contact with it. It was trying, Mim supposed, to look sunny with its terracotta paintwork, but it was a bit forlorn with peeling window frames and grubby net curtains.

Trisha consulted her phone, then frowned up at the property. "Looks better in the picture." She jammed her phone in her pocket and shrugged. "It'll do."

They carried their bags through the open front door, greeted with the scent of burnt toast and carpet shampoo. Nestled between dusty, overbright artificial flowers was a bell which Trisha dinged, summoning a tiny woman from the shadows. She glared at them, then indicated that they follow her. They smirked at one another and trotted dutifully through to a room. Five small round tables squatted obscenely close to one another, each topped with yet more artificial flowers. A pine-clad bar teated with optics lurked in the corner. Every wall had ten or more pictures in ill-assorted frames - lurid oil paintings of donkeys, the Blackpool Tower, and yet more flowers - interspersed with glimpses of a browny-yellow flocked wallpaper.

"I'm Mrs Gatherer." She examined them with mousey-little eyes. "We only do double beds here."

Trisha shrugged. "That's fine."

Mrs Gatherer scowled, dipped a hand in her cardigan pocket and lifted out a scrap of paper. She examined it thoroughly, before sighing and beckoning them back out of the room. They followed her up the squeaking staircase as she rattled off 'house rules' over her shoulder.

"Breakfast is at seven-thirty sharp. No latecomers. No vegetarians. If you come in past eight pm, use the silver key." She stopped on the stairs, rotating to glare from a height. "If you come in past eight pm, you do it silently. Our guests like to sleep." A mangy grey cat on a chair meowed its agreement, as Mrs Gatherer continued up the stairs, leading them up a second, narrower flight. "No guests. No funny business." Reaching a tiny landing with two plain MDF doors, she produced a key with a plastic fob attached and fumbled one open.

The door coughed to reveal a tiny attic room whose double bed took up the majority of its space.

Trisha poked her head in. "Do you have anything bigger?" She turned back, but Mrs Gatherer and her cardigan were thumping down the stairs.

Mim laughed, clamping her hand over her mouth and edging inside. "Cosy!" She plopped onto the yellow bedspread, sinking deeply in the middle. "It's trying to eat me."

Trisha joined her, rolling into a heap in the sunken centre of the bed. "I think they call it bijou." She pulled a rabbity face at Mim. "She thinks we're lesbians."

Mim laughed. "What's the plan, Stan?"

Trisha stood. "Let us go forth and Blackpool!"

Over a hearty pub lunch of sausage, chips and peas, Mim was starting to feel a little better. The three pints of Heineken were probably contributing too. Trisha popped her last pea in her mouth and took a long gulp of beer.

"So, how bad was it?"

Mim groaned and hid behind her hair. "You remember

that time you had your ingrown toenail removed?" Trisha shuddered. "Worse than that. Like, if you'd got gangrene. And then your toe had fallen off and you had to walk on crutches forever. And had to take Colin with you to the toilet for the rest of your life because you couldn't manage anymore."

"I get it. Awful." She downed the rest of her pint. "I'll get us another, but then I want details." Trisha skipped to the bar. Mim very much wished that Friday night had not happened, and that she never needed to think about it again. But it had, and she did, because Trisha would never let her off something so significant without all of the mortifyingly dreadful details.

Trisha returned, slopping beer all over the table in her eagerness. "So, he called you Thursday."

Mim nodded. Steven had called her Thursday, his voice syrupy with persuasion. *"You know I still respect you, Mim. And Uncle Paul loves you."* She had muttered, *"unlike you."* Somehow, he had talked her into it. *"But I'll meet you at The Nelly before we go."* At their old local, he had explained that his family would be *"utterly devastated"* to hear about their golden boy and his childhood sweetheart breaking up.

"So you agreed to go along with it?"

Mim sighed. "It seemed like the easiest option."

"So you got there?"

"So we got there…"

Uncle Paul had indeed been delighted to see her, insisting immediately on a dance. *"You've a lovely rump, Miri-am,"* he declared, weighing it up with both hands. She made a polite exit to the toilet.

Steven's Aunty Jean was emerging from a cubicle with Nanny Peg. *"Oh, she's got terrible trouble with her irritable bowel nowadays. Can't stop crapping at the mo!"* She had deposited

Steven's gran at the sink and pulled Mim to one side, without, Mim noted, washing her hands. *"Now then Miriam, we're all dying to know when you and Steven are going to pop out a sprog."* Mim caught sight of her fuschia visage in the mirror and for a moment, panicked that she was about to cry. *"Oh no Miriam! Is it true? We all guessed you must be barren."*

"Fucking hell Mim! That's the worst!"

"Oh, it gets better."

Aunty Jean evidently passed on the news that Mim's womb was an inhospitable cavern of emptiness, as she was touched sympathetically by all of Steven's female relatives at some point during the night. Gabby Torrence from the corner shop whispered *"mine's adopted. Don't tell anyone. You can always move somewhere else, pass it off as your own."* Uncle Jeff suggested she could *'try going at it a bit more."*

Trisha barked a laugh. "Sorry Mim. It's awful. Just awful." She sniggered again, taking another sip of her beer. "Please, carry on."

Uncle Paul had got trashed and grabbed her boob. Joan Kelly got her heel caught in Mim's skirt and ripped it. And Kerry Kelly spent all night flirting with Steven. To his credit (Trisha snorted), he didn't do too much flirting with Kerry Kelly ("That's because she looks like a goat in a human costume") but he also didn't pay much attention to Mim until after the cake. While Uncle Paul was murdering *Please Release Me* on karaoke, Steven insisted on slow dancing with her. She fluttered at his touch, and for a moment, resting her head on his shoulder, it felt like nothing had happened. That after Uncle Paul cried as he did near the end of every party, they'd return to their little lego semi and laugh about how crap everyone was.

"Right," he'd said. *"I've got a taxi booked. You'd better come outside."* The pair had climbed into the cab, waving their

goodbyes like a royal couple and pulling off into the night. *"Where to from here mate?"* asked the driver.

"Just pull up around the corner please," Steven had instructed. They pulled up outside of a kebab shop. *"You'll be alright to walk from here."* It was a statement, not a question. Steven started humming, tapping out a message on his phone. Mim tutted, then leapt out of the car, before Steven could see her tears.

"He's such a cock Mim! I hate him." Trisha rubbed Mim's hand as she watched the tears drip from her best friend's lower lashes.

"He went the wrong way."

"What?"

Mim dabbed her eyes. "In the cab. He went the opposite way to home. He didn't go home."

"Jesus Fuckbollocks." Trisha swallowed a glob of beer. "Where do you suppose he went?"

Mim shrugged, grimacing. She sniffed hard. "Yay for freedom." She raised her glass and downed the beer. "Now let's get our serious Blackpool on."

Gypsy Carmella Rose: World Famous Teller of Fortunes had a narrow shop wedged between a newsagent and a donut stall. The orange and red paint was illuminated by two rows of bulbs, that seemed like a bit of a waste during the day. Photographs hanging in the window showed a tiny woman with a brillo pad of dark hair smiling between an array of celebrities. They were all there; Cannon and Ball, Cilla Black, Frank Bruno, The Chuckle Brothers, Max Bygraves, Bruce Forsyth and even The Nolans.

"Remind me again why we're here."

Trisha started bouncing on her heels. "To see what your future brings, Mim. To see if you'll find real love."

"I did, remember." Mim rolled her eyes. "You don't actually believe in this crap, do you?"

"If it's good enough for a Chuckle brother," Trisha grinned, "it's good enough for us."

Mim poked her head around the open door. "I don't think there's anyone here."

"I am!" A man of around forty with brown floppy hair and a paunch stepped from behind a curtain. "Come in. Sit down while I sort myself out."

Mim and Trisha exchanged a glance.

"Is Carmella Rose here?"

The man shook his head. He looked tired. "No. Her gout's playing up something chronic. I'm her son, Graham. I do readings too." They took in his pastel-shaded Pringle jumper. "Who's first?"

Trisha pointed at Mim, who shrugged. "Me, I guess."

Graham dipped behind a curtain, gesturing at Mim to follow. She turned to Trisha, crossing two fingers hopefully.

Inside the inner sanctum, things were a little more gypsyish: Turkish rugs, soft lights draped with scarves, mirrored cushions and gilt framed images of yet more celebrities. Mim sat on a plastic seat covered with a crocheted blanket. Graham took the other, a velvet covered table resting between them.

"What'll it be? Palm, tarot or crystal ball?" He was rearranging a chiffony-coined scarf over a picture frame.

"What's the cheapest?"

"Palm. Twelve pounds."

Mim examined her palms. "Right then. Palms."

"No, just one palm for twelve pounds. It's twenty for both. You want both?"

"What's the difference?"

Graham sighed, combing a hand through his hair. "Well, two's better, obviously. But I'll do the two for twelve because my mum's not here."

"Thanks."

"Now, pay first, then you just pop them here on the table."

Mim dug two fives and a coin from her purse and put them on the table in front of Graham. She placed her hands on the velvet cloth, palms up, peering at them like Graham was doing, wondering what he could possibly see in the pink rivery valley of her hands.

Graham ran a finger across her left palm. It tickled a bit. Mim shivered.

"Hmmm." Graham frowned. "Right, well. We've got all the major bits covered here. Travel first. You're planning a big trip, aren't you?"

"No."

"Ah. Well, you will. You'll go on a big trip. All over. Far and wide."

"When?"

"Really soon."

"Who with?"

Graham leaned in closer. "A man."

Obviously not, thought Mim.

"And death. There's a death coming up."

"When?"

"Really soon."

"Who?"

"A man." He paused and licked his lips. "And you're doing something educational now?"

"No."

"Well, you did some education?"

"I went to school. Is that what you mean?"

"Yes, that's it." Graham licked his lips. "You like your job, don't you?"

"Nobody likes their job."

"Well, you'll get a new one. Later. You'll like that."

"What about love?"

Graham drew her hands close to his face, then put them back down on the table. "You married?"

"It's complicated."

"Yes. There's someone you like, isn't there?"

"No."

"Well, there has been. Am I right?"

"Yes."

"And you've had a heartbreak, haven't you?"

"Hasn't everyone?"

Graham smiled sadly. "Not everyone, no."

"So, the love thing? Am I going to get some?"

"Probably."

"What do you mean 'probably'? Can't you see a big love in there? A handsome stranger?"

Graham wrinkled his nose. "Yes. No. I'm not sure. It's a bit fuzzy."

"Great." Mim sat back in the chair and folded her arms. "So a lonely future, a marginally less boring job and death. That's all you've got for me?"

Graham grinned. "No! Not lonely." He flapped his hands at her. "Give me them back, I'm not done."

She sighed and handed them over, his thumbs on her pulse, her wrists cradled in his palm. Graham leaned in so that she could feel the air from his nose brushing her skin.

"There is a man. Very important. Not love though. Companionship, I think."

"Am I going to get with a gay fella?"

Graham chuckled. "Whoever you get with, they'll be the lucky one." He glanced at her. "Sorry." He dropped her hands. "That's all I've got."

"So, he said I'm going to marry Colin, we're going to live long and happy lives on the farm and I'm going to have a big fat lottery win with the numbers nineteen, seven and thirty five, as long as I don't tell anyone." Trisha clamped her hand over her mouth. "Crap. Do you think I've cursed it?"

Mim swatted Trisha's arm. "I think you're a gullible idiot." She glanced around the pink and blue lights illuminating a sticky-looking dance floor. Four women, who were possibly having trouble remembering their fortieth birthdays, were jiggling out of time to *Karma Chameleon,* observed critically by two sniggering bespectacled men. Other than that, they were the only patrons at *Rewind!* "This place is a hole."

"But the music! It's epic. We should dance."

Mim shook her head. "I am quite drunk and not in the mood." She gestured at the women on the dance floor. "I'm sure they'd be happy for you to join them though."

Trisha beamed. "You won't mind?"

"Not at all. Go."

Trisha took a greedy suck on her straw, topping herself up with Pina Colada, before shaking her bum and wiggling over to the women. They hugged her delightedly, one toppling on her diamante-studded heels. Mim smiled and concentrated hard on her Sex on the Beach.

"Hello." One of the sniggering bespectacled men had

apparated at the end of the booth. He gripped a nearly-empty pint glass with both hands.

"Hello."

"Can I sit with you?" He gestured at the purple vinyl with his double-gripped drink.

"Oh!" Mim searched for a reason why he couldn't. She was waiting for people? There was no space in between her invisible friends? She had leprosy? "I suppose so."

She wiped a sticky finger on her jeans. "I'm not feeling very sociable though."

Bespectacled sniggerer put his glass down on the table, removing his hands very slowly. "That's okay. I'm not either. You just looked like the sanest person here."

"It's a pit, isn't it?"

He shrugged. "Darren's just broken up with his fiancee." He indicated his companion, who had now infiltrated the dancing group. "He just wanted to go somewhere cheap and cheerful." Darren resembled one of those inflatable people they blow up outside of car sales yards. He danced as though he had left his bones at home with his inhibitions, though his face registered a steely determination.

Mim drained her Sex on the Beach. "Well, it's got cheap covered."

A shriek loped from the dance floor as the DJ threw on *Don't You Want Me?* The women formed a circle around Darren and shimmied around him as he mouthed the lyrics to each of them in turn.

"Can I buy you a drink?" The man indicated both of their glasses with flat palms. "Don't worry, I'm not coming on to you."

Mim shrugged, wondering why he wasn't coming on to her. "Erm. Okay. I'll have a Blue Lagoon please."

The DJ had assaulted them with Rick Astley, Wham!, and a spot of Duran Duran before Mim learned the man's name. Nigel was twenty-eight, worked in 'pest-control' and was in Blackpool on a conference. "Rat catching. You'd be surprised." Mim shuddered. "The conference finished yesterday, but I thought it would do Darren some good to have a night out."

Mim had finished her Blue Lagoon. "Can I get you another drink, Nigel?" She leaned in to him, casting a surreptitious glance at Trisha. Her friend was still on the dance floor, hair clinging sweatily to her forehead. Nigel shrugged.

"I'll have what you're having."

"Said the actress to the bishop!" Mim snorted. "Sorry. I've drunk a lot and forgotten how to flirt."

Nigel raised his eyebrows, hitching them up over the rim of his glasses. "That was flirting?"

Mim grimaced. "Pretty bad?"

"Woeful!"

"Aw." Mim pressed her head on the table. "Sorry." She kept her head there.

"Well, if it's any consolation, it wouldn't have worked anyway. I'm sort of gay."

She sat up. "Sort of gay, or actual gay?"

"Actual gay."

"Graham was right! Are you in the market for a beard?"

Nigel laughed. "Who's Graham? And no thanks, I'm all good being beardless."

Mim sagged. "Ah well. I guess I'll just be alone." She slid out of the booth to get the drinks. Trisha was shim-

mying around Darren, who was being spanked by one of
the other women. Mim waved, pointing at the bar. Trisha
flapped a dismissive hand and put her shimmy face
back on.

The barman ignored her and carried on looking at his
phone. "Excuse me." He held up a finger, eyes glued to the
screen. Mim folded her arms on the bar, something tacky
glueing itself to her elbow. "Excuse me."

He looked up. "Wait."

She tutted. The barman slowly placed his phone back
into his pocket, took a languorous stretch before ambling to
where she stood. "Yes?"

"Two Blue Lagoons please."

The barman sighed. "They take too long to make."

"Oh, and you're rushed off your feet, are you?"

"I am actually." He put both hands on the bar like an
A-frame easel. "Couple of pints do you?"

Nigel and Mim had almost finished their pints.

"Miiiiiiim! You should totally get with Darren." Trisha
dragged an equally sweaty Darren to the booth. "He's all
messed up too." She flung Darren into the seat beside
Mim. He grinned, showing a set of undersized, jagged
teeth. Mim wondered how his fiancee had managed to kiss
him without shredding her lips into a million pieces. *No
wonder she left*, thought Mim. Then she felt bad. Darren was
still showing her his weird teeth, a mixture of hope and
desperation bulging behind his glasses.

"So Mim. They've got a pool table at their guest house.
We should go and play pool."

Darren and Nigel exchanged an unreadable look, before shrugging simultaneously.

The intrepid pool-table hunters trotted up a street remarkably similar to the one Trisha and Mim were staying on. These guest houses were set apart in their prestige by having steps up to their front doors instead of being flat to the street. Most of the windows were darkened save for a glowing blue or red vacancies/no vacancies bulb in their corners, though their doors stood open.

"Here we are."

Darren led the way. They teetered up in single file, Trisha, then Mim, then Nigel. Mim stepped over the threshold when the line halted.

"Wait! This isn't our guest house."

Nigel called from the back of the line. "I think we're next door."

Mim and Trisha giggled as they turned and tottered back down the steps, onto the street, conga-ed along a little, then up the steps next door. It did look identical.

"Dolphin's Retreat. This is us."

A large velvet dolphin picture hung above a table in the entrance hall, seemingly coloured in with some felt-tip pens that were on the brink of running out. Trisha prodded its snout as she passed.

"I used to colour those in when I was a kid."

Nigel led them into a large drawing room with a yellowy wallpaper dizzyingly adorning every wall. Most of the space was taken up by a full-size billiard table: a tiny chaise lounge in green satin and a Bontempi electric organ in the corner being the only other items of furniture that had managed to squeeze their way into the room.

"All right. Doubles." Trisha thrust cues at Mim and Nigel. "Me and Nigel against Mim and Daryl."

"Darren."

"Darren. Me and Nigel against Mim and Daryl."

The game was slow. Nobody potted anything for about ten minutes. Evidently none of them had a career as a pool hustler in the making. Trisha whooped gleefully anytime Nigel managed to get a ball anywhere near a pocket, and booed, pantomime audience style, whenever Mim or Darren got close. Trisha barely managed to hit a ball, but declared it 'tactical' when she did. Darren disappeared to their room to fetch their bottle of Frangelico, which they set about demolishing.

About twenty minutes into it, the door sprung open. Three men, clad only in their boxers nodded politely, before edging around the table to the Bontempi organ in the corner. One sat, the other two stood at his shoulders. He flicked the *on* switch, cracked his knuckles, and sounded out a flat chord. Satisfied with what he heard, he proceeded to play. Mim recognised the tune, but couldn't remember what the song was. The two standers took a deep breath.

"Oh little town of Bethlehem, how still we see thee lie."

Their voices were rich, tremulous and confident. Mim, Trisha, Darren and Nigel looked on, utterly unable to react. The organist bashed out the notes, which sounded more like an accordian than a piano, the plasticky twang of the keys flicking up at the end of each push. The singers closed their eyes, lips moving as though in prayer.

"Oh come to us, abide with us, our lord Emmanuel."

The organist flicked the off switch. He stood. The

three men turned to face their audience, dipped a bow and headed for the door. The watchers smattered a tiny round of applause waiting for the door to close behind their impromptu entertainers.

The door clicked shut. The foursome glanced at one another.

"Did that just happen?"

They exploded simultaneously, laughing so hard their guts ached. Mim felt tears rolling down her face. Trisha clutched her, legs crossed, face purple. Nigel was doubled over, while Darren had to prop himself up with a billiard cue. Mim stepped backwards and fell over a stray ball, landing in a pile of mirth on the carpet. They roared harder, Mim too.

Mim's ringtone hollered from her handbag. She scrabbled to find it, eyes not working properly. She plucked it from her bag.

"Who is that?" Trisha was now clinging onto the side of the billiard table.

Mim squinted. "Geraldine."

"Don't answer!" shrieked Trisha.

Mim fumbled for the answer button, swiped it across and whipped it to her ear. "Geraldine!" She rolled her r's, singing the woman's name at her down the line. The laughter of the other three continued.

"Oh Mim! He's dead!"

5

SAUSAGE ROLLS

Mim chewed on a sausage roll. The grease formed a film on the roof of her mouth and had coated her fingers in more of the same. She wiped her hand on the hem of her dress, scanning the room for Trisha or her dad. Dad was wedged in a corner by Geraldine and Nanny Peg. She watched him sigh. Mim knew that he was deciding if he had enough alcohol to drag him through the endurance sport of conversing with Steven's family. Sandra fed another pint of John Smiths into his free hand, before disappearing with a wink.

Trisha's laugh gave up her location. A hearty guffaw, accompanied by wild waving paws drew Mim's attention to a table by the door. Her best friend was regaling something hilarious to Uncle Pat, who looked confused. She tried to catch Trisha's eye, but she was too caught up in her own oration. Mim sagged, trying hard to blend in with the curtain.

"Hello Mim."

"Dennis!" Mim sloshed the remnants of the port Aunty Maud had bought her, all over her jacket. Steven's older brother, immaculately clad in a well cut navy blue suit plucked a napkin from a table and handed it to her.

"I thought you weren't coming. Your mum said…"

Dennis waved a hand. "Flights, complications, you know how it is."

Mim didn't know how it is, but nodded anyway. She dabbed at the sticky liquid with the napkin, but that only made flecks of paper stick to the port. Deciding she didn't care about the stupid jacket, she tossed the napkin on the table and shrugged. Dennis stared at her. She coughed, bringing herself back into grieving widow mode.

"Thank you for coming Dennis. It means a lot."

He leaned close. Mim felt his breath tickling the little hairs in her ears.

"I know you'd split up, Mim. And I know he didn't want anyone to know." She felt her breath quicken. "And here you are, still covering for him. He always was an insufferable arse." He straightened up, still close enough to smell his aftershave. It smelled like the sea and sandalwood. "You always were too good for him, Mim." Dennis pecked her on the cheek, before being engulfed in a blobby aunty.

"Oh my God, Dennis is so hot!" Trisha sidled over, tugging Mim's arm. "John reckons he's doing really well in America. You picked the wrong brother Mim! I'd totally have a turn if it wasn't for Colin. Hey, is your Uncle Pat going a bit deaf or something? He didn't even laugh at my Barbara Windsor impression."

The sound of the assembled crowd dropped, the faint tinging of a fork striking a glass piercing the room. Geraldine, on tiptoe, was poised on top of a blue cushioned chair, hat slightly askew. She stopped tapping the glass as the room fell silent. For a moment, nothing happened. Her face blank, as though she had quite forgotten that she was standing on a chair in a room at her son's funeral, she suddenly roused herself.

"Oh. Right. Dear friends. My son Dennis would like to say a few words and raise a toast."

Dennis, startled, gathered his features together, taking the glass and the fork from his mother and helping her down from the seat. He cleared his throat.

"Friends, family. We come here today to say goodbye to Steven. My brother. My mother's youngest son. Husband to the beautiful Miriam." Dennis looked straight at Mim. "Sometimes we don't realise how precious something is until it's too late." He took a sip of his mother's wine and grimaced. He lifted the glass. "Steven Ian Webster."

The room collectively lifted their glasses. "Steven Ian Webster," they muttered. Mim vomited into her handbag.

6

CRAFT ENTHUSIAST

"Do you want tea or Buck's Fizz?"

Trisha loitered halfway between the kettle and the fridge.

"Both, please."

Trisha shrugged, flicked the kettle switch and swung the fridge door open. The Buck's Fizz cork yielded with a disappointing pop. Trisha peered down the neck of the bottle before tipping its entire contents into two bulby wine glasses.

"Get started on that while we wait for the tea."

She deposited one in front of Mim, took a slog of her own before parking her rear on the table. Mim wrestled a packet of chocolate Hob-Nobs open and flashed her friend a half smile.

"Trish, we're so British." Mim took a bite of a Hob-Nob, oaty biscuitiness crumbling brazenly onto the table. She washed it down with a gulp of Buck's Fizz, before continuing. "Tea and biscuits in a crisis. Such a cliche."

Trisha's eyes widened.

"You didn't say it was a crisis! You just said 'come now,

bring booze'. If I'd known it was a crisis, I'd have brought, I dunno, brandy or something a bit more crisis-worthy."

Mim shrugged.

"Buck's Fizz is fine. And I'm not sure it actually is a crisis. Not really."

Trisha transferred from the table to a chair - which was of course a more potential-crisis-worthy item of furniture to be sitting on - and began aiding Mim in the important business of eating Hob-Nobs. They each finished their first biscuit in silence, took a swig of the sticky orange drink and waited for the kettle to reach its crescendo. The switch flicked to *off.* The friends looked at it, then back at one another.

"Screw the tea. What's going on Mim?"

Mim reached into her cardigan pocket, pulling out a compact black mobile phone. It was an older style, nothing fancy.

"I found this. It was wedged in the back of his sock drawer."

Trisha turned it over in her hands.

"You think it's his?"

Mim took it back, pressed a few buttons and presented the screen to her friend.

"It's to CT: 'SHE'S GONE. SHE TOOK SHUBERT. GUTTED. NEED "COMFORT" ;-)'. Who's CT?"

Mim took it again, scrolled and handed it back.

"It's the only contact in there. And look at that!" She jabbed the screen hard.

"'CAN'T WAIT TO GET YOU NAKED AGAIN, YOU SAUCY MINX.'" Trisha gasped. "What a total dick, Mim!" She worked through the messages. "Oh Mim! He's been screwing this harlot for ages!"

She glanced up from the messages. Mim's eyes were wet.

"Mims, don't cry. He's a total dog!"

Trisha wrapped her arms around her friend and let her sob hot tears onto her shoulder. Mim swiped her eyes and unlaced herself.

"I don't know why I'm surprised. The cockwaffle lied about why he wanted me out. But I should have known. I'm so stupid. It hurts. I did love him."

Trisha roared to her full height.

"You can't waste any more tears on him, Mim. He kicked you out of your own home, banged this woman, was too cowardly to tell his mum what he'd done, made you pretend you were still together at his stupid uncle's party and then, then that bastard went and did what he did."

Trisha was marking the indiscretions off on her fingers, pulling them so far back, they looked on the brink of snapping.

"Trish, technically we can't blame him for the last bit. That bit wasn't his fault."

Trisha's rant was not yet over.

"The pathetic little turdburger went and got himself killed. Selfish. Bastard."

Mim snorted.

"Why does him dying make him selfish?"

"Aha! Because now you've got no closure. No proper end. You can't go shouting at him. Well, you could shout at a headstone, but my Aunty Bibby got sectioned for doing that." Trisha paced. "Oooh, you could punch CT!"

"I'm not going to punch anyone."

Trisha sank back to her seat, chewing her thumbnail.

"You do need closure though. I read it on this blog. Otherwise you'll get all weird next time you've got a fella."

Mim didn't want a fella. She also didn't want to 'get all weird' though either. Perhaps she did need some closure. She reached for another Hob-Nob and sank her teeth into the buttery oats.

"I will think about the closure thing. But right now I want to get day-drunk with my best friend and cry a bit more."

———

CT, it turned out, was Cheryl Tiplady. She was a 'business administrator' - which apparently is some sort of receptionist who needs a fancy title to make herself feel important - at Steven's insurance firm. Steven had no hobbies and never went anywhere socially with the exception of work functions, which Mim found buttock-numbingly dull, and he had been increasingly keen to attend them alone of late, so it stood to reason that CT the SEXY MINX might be someone he worked with.

She found a 'Business Administrators Team' shot from his firms' website of four women smiling in front of a tree (which was odd as there were no trees anywhere near Steven's office. They must have gone on an outing to have their picture taken by a tree). Two were tall, one was wider than she was tall and the last one was shaped like a robin: round body, spindly legs and a head that sprouted straight from the torso, forgoing any suggestion of a neck. The three with necks wore jauntily-angled red scarves. The other one possibly regarded scarves as discriminatory. Mim scanned the names at the bottom, hoping that the neckless one might have the initials CT. Sadly, it appeared that

Cheryl Tiplady was one of the tall ones and was probably better looking than her, but only very slightly, and mostly because Mim had been doing a lot of crying of late. Mim wouldn't have described her as a SEXY MINX though. She looked, at best, competent.

A quick Facebook stalk confirmed her suspicions. Aside from a naively public profile, Cheryl clearly had far too much time on her hands. Big into *crafts*. Not just one craft, but a whole cacophony of crafts; stencilling, cake decorating, crochet, knitting, glass painting, plasticine modelling. And she clearly wasn't very good at any of it. Mim clicked on a picture of what appeared to be a knitted green ghost. The caption read: *So proud of how my octopus turned out!* It had five likes, which Mim thought was at least five too many. She squinted to make out what a pink lump on another picture was supposed to be: *Peppa Pig cake! Nailed it.* Mim snorted.

She opened another picture which was of a glass vessel, decorated with a childish painting of an orange fish puttering about a blue background. The vase was filled with chrysanthemums and captioned: *Flowers from my man, in hand painted vase!* There were three comments.

Dreamy! read one.

*Aha! Your mistery (*this was an actual spelling mistake on the comment) *man does exist!*

The third comment read "*Did he 'lose points' avec ladies for not wanting a woman with cellulite? Hahahahah!!!!!!*

Mim had no idea what that meant. She typed that weird missive into Google. About halfway down the page, she found *Ben Folds Five - Steven's Last Night in Town Lyrics*. She sagged a little then clicked back to the picture. There it was in the background: the knob tie.

She pressed her head onto the keys of her laptop.

"Uuuuuugggggghhhhhhhh!"

————

A tray would have been a good idea, grumbled Mim's brain, balancing two mugs of tea and a plate of custard creams in lethargic hands. One custard cream was wedged in her mouth, but multi-tasking was proving a bit much, and she had forgotten how to eat and walk. She pushed open the living room door.

"Tea," she announced, though what came out was "uguee", crumbs projecting themselves artfully on the carpet. Schubert hoovered them up.

Geraldine twisted awkwardly from her position on the floor, startled. Her eyes were rimmed red, her pointy nose dripping. Mim had only been gone a few minutes to make the tea, but evidently her mother-in-law had found something else to weep over. An hour ago, it had been a sock. Before that, a postcard that she had sent to them from the Algarve ("such a wonderful holiday"), and earlier in the day she had bawled at a photo of their old cat, Lemons. Mim resigned herself to this being the longest two days of her life.

She popped the tea and biscuits onto the coffee table and patted Geraldine's back dutifully.

"Look Mim." Geraldine pushed a glass paperweight into Mim's hand. She enjoyed the cool weight for a moment before glancing at the familiar Lightwater Valley logo. The theme park had been a favourite place for every kid from the area to spend a day or two during the summer holidays. Geraldine waited expectantly.

"Lightwater Valley. Great place. Fun times."

Geraldine burst into a fresh round of tears. "He loved

that place." She snuffled around for a new tissue as the previous one dissolved soggily on her trouser leg. Mim handed her one.

So did everyone, thought Mim meanly. *It's a theme park. That's what teenagers like.* The forlorn figure on the floor was making the task ten times harder and at least fifty times longer. Mim wanted everything out by the end of the week. She had an estate agent coming to value the place and wanted it to look like the bland, sellable box they had been shown eight years ago. Geraldine didn't know about the estate agent, or the photos of furniture ready to post on Durham Buy, Swap, Sell, and Mim had no intention of mentioning it until they had got rid of Steven's things.

"I should really let you keep this." Geraldine touched the paperweight with her fingertips.

"Honestly Geraldine, you take it." She put the paperweight in an already densely packed box. "We never went there together anyway."

Geraldine's face crumpled again. Mim jumped in before yet another round of weeping.

"Drink your tea and have a nice custard cream." She patted the woman's shoulder again and grabbed another biscuit.

The doorbell buzzed. Mim hoped it would be Trisha, here to save her from more weeping over inanimate objects.

She pulled open the door to be greeted by a face that was largely obscured by a bandage. It took her a moment to place the rest of the face.

"Oh, hello. I'm…"

"I know who you are, Cheryl Tiplady."

The eyebrows shot up, the eyes widened. The effect was disconcerting, the white of the dressing standing out against her sunbed-tanned skin. Cheryl followed Mim's gaze, rendering her temporarily cross-eyed.

"I broke my nose."

"Yes. At my husband's funeral."

Cheryl's eyes darted. "Can I come in?"

"No, Cheryl Tiplady. You cannot come in."

Cheryl edged closer, placing a foot on the fluffy carpet. "Please. It won't take long." She straightened up, both feet now inside Mim's house. Mim took a step towards her, placing her in a position where Cheryl could either topple out of the house, or would have to push past her to get in.

"Mimmy, I found his Dennis the Menace pencil case!" Geraldine's quivering voice distracted her, giving Cheryl time to squeeze by and into the living room.

"This won't take long."

Mim sighed and followed the bandaged thing into the living room, where Geraldine now cradled a karaoke dvd featuring songs by Elton John. Schubert growled at the odd-looking stranger.

"Geraldine, I wonder if you could pop to the shop for me. Cheryl and I need some, erm, cake."

Geraldine blinked at the stranger then back to the dvd. "He loved Elton John."

Mim hoisted the woman to standing, the dvd dropping to her feet. Geraldine scooped it up and plopped it into her box.

"Right. You want cake?"

"Yes please."

"Fondant fancies?"

"Perfect."

Geraldine turned to Cheryl. "You can never go wrong with Mr. Kipling." She picked up her handbag. "You should get that looked at, dear. Whatever it is that you've done."

Mim bustled Geraldine out, slamming the door and turning back to her lurking nemesis. "Well?"

"I was his friend. From work. I just needed to...Well, I..."

Mim sat down heavily. "I found his phone Cheryl. I know what was going on."

Cheryl blanched and leaned into an armchair. "I'm sorry?"

"Is that a question or a statement?"

"Neither. Both. I don't know." Cheryl pressed her hands to her eyes. Mim almost felt sorry for her. Almost.

"You knew he was married, right?"

Cheryl whipped to face Mim. "Look, I didn't come here to talk about my relationship with Steven."

"Oh! So you came to the house of the widow of the man you were bonking to discuss Claudia Winkleman's new hairdo, I suppose? Or who's going to die next in Emmerdale? Or the truth about why the Spice Girls disbanded?" Cheryl flinched as Mim leapt to her feet. "So tell me, Cheryl Tiplady, what exactly did you come here to talk about?"

Cheryl stood, the women face to face. Steven's lover was taller than Mim, not helped by the neat pointy heels that she was wearing. Mim, head tilted slightly upwards, regarded the woman squarely. Cheryl would have been looking down her nose at Mim, had she still had a visible nose. As it was, she squeezed her eyes tightly shut.

"I have come to collect something of mine."

"And what might that be?"

Cheryl stepped back, indicating the stairs with her arm. "I know where it is. I can just go and get it."

Rage welled in Mim's stomach. "No you can't. You are going nowhere. Tell me what it is and I'll decide whether you can have it or not."

"I'll grab it and be gone in a minute." Cheryl took her first few steps towards the stairs before Mim leapt on her, bringing her down to the floor. Schubert barked with delight.

"What is it? Where is it?"

"It's mine. I need it. Get off me."

"What is it?"

Mim sort of sat on Cheryl who tried to wriggle free. Everytime Cheryl got a limb out of the melee, Mim had to change her position to grab it. It was a little like *Whack A Mole*, just altogether more suburban. Cheryl poked Mim in the armpit. Mim pulled her earlobe.

"Ow, get off me."

"You get off, you noseless slapper."

"No wonder Steven didn't want you anymore."

Mim growled, grabbed her ponytail, and waggled her head from side to side, bits of carpet fluff getting stuck on her stupid bandaged face. Schubert ran around the pair barking and wagging his tail. At one point, excited by Cheryl's flailing and now shoeless foot, he took it for a mate, enthusiastically jabbing his pelvis into her calf.

The door clicked open.

"Oh!"

Geraldine dropped the box of Mr Kipling's Fondant Fancies. "What's happening Mim?"

"She's trying to steal some of Steven's things!"

Geraldine shrieked. "The nerve!"

She hit Cheryl's kicking legs a few times with her hand-bag, before tossing it aside and grabbing her ankles. She pulled Cheryl, bringing Mim with her with a scary amount of strength for a small birdlike woman. She made some good progress in dragging her to the door. Mim hopped off so that Geraldine had less weight to pull and leaned into Cheryl's bedraggled face.

"What was it?"

Cheryl sagged. "Holiday fund. Under the mattress."

Her face was pulled along the carpet where she was unceremoniously dragged into the street. Geraldine deposited Cheryl Tiplady on the wet path and stepped back into the doorway.

Mim and Geraldine watched the figure pick itself up, attempting to salvage a shred of dignity, and retreat with a slight hobble into the closing afternoon.

"Good job Geraldine."

———

The bulging envelope sat on the table between them.

"Open it," Mim instructed. Trisha did as she was told, sliding a finger under the tacky seal. She peeked inside, before drawing out the contents and placing it reverently down.

"Have you counted it?"

Mim nodded. "Four thousand pounds. In fives, tens and twenties. That's a lot of pounds to count."

"Wow."

"I don't know whether he'd saved it, or they'd both saved it together."

"Either way, it's yours now. Right?"

Mim stretched a small grin across her mouth. "Well, it was under my mattress. What is she going to do? Sue me?"

"She won't. She'd have to admit to being a homewrecker, and she clearly has no backbone." Trisha smirked. "Or nose."

Mim tapped a finger on the hefty pile of notes. "With this, what I got for his stupid car and selling the house, I'm going to be okay for money for a bit."

"And…?"

"And, I've been thinking about the book. You know, maybe doing something like that."

Trisha whooped and ran from the room. Returning a few seconds later, she had a heavy looking shopping bag dangling from her arm. She hefted it onto the table, squashing the neatly arranged four thousand pounds and proceeded to unload the contents.

"I got these out of the library." She lifted out some dog-eared Lonely Planets, piling them up in front of Mim. "I thought we could at least think about planning a trip for you."

Mim picked up *Vietnam*. "Oh! I don't know if I could go anywhere like that!"

Trisha opened the kitchen drawer where they kept oddments, like elastic bands, bits of string and internet bills that didn't need to be sent anymore. She fished out a spiral notebook filled with old shopping lists and doodles of rabbits and birds and a chewed biro. "Here we go! Let's plan you a trip."

"Do they eat much cheese in Vietnam?"

"I don't know. I doubt it. I think they eat spring rolls and noodles and things." Trisha flipped to a blank page near the back of the notebook. "Mim, you can't plan a trip based on whether or not they eat much cheese there. You might as well not go on a trip if that's your main criteria."

"I suppose." She flipped through the book, pausing to

examine a picture of a turquoise wash with green lumps poking out of it. "That looks pretty."

Trisha was earnestly writing something in the notebook. Mim flicked further, a picture of a grinning woman in a pointy hat making her smile. Maybe she could go somewhere like that.

"Right." Trisha put her pen down. "We've got Vietnam, Bali, Andalucia and Australia. Spot anything you like, I'll write it down."

Mim liked the look of it all. Trisha wrote it all down in the notebook. Three hours later, she had flights booked to Vietnam, Bali, Andalucia and Australia.

7

OH GOD, WHEREFORE ART MY SPIRIT?

Mim kicked a stone into the gutter. The heavy door appeared to be locked and she was reluctant to try the fat, brassy knob. *Friends Hall* was etched into the stone lintel above the entrance in a distinctly unfriendly font. She dug her hands in her coat pockets and wondered for the seventh time why she had even come here. Trisha's dulcet tones echoed around her skull. *Closure.* She reached into her bag to check the time on her phone (again!), poking her dog-eared copy of *Eat, Pray, Love* into the depths next to the half-eaten, fluff-wearing stick of Edinburgh Rock she had discovered at lunchtime.

"Are you here for the service?"

A thin voice floated out of the door that had opened - just a crack - silently. Mim cleared her throat, making her way up the unswept path, crisping wafer-thin leaves beneath her boots.

"Erm, yes. Five o'clock. The *Divine Service.*"

The words felt clunky and alien in her mouth. A small turtleish head poked out from behind the door jamb, carrying a face that must have been at least eighty years old. Somewhere beneath the folds and creases, a mouth opened.

"Well, you had better come inside."

The door swung wide. Mim glanced at the empty street, willing some friendly looking congregationers to skip up the road. She plucked her phone out and took a deep breath. Four fifty-seven.

Oh, you'll enjoy it. It's all joyful and supportive.

She cursed Sandra under her breath. It all sounded well and good in her dad's cosy kitchen, but three minutes to go and she seemed to be the only person here. She scowled and stepped over the threshold.

Mim traipsed through the grey-walled entrance area and into the church itself. She was surprised to see that it looked a bit like an actual church. Her breath caught in her throat remembering the Easter Methodist Services her mother used to take her to when she was small. The same dusty, papery smell, with a hint of mildew tickled her nostrils. She cleared her throat again, eyes adjusting to the subdued light. The turtleish person turned out to be a very small woman in a red skirt, moving painfully around the space, distributing hymn books onto chairs.

Mim shuffled into a seat near the door, examining the leather-bound hymn book on her chair. She flipped through it, pretending to be fascinated by the perks of *Dwelling in Beulah Land*, hoping that the turtley woman would not make conversation.

She needn't have worried. The turtley woman was inching through a curtain behind the altar. Mim let her eyes wander. There was an unhealthy predilection for velvet - the curtains, cushion covers, bits of material draped over the altar - in dark, mossy colours and adorned with tassels. The walls were painted a sickly mustard with an assortment of crosses dotted about, seemingly without any design integrity. Perhaps, they had been placed randomly to hide holes in the walls. There were wooden crosses, paper crosses, knitted crosses and - most weirdly - a cross made out of glued together pasta shells. Mim stifled a giggle and made a mental note to regale every detail to Trisha.

Uneven footfalls interrupted her thoughts. She watched a curly-haired man with a pronounced limp make his way down the aisle and sit in the front row. *Ah good! Somebody equally as tragic as me*, she rejoiced, although she sincerely hoped that she was actually the least tragic person in the room.

Two more pairs of feet trod dully onto the carpet. A middle aged couple in matching rotundness waddled toward the front, parking their ample rears on three chairs at the opposite side to the limping man. The rotund man blew his nose loudly. Mrs Rotund tutted and shook her head, her helmet of backcombed hair staying exactly where it was. Mim was glad there were no candles.

The turtley woman poked her head from behind the curtain and examined the congregation. Satisfied that this was as good as it was going to get, she slid out and took her place behind the altar. A long (velvet!) scarf was draped around her neck, reaching to the floor on both sides.

"Mr Ketchen, please close the doors."

Mim swivelled to see a gargantuan figure in a too-small suit pushing the double oak doors closed. She felt a jolt of panic. She did not want to be shut in a room with these weirdos. She swallowed and took a deep breath. *Closure. Closure.*

"I am Minister Dorothy Ogden. Welcome."

Minister Dorothy Ogden scowled at them. Mim

wondered how glarey she got when she was in an unwel-
coming mood.

"We close the doors so that the spirits may enter and
feel safe, and so that Satan knows that he is unwelcome
here."

Dorothy Ogden leaned forward and glared at the door.
Mim frowned. *The spirits can get in, but Satan can't? Why, she
wondered? Does Satan have some kind of door phobia?* She
disguised her snort as a cough and arranged her face into
neutral.

"We begin by singing hymn number forty from your
hymn book. *Oh God, Wherefore Art My Spirit?*".

The limping man pushed himself to his feet, while Mr
and Mrs Rotund had to help each other up. Mim stood
awkwardly and flicked through her hymn book.

"We must sing loud! We must sing clear! Let our vibra-
tions gather the spirits into this space tonight!"

Minister Dorothy Ogden threw her arms wide and her
head back.

Mim was not sure whether she was meant to start
singing or not. She looked at the unfamiliar words in the
book as the pause dragged on.

Honnnnnnk!

Mim dropped her hymn book as a discordant note
punched onto an organ broke the silence. She hadn't even
noticed the wizened elf of a man wedged amongst stale
pipes. He was at least one hundred and seven years old; he
made Minister Dorothy Ogden look positively youthful.
Apparently, the introduction ended and it was time to sing.
Mim was made aware of this by the unusual mixture of
sounds floating out of the congregation. Limping man's
voice was around two and a half notes above where it was
meant to be with a precarious wobble to it. A low growl

tumbled out of Mrs Rotund, a little like an irritated gorilla, while Mr Rotund's squeak belonged under the sea, communing with the whales. Minister Dorothy Ogden had the most impressive voice though. It appeared that there was no connection between her vocal chords and her ears, so far removed was it from the actual melody. It wiggled and vibrated somewhere a long way from the actual notes.

"When Satan springs from here to there,
May we open up our heart for prayer."

Mim pressed the giggle down that was threatening to escape. The organ tried to drag the singers with it, but to no avail. She opened her mouth in a futile attempt to join in, but had to close it again when the ripple of laughter surged once more.

"Oh God, oh God, oh God! Wherefore art my spirit?"

Oh God indeed! Mim covered her mouth with the book. God, if he existed, would certainly not be looking for their spirits. More likely he would be looking for a cure for chronic singing enthusiasm whilst removing his ears and weeping into a Margarita.

She snorted, wishing she could join him. Mercifully, her snort went unnoticed as the organist's weedy arms pumped - brow furrowed, armpits moistening - in preparation for the crescendo.

"Oh God!!!!!"

They chorused with zeal.

"Oh God!!!!!!"

They squeaked, honked, growled, warbled. Mim's body shook.

"Oh Goooooooooooddddddddddddd!!!!!!!!!!"

They climaxed, holding that last note for all it was worth. Mim was racked with the silent heaves, willing herself to hold it together. The organist let the last note go, spent, dropping back into his chair. One by one, the congregation dropped off, except for Minister Dorothy Ogden, clinging onto the note like a lover dangling from a cliff.

"*Goooooooooooodddddddddddddd!!!!!!!!!!*"

The note was somewhere between a chainsaw and a hornet attack. She finished, dropping her head to her chest, eyes pressed tightly shut in ecstasy.

And that's when Mim lost it. Right in the silence. Stabbing the heart of the post-choral glow they were basking in, Mim laughed uncontrollably. Tears poured from her eyes, her mouth stretched so far she could have swallowed an ocean and she had to cross her legs to stem a wee. The laugh echoed about the weird chapel, bouncing off the walls, burrowing into the velvet, rattling through the pasta-shell cross. She knew they were looking at her, but her eyes were screwed so tightly shut that she couldn't see them. She had to get out.

Legs still crossed, she shuffled out of the aisle with as much speed as she could muster. She elbowed Lurch out of the way to pull the door open.

"*Aaaagghgh!*"

It was locked. She burned with shame, but the laugh was going nowhere. A key protruded impudently from the lock. She turned it and stumbled out into the street.

Mim half ran, half fell like a hunchback with two broken legs as far as she could, before sitting down on a wall. She gulped some air, wiped her eyes and sighed.

"Well, that went rather well."

She giggled again. Trish would love this. She might insist that they come back together. Mim coughed. Nothing on the planet could ever convince her to go back there again.

Mim sighed. No closure today. Not for Mim. Hopefully, the Rotund's or Limpy would get some lovely message. Maybe Minister Dorothy Ogden would get divine instruction to never sing again.

A final giggle floated out, and Mim realised that this was the best she had felt since Steven died.

A few exploratory plops of rain parachuted to earth as the bus appeared at the end of the road. The droplets, delighted with what they found, summoned all of their relatives and treated Mim to a right good soaking. By the time the bus drifted to a halt beside her and sighed its doors open, the bottom of Mim's jeans were drenched, water sucking from the gutter to her knees like a heavy boot. She went to leap on the bus, but found that her feet would not move.

"Haway love. A haven't got all day y'kna."

She glanced at her feet, deciding that they must have got sucked into a puddle. Shrugging, she squelched one up into the air, relieved that it did move after all, and hopped on the bus. She dragged a wet strand of hair out of her eye and fumbled for her bus pass while a puddle formed at her feet.

"Ya pass has expired."

"What?"

"Ya. Pass. Has. Expired."

The purpley, balding bus driver plucked the pass from her fingertips and tossed it, the offending article landing semi-submerged at her feet. She stooped to retrieve it, catching a glimpse at her face reflected back from the puddle.

"Wah!"

She stood. Her reflected face looked like a middle aged man. Glancing back down, she saw nothing but her drowning pass. She whipped it up, examining it closely. She frowned. There was still another three weeks on it.

"Look. It's still got three weeks on it."

The driver pursed his lips, a cursory flicker of the eyes searching out the date. He purpled harder.

"My mistake."

He glared. Mim shlopped out of the puddle and trudged to a seat. There was only one other passenger on the bus. A tiny woman who was more coat than person peeked out of an oversized puffer jacket that would have looked more at home on a nightclub bouncer than a shrunken-headed little pensioner. Mim smiled at her, rewarded with a startled little "oh!" and headed to a seat near the back. A navy-grey wash hung heavily outside. She watched the closing shop lights slide by, slowly at first, then stretching out as the bus picked up speed. She let her eyes relax, and town slipped away blurrily.

Her phone pinged. Trisha. A simple

well????

She threw back a quick reply.

On the bus. I'll call when home. Too funny!!!!

She peeked back out of the window as they shot across the brief countryish divide to the sprawling development of Lego houses. It was dark now. Her pale reflection ogled her in the window. She looked like crap on a stick.

A second reflection joined hers. She shrieked, twisting in the seat. A man sat on the seat beside her, peering with bald curiosity. Mim glared pointedly at the array of empty seats stretching in every direction. "Can I help you?"

"You what love?" The swaddled old woman in front twisted in her seat.

"Not you." She jerked a thumb at the man beside her. "Him."

The old woman frowned, muttered something about *"young 'uns and the drugs"* before hunkering further into her coat.

Mim watched the stranger beside her. The man wrinkled his brow, causing a clump of greying hair to flop forward, coming to rest on his nose. Perturbed, he did not appear to know how to move the hair from his face. He blew a few times, a foosty waft sailing out of his mouth, but to no avail. He tentatively prodded it with a finger. Delighted that the hair acquiesced, he tossed it back onto his head, before examining the finger with wonder.

Mim cleared her throat. "Are you okay?"

The man grinned and held the finger aloft. "Who would have thought it? That this finger would have life again." He chuckled, before poking himself in the leg a few times. His voice was soaked in the plummy tones of a television period drama, and though he was shabby and smelled a bit like a bin, his clothes growled with high quality.

Mim wriggled closer to the window, making herself as small as possible to avoid contact. She gazed outside, but kept an eye on his reflection in the window. He was exploring his face with the wondrous finger now. He poked his cheeks, before having a little quarry into his nostril. Mim tutted and shook her head. "Every time." Trisha had once bought her a birthday card that said *Psycho Magnet* on it. If there was a crazy in the room, they would find Mim.

"Can I see if it works on you?" Mim pretended to be deaf. "I want to see if it works on you."

The finger jabbed her in the ribs.

"Ow! How dare you!" She stood, hugging her handbag to her chest. She tried to squeeze by, but the man was too ecstatic about his working finger, and to get by, she would have had to straddle him. "Could you let me past please?"

He grinned up at her. "Of course. Where are we going?"

The old woman was peeping over the collar of her coat, eyebrows raised in alarm. Annoyed as Mim was, she was glad this weirdo wasn't picking on an old woman. Mim flashed her a look of reassurance.

"I am going to sit somewhere else. You can stay here."

The man shook his head. "I do not think that that will work. By all means, give it a jolly good whirl, but I think that you are barking up the wrong tree." He shifted his knees to the side, though made no attempt to stand. Mim turned to face him, so that her buttocks would not be too close to his head. She edged sideways and scarpered up the aisle closer to the woman. *Safety in numbers*, she thought. Sliding into the seat opposite, she swung around.

"Agh!" The man was right beside her. "Why are you following me?"

The old woman squeezed out of her seat, waddled up the aisle and muttered something in the driver's ear.

"How lass, who ye talking to?" The driver regarded her warily in the mirror, the bundled woman hanging onto a plastic rail by his side.

"Him! He's following me!"

The driver tutted, shaking his head with the old woman. "Frickin mental that one." Bulkily, the old woman sat as close to the driver as she could

"Why are you following me?"

The man frowned. "Following you? Heavens woman! Got a bit of a high opinion of yourself, have you not?"

Mim leapt up and darted to another seat. He was right beside her once again. "I'll scream if you don't stop it." She jabbed her handbag at him. The man shrugged, a thin smile tugging the corners of his mouth. "I'm taking a picture. I'll show the police." Phone in a shaking hand, she clicked. "I'll do it. I'll scream."

The old woman shuffled back to the driver's side, eyes glued to Mim.

The man folded his arms. "So you said. Please do get on with it."

Mim opened her mouth. The man nodded encouragingly. She closed it again. Then opened and closed it once more. He snorted.

"Waaaaaaaaagggggghhhhhhhhhh!"

She punctured the air with one of the most impressive screams she had ever released.

"Will you pack it in?" The bus jerked to a halt, the old woman nearly catapulting through the windscreen. "I've had enough of weirdos for the day. Either you pack it in or ya walkin' in the rain."

"Tell him!"

"What's it to be? Shut it or walk?"

Mim pressed her lips together. The driver snarled like a deformed pug, then ground the bus into gear again.

"I have to say, that chap is frightfully rude."

Mim glared at her stalker. Pulling her jacket collar around her mouth, she hissed at him. "Why are you following me? If you're planning to rob me, I haven't got anything worth stealing."

"Rob you? What on earth makes you think I want to rob you?"

"You'd better not be trying to rape me, then."

"Good lord, woman! I am a gentleman!"

Mim examined him. He looked like he was telling the truth, as well as being highly disgusted. Mim hoped that his disgust was at the idea of him being a rapist, not of touching her specifically. "Then why are you following me?"

He sighed. "Following you, I am not. Stuck to you, I am." Mim shrugged. "I am stuck to you. I have been stuck to you for about twenty minutes, but you only just appear to have noticed."

Mim looked at the small but clear gap between them, no stray fabric, no loose threads. She waved her hand in the space. "Nothing there. You can go now, see. Not stuck."

He smiled indulgently. "Okay then." He stood and took a few little side steps from her. When he was about a metre away, Mim felt a tug down the side of her body. As though attached by an invisible elastic bungee cord, the man twanged back to the seat.

Mim shrieked. "How did you do that?"

The brakes slammed on again. "Right, ah've had enough of ye. Ya freakin' us out lass. Get off." The doors slapped open, cold sheets of water tumbling in. Mim stood, bewildered and trudged to the front of the bus, the stuck man just behind her.

"Look! He's following me!"

The old woman flinched, the bus driver's face pucing up.

"Get. Off. The. Bus."

"But look! Look how close he keeps sitting!" She jabbed her phone and pushed it in his face, bringing it around to the old woman. "See! Look! I've got evidence." The old woman scuttled away. The driver frowned.

"Yep. Terrifying. It gives y' a double chin." Mim pulled the phone to her face. It was indeed a deeply unflattering selfie, but she had managed to cut her stalker out completely.

"Tell him to leave me alone." She flapped a hand at the man, standing slightly apart from her, arms folded, a smirk playing on his lips. "It's not funny! He thinks its funny."

"There's nowt funny here. Ya scaring me passengers." A little squeak floated from the folds of the puffy coat. "Now get off the bus, before I call the police."

"Call them. I'll tell them that you failed to protect me from a dangerous stalker." She grabbed the rail. Something spikey poked her in the side.

"Ow!"

The coat was advancing towards her, a minty-striped golf umbrella jousting from the quilty lump. The umbrella jabbed her, once, twice.

"Aaagghhh!"

"Then get off the bus!"

"But it's wet."

"Yep, and you're weird, so get off me bus."

Mim glanced between the hammering rain and umbrella assassin, stuck to the spot. Just as a particularly ferocious jab was careering in the direction of her belly, she felt two firm hands on her shoulders. The stalker lifted her, depositing her onto a mushy grass verge. They watched the bus disappear, driver muttering, the old woman waving her umbrella.

"I don't get it."

The man glanced at the sky then at Mim's wet jean legs. "Perhaps we can go somewhere dry to talk about it."

"No! You can't come to my house!"

"Well I cannot *not* come to your house if we are in fact stuck together and that is where you are going." She frowned at him. "Look, if you allow me to explain, we may be able to figure out how to become unstuck."

"Why is my life so crap?"

He frowned. "I doubt I can help you with that one."

As soon Mandy Horspool got home, she called her mother. "Do you remember Mim Webster? Used to be Angus? She was in Derek's year at school? Well, you'll never guess what's just happened…"

After a particularly trying day at the furniture shop where she had worked since leaving school, Mandy Horspool, had wedged herself into her Fiat Punto and headed for home. On the road snaking across the gap between town and the new development she spotted something a little odd, so odd in fact that she forced the reluctant Punto into a crawl, where she observed a woman behaving strangely by a tree. The woman looked as though she was in the section where they pull a truck in The World's Strongest Man competition. Mandy stopped the car a little distance away. She uncorked herself and stood, keeping the door as a shield between her and the oddness. It was raining, but she did not want to miss being the first to report on something exciting. It would make up for that horrible woman calling her a lump at work. Squinting through the drops, she recognised Mim Webster. Hadn't her husband just died?

Mim seemed to be tied to the tree. She was standing against it, then launching herself forwards, but only getting a little way, before it became too difficult. Mandy shook her head. Who would tie Mim Webster to a tree? And just after her husband had died? She closed the door.

"Mim!" she called. "It's me, Mandy Horspool. Do you need some help?"

Mim stopped struggling. "Oh! Mandy." She leaned against the tree, folding her arms across her chest. "No, we're alright thanks."

Mandy wiped some rain off her face. "Are you sure?"

"Quite sure." Mim grinned. "We're just resting. Here. By this tree."

"In the rain?"

Mim glanced at the sky as though she had not even realised that it was raining. "You know, I hadn't even noticed."

Mandy stepped closer to Mim, remembering to be sympathetic, because it was very important to be sympathetic to the recently widowed. "Are you tied to this tree?"

"No! We're just resting."

"Well," Mandy started slowly, "perhaps you'd like to rest in my car, where it's dry. I can drive you home if you like? Wouldn't that be nice?"

Mim shook her head. "We're all good thanks. Nice to see you again."

Mandy raised a hand, then let it flop back down. "Well, if you're sure?"

Mim nodded, adopting a casual expression.

"Honestly mum, I think she's gone proper loopy. Either that or she was embarrassed that she was tied to a tree. It was all a bit weird. Anyway, I drove off really slowly and she just stayed there! She'll catch her death in this." The rain was teeming harder now, throwing watery patterns across the glass. "Do you suppose it's a breakdown? Haha!

Yep, I'd have had a breakdown earlier if I'd been married to that idiot too!"

She hung up, staring for a moment at the blank screen, wondering who she should call next.

"Well, that didn't work."

"I could have told you that before you tried it. Now can you please untie me and take me somewhere civilised." Mim frowned, but set about unknotting the sleeves of her jacket. "I cannot believe that I let you tie me to a tree. Utterly degrading. Who was that lardy sprout?"

"It's not okay to call women insulting names, you know."

"Unless they're lardy sprouts."

"No!" Mim sighed and pulled her jacket back on. It was soaked through and clung wetly to her arms. She picked up a stick and started whacking the gap between them. "She's some girl I went to school with."

"That's not going to help either." He knocked her hand, the stick skittering to the ground. "Why did you not want to get into her car?"

"Why? Oh, let me think. Well, firstly, I appear to have a man stuck to me. Secondly, I had tied him to a tree, which I think might be illegal, but we're in a murky area with that stuff anyway. Thirdly, she always smells a bit like corned beef, so I bet her car is rank."

The man shrugged. Mim examined him. He was tall, around her dad's age with visible bones in his face. His hair was the colour of mushroom soup. Mim sighed and started slopping through the mud, conscious of the tug of the man stuck to her.

"And also the fact that she cannot see me may have been a bit awkward."

"What?" Mim swung. "What do you mean 'couldn't see' you? Are you saying there's something wrong with her eyes?"

He chuckled softly. "It is not her eyes that are the problem. Why do you think that you were so mercilessly ejected from the bus?"

"Because you were harassing me, and society doesn't support women who are being harassed by men!"

"Oh dear, one of those are you?" Mim opened her mouth to protest, but he held aloft a hand. "Back to the issue in hand. It's nothing to do with her eyes. It's more about the fact that you do not really see them unless they happen to be stuck to you."

"Who's them?"

"Dead people dear. Keep up."

8

WHAT IS PIERS MORGAN?

Mim needed a hot shower urgently. And a vat of wine. And for the dead guy not to be stuck to her. On the wet walk home, she kept repeating *I don't understand*, sort of to him, but mostly to herself. He had been more concerned with getting indoors than answering her questions, remarking that it was '*most uncivilised*' to have important conversations in the rain.

She paused on her doorstep, key halfway in. "I don't even know your name."

"Arthur Patrick Wallop Wiggleton. But you can call me Wiggy. And you are?"

"Mim. Miriam Webster. Or Angus. I'm not sure which one to use these days." She turned the key and they stepped inside. Her usual response to a new visitor was to apologise profusely for the mess, despite having spent three hours cleaning, but bringing a man who professed to be dead into one's house was definitely not a setting for a usual responses.

Wiggy appraised the house. There was little left in it

and certainly nothing that gave any clues to the occupants. All of Steven's personal effects were now on shrine-like display in his childhood bedroom at his mother's house, and Mim realised that after she had got rid of the pointless crap she had once thought she needed, she actually owned nothing much of value. Most of the furniture had been sold and was now gone, apart from the kitchen table, a sofa and her bed, which would be safely ensconced in Jane Kemp's granny flat by the end of next week.

"You live here?"

"Well, sort of. I did. I've sold it. I'm going away." Mim dropped her keys into her bag and threw it on the bottom step.

"It's no bigger than a shoebox, Miriam. Where do you entertain?"

"I don't. Not really."

Schubert yawned his way down the stairs, tail wagging behind him. He stopped on the last one giving himself a shake before staring at their visitor.

"What's up, Schubes?" Schubert growled, baring his teeth. "Schubert, no." The hound snarled, and before she could grab his collar, he leapt at Wiggy. "No!"

The wolfhound sailed through the air, then continued, shooting straight through the middle of Wiggy and into the wall. Schubert crumpled.

"Schubert! What just happened?" Mim dived to the dog's side, stroking his large head. Schubert blinked. She turned back to Wiggy. "He went through you! My dog jumped through you!"

"Yes. And I think that's frightfully rude. You should learn to control your animal."

Schubert gave his head a shake, licked Mim's knee, then padded to the window.

"But…" Mim prodded Wiggy. He felt entirely solid. "How did…? I mean…And how are you dry from the rain? I'm drenched!"

"Rain doesn't fall on dead people, Miriam. Stop being hysterical. Now, may I recommend that you take a hot bath and we have a proper conversation when you are dry? There's nothing more pitiful than a soggy woman."

The odd pair ended up in the bathroom together. Mim, armed with newspapers and blue tack that she had to go next door to borrow, was attempting to completely cover the shower cubicle in yesterday's forgotten stories. The perspex cubicle was a stupid curved shape over the bath, and the paper got caught every time she tried to slide it open.

"This is a little ridiculous. Are you going to go through this charade every time you wish to bathe?"

"No, not every time. Just every time until I've managed to get rid of you." She smiled lightly. "No offence."

Mim clambered in fully clothed and slid the door shut, scanning the inside for any breaches in her newspaper defence. Satisfied, she tugged off her jumper and t-shirt. Tossing them over the shower, she already felt self-conscious. The jeans were heavy as she flung them over. She balled up the socks and threw them too. Down to just her underwear, she flashed a second sweep at the wall of paper between her and the dead man. She sighed. The bra came off. She would usually give her boobs a friendly little massage after a whole day in a bra, but not that night. The boobs drooped sadly floorwards. She tugged off the knickers, then rolled them together with her bra. She popped

them on the small, letterbox shaped window above her and
turned the taps to scalding.

Mim squirted a good dollop of shower gel into her
palm and stared at it for a few seconds. It just seemed too
obscene having a shower with a total stranger in the room.
She shrugged. Life was getting weirder and weirder
recently anyway. Just a couple of months ago, she had been
a happily married woman. She rubbed the gel onto her
skin. Had she? Been happy, that was. Certainly things had
been easy. She had a routine. But had she actually been
happy?

Her mother flashed into her head. Sweet, smelling like
biscuits and with an always toasty warm spot between her
ear and her hair where Mim had loved to burrow. That
was what happy had smelled and felt like in her mind.

Mim shook her head and scrubbed her armpits,
enjoying the lather. *Feel Active*, the gel was called. Mim
didn't feel at all active, just tired, confused and a little bit
frightened.

"What's Piers Morgan?"

Mim blinked. "What?"

"What is 'Piers Morgan'?"

"You mean 'who'. Piers Morgan is a person. Or so he
claims."

"Oh, I thought it might be a bank."

Mim shook her head, prickling pleasantly under the
sting of the hot needling water.

"Theresa May. Is she somebody's secretary?" She
jumped as Wiggy struck the perspex of the cubicle. "Has
she had an affair with someone important?"

"Ha! She wishes! She's the Prime Minister!" Mim
snorted, as a vision of Theresa May gyrating on some

terribly English chap in a wheatfield bulldozed into her head. "Can you please let me shower in peace?"

Wiggy began to hum tunelessly. Mim sighed. She wondered if she should shave her legs. They were prickly, but she would mostly be wearing tights until she went away. She rubbed a shin with a finger. Would the hairs poke through her tights? She didn't enjoy looking like a cactus.

"Is a Hard Brexit like what the prefects used to do?"

"What? Prefects? What era are you from?"

"This one. Sort of. Well, I may have still been around. If I hadn't died."

"You may not have died if you hadn't already died?"

"Yes!" She heard him chuckle. "She understands. What's a drone? Is it those worker bees? How are people getting them under control?"

Mim sighed. "Hang on. I'll get out now. Can you pass me a towel?"

"I doubt it."

"What? Why won't you pass me a towel? Are you some sort of perv?"

"I have no idea what a 'perv' is, but no, I can't hand you a towel. I physically cannot pick anything up. I've been trying to pick up some of this tat you've got in here, but to no avail "

"You picked me up and threw me off a bus!" Mim sulked.

"Clearly, I can touch you. And you can touch me. Other people evidently can't." He snorted. "Your dog jumped through me! If I could pick things up, I would have removed that umbrella from that marshmallow woman on the bus."

"So you can't get me a towel?"

"Correct."

"And I'm here in the shower."

"Gosh, how observant you are, Miriam."

"Then how do I get out without you seeing me naked?"

"Miriam, stop. I have seen naked women on many occasions, all of them significantly more magnificent than you. I have no desire to look at you. Just get out and get your own towel."

Mim seethed. "Close your eyes."

"As you wish madam."

Mim pulled back the door, a cloak of steam enveloping Wiggy who had glued his lids firmly together. She shot across the small bathroom, pulling him with her towards the shelf. She briefly forgot that it was necessary to waddle slowly across the tiles and skittered clumsily, careening painfully into the jagged corner of the shelf.

"Ow!"

Wiggy slammed into her, knocking her to the floor.

"You're on me! Get off me!"

Mim's nude form was sandwiched between the tiles and the dead man. Wiggy made a show of scrunching his eyes even more firmly shut.

"I can't get off. I can't see." He waved his arms around in front of him like a blind man.

"Get off! Get off me!"

He heaved himself to standing, turning his back to her.

"God! What a cock up."

She reached for the lone towel sagging on the shelf. Glancing cautiously at his back, she gave herself a quick rubdown. Wiggy hooted.

"Oh, so you think this is funny, do you?"

"Well, it does have a certain farcical value, you must admit."

"You're such a dick!"

"I demand that you take that back." He spun, eyes blazing.

"Stop looking at me, you pervert!" Sheathing herself in the towel she punched Wiggy in the arm.

"Ouch!" He gripped the spot where she had hit him. "What was that for?"

"Oh, where to begin! Perving at me, knocking me over, insulting me."

"Pardon me, but you were the one hurling insults. And you fell over like a clumsy oaf, not I!" He rolled his eyes upwards, speaking to an invisible audience. "This is why I never married." He looked back at her. "And as for perving! Even the notion! I kept my eyes shut until you started spouting obscenities."

"My arse!"

"Is a tad on the bony side, actually."

She punched him again.

Mim poured tea into two cups.

"You do realise that I can't drink that, don't you?"

Mim nodded. "Yes, but I can't just make myself a cup of tea. I'll feel like a bad hostess."

"You've set your dog on me, flashed your dillypot, and punched me in the arm. I think you are failing spectacularly as a host thus far."

Mim cradled her hot teacup. She had a headache. "So,

what now? This is just so surreal. Am I going to wake up tomorrow and find this has all been a messed up dream?"

"No."

"Have you ever been stuck to anyone before?"

"No. Well, not really. Not like this."

"Then why me?"

"Well, you ran off, while I was still there." He eyed her cup of tea longingly. "That looks nice."

"What do you mean?"

He sighed. "I am just there sometimes."

"What for? Do you want to get a message to someone?"

"There is not a great deal else you can do when you are dead. Oh, I do get a laugh at the singing."

"Can't you just like, go to heaven or something?"

Wiggy laughed. "Ah, beliefs and notions! Pile of horse dung, dear."

Mim sipped her tea. It was too hot and burned the roof of her mouth. "Have you seen anyone you knew?"

Wiggy glared. "Us Grantham House boys are not the sort to believe in supernatural nonsense."

"Right. And yet here you are."

"Here I am."

"You haven't said how you got stuck to me."

Wiggy's face twitched. "I was just looking."

"Looking at what?"

"In your handbag. You carry an awful lot of bumf around with you Miriam."

"And…?"

"And then you ran off, and I was stuck. I thought I may have been stuck to your handbag, but it would appear that it is actually you that I'm stuck to."

Mim stood. "Ok. So." She sat back down. "We've got to figure out a way to unstick you, then you can go on your merry ghosty way while I trip across the globe finding myself, or some crap like that."

Wiggy spread his hands in front of him. "Be my guest."

9

RUSSELL HOBBS

Minister Dorothy Ogden glared from the crack of the door.

"We're closed."

"I told you Miriam. You cannot bring me back to this weirdo."

"Please, Minister Dorothy Ogden. I have something of yours. I need to return it."

Minister Dorothy Ogden glared, but tugged the door open just a crack. Mim squeezed through it, Wiggy in tow.

The odd threesome moved obscenely slowly through the door to the churchy-bit. In daylight, the place looked even dustier than it had in the wintery evening light. Minister Dorothy Ogden was wearing lime green satin pyjama bottoms that looked fairly flammable and a jumper with huge red roses knitted into it. Despite the chill, her tiny gnarled feet were bare.

Minister Dorothy Ogden shuffled them through the curtain. Wiggy scowled the whole way, but remained silent.

The back room was dominated by a solid mahogany desk, piled high with books and scraps of paper. A small kitchen area lurked in the corner. Splintering wooden units had been painted yellow and green sometime around the nineteen fifties and had never been updated. No white goods showed themselves, no hint that the kitchen had stepped into the next century with the rest of the world.

The saddest thing in the room was a cheap pine single bed, topped with a pile of crumpled blankets. Minister Dorothy Ogden seemed to live here, and Mim wanted to cry.

The little woman ensconced herself in an antique leather chair that cupped her like she was a doll. Mim scanned for somewhere to sit. There was not another chair in the room so she leaned awkwardly on a pile of books. Minister Dorothy Ogden pierced the desk with her elbows and glowered at Mim.

"Well?"

"Can't you see him?"

"See who?"

Mim gestured vaguely at Wiggy, who had angled his body away from the glary woman and her big desk. The woman shrugged impatiently.

"I got him from here."

Wiggy sighed. "She can't see me, Miriam."

"Right, but I thought she'd be able to hear you."

Minister Dorothy Ogden frowned suspiciously. "Who are you talking to?"

"Him. Wiggy. Can't you hear him?"

"I hear nothing but you talking crap."

"She can't hear me, Miriam."

"Why can't she hear you?"

Wiggy looked at the floor. "I don't know. I've tried. She's never been able to hear me. Maybe she's just a bit deaf?"

Mim remembered Minister Dorothy Ogden's singing. "Yeah, she might be a bit deaf."

"Or a massive charlatan."

Minister Dorothy Ogden stood, hand slapping the desk. "I'm not deaf. Who said I was deaf?"

"Wiggy did."

"What's a Wiggy?"

Mim sighed. "Not what, who. Wiggy is a person. A dead person. I got him from here."

Minister Dorothy Ogden blanched. "Get out! Get out of here now." She stalked around the desk with an unprecedented agility. "No returns." She started pushing Mim towards the curtain. "Don't bring them here! Are you insane?"

Mim, not sure where to put her hands or whether to fight the push raised her eyebrows at Wiggy. "What's going on? Why won't she have you back Wiggy?"

"Stop doing that!" Minister Dorothy Ogden's voice had risen an octave. "Stop pretending!" She continued shoving Mim towards the exit, successfully propelling her back into the church.

"Let's just leave Miriam. This old bat is certifiably insane." Wiggy was no help whatsoever, trotting beside Mim's forced ejection.

"I don't get it. Your job is trying to coax dead people out of the rafters, yet you don't believe I've got one with me."

Minister Dorothy Ogden shrieked. "Stop it! Just stop it!"

"Okay!" Mim shrugged the little woman off. "Okay, we'll leave. Just stop pushing me." She stalked to the door, Wiggy galloping gleefully by her side. Turning, one hand on the brass knob, she regarded Minister Dorothy Ogden, reduced to a tiny speck in her velvet empire, arms wrapped tightly across her rose jumper. "Are you scared?"

"Get out!"

"I tried to tell you Miriam."

Back in the kitchen Mim opted for a glass of old Kahlua instead of tea, wondering why there was a sticky bottle of Kahlua in the kitchen. She definitely hadn't bought it. It tasted rank. It was entirely possible that it would make her headache worse.

Last night, she had teetered between a shallow sleep and panic, waking every hour or so. Her body right on the edge of the bed, she fell out twice and landed on a disgruntled Wiggy, who had taken up the floor on the boring grey carpet. When she woke, she was in the middle of her bed, Wiggy snoring gently by her side. In his sleep, he looked almost sweet. Almost.

She licked the roof of her mouth.

"Are you drinking alcohol Miriam? It's ten am!"

Mim stuck out her tongue, blowing him a perfect wet raspberry. She knocked back the Kahlua and refilled her glass. "Hmm, what to do next. If the spirit woman won't take you back, there has to be something else we could do." She tapped her chin thoughtfully.

"Well, there is something we could try."

"Really? What?"

"I have this old friend." He paused. "Well, acquaintance really. Another good old Grantham House boy."

"Go on."

"Digby. Old Digby Bullhorn. Frightful chap. We should go to see him."

Mim stood. "Great! Where does he live?"

Wiggy grinned. "Oh, he's got a rambling pile in Hert-fordshire. Family seat and all. Ghastly place."

"Hertfordshire? But that's...where even is Hertfordshire?"

"You do not know where Hertfordshire is? What do they teach in state education? It is near London. Candle-ford House." Wiggy chuckled. "Very atmospheric. Perfect spot for a deceased personage such as my good self."

Mim sat back down. "Sounds like a long way. And you think he'll be able to help?"

"Help? Not a chance. The man's a complete fribble! Couldn't extract his own spoon from a boiled egg." Wiggy giggled. "Oh dear."

"Then why would we go to see him then?"

"Why?" He chortled. "For sport of course! Give him a damn good haunting. To see if he's still a great big lumbering poltroon. Haha! I'm pretty certain I could make him cry like an ugly lady. It's no less than he deserves."

Mim narrowed her eyes, shaking her head. "Aha!" She turned suddenly and whipped out of the back door, yanking Wiggy out of his ignoble reverie. They stalked across the frosty-tipped turf to the shed. Groaning on its hinges, the splintering wood creaked aside and Mim peered in. She hadn't quite got around to clearing it yet. She was contemplating just burning it instead.

"Is this the servant's quarters?"

"Hah! Yes, I keep a scullery maid called Petunia in here, along with a cook, gardener and a butler!" Wiggy shot her a withering stare.

Boxes were piled dustily. She poked in the first one. Old shoes meant for a cobbler, life saving operations to save the sole never performed, left to languish in a dusty box. She pushed that one aside. The next box held what she wanted. Hoisting it up, she staggered back towards the house, kicking the door shut behind her.

"Careful! You nearly slammed that on me."

"So? What's the worst that can happen? You might die?" She laughed.

Back inside the house, Mim plopped the box on the table and ripped it open.

"What are we looking for?"

Mim poked a hand in, pulling out a vase with a badly painted lion on it. She dumped it on the floor, plunging her hand back in for another rummage. A glass decanter, an ornament of an old fashioned shepherdess and a Charles and Diana commemorative tea towel were dragged out of their dusty slumber. "Aha!" She held her bounty aloft with a triumphant grin.

"My word Miriam! What is this weaponry?"

She grinned, gripping the Russell Hobbs electric carving knife in her hand. Wiggy shrunk back.

"This, *Wiggles*, is an unwanted gift that's going to finally get some use." She marched to an empty socket where the microwave once roosted and plugged it in. "Behold, Russell Hobbs at his finest!" She flicked the switch, proffering the knife into the air. Nothing happened. "Oh. Hang on, there's a button." She pressed it. The blade whizzed into life. "I haven't actually used it."

"Turn it off!" Wiggy covered his ears. "Please!"

Mim shook her head. "No." She took a step towards him, the angry saw buzzing close to his ear.

"Please don't kill me!"

She let go of the button, puzzled. "You're already dead. Besides, I'm not trying to hurt you. I thought I might saw this invisible sticky thing off."

"Oh. Okay. Let's try."

He nodded complicitly, and Mim depressed the button again. Wiggy stood very still, staring straight ahead. She circled the blade around so that it pointed to the space between them.

Clunk.

The blade hit something.

"Did you feel that?" Mim jabbed it again.

Clunk.

"I can feel the thing!" she shouted excitedly. Wiggy nodded, and bit his lower lip.

Eeeeeeeee.

The blade made a screech, small orange sparky globules flying out of it, before the Russell Hobbs launched itself out of her hand. It bounced, blade down, pulling the cord from the wall, then landed in a twisted heap on the floor. The blade was bent, reminding Mim of a swordfish she'd once seen outside a restaurant in Greece with her mum, that made her cry for hours.

"Well."

Mim sighed. "I thought that would work. I felt the thing. Did you feel the thing?" Wiggy nodded. "Maybe a chainsaw. Who do I know with a chainsaw?"

"You are not coming near me with a chainsaw. You can't even cut your fingernails straight!"

Mim sank to a chair and poked her tongue into her kahlua. Her dad would probably know someone with a chainsaw, but how would she explain needing one? If she said she wanted to chop wood, he'd insist on doing it for her. She rested her chin on her hand. Maybe Colin would have one. Colin never asked questions.

"Who's Dennis?"

"What?" Wiggy had his head in the box, his voice muffled.

"And Steven. Who is Steven?"

Mim sighed. "Steven is my husband. *Was* my husband."

"Ah. Did he divorce you because of Dennis?"

"What? No! He died. What are you looking at?"

Wiggy popped his head out. "A card from Dennis."

"Give that here."

"I can't."

"I know." She elbowed him out of the way and tugged the card out. It was crumpled and had been wedged in the open box. Dennis's neat, square writing glowed inkilly from the thick card.

To Steven and Mim, may you always treasure one another. Steven, you are the luckiest man in the world. Keep that precious jewel in your heart forever. If you don't, I will! (Just kidding!). Love you, Dennis.

"I don't remember reading that." Mim turned the card over. Two gold embossed lovebirds were wrapped in a heart. "Dennis has always been funny."

"You mean Dennis has always wanted a bit of how's your father from our little Miriam?"

Mim felt a hot pulse rising through her ears. "Shut up. He's Steven's brother. What a terrible thing to say." All the same, a little something throbbed just south of her belly button. "Stop it."

"I already have."

She was rescued by the doorbell. "Oh! I'd best get that."

"Do not let them in if it's bloody Mormons. Frightful bunch."

Trisha loitered on the step shivering. In one hand was a bottle of Cherry Lambrini, in the other, a small gift wrapped in Santa Claus paper.

"Hola, sinyoreeta! I bring glad tidings of comfort and joy."

"Get rid of it!" Wiggy hollered. Mim glared.

"You'd better come in, Trish. I've got something weird to tell you." Her eyes slid sideways to Wiggy lurking just behind the door.

"Well hurry up! I'm bloody freezing!"

Mim glanced furtively up and down the cul-de-sac, before yanking Trisha inside. She took the gift and Lambrini from her friend, who shivered out of her coat, stamping slush onto the mat like a disgruntled pony.

"You didn't call last night."

"Because you were busy flashing your patootie at me!"

Mim slapped Wiggy on the arm.

"Was that a fly?" Trisha's eyes hunted out a flying beast.

"Yes. No. Sit down."

Trisha sat. "Sounds serious. Shall we open the Lambrini?"

"Miriam, it's still morning!"

"Yes Trisha. We shall open the Lambrini." She raised an eyebrow at Wiggy. "We shall open and enjoy the Lambrini, because you only live once, and *I'll* sleep when I'm dead." She flicked a stray lump of fluff from her cardigan at Wiggy. "And not harass people."

She fetched two glasses, hers still with a swig of Kahlua in the bottom.

"Cheers!" They clinked. Wiggy scowled.

"You're just jealous."

"What?" Trisha wrinkled her nose. "Jealous of what?"

Mim poked out her tongue. "Sorry. Not you." She sat, sandwiched between her best friend and her resident dead chap. "Now, the thing I have to tell you is weird. Very weird indeed. Probably the weirdest thing that's ever happened to me, and that's saying something."

"Weirder than when you got stuck in the train toilet with a Rabbi and ended up in Aberdeen?" Mim nodded, Trisha's eyes saucerish. Wiggy reached across Mim and tried to poke Trisha in the arm. Mim slapped his finger.

"Stop it!"

"Stop what?"

Mim took a deep breath. "I went to the spiritualist church, like you wanted me to. The singing was horrendous. I got the giggles, nearly wet myself and had to leave."

"Classic Mim."

"Well, that was all good and I got the bus and then realised there was a fella sitting next to me. The bus was practically empty, so it was a bit strange."

"Mimmo, petal. You are a psycho magnet." She took a swig of the pinky fizz. "Carry on."

"Well, you could if she would stop interrupting. Bloody woman!"

Mim popped a finger to her lips, shushing Wiggy. He folded his arms sulkily. "So, I tried to move, but he kept following. Then I got attacked by an umbrella and thrown off the bus."

"Oh Mim! You should report the driver. Beryl Martin did that and she got a year's free bus pass."

"Why can't she just close her tunnel and let you tell the

story?" Wiggy threw his hands in the air, shook his head, then returned them to his sulky fold.

"Yes, well. So we were by the road…"

"Oh, the fella got thrown off too?"

"Yeah. So we were by the road and…"

"So the bus driver left you on a dark road with a potential rapist?"

"Oh God Miriam. What is this thing? Make it stop!"

"Trish, I…oh fuck it! I've got a ghost stuck to me."

Trisha's jaw dropped. Then her nose wrinkled. She closed her mouth, smacked her lips together a few times, then took a huge glug of the Lambrini. "A ghost?"

"I have never introduced myself as a ghost, Miriam. Even the notion!"

"Well, what would you call yourself then?"

"Wiggy! You know my name. Use it!"

"Yes, but what are you?"

Trisha stood. "Mim, you're scaring me. Are you talking to the ghost?"

"I'm not a ghost."

"You are though." Mim turned to Trisha. "Yes, I'm talking to him now."

Trisha laid a cold palm across her friend's forehead. "You're not having some kind of breakdown are you? Because of the grief? Mandy Horspool said you were."

Mim swatted her hand away. "I'm not. And Mandy Horspool doesn't know whether she's batting or bowling. He's here. His name is Wiggy."

"Wiggly," breathed Trisha.

"Wiggy! Miriam, your friend is a veritable arse."

"She's not. She's lovely."

Trisha gasped. "Did he just insult me?"

"Yes I did, you boring miscreant!"

Mim frowned. "Yes, he did. Stop it Wiggy. Trish, I need your help. I tried to take him back to the church, but she threw me out."

"You should go to the paper. That's unfair dismissal."

"I think that only works when you work somewhere, not when an old lady throws you out of a spiritualist church because she is scared of your ghost."

"Right."

"I tried to saw him off with the Russell Hobbs carving knife, but I broke the knife."

"That's a shame. They're meant to be really good."

"At carving a brisket perhaps," Wiggy muttered.

"Do you think Colin would lend me his chainsaw?"

"I have told you, Miriam, you are not coming at me with a chainsaw, especially one that's been anywhere near this thing."

Trisha paced, eyes sweeping around Mim, searching for signs of the ghost man. She stopped, wafted a hand around Mim, who pointed her in the right direction, brow furrowed in concentration. Wiggy tried to slap her repeatedly with both hands, matter sliding straight through her very real and solid arm. "I've always been very intuitive about these things. I'm not getting much, but yes, definitely a sense of him." She stood up straight and tapped her lower lip. "Aha!" Her eyebrows shot up to somewhere around her hairline. "We'll have an exorcism!"

Mim frowned. "Like in the film?"

"Yes! We'll cast the demon out."

Wiggy snorted. "Demon, I am not. Miriam, don't listen to this fruitcake. Look, she doesn't even have matching socks on."

Mim nodded. "Yes. Yes, that's a great idea. Shall we get a priest?"

"Oh cripes! You cannot be serious Miriam."

"Yeah, don't worry. I'll sort it. Hazell's brother is a priest. I reckon he'd do it."

"Great!" Mim leapt to her feet, dragging Wiggy upright too. "It'll have to be before I move into dad's though."

Trisha patted her friend's arm and smiled. "We'll have you right in no time, petal." Her grin fell. Mim's finger was up her left nostril.

Wiggy, hand gripped firmly around Mim's chuckled. "Such fun!"

10

WHAT AN EXCELLENT DAY FOR AN EXORCISM

It was hard having a dead man stuck to you, Mim decided. Probably harder than your husband throwing you out, cheating on you and then selfishly dying. For a start, there was going to the toilet. Public toilets were fine. They seemed to be able to stretch just about far enough to close the door and have him on the other side. But the toilet at home was an issue. Tucked right in the corner of the bathroom, there was nowhere to put him while she did what she needed to do. She wasn't keen on the trust agreement after the whole towel debacle, but really, she had little choice. She very much could have done without the commentary though.

"Was that worth your while? You couldn't have held onto that one a bit longer?"

She was looking forward to getting rid of him and being able to wee in peace again. Friday couldn't come soon enough.

Mim prepared by buying black candles. She also ironed a nice black dress she had bought but never worn. She had been planning to wear it on Steven's birthday, because it was a bit sexy with cheeky little lacy bits, but of course, that had never happened. Trisha had instructed her to get white sage too, but they didn't seem to have any in Tesco. She just got a little packet of sage leaves from the salad section instead. She was sure that would be okay. She even got a special edition bottle of Freixenet prosecco so they could celebrate after they'd finished. She was going to get two but wasn't sure whether Hazell's brother was allowed to drink, him being a priest and all.

"But they drink all of that sacrificial wine stuff don't they?" She was deciding whether or not to get a thank you card for the priest.

"Who cares? Nothing's going to happen anyway."

Mim tutted and chose a pretty one with a peacock in front of a cloud. "You're so negative. Why are you so negative?" She popped it into her basket with the sage and the Freixenet.

"Because, Miriam, it is not going to work. It is yet another dreadfully predictable waste of everybody's time, especially mine. I'm languishing here Miriam. Languishing! Take me to Hertfordshire! Give me some purpose, please!"

Mim ignored his appeal. She picked up a glittery bow and held it to the front of the envelope. "Too much?" She took his lack of a response as a yes and threw the bow in her basket too. "Priests know all the special language to get rid of a spirit."

"Miriam, Miriam, Miriam." Wiggy sighed. "I am not here because of a lack of special words being uttered dramatically while some repressed homosexual in a dress waves burning plants at me. I am stuck. I would be delighted to bugger off and leave you to your sad little existence if I could. But I cannot. And if it was as easy as lighting a candle and chanting in the moonlight, I would have done it by now."

Mim shook her head. "Well it might not work with that attitude. Buck it up Wiggy. Get in the zone."

A passing toddler wiped his nose on her skirt.

"Ugh! Little grub."

Wiggy laughed and patted at the boy around the general head region. The boy glanced up, before his face crumpled into a tearful wail. A tired looking man scooped the child up, glaring at Mim.

"Roll on Friday."

Friday rolled on. The living room looked a bit spooky, all candlelit but the first sage leaf that she had burned smelled acrid and nasty.

Mim thought she looked pretty good in her outfit. A bit witchy. She had dabbed on a darkish lipstick to complete the effect and was enjoying pouting in the mirror. Wiggy hadn't let her put eyeliner on him though, which was a shame, and to cap it off, he was looking extremely sulky.

She had placed a single chair in the middle of the living room and covered it with a white sheet. The Freixenet was in the fridge, the card written out (*To Reverend, Many thanks for exorcising this pesky spirit away from me. Love Mim ~~Webster~~ Angus*).

"I don't know what type of music is suitable for an exorcism, do you?"

Wiggy made a sort of harrumphing noise, but didn't actually answer her question. The doorbell rang, and Mim skipped, Wiggy slouched, to answer it.

"Hi!"

Trisha had got herself dressed up too. She was wearing a ruffley-necked black blouse with a skirt who's hem was trailing in the slushy gutter. "You look great!"

"You too!"

Wiggy rolled his eyes between the two women.

"What time's Hazell's brother getting here?"

"Yeah, so, small hiccup, but no biggie." Trisha pulled the door shut and shrugged a large shopping bag off her shoulder. "Hazell's brother has moved to Margate. His pal Father Trimmings doesn't do occult stuff after a bad experience with a former leper or something. I didn't quite catch the details. He smelled of pork. So, long story short, I'm doing it."

"You're doing it?"

Trisha nodded.

"Well, I suppose that you are stuck with me then, Miriam," Wiggy snorted.

"But, you're a dog groomer! What do you know about exorcising ghosts?"

"Not a ghost."

"Bit rude Mim." Trisha folded her arms. "I know I'm not an expert, but I got a book," she dug into the shopping bag, "out of the library. See!" She wafted a fat battered paperback like a fan. *Loosening Satan's Grip: A Practical Guide to Exorcism and Expelling Unwanted Spirits* was the ominous title. Mim frowned.

"Miriam, you cannot allow this to happen. She is a nicompoop! She might do some actual damage."

Mim shrugged. "What choice do we have?"

"Is he complaining?"

"Of course I am bloody complaining! A shrew who cuts dog toenails is going to chant Satanic vitriol at me, while you are going along with it dressed like Lady Macbeth! Why has she got a book about Satan?"

"Yes. He's complaining." Mim turned to Wiggy. "And if you read the subheading, it says *unwanted spirits*. You are an unwanted spirit. No offense."

"Saying no offense after an offensive statement does not make it less offensive Miriam."

"Aw, have I hurt wittle ghosty man's feelings?" Wiggy turned away. "Right, let's do this thing." Mim hooked her arm through Trisha's and they marched to the awaiting chair, Wiggy stumbling reluctantly across the carpet.

Half an hour later, Mim was getting fidgety in her exorcism seat. She had to keep adjusting the sheet, which was in constant danger of falling off. *A cushion would have been nice*, she thought.

Trisha was consulting her book at each juncture. Pink post-its peeped reassuringly from between the pages of the book, but Trisha had to squint to find what she needed. The candlelight maybe wasn't such a good idea, but it was very atmospheric. They'd done the first three steps from Chapter 17: A Step by Step Guide to a Successful Exorcism.

Step 1: The subject must be briefed. Mim had duly been briefed: *"Now Mim, I understand that if voices take over, that it's not you talking."* Wiggy had been delighted. *"You can say whatever you've always wanted to say to her and get away with it. Brilliant!"*

Step 2: The demon must be engaged, his presence noted. Wiggy had been engaged: *"If you are there spirit, give me a sign."* Wiggy had responded by whipping Mim's pony-tail in Trisha's face. *"Oooh,"* said Trisha, *"feisty."*

Step 3: The Heavenly Father must be invited in. Trisha had invited the heavenly father in: *"I don't think he's coming, Miriam."* Wiggy was all mock-solemnity. *"He is probably doing something more interesting like working out how he might next imprint his face on a slice of toast."*

Trisha appeared to be figuring out what step four was.

"Right, here's the bit I want." She folded the book back, pulled a Lemon Fanta bottle from her shopping bag and stood in front of Mim.

"What's in the Fanta bottle?"

"Holy water. I pinched it from a church."

"Bit naughty."

"I know." Trisha laid a hand on Mim's head. Realising that she couldn't hold Mim's head, the book and the Fanta bottle all together, she wedged the bottle into her armpit. "Right, here we go." She and Mim took a collective deep breath. Wiggy watched, but grew silent and still. "Lord God and Saint Michael the protector, defend this woman against the forces of evil." Her voice was low and loud. "By the power of…erm..." Trisha lost her place in the book.

"Greyskull?" Mim suggested.

"Shh. Got it. By the power of God, cast Satan and his other unclean spirits back into the mires of Hell. Behold, the holy water of the Lord and begone, ye hostile breasts. No, beasts." She had to take her hand from Mim's head to unscrew the Fanta bottle. She held it in the air, squinting back at the book. "Ah, right. I'm going to tip some of this on you now." Trisha slopped a good splash of the holy water on Mim's hair. It smelled faintly stagnant as it dripped past her face onto a lacy bit of her dress. Trisha put the bottle on the floor, placing her hand back on Mim's forehead. "Lord, may you be merciful to her soul."

Trisha flicked the page over. "Ah, yeah, some of this is missing, but I've got it covered." Mim raised her eyebrows, but her head was gently pushed forward, tilting so her chin was tucked into her chest. "Right. The power of Christ compels you. The power of Christ compels you. The power…"

"Is that from The Exorcist?"

"Yes. Shush. I think it's working. How many have I done?"

"Erm, three I think."

"Oh, that should be enough. Hang on, I'll do one more." She cleared her throat. "The power of Christ compels you. There."

Trisha stepped back, her hem taking down the holy water, making a mushy spot on the carpet. "Well?"

Mim glanced up slowly. Some of the candles had gone out, so it was really quite dark. She turned left, then right. "Wiggy?" She held her breath. "Wiggy?" Trisha opened her mouth to speak, but Mim shushed her at once. "Wiggy? I think it may have worked."

Mim blinked a few times. She smiled at Trisha.

"Blaaaaagghhhh!!!"

"Wah!" Mim shrieked and fell off her chair. Wiggy fell to the carpet beside her.

"Hahah! Your face Miriam! Priceless! Absolutely priceless."

She shoved him hard. "You're such an arse! I nearly wet myself."

"Oh Mim! Did it not work?" Trisha knelt beside her.

"Of course it did not work," Wiggy chuckled. "It was possibly the funniest thing I have ever witnessed though!"

11

SHOULD OLD ACQUAINTANCE BE FORGOT?

"Do you promise to behave yourself tonight?"

Wiggy thought for a moment. "No."

Mim swivelled on the bed, fixing him with her deadliest stare. "Why do you always have to be such a dick?"

"Because, Miriam, had I realised how very provincial and dull you were, I would have made a more concerted effort to avoid your fake designer handbag and consequently getting myself stuck to your miserable self. Unfortunately, here we are, and I need all the japes I can get just to drag me through each of your tragic little melodramas."

Mim rotated back to the mirror. It was squashy under the eaves in her old childhood bedroom. The mirror was still stuck to the wall above the bed where it had always been, meaning that applying make-up could only be done sitting on the bed. The tiny room was rendered even squashier by her backpack, stuffed full like the Very Hungry Caterpillar, taking up the only available square of carpet. Furthermore, Mim was sharing her little-girl bedroom with a sixty-two year old dead man who had been floating around in some sort of limbo for more than twenty years and had been glued to her side for nearly a month. Claustrophobic did not even begin to cover it.

"So what delights do we have in store here at the Chateau Angus? How do you ring in the New Year? Do you gather round a piece of coal to share a slice of stale bread? Get drunk on homemade potato wine and punch the local vicar?"

Mim threw a used cotton ball at him. "You're a snobbish pig." She puckered her lips to dab on the Glam Shine Trisha had got her for Christmas. It really was exceptionally sparkly. "Why, what did the hideously repressed and massively dysfunctional Wiggleton's get up to on New Year? Did you all weep silently into your plum brandy because you were all so starved of love, except your dad who was diddling the maid?"

Wiggy stuck out his tongue. "You are just jealous because you grew up in a cupboard."

"You're just jealous because I have a loving family."

They glared at one another. Her dad hollered from downstairs.

"Mim! Come down. Trisha and Colin are here."

Mim hopped onto the bed, pulling her sparkly green jumper down, twisting to try to fit in the small glassy frame. "How do I look?"

"Like the Wizard of Oz vomited on a munchkin."

"Charming."

They headed downstairs, a most odd couple.

———

Sandra proffered an Iceland mini deep dish pizza at Mim. "Go on. It's ham and cheese."

"Thanks Sandra."

Sandra sipped her Mateus Rose. "He's going to miss you, Mim."

"Who is?"

"Your dad."

Mim glanced at her father, chatting to Mrs Dibley from up the road. There was always some waif or stray random on New Years Eve, as far back as she could remember. Mrs Dibley was wearing red sequined Minnie Mouse ears and, unfortunately, the same jumper as Mim. *"Hah,"* Wiggy crowed. *"You are dressed like a pensioner!"*

"I'll miss him too." She bit back a little sob. She had never been away from her dad for more than a week or so and was not looking forward to the ache that had already started to form in her gut whenever she thought about the distance she was going to put between them. "He's got Schubes though. He'll look after him. And you of course."

Sandra blushed and turned away. "Colin, do you want an Icelands mini deep dish pizza?"

Mim took a glug of her wine.

"Careful Miriam. We do not want you getting squiffy and doing something silly, do we?"

She elbowed Wiggy in the ribs, but didn't answer. She was proud of how well she was doing at not looking crazy in front of her dad.

Trisha trotted over, sunny Snowball in hand. "So exciting Mim!" Her cheeks were flushed as she squeezed her friend. She leaned in close. "And how's our ghostie? Behaving himself tonight is he?"

Wiggy pushed Mim's hand forward, tipping Trisha's glass. The sticky yellow liquid cascaded all over her glittery cardigan.

"Mim!" Her dad turned from Mrs Dibley. "What was that?"

"It's okay Terry, it was an accident." Trisha accepted a gingerbread man napkin from Sandra and gave it a quick wipe. "Why's he so grumpy?" she whispered. "It's New Year's Eve."

"Perhaps, Miriam, it is because I am stuck in this hovel with a collection of glitter clad ninnyhammers!"

"He's just a miserable arse, Trish. Ignore him."

"Ahem." Terry cleared his throat. "Sandra, could you get Trisha a top up please?" Sandra scuttled to the kitchen, returning seconds later with the bottle of Advocaat. Terry turned down the stereo, now playing 'Last Christmas' and spread his hands in front of him. "Now, I'm not one for speeches, but I do want to say a little something. Mim, apple of my eye. You've had a tough year. A really tough year. But this one, this one's going to be the making of you. I will miss you so very much when you're away, but, you know, I've got Schubert. We'll be okay." Schubert yelped. Everyone giggled. Terry coughed again and looked straight at Mim. "You're a brave one Mimsy. Your mum would've been proud." He poked a calloused finger into the corner of his eye. "To Mim and her grand adventure."

"Mim and her grand adventure."

Everyone raised their glasses. They went to sip, but Terry wasn't finished.

"And." The guests lowered their glasses. "Well, I don't really know how to tell you all this, but Sandra and I...well, we are more than just friends." He wrapped an arm around the short, grey haired woman. "We're a couple."

Terry and Sandra glanced nervously at Mim.

"Ha! I know! We all know, you pair of donkeys! What's it been, like, six years?" Mim laughed.

"More like seven," Trisha countered. "I'd say I'm happy for you, but I have been for ages anyway."

"Oh!" Sandra blushed some more. "So you're okay about it?"

Mim felt a bubble rising through her. Joy? Excitement? "More than okay Sandra. Happy. Very happy."

"Look, it's five to twelve!" Colin, man of few words but great on time keeping, sounded the alert.

"Oooh, quick!" The party goers headed to the front door, Terry scooping up the basket by it. Mim grabbed Wiggy's hand, dragging him with the small throng.

"What's going on?" Wiggy wrinkled his face.

"I love that we still do first footing in this house. Where the eldest male of the group is the first to step over the threshold carrying gifts for prosperity."

"You sound like you're on a documentary Mim," laughed Mrs Dibley.

They gathered, shivering on the doorstep, waving to other families gathering on their own doorsteps with their teeth chattering. Schubert nestled into the throng for warmth.

Wiggy peered into the basket. "See, I was right about the coal and the bread!"

Terry poured a small measure of whiskey for everyone from the bottle and the little shot glasses that had also been in there.

"Them whiskeys were two for one in Tescos," remarked Sandra to Mrs Dibley.

"Ten...nine..."

The McAlindon's next door started the countdown. Mim's group joined in, as did the other assembleages of people dotted along the terrace.

"Eight...seven...six..."

Mim grinned at Trisha.

"Five...four...three..."

She even flashed a smile at Wiggy, who reflected it back.

"Two…"

A small tear pricked her eye. *It's going to be okay,* she thought.

"One…Happy New Year!"

Before she had a chance to be swallowed in the collective embrace of their little party, Wiggy had picked her up and thrown her over the threshold. She landed face first on the hall carpet.

"Ow."

"Mim! What did you do that for?"

"Now we'll have bad luck for a year."

"It's the grief I think."

"Poor thing."

"All the same, though…"

She stood, dusting off a bit of gravel that her knee had dragged into her tights. She swung out her arms, ensuring that one hit Wiggy right in the throat. "I'm so sorry. I fell."

The group nodded, unconvinced. Only Trisha flashed her some genuine sympathy. Terry picked up the basket and walked quietly into the house. Everyone else trooped in behind him.

"Right." Terry clapped his hands. "No harm done. Auld Lang Syne." He avoided looking at Mim while he flicked the volume up on the TV. Jools Holland was Hootenannying into the New Year. They all crossed their arms and joined in a circle.

"Should old acquaintance be forgot…"

"Wish I could forget you," murmured Mim to Wiggy.

"Not a chance dear." he grinned. Not. A. Chance."

PART II

12

TRANSPORTING PENGUINS

Mim uncapped a bottle and tipped the water greedily down her throat. Sangria was very moreish, but she hadn't reckoned on feeling like she had been licking a badger in the morning. Her tongue was fuzzy, her throat sandpapery. Three, four glasses tops, and she had been left feeling as though she had swallowed a gallon of neat vodka. Okay, maybe it was five. Or seven. Somewhere around there. Eight perhaps?

She shook away the booze-maths and tilted her

sunglasses down; a futile attempt to focus on the bus timetable.

"Feeling a bit delicate, my lady?"

She grimaced. "I'm holding you responsible, Wiggy. *'Just one more Miriam. You're on holiday Miriam.'* And now we've got a four hour bus journey and I feel like death on toast."

Wiggy grinned impishly."Dear girl, nobody made you drink the sangria. Nobody made you dance like a spasticated ox. And nobody, but nobody, made you plant your piehole on that shrunken greasy elf."

"He was a matador!"

"And I am the pope. Now, pick up your bags and pull your chin up off the floor. The bus is coming." He curled his lip when he said the word 'bus'.

Mim took another gulp of water and slung her backpack over her shoulder. The bus sprayed an arc of dust as it rounded the corner.

"Watch out for the penguins."

Mim turned to where Wiggy was pointing. Three elderly nuns waddled across the concourse clad in their finest black and white garb, finished artistically with a range of grey cardigans. Two of them pressed hard into flagging walking sticks, bowing to take their weight.

Wiggy snorted."Too much paella."

"What have you got against nuns?"

Mim didn't have any strong feelings either way about nuns. She was just hungover and waspish.

"Where do I begin? The God thing is unhealthy for a start…"

"I acquired you in a church!"

"Do not interrupt please Miriam. It is not ladylike.

Secondly, they have the most dreadful sense of entitlement…"

"This, from a man born with a silver spoon up his arse!"

Wiggy glared.

"Miriam, mark my words, these women are the personification of devillment. All lumpen repression and piety."

He shuddered, as Mim laughed and turned back to the bus, coughing its way into the bay. The door creaked open on a mechanism that was at least fifty years older than the rest of the decrepit vehicle.

"Wiggy, you're insane. There's nothing sinister about a bunch of…"

She would have finished the sentence with the word 'nuns' had her face not made contact with the bottom step. A dusty orthopaedic shoe stomped by her face, followed by another. More feet, brown sandals and bulging cankles thundered by.

Mim hoisted herself upright, rubbing her jaw, blinking at the metre wide posterior of the last nun.

"See."

"Wiggy, did I just get pushed over by three nuns?"

He nodded gravely. "Cannot trust them Miriam. Disgusting creatures, they are."

"But…but…but…"

Wiggy shook his head with the unfettered air of one who was sadly vindicated. "Ah young lady. You will learn." He squeezed past her and tripped up the steps.

"Vienes?" The driver glared at her, an ashy cigarette stuck to his bottom lip.

"Si." She flashed her ticket and trudged to the seat at the front rubbing some dust off her t-shirt.

The nuns were inching down the aisle towards the back

of the bus, large hips squeezing bulkily between the seats. Mim glared at their retreating bums.

"I'm with you. I hate nuns."

The driver flashed a glance at her, question hovering on his mouth. Mim waved a dismissive hand, and he ground the bus into first gear. She swung her backpack onto the overhead luggage rack with neither ease nor grace.

"Delighted to hear that Miriam. Now, what are you going to do about it?"

Mim popped her sunglasses onto her head. "What do you mean *'what am I going to do about it?'*? I'm going to whinge for at least ten minutes, then I'll fall asleep and you will leave me alone. That's what I'm going to do about it."

She flicked the sunglasses back down onto her nose and wedged her knees onto the barrier separating them from hurling through the windscreen. Wiggy tutted. "Typical woman."

Mim tore the glasses from her face and reeled towards him. "I've told you to quit it with that sexist shit." Her voice was too loud for the sparsely inhabited bus. The driver swivelled in his seat, almost careering into an oncoming bin lorry. "Watch the road, not me!" She lifted a hand to her mouth, dropping her voice to a barely-whisper. "I'm not in the mood for arguing this crap with you."

Wiggy grinned indulgently. "My dear Miriam. No need to get hysterical." She opened her mouth to argue, but Wiggy raised a judicious finger. "You would be better employed ploughing your mental resources into a revenge theory. That is all I am saying. Do not just complain. Do something."

He settled back into his seat, folded his arms and flashed a self-satisfied grin at the dusty landscape flashing by. Mim allowed her mouth to flop open, a half-hearted argument summoning itself from the depths of her soul, before the desire to sleep took over, her leaden eyelids slamming shut.

An hour and two deeply unsatisfying mini-naps later, Mim realised that she was still incandescent with rage. At the back of the bus, one of the nuns chortled. *Probably laughing about how they shoved Satan off a train in Barcelona*, Mim grumbled. She tipped her empty bottle upside down, smacking her parched lips together.

"It's not that I'm not assertive…" Wiggy pushed open a reluctant eye, winking crookedly at her. "It's just that I don't harbour grudges like you." He opened his other eye, raising both eyebrows, a grin threatening his lips as Mim warmed to her theme. "I mean, what is the point in this Major Hornbull thing?"

"Bullhorn."

"Major Bullhorn, That's what I meant. I mean, what will you gain from trying to spook him? Wouldn't you be better off spending your eternity doing something fun?"

Wiggy shook his head. "Purpose, Miriam. Purpose. We all need a purpose. Besides, it's such fun!" Wiggy chuckled, no doubt recalling just a few weeks ago, when he had scared the willies out of Mim herself.

Mim shuddered and fished yesterday's potted salad out of her handbag.

Mim poked Wiggy in the ribs, rousing him from a fantasy where Major Bullhorn was begging him for mercy in the centre of a *plaza del toros*.

"Move Wiggy!"

The bus had made a stop a few hours before Seville. The sign read Antequera. A very attractive man was getting on the bus. His hair stood up in all directions, as though it had no particular compass allegiance and had vowed to face all ways simultaneously. Perhaps the hair feared that it was going to be ambushed and wanted to cover all bases. He was wearing an olive green tracksuit with brighter green stripes and had the air of a startled vole surfacing for the first time.

He glanced about the bus, stopping his gaze on the space beside Mim. She slapped the lid back onto her salad, cursing the wayward fork as it disgorged half of her salad and launched it in the direction of her head.

"Fuck off Wiggy!" She kicked her wispy companion and watched him land awkwardly in the aisle, before flashing her most winsome grin at the new arrival. He rechecked his options, then, recognising that they were limited to a rowdy bunch of nuns, a man dressed head to toe in powder blue clutching a cactus or Mim, made his choice and slid apologetically into the seat beside her.

Mim slipped her sunnies onto her head. She smiled her best smile, then panicked that her teeth might be gunky. She hid her teeth and proffered a hand.

"Hola. I. Am. Mim."

The stranger dutifully wagged her fingers up and down before pronouncing "I. Am. David."

He pronounced it *Da-vv-id*. Mim grinned. He was much more attractive than the greasy little man she had kissed last night. *Ugh,* she shuddered. *Never again would she lower her standards that far just to annoy a dead guy.*

Wiggy, still sprawled in the middle of the aisle, glared at her.

David was from Seville. He was twenty eight, lived with his best friend Horgay (*stupid name,* Mim thought) and worked in the contracts department of a real estate rental agency. He also had a highly pronounced cupid's bow on his upper lip and a very slight lisp. She wasn't sure whether this was just the Spanish in general or a unique little quirk. Either way, she liked it. Wiggy glared from the aisle.

David was studying her intently. Really gazing hard at her face. Mim licked her dry lips in what she hoped was a devastatingly sexy move. David leaned in close. Her vital organs fluttered in response. She could smell the tang of strong coffee on his breath.

"Excuse me, you have vegetables on your face."

Vegetables.

Mim burned. She swiped at her cheek. Sure enough, she dislodged three strands of carrot, a slice of cucumber and seven tomato seeds nestling in their gelatinous sac. Mim dug in her bag for a wiping implement, angling her hot face away from him.

David shrugged as Wiggy, no longer sulking, guffawed. Mim glared past David at Wiggy, by then clutching his sides with mirth.

"Vegetables! On your face!" Wiggy wiped his eyes. "*Excuse me, you have vegetables on your face.* Ha!"

"Fuck off!!!"

David shuffled as far as he could away from the screaming Mim on the seat, before deciding that the powder-blue cactus owner was a preferable option. He darted across the aisle and slinked into the seat beside a delighted powder blue chap. Mim died a little inside. Overjoyed by the arrival of a companion besides his spiky plant, the blue chap proceeded to launch into something lengthy and very Spanish. David pretended to be fascinated by his own kneecap.

He was fascinated by his own kneecap for another two hours and forty-three minutes. Mim spent two hours and forty-three minutes pretending not to exist anymore.

"Se Bee Yah". Murmurs throughout the bus alerted a sulky Mim to their impending arrival. Despite still being in traffic and out of sight of anything that vaguely resembled a bus station, most of the passengers were standing, gathering their bags or stretching crumpled limbs. They inched through the city, jerking everytime the clod-footed driver stamped on the brake.

"You have to get off before those God-bothering magpies Miriam."

Mim shook her head, although she fully intended to be first off the bus. That was more to do with hoping to avoid any form of eye contact with David. She stood as inconspicuously as she could manage and slipped her backpack off the shelf. This coincided with a particularly shire-horseish stamp from the driver, so her bag smacked her in the face. Wiggy grinned. She sat back down.

"No! Don't sit Miriam. They're on the move."

Mim swivelled to the back of the bus, where indeed, three round human mint humbugs were squeezing their well-padded hips between the chairs.

"Come on Miriam! Let's get off in front of them."

She hopped up and swung her backpack onto her shoulders, edging sideways into the aisle.

"Sentar!" Roared the driver, turning to Mim, almost taking out an old lady with a poodle crossing the street. "Seet dohn crezy!"

Mim sidestepped back to her seat, and half slumped, wedged into an awkward lean by her backpack. Still, it was giving her core some kind of pressurised exercise. The nuns continued squishing forwards.

"How come he didn't tell them to sit?"

"It's the Jesus thing, Miriam. They can get away with just about anything."

The bus squealed to a halt in a bay.

"Go, go, go Miriam!"

And she did. Or at least she tried. She was quite firmly wedged against the back of the chair.

"Come on Miriam."

"I'm stuck!"

Wiggy wedged his shoulder into Mim's side and began to push. The nuns were fast approaching the front.

"Push harder Wiggy!"

He did, and she popped out like a Lambrini cork into the aisle.

"Damnit!"

One of the nuns had just pipped her to the front spot, and she found herself and Wiggy sandwiched between two of them.

"Agh, Miriam. I can't stand it."

They moved as one lump towards the front of the bus. The first descended the top step with a painful lowering of her fat foot. Mim waited politely for her to clear the top one with a patience she wasn't really feeling. A wave of sangrian nausea ripped through her stomach. The nun at her back started to try to edge around Mim, causing a serious bottleneck.

"Back off nun," Mim warned.

"You tell her Miriam!"

The nun paid no heed to the pale woman in the large backpack and wriggled harder.

"Do something Miriam!"

The third nun started jostling the second. The first was only just bringing her second foot to join the first on the step.

"Right!" Mim executed a writhing twist which unwedged her and brought her face to face with nun two.

"Stop pushing me! Just because you've got your stupid headscarf thingy on, doesn't mean you can push me around."

A whimper behind her. Mim turned her head slowly. Nun one was lying in a heap on the concrete. "Oh shit!"

"A backpack to the face with force will do that to a geri-atric badger, Miriam." Wiggy sniggered. It was, however, the only sound. The rest of the bus had fallen silent. The other two nuns glared at her and the driver had stood, rolled up timetable gripped batonesque in his hairy fist. The other passengers pushed to the window to view the fallen nun. David was shaking his pretty head.

"Oh shit."

Whispers rustled through the passengers. The prone nun squeaked piteously.

"Oh shit. What now?"

"I suggest, Miriam, that we RUN!"

She did. Mim leapt down the stairs, propelled by Wiggy. They cleared the flattened nun like Olympic hurdlers. They barged through some onlookers who had gathered by the bus. They galumphed past a sock vendor, clipping his stall and sending a couple of pairs of knee-lengthers skittering across the concourse.

"Oh crapping hell," called Mim, struggling to get her lungs to keep up with her exertions. "Is anyone following us?"

They jumped down the steps, rounded a corner and ducked into an alley. Breathlessly, they peeped about.

"I think that we escaped a potential lynch mob with a semblance of dignity." Wiggy grinned. "Well, I must say, that was not quite the revenge I expected you to take."

Mim crumpled, her face hot. She raked a hand through her dishevelled hair and took a few steadying breaths.

"I knocked a nun off a bus."

"Yes Miriam. You knocked a nun off a bus."

"I knocked a nun off a bus." She heard the sentence and it sent a funny little bubble into her stomach. "I knocked a nun off a bus!" The bubble burst and a laugh exploded out of her. "Oh my god, I'm going to Hell! Hah!"

Wiggy laughed with her. "Bloody Hell Miriam! We have been away three days, and you have smooched a midget and flattened a nun."

13

FLAMENCO EGGS

The waiter frowned.

"Mesa para uno?"

"Si."

He furrowed his brow further, then rearranged his features into those of pitying disdain.

"Ingles?"

"Si."

This definitely made things worse.

"Come sit at the table, please." He gestured to a small round table, lone chair poking from beneath it lurking in the shadows near the toilets. Mim was about to follow him.

"Miriam! You cannot sit there. You will not be able to see." Wiggy scowled at the waiter. "Tell him you categorically will not. You want to see this, do you not?"

Mim cleared her throat. "I don't want to sit there. I want to sit over there." She pointed at a small free table near the stage. The waiter curled his lip.

"Estarias mejor sentado en la esquina."

Mim shook her head. "I don't know what you just said,

but I'm going to sit over there. I paid the same as all of these other people."

The waiter glowered. Mim's heart pounded as she snaked through the tables to the one at the front. She tucked herself in, hands trembling.

"That was good, Miriam. Though you could have been a tad more acerbic."

"Shhhh." The waiter was muttering into the ear of a dark haired waitress who grinned and nodded. "He might be sending this woman to throw me out."

"Lawks!"

The woman was making her way to Mim. She was tall, broad and haloed by gleaming black hair.

"Don't mind Pablo. He is an idiot." The woman whipped a notepad out of an apron pocket. "The set menu for you? Andalucian specials and sangria?" Mim nodded, though the thought of sangria was still making her queasy. "Benito will bring you some *jerez* before the show. On the house." The waitress raised an eyebrow at the rude waiter - Pablo - before she sauntered away, all soapy and efficient. Mim hadn't even looked at the set menu, but hoped it included some kind of cheese.

"You should be more like her, Miriam." Wiggy stared baldly at the waitress. "Magnificent. I for one would very much like to give her a really good…"

"Stop it!" hissed Mim. "So inappropriate!"

"What?" Wiggy shrugged in mock innocence. "I was going to say really good night out, for your information." He grinned. "Before saucing it all up with a spot of rumpy pumpy."

Mim did a fake retch, although there was actually bile swirling at the notion. "Vile."

"Madam, *jerez*." A young waiter with none of the first

man's sneer appeared by the table. He had chasmic dimples burrowing down each side of his mouth and skin like a freshly picked apricot. He proffered a bottle of Tio Pepe at her with a grin. "Low cal."

Mim frowned, before realising that he had said local, not low cal. "Oh, ha! I thought you were implying that I needed sherry for fatties."

He cocked his head, puzzled.

"Miriam, you are an embarrassment to yourself." Wiggy shook his head.

Mim burned, nudging her glass forward for the regionally-produced beverage. He poured swiftly and danced away. Mim vowed never to open her mouth anywhere in the vicinity of an attractive man ever again.

She sipped at the sherry. It was crisp, dry and coated the roof of her mouth. Mim wasn't entirely sure she liked it, but didn't quite hate it either. It reminded her of Nan, who loved a sherry at Christmas while watching the Queen's speech. *"Eee, she's a good un,"* she'd hiccup at the TV before falling asleep, leaving Mim free to drain the dregs of the sticky glass. Mim smiled.

This place couldn't have been more different from Nan's draughty living room. It was at once cosy and caveish: arched ceilings partitioned by rosy wooden beams crossed overhead like the ribcage of a whale. The limey walls were painted a sunny yellow and bricky little alcoves were lined with dusty bottles. It glowed in a candley orange light, though the stage was lit in silver.

She had done the right thing, objecting to that table by the toilet. She twisted to look at it. Yes, she wouldn't have seen much, just the backs of people's heads from there. She stretched out a foot, the tip of her shoe reaching the low stage. This, she marvelled, was an excellent seat.

The food was delicious: crisp *gazpacho* (*"your soup is cold Miriam, send it back!"*), *huevos a la Flamenca* (*"eggs are not dinner Miriam, they are breakfast!"*), *piononos* (*"A moment on the lips Miriam…"*) and washed down with a particularly fruity sangria that was even more moreish than the one she had overindulged on in Malaga.

Mim licked her lips as Benito brought another cheeky Tio Pepe to palate cleanse.

"You are drinking rather a lot of alcohol Miriam."

"Oh hush Wiggy. You're just jealous."

The tables around her fell silent as five people walked onto the stage. Two women, clad in ruffles that cascaded about their shoes and three men clacked into the space, taking their places on chairs at the stage's periphery. One of the men picked up a guitar and settled it onto his lap. Another, perched very upright on his chair, angled a microphone to his lips. One of the women wrapped a shawl around her shoulders and crossed her legs, the other clasped her hands to her chest, head bowed as though in prayer. The third man hooked an ankle across his knee, moored his elbows on the back of the chair and raised his chin heavenwards. There was a solemnity, which under normal circumstances would make Mim giggle, but a crackling fizz in the air kept any characteristic mirth at bay.

The man with the microphone mumbled something in fast Spanish, before clearing his throat and rubbing together the palms of his hands. A nod to the guitarist with just a fraction of pause. Mim realised that she was holding her breath.

He clapped. A deep, dense echoing clap that spoke of caverns and secrets. A rhythm built, pacy and unforgiving and the guitarist joined him. He, the clapper, began to stamp, square heels on wood. The rhythm galloped. The strings of the guitar were metallic, harsh, ringing hardship through the woody heartbeat giddying it along.

Mim felt her blood roaring in time. She studied the face of the clapper whose eyes were closed. There was a story of pain etched into the creases, twitching and jolting. His lips parted. He stretched his jaw wide and out came a sound. It was like no singing Mim had ever heard before: scratchy, resonant and sad. It reverberated across the unfamiliar words causing the hairs on her arms to prickle to attention. Mim closed her mouth, afraid that her soul would leap out of it if she didn't keep a firm handle on herself. He sang and rallied and railed, shredding his being on stage with more passion than Mim had seen in a lifetime. Something cracked.

He finished. The audience applauded, but Mim was scared to move in case parts of her body started to spontaneously fall off. The man was sweating as he popped the microphone out of its stand and handed it to the beshawled woman.

Mim let herself take a deep breath as the other woman moved to the centre of the stage. She was sheathed in a body hugging turquoise brocade dress that fell from just below the knee like a fountain in swathes of green-hued frills. Her feet were encased in what Mim regarded as sensible-looking shoes with a blocky heel and her gleaming oil-dark hair was fastened in a tight bun at the nape of her neck. Mim wanted to be her.

The woman licked at red lips and arranged herself side on to the audience. The other woman cocked a head to the clapper and guitarist who set about messing with Mim's heart rate once again. When the seated woman opened her mouth, the word *naked* flashed through Mim's mind. It was so raw and exposed, like she had torn herself open at the ribs and screamed *"this is my heart. Take it!"* The turquoise woman started to move. She twisted her body, wrists rolling, fingers quivering before arching her back. Her face was at once tortured and soft. The heels on her shoes began to hammer out a rhythm, both at odds with and perfectly complementary to the rhythm of the clapper.

Mim, mesmerised, shivered. Fire and ice swirled in the pit of her stomach. Her heart thudded so loudly she was certain it could be heard across the room and then, something deep inside like a seed pod, burst. She lurched forwards, winded, hands slapping the table. She gasped for air, choking. Her eyes burst like a broken faucet, sobs wracking her body.

Mim was at once embarrassed but completely powerless over her response. It just kept coming in waves. A few curious onlookers turned their chairs to peer at the strange sobbing girl.

She felt a hand on hers. Wiggy's wrinkled hand lay across hers, and for a moment, she quite forgot that she was convulsing in the front row of a flamenco performance. She gazed at the withered knuckles and took a couple of large breaths.

"That's good. You're okay Miriam."

Mim swallowed hard, drew herself up to a normal seated position and attempted a smile at the audience members staring at her.

"All good now Miriam."

She took a swig of her sangria and focused her eyes back on the dancer, swirling now, concentration unbroken by the weeping girl at her feet.

"It happens a lot," the kind waitress had reassured her as they were leaving. "Flamenco stirs something in the soul that words cannot." Mim could certainly attest to that.

She and Wiggy were strolling back to the pretty pension along the cobbles. There had been a light rain and the dark stones reflected the light of the streetlamps back to them.

They hadn't spoken since they left the bar. Mim was feeling the odd sensation of heavy and light: like she was holding an encyclopaedia in one hand and had a helium balloon tied to the other wrist. It was odd, but not entirely unpleasant.

Wiggy was looking steadfastly downwards, as though the cobbles held a secret that only he and they knew. Mim glanced at him.

"Um, thanks," she muttered, "you know, for being nice back there."

Wiggy nodded, a gesture that involved most of his upper body because he had been looking down, before resuming his deep study of the ground.

Mim felt as though she hadn't quite said enough. "I expected you to be, you know, a bit more upper class English repression about it all. You know, a bit '*suck it up Miriam*' sort of thing." Wiggy tipped his head from side to side, but continued looking down. "But you weren't. You were nice. A bit like my dad would have been."

"All right Miriam, you can stop now. No need to gush."

She glanced over. A very tiny upcurl in the corner of his lips suggested that he had, in his Wiggyish way, accepted the thanks.

14

I DID NOT MAKE USE OF INTELLIGENCE, MATHEMATICS OR MAPS.

"It's got an orangery."

"Well, hose me down! The excitement is just too much."

Mim was reading to Wiggy about Seville cathedral from her Lonely Planet. She wondered vaguely how big Trisha's library fine would be on their return.

"I am not at all excited about entering a church, Miriam. It gives me the willies." He turned to face her. "You people," he began, "feel the need to visit churches and whatnot, when none of you go to one back home. Why is that?"

"By *'you people'* I take it that you are referring to commoners such as myself."

Wiggy tutted. "Such a reverse elitist Miriam. Always desperate to bring class into everything. No, I meant," he rolled the word in his mouth as though it was a curse before spitting it at her, "tourists." He finished this with a dramatic shudder to demonstrate his disdain for the sub category of human.

Mim grinned. "Us *'tourists'* enjoy seeing the wonders on

offer in the world and, you know, don't confine ourselves to exclusionary boys clubs or *'dear Percy's little manor in the country.'* Ooh, I did your accent quite well there!"

Wiggy scowled. "The backchat is somewhat tedious, Miriam."

"It says here that it's the third largest cathedral in the world and Christopher Columbus is buried there." She scanned the text. "It also says that children have to be accompanied in the bell tower. Doesn't say anything about ghosts though. Perhaps you'll spontaneously combust on arrival."

The cathedral was magnificent. Wiggy was not. From the outset he objected to her plan to go during a mass.

"You know, to see the place properly in action. *"*

Wiggy shot her a withering stare. "Zealous Jesus-fanciers trapped in a confined space! No thank you, Miriam." He glared at a pigeon picking crumbs from between the cobbles. "And you just know there will be hoards of nuns, don't you? Castrated choir boys that they keep locked in a tower. And a bishop with a golden Ferrari. Ugh!" He shuddered dramatically.

Unfortunately, and loathe as she was to admit it, Wiggy was absolutely correct. Not about the bishop with a Ferrari - although he was heavily bejewelled - but about the rest. Mim probably would have been happier amongst camera-wielding tourists with no sense of personal space than wedged shoulder to shoulder with the repentant.

There were lots of shawls. Mim hadn't really expected lots of shawls. Shawls were reserved for plucky village women doing marvellous things in films, or so she believed. But no, shawls were draped abundantly on the shoulders of women young and old. Mim wondered if she needed a shawl in her life.

"See!" hissed Wiggy. "I told you there would be nuns."

A particularly stooped one with an unfeasibly long whisker jutting out of a chin mole barged Mim aside.

"Bloody nuns!"

Wiggy snorted. "Well, you are probably going to go to Hell for that comment. Oh, hold the fort! We are already there."

Mim nudged him as they shuffled on; little boats on the sea of the converted. The pious were taking their seats. Mim and Wiggy ducked out of the stream of people to explore the cathedral. A man in a smart jacket and maroon tie stepped in front of them.

"No turismo durante la misa."

Mim glanced at Wiggy.

"Do not look at me! You know that I do not know a word of this ghastly lispy language."

The man repeated his question, or statement, or whatever it was, an intolerant smile developing nowhere beyond his pursed mouth.

"Ingles?" Mim nodded. The man sighed. "No tourism in the mass. You are welcome to join mass and tourism after." He showed her his teeth, putting a palm on her elbow and politely shoving her in the direction of the door.

Swarms of the virtuous buzzed onwards, completely obscuring their path to the exit.

"Looks like we're churching it Wiggy."

It was all in Spanish. Mim was vaguely disappointed. "I have no idea what they're talking about," she whispered behind her hymn book.

"I thought that you could speak a little Spanish. Can you not?" Wiggy didn't need to keep his voice down so he didn't. He seemed to be enjoying its echo as it bounced off the stone walls. "I thought that you had been here before."

"Steven and I went to Majorca once."

"And did you learn Spanish for that trip, Miriam?"

"No. Everyone's English in Majorca."

"Ssshh!" The old man to her left - inexplicably cradling a pomegranate in one hand - evidently wanted her to be quiet while he reflected on all of the terrible Spanish things he had done. Perhaps he had stolen the pomegranate.

Mim settled in, resigning herself to - she glanced at her watch - how long did these things go for?

The castrated choir boys did sing rather well. Mim felt a prickle somewhere in the back of her eye as their sweet voices soared, unencumbered by the weight of puberty. A tear threatened to leak.

"Are you about to cry again? What is it with you crying all over Spain, Miriam?"

Mim flashed Wiggy a steely glare, but the tear still lurked ominously.

"Oh God, what is it with all these bloody nuns?" Wiggy was singing, really badly. And really loudly. *"Too many virgins in one place! If the bishop was diddling them, instead of choir boys,"* his voice went up screechingly high. Mim pressed a snort down deep into her belly. *"It might put a smile on one's stupid potatoey face!"*

The snort rumbled in Mim's belly. It popped out, but she disguised it as a cough. She punched Wiggy lightly in the leg. Pomegranate man drew his precious fruit closer to his body and glowered.

"I can't eject myself from another church because of a bad singing induced giggling fit!" Mim muttered.

"Once is an accident," Wiggy agreed. "twice is a habit."

The service had been running for at least thirty five years when Wiggy decided that he could take no more. His eyes danced in their sockets and his hair was particularly dishevelled due to the fact that he'd ran a hand through it about fifty seven times.

Mim grinned. "You look like a comprehensive school geography teacher limping to the end of a rough year."

Wiggy grabbed the lapels of her cardigan and shook her. "I am going crazy here, Miriam. Out of my tiny little mind! Please get me out of here!"

Mim jiggled, much to the alarm of pomegranate man, who tucked his precious offering into his pocket.

Mercifully, the longest church service in the world ended with a gruesome organ murder, and the congregation - those with shawls, those with pomegranates and those with neither - pushed themselves to their feet.

It was slow going, getting out of the bit where the mass was. Smart jacketed bouncers stood at every available escape point presenting offertory plates. Mim, being too British to brazen out a non-compliance act, dug a couple of rogue coins adorned with bag fluff out of her backpack.

"They've got envelopes!" she panicked, glancing between her sad coins and the neatly packaged contributions.

An old woman with an overstock of chins was taking her time placing her envelope on the plate. The bejacketed bouncer smiled indulgently at her.

"Lawks," groaned Wiggy, "she is taking forever." She was. But the crowd coming up behind them was slowing their unified crush for no man, or woman, shawled, chinfull or otherwise. "I am getting squashed Miriam!"

Mim felt Wiggy's fingers encircle her wrist. She presumed he just wanted to anchor himself to her. He didn't. And then it all moved into slow motion.

Wiggy swung her upturned palm - coins and all -

toward the bottom of the plate. Her hand made slappy contact with the underside of it, propelling it into the air. As it left the attendant's grasp, his face contorted in waxy horror. The coins and envelopes liberated themselves from their platform, sailing into the air with abandon, before cascading onto the multi-chinned woman's head. A heavy financial rain drenched her. Drooping jowls flapped in the wake of her shaking head, chins quivering, envelopes littering her ample bosom.

The plate hit the floor with a clunk.

Eyes swivelled to a horrified Mim, palm still out.

"I am so sorry," she whispered. "I am so, so sorry." Spanish voices swelled angrily around her. "Agh, I really am. I'm so sorry. Je suis desolee. Ah crap! That's French."

She stooped to retrieve some of the debris but the attendant hissed at her, shooing her with a gesture usually reserved for dogs or geese.

"I'm sorry." She touched the chinny woman on the shawl. Chinny woman recoiled in horror.

"We should leave Miriam."

Mim's face burned. Her eyes were hot and wet. She picked her way through the crowd, random angry people shouting at her as she passed. Wiggy squeezed behind her.

Out in the square, she picked up her pace.

"Bit fast Miriam. Perhaps we could slow down?"

She didn't. Mim wove through the maze of pretty streets, heeding none of the charm of the cafes and shops that had been enthralling her. She turned into a dingy alleyway and ducked behind a bin. Leaning back against the wall, she screwed her eyes tightly shut.

"I thought that was never going to end," Wiggy chuckled. "Did you see her chins? I counted five."

Mim drew in a raggy breath. "You are ruining this for

me." Her jaw was clenched, lips pressed white. Her voice came out low.

"Steady on, old girl. That is a bit harsh."

Mim opened her eyes and fixed them on Wiggy. Her lashes were moist. "This trip was for me. For me to get over the shit show that has been my life for the past six months. Maybe longer. And you are wrecking it." Her mouth twitched. "We're a few days in and already I'm wishing it was over." She shook her head and stared at the ground. "How am I supposed to find myself if you keep getting me into trouble?"

Wiggy muttered something.

"What was that?"

His eyes gleamed. "Find yourself? Have you any idea what a pretentious, self-absorbed arse you sound? Find yourself? You should be trying hard to lose yourself."

"If you had bothered to find yourself, then maybe you could have died properly. You know, buggered off to where normal dead people go instead of cocking up my trip of a lifetime."

"I'll thank you not to allude to my death Miriam. It was a most upsetting affair."

Mim wanted to go on. She was still furious, still fluttering with incandescent, impotent rage. But she just wasn't well versed enough in the ethics of discussing a dead person's demise without being too insensitive.

Mim glanced around the alley. It smelled of old fruit and baby sick.

"I thought you were as bored as me, Miriam. Thought that perhaps you wanted to get out of that sanctimonious scrum as much as I did."

"Yes, but not like that!"

"Miriam, it's hard being squashed by churchgoers

when you're dead. You have no idea." He waggled his head. "Are you amused? I mean, even a tiny, little, weeny bit entertained?"

"The singing was funny," Mim conceded. He grinned. "But seriously, no more treating me like a puppet to get me into trouble. It's not okay to be a pain in the arse."

"As you wish, ma'am." Wiggy bowed. "Can I just have a bit of clarification of where the 'getting you into trouble' boundaries lie?"

Mim trod on his toe.

15

I'LL BE THERE FOR YOU

Hi Trish,

All good here. Spain lush and the men hot. Making loads of friends and memories. W annoying, but looking over my shoulder as I write so won't say more than that! Knocked a nun off a bus and caused a ruckus in a church!

Say hi to dad and give Schubes a big pat from me.

Love Mimosa xxx

She wasn't making loads of friends. That was a bit of a lie. But she was befriending the local tapas: her relationship with albondigas and manchego was blossoming, though she was struggling to button her jeans, which was a bit problematic.

The friends thing was eluding her. Mim realised that she hadn't needed to make any for years. She'd made friends at school and sort of stuck to them. Mim and

Trisha had been in the same form - so had Steven - and they had always spent time with their group. At uni, Mim hadn't really bothered making friends because she'd lived at home and was already part of a long term couple.

She and Wiggy were at a corner table in an Irish bar in Ronda. A loud group, comprising a few local looking women and an assorted selection of young, attractive Europeans chatted and laughed in broken English. One of the males appeared to be impersonating a crocodile, much to the amusement of everyone. *It isn't that funny,* thought Mim sourly.

"Bloody obnoxious bunch over there, Miriam."

"I know. So loud. Inconsiderate really." They sighed in unison. "My friends are much funnier and more sophisticated than that."

Wiggy raised an eyebrow. "By 'your friends' I suppose you mean that ageing mooncalf Trisha?"

Mim frowned. "I don't even know what that means. I have excellent friends."

"Name one friend that is not that Trisha thing."

"Colin."

"Colin the mute milksop?" He snorted. "Next!"

"Um, Wendy Tuck."

"I've known you for a month and I have never seen or heard you mention Wendy Tuck."

"That's because she moved to Grimsby. She doesn't get back much."

Wiggy nodded, unconvinced. "Right. Anyone else?"

Mim thought. "Yes! Claire Hamilton. Laura Leeks. We were all in French together." She sighed. "Good times."

"You left school, perhaps, twenty years ago? When did you last make a new friend?"

Mim paused. "Oh! Lionel. At work. Yes! I befriended

him." She nodded. "I had to show him how to use the coffee machine. He didn't know." A grin signalled this was incontravenable evidence at her excellent friend making skills.

"What's Lionel's surname?"

"Um, Smith. No, Murdock! Peck. Yes, it's definitely Peck."

"Right. And you and Lionel Peck spend lots of good, quality time together, I suppose? Chuckle at gaudy arrangements in the back of flower arranging classes? Share recipes for a hearty minestrone in your designer kitchen? Shame he could not make your little New Year soiree. Still, I am sure he sent his heartfelt apologies."

Mim glared. "Well I don't hear you talking about friends. In fact, the only person you ever mention is that fella you hate."

"Ah, Diggers! Good old Digby Bullhorn." Wiggy gazed into the middle distance. "He is a lardy cumberwold."

"I suppose you had loads of toffish friends? Spend your weekends hunting defenceless creatures, did you? Loitering pointlessly in some fusty club with young Tories and colonial relics?"

"Sport of gentlemen! Ah yes, Weekend hunts were quite exciting. And Boodles was an excellent club full of fine gentlemen. So, yes, Miriam, I had a glittering array of well-bred, well-educated friends." He coughed. "Besides, when you are thrust into a boarding dorm aged eleven, it is absolutely crucial that you not only make friends, but that you make the right friends."

"What do you mean? You needed to be friends with the popular kids?"

Wiggy snorted derisively. "Popular! What a terribly funny perception you have of the world Miriam. Some of the 'right friends' were a long way from 'popular', I can assure you."

"Right." Mim nodded vaguely, but didn't really get it. "So I bet there was a good turn out for your funeral."

Wiggy waved a hand at her. "The best. Crammed, the cathedral was. Absolutely crammed."

Mim leaned forward eagerly. "It's amazing. You got an actual chance to see what people thought of you. I mean, properly. Not just what they said to your face. Tell me what it was like. Were you there? Did you see it all? What did people say?"

Wiggy rolled his eyes heavenwards. "You are too maudlin, Miriam. I will not fulfil your Gothic yearnings for grubby details." He glanced back to the group by the bar, now flicking peanuts through thumb-and-finger goal-posts. They roared as one of them missed the goal, the bouncing nut instead hurling itself into a Scandinavian-looking man's eye. He feigned dramatic injury by pitching to the floor and writhing. "I think that this sort of high-jinx looks exactly like the sort of guff you would be excited by." Mim shook her head. "You want to join them, admit it?" Mim shook her head again, looking back to the group. "What thirty-something woman in a bar would rather be talking to a deceased gentleman than getting squiffy with Northern European backpackers?"

One of the Spanish-looking women placed a foot either side of the writhing man and hauled him to his feet, both laughing easily. Two of the group headed to the toilets, another to the bar. The remaining group members split into a few smaller conversations.

"Here is your chance Miriam. I think that you should go and befriend them."

"What? No! They're young, they don't want a weird middle-aged lurker spoiling their fun."

"Oh stop it. You do not look a day over thirty eight."

"I'm thirty five!"

Wiggy flapped flaccid fingers at her. "It'll be fine Miriam. What could possibly go wrong?"

"I worked in a call centre," Miriam explained to Lucas.

"What is that?"

Mim had managed to commandeer the attention of one of the group. Actually, she had sort of assailed him at the bar and left him with little choice but to talk to her. He was very tall with icy hair that shivered past his shoulders and the beginnings of a fluffy beard on his chin.

"Maybe you don't have call centres in... where is it you come from?"

"Egmond aan den Hoef."

"Right." Mim had no idea where that was. Lucas was peering over her shoulder at his fun friends.

"Say something, Miriam. It's getting a bit awkward."

"So, you all look like you're having fun." She did her best young person grin. A bit throwaway, a bit cool, like she didn't care if he invited her over to meet his friends or not. She thought she was pulling it off pretty well. She tossed her hair for good measure.

"Yes." Lucas' eyes glazed a bit. Mim pointedly looked away from the raucous group. "Erm, you might like to join with us, yes?"

"Oh. I suppose I could. Just for a bit."

Lucas indicated the way - perhaps fearing that she was too geriatric to find it for herself - and Mim made her way shyly to the group. He greeted his friends with handshakes as though he had been gone for a year. Mim hovered by his side, Wiggy by hers. She grinned at the group, all of whom peered quizzically. Lucas, seemingly having forgotten that she was there, inclined his head curiously too.

"Oh, guys. Tim." He patted Mim on the shoulder.

"Erm, Mim actually." She gave a toothy grin, which she felt morphing into that stupid rabbit face she was in the habit of doing: exposed gums and googling eyes.

"Why are you pulling that face Miriam? Nobody wants a friend with a face like that."

She let her face relax and shrugged. "So, what are you all doing here? Where have you all come from?"

A squat man wrapped an arm around one of the Spanishy women. "Oh, we've told the travel stories already. Now we have a fun night." Inspiration bloomed on his face. "Tim, you can make a picture of us!" He proffered a camera at her, disengaging it from a weird metal stick. "Here! Make a picture of the gang."

"Oh. Okay." Mim took the unfeasibly little camera from him. The group assembled - seven of them in total - and arranged themselves artfully as though they had rehearsed their positions already. Some pouted, some grinned, one made a weird hand gesture while sticking out his tongue. Mim clicked a few snaps, then popped the camera on a damp table.

"Well," she beamed. "Who's up for shots?"

They were lost. Or rather Mim was lost. Wiggy was lost by default, being attached as he was to a drunk woman too inebriated to listen to his directions. He did actually know the way, Mim just wouldn't listen.

"Do not cross this damned bridge again Miriam." She blinked at him. "We have crossed it twice already. We are staying on this side of it."

Mim grimaced and pushed him aside. "Utter crap. Why would I listen to you? You're not even alive?" She snorted, starting across the Puente Nuevo for a third time.

Wiggy stood his ground. It usually did not work, Wiggy trying to control Mim, but she was drunk enough that her wobbliness gave him a little advantage. She struggled forwards, straining as their tethers tugged.

"Ugh!" She sagged onto Wiggy and slid to the cobbles. "I give up."

"Oh for pity's sake! Get up woman. You truly are a mess."

Mim sniffed and looked up at him. "Will you help?"

Wiggy hoisted her to her feet, hooking his arm through hers. "You are going to have to walk. I will help, but you will have to do the stepping yourself. Understand?"

She nodded, a bit pale and pathetic in the glow of the streetlights. The cobbles gleamed: a light shower had polished them to jet, and consequently, the wet stones had left an attractive blob on the bum of her jeans.

They walked in silence for a few minutes, Mim's uneven footsteps being the only sound. A few passers by skirted away from her, presumably seeing a woman walking who may well have had some form of motor disease.

"Why do you do this to yourself Miriam?" Wiggy tutted softly. "I encouraged you to make friends, not cry all over a bunch of strangers." He chuckled. "Well, after you'd finished gyrating on them." Mim shook her head. They turned into the narrow street where her pretty pension wrapped itself around a tiled courtyard. It was still, quiet, lit by fairy lights and a little bit magical. Mim paused.

"It's just so pretty."

Wiggy nodded. "Let's get you inside, you tippled bumpsy."

Mim struggled with the key, struggled with the door and then struggled herself into an undignified clump on the bed. "I cannot," she declared, "take off my shoes."

"Well, Miriam, you are right royally stuffed then, are you not."

"Take off my shoes!"

"I cannot. We have established this." He pulled her by the hand to a seated position. He led her hand to her foot, clamped it around the back of her boot and pulled.

"See, you can!"

Wiggy sighed and took her hand to the other boot, repeating the awkward yank until Mim was boot-free and moist-socked. She flopped back onto the bed and waggled her feet in the air.

"Free at last! My feet are free." She giggled, hiccuped, and then giggled at her hiccup.

"Miriam, how did Steven die?"

"What?" Mim flopped up, regarding him quizzically.

"Well, you were talking about it to that Viking chap. Only you weren't really making much sense. Something about ogres, you said."

"Monsters!" Mim nodded sagely. "Yes, it was the monsters that killed him."

"I do not understand."

"The monsters. The munching monsters."

"Monsters ate him?"

Mim grinned manically. "Yes. Sort of. He'd been to

hers, see. Ladytips. That's where he must have been. She's by the station. Must've got hungry. And they've got them there at the machine, at the station. He had his arm in. They mustn't have come out. And then it squashed him. The machine." She sighed. "He always did love a Monster Munch. And then the monster munched." She giggled, flattening herself onto a pillow.

"Steven was crushed? By a vending machine?"

"Yes. Crushed dead."

Wiggy sighed. "Terrible way to go Miriam. Crushing. The absolute worst."

"Worse than a shark attack?"

"There are not too many shark attacks on the shores of our green and pleasant land, Miriam." He shuddered. "No, crushing is definitely the worst. I wonder if he suffered. I wonder if he felt the air leaking out of him like a hole in a balloon."

Mim hit him with a pillow. "Not helping Wiggy. I'm still mourning. Listen to the grief!"

"You are not mourning him. You are mourning your security blanket." He lifted Mim's head, directed her fist still clutching the pillow towards the gap and released her. Mim sunk into the marshmallowy depths. "You know that you would have pottered on in an oblivious cloud of dullness, until your own untimely death from abject misery had he not booted you out, had an affair and died. He did you a favour, Miriam, and you know it." Mim was snoring softly. "He did us both a favour."

16

GOOD MORNING VIETNAM!

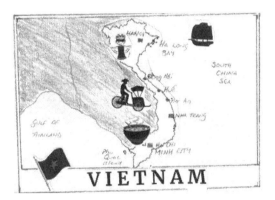

Ben Thanh Market was categorically the hottest place on earth. They had been there for approximately four minutes when Mim decided that she was likely to die in a puddle of sweat on the floor if she didn't immediately leave.

"I'm dying," she declared. "But I need one of those vests otherwise I'll have armpit death to deal with too."

Her backpack full of clothes, which had been more than adequate for a European winter, contained nothing that wouldn't immediately melt her in a South East Asian climate. She needed vests and shorts, and she needed them fast.

Wiggy rolled his eyes. "Miriam, must you be so dramatic?" He flashed her a smug grin. "I am so lucky that I cannot feel the temperature." He shivered in his smart jacket and fastened a button for good measure. "Hot, you say?"

Mim glared, before immediately being distracted. "Oh, look. That's what I want." She indicated a little stall, *almost identical to all of the others*, Wiggy thought, with cheaply made vests hanging from every available inch of space. Mim dragged him through the dense crowd.

She rifled through a rail bulging with a rainbow of otherwise identical vests, emblazoned with SAI and GON on two separate lines. Mim pulled out a purple one, a blue one, a green one and a black and white striped one whilst stating "ooh".

"Xin chao." A small smiley woman apparated from behind some t-shirts. "What you like?"

"Oh, I like them all."

"Too keen Miriam. Too keen. You need to bargain, or haggle or whatever it is called in this part of the world." He looked the woman up and down. "Criminals, the bloody lot. Look at her, smiling as though she doesn't despise you."

Mim elbowed him in the ribs, but straightened her face all the same.

"How much for these four?"

"One for one hundred thousand dong. Special price I do you five for six hundred thousand."

"Great!"

"Haggle Miriam, haggle!"

"I can't work out the conversion," she hissed. "So

many zeros!" She glanced back at the woman. "Erm, how about I give you one hundred thousand for the five."

"Oooh! You went in low, Miriam!"

The woman flapped her hand in front of Mim and shook her head. "Five hundred for five."

"Stand your ground Miriam."

"Oh, okay. Erm, I still only want to pay one hundred thousand." Mim had a vague idea that this was not how haggling worked, but she had never done it before. Wiggy seemed to know though, so she was willing to follow his lead. She wished she had been good at maths.

"Tch." The woman sucked her teeth and pretended to think it over. "Four."

"Okay, so now Miriam, you put them down and shake your head."

"But I want them."

"Fine. Then let her rip you off Miriam. Let her make a real mockery of you. Be the pathetic tourist."

Mim pushed the vests back onto the hanger and shook her head. "No thank you," she said primly, and turned from the stall.

"Good work Miriam. She'll come after you, mark my words."

She didn't.

"Well, that went well,"

"No it didn't! I haven't got any vests and still have to wear this sweaty garb!" She flapped her Marks and Spencer's button down, trudging to another stall. She picked up five vests. "How much?"

"Eight hundred thousand."

The stall holder looked ridiculously fresh considering he worked in the sixth circle of Dante's Inferno. Even he looked surprised when Mim fanned out the notes. He tried to appear nonchalant as she grabbed the plastic carrier bag and stalked away.

"Wow," breathed Wiggy darting through the melee. "No bargaining for you then. You just paid nearly thirty pounds for a pile of tat that is arguably worth about a pound."

"It's not nineteen fifty any more Wiggy. These people are not your slaves and deserve a living wage."

"Said the woman who tried to buy five tops for less than four pounds."

"Oh shut up," she swallowed, "and get us out of here."

17

COME ALONG, KIDDIE-WINKIES!

The platform at Ho Chi Minh station was bustling. Families laden with luggage intertwined with young backpackers and a few jaded-looking business types. Mim clutched her ticket and wondered if she had weed sufficiently to ensure that she wouldn't need to use the toilet on the seven hour overnighter. It was a long shot, she supposed, but worth a try. She hated train toilets and as a rule, avoided them at all costs. The air was hot and wet; she yearned for some form of air conditioning on the train.

Wiggy was in a terrible fettle.

"All of these short foreigners give me the willies, Miriam." She rolled her eyes, but stayed silent. A crowded train platform was not the best forum for berating an invisible dead man for his sneering racism. "They smell of noodles and desperation. Why have you brought me here to this infernal hellhole, and why do we have to get a train?"

Mim glared at his profile and tried to telepathically communicate her reasons behind getting a train.

Firstly, she wanted to feel like a proper traveller. Spain had felt like a holiday: here, in Vietnam, she was going to channel her best Elizabeth Gilbert and to do it properly. *Bring on the discomfort!* She rallied, although secretly she hoped that a 'soft berth' would live up to its moniker. And besides, flying with this cantankerous dead man had already been an ordeal on three occasions. She categorically was not planning on putting herself through it any more often than strictly necessary.

Logistically, the flight to Spain hadn't been too bad. She flew on a Tuesday, so there were a few spare seats on the plane, one of which, she had managed to be beside. Wiggy had been able to loiter in a space of his own, albeit a budget-airline, cramped sort of space. He had however insulted just about every other passenger and member of the cabin crew before the flight was over. "Bent as nine bob note," or "Oompa Loompa" or "is that a he or a she?" were amongst his most memorable comments. At points, Mim had wanted to laugh, but didn't want to give Wiggy the satisfaction.

The two flights to Vietnam however had been an entirely different story. On the first one, her request for an aisle seat, at which the check in attendant had nodded politely, in fact manifested in a window seat. Mim would have enjoyed looking out of a window, had she not had to endure a dead man standing in front of it for four hours. After a three hour wait in Istanbul, during which time she ate so much Turkish Delight that she needed to unfasten her trousers, they boarded their final flight to discover that she was sharing a row of four in the middle of the plane with three wide men. She was as far from the aisle as she could be: too far for Wiggy to have stood in the aisle. Instead, she made do with his skinny buttocks in her face for eleven hours.

Mim was definitely done with planes for the time being.

Besides, she had never been on a sleeper train before. *Real travelling*, she shivered happily.

The red-white-and-blue locomotive snaked into the station and there was a flurry as everyone searched for their berths. By sheer chance, Mim was standing in exactly the right place for hers. She hopped on to coach four, the first one on the train, as the rest of the platform scurried like ants to find their bed for the night. Mim found her berth.

The cabin was tiny. Someone with big hips like Mandy Horspool would never have been able to squeeze her bulk into the space. Mim grinned. It looked okay. A window directly in front, two sets of narrow bunks to either side. She would definitely get a good night's sleep in here. The numbers on the bunks seemed to indicate that she was up top on the left.

"Pretty nice, huh, Wiggy?"

"Delightful. If you have spent the last few years detained at Her Majesty's Pleasure."

Mim grinned. Even Wiggy's sulkiness couldn't sully the thrill tickling her spine. *Adventure*, she murmured softly.

"With any luck, we'll end up with this place to ourselves, Miriam."

Mim shrugged and swung her backpack onto the bunk. "Come on." Mim stepped on the metally rung of an extremely narrow ladder. "You'll have to come up. I don't think we'll stretch that far."

"I'll do no such thing, Miriam."

"No choice," she heaved, and pulled him up with her. "There. Nice, right?"

She had to tilt her head sideways, and it still pushed against the ceiling. Wiggy scowled.

The chatter of local voices preceded the arrival of a

family into the cabin. Three adults, a smallish boy and a baby. Mim was mildly disappointed, but pasted on her best smile.

"Hello!"

The family smiled warily, before bustling right in with all of their bags. The man, presumably the patriarch, glanced at the numbers stuck to the sides of the bunks, then flashed a glare at Mim before becoming distracted by the toddler.

One of the women was examining Mim baldly. She looked fairly old in her flannelette trousers and gaudy blouse, stooped from the waist with wispy gray tufts sticking out of her head at funny angles. She placed a large basket on the floor between the bunks, folded her arms and continued to stare.

The younger woman clutching the baby fired out some rapid Vietnamese at the other two, who turned to leave the boxy space. She bopped the baby on the nose with her own and hauled its fat little bulk up to Mim. She took it, surprised. The woman followed the other two out.

"What in God's name have you got in your hands Miriam?"

Mim frowned. "A baby." She turned it to face her.

It was pretty cute. Mostly smooth cheek with blinking alert eyes and crowned with a feather of dark hair. It poked out its tongue and made a gurgling sound at her.

"Hello cutie," she smiled.

"Oh please!" Wiggy rolled his eyes. "You middle-aged cliche you. Look at you, fawning over what is essentially a parasite like some broody hen."

Mim glared at him. Something poked her toe. Glancing down, the toddler, it appeared, had also been left here with a total stranger. He was brandishing a stick: his weapon of choice for poking her in the toe.

"Hello," she said to him. "I. Am. Mim."

The little boy wrinkled his face and laughed, before hitting her on the toe again.

"You would not get this back in good old Blightly, Miriam. People leaving their children with strangers who are not even a paid nanny. It's ludicrous!"

The baby grabbed her hair and popped it into its mouth. "Don't do that baby!" She fished it out. The little boy burst into peals of laughter and whacked her again with his stick. "Erm, stop it?" she ventured. She glanced at the door, wondering when the adults were planning to return.

A jolt ran through her and she gripped the baby harder. The little boy's eyes widened. Mim and the boy glanced to the window to note that they were crawling slowly out of the station. Mim looked at the boy, the baby and then to Wiggy.

"Oh no, Miriam. Oh no, oh no!"

The train began to pick up speed, the station blurring by.

"Where are those adults?" Mim whispered. The little boy frowned.

"Oh heavens Miriam. You're a kidnapper!"

"Shush," Mim hissed. The boy's brows knitted in confusion. The baby hit her in the ear.

The train moved faster, the station now behind them.

"Oh crap Wiggy. Where are they? What do I do?"

"Ooh, those villains! Spotted a nice white girl and decided to foist their offspring on her. I hate the Vietnamese."

"I'm sure that's not the case."

She was worried though. Although everyone had been lovely so far and using English when speaking to her, she doubted the nuances of 'I appear to have accidentally kidnapped two small children' would have been easy to communicate.

"Little barnacle," said Wiggy viciously to the baby. She (Mim wasn't sure if it was a she or a he) squeezed her eyes shut and stretched her mouth.

"Oh no, no, no! Don't cry, baby!" She jiggled it up and down. "Why were you mean to it?"

The baby took a deep breath, and Mim steeled herself for the barrage of noise that was to come.

"Waaaaahhhh." It wailed. "Waaaahhhh. Waaaaaahhhh."

"Shush, baby, shush." Mim rocked it from side to side, then popped a little kiss on its head.

The boy, witnessing his sibling's distress decided to join in the wailing fun. His was more of a dry-heave sob than a full blown wail, but it still had some serious volume in it.

"Oh Christ, no!" Mim waggled her foot at the little boy. "There, there, little chappy." He sobbed more.

A frowning train guard poked his head around the door. He reminded Mim of Sam Eagle from The Muppets, so downturned was his mouth. He uttered something in sharp Vietnamese, shaking his head disapprovingly.

"I can't help it!"

"Oh, this is very bad, Miriam. Very bad indeed. I can't imagine the prisons are particularly luxurious over here."

"It's a mistake!"

The little boy had at least quieted down in the face of an authoritarian in a uniform, but the baby was wailing with abandon.

The train guard began shouting into a walkie-talkie,

crackling voices on the other end responding with the same ferocity. Mim was scared.

The boy's face broke into a wide grin. His mother stepped around the guard and into the cabin. Mim breathed a sigh of relief. His mother patted him on the head, frowned at the wailing baby and swiped it from Mim's arms. The baby immediately stopped crying, but glanced back to the top bunk with suspicion.

The other two adults in the party arrived laden with bags and boxes, chattering quickly and sharply to one another and the guard. The luggage was piled high as they talked, ensuring little floor space remained. At once they all stopped talking: their heads swivelled to regard Mim. She smiled, trying to look as harmless and non-child-snatching as possible.

"You see Miriam. These people are scoundrels."

18

FEELING REFRESHED AND GRATEFUL

Mim needed to wee in the night. Thankfully, neither she nor Wiggy had been asleep, due to the family they were cohabiting with in the smallest train carriage in the world. An array of battery-operated offenders conspired to rob Mim of some much desired rest: a radio playing some dirgey pop covers, a wind-up plastic dog that barked and panted, some kind of music box spewing out a tinny lullaby and a computer game console from the early nineties that was keeping the father amused. The grandmother (she assumed) maintained her vigil of glaring at Mim, which was highly unnerving, adding tremendously to her inability to sleep. To cap it off, there was nowhere to put her backpack as the family were taking up all of the floor space so it was currently lying at the foot of the smallest bunk in the world, Mim's legs draped over it. Wiggy was hanging off the edge of the bunk, head twisted to fit the little space. Comfortable, they were not.

"I need to wee," she murmured as surreptitiously as she could.

"Praise the lord! Get me out of this circus of horror Miriam!"

She climbed gingerly down the ladder, very aware of her sweaty-toed sock and its close proximity to the dad bunking below her. He sniffed as she reached the bottom. Mim smiled and was rewarded with a glare akin to one you might bestow on someone who had just murdered everyone you had ever loved, stolen all of your clothes and sent the photos to *The Daily Mail*.

They found their way to the bathroom by following their noses. A large room, clad with metal walls and ceiling was, it appeared, the train toilet. Singular. *And how much it has been used!* The actual receptacle of waste was a toilet lid lurking apologetically over a hole in the carriage floor.

"Oh!" remarked Mim.

"Lovely." Wiggy cast a sneer around the space. "I imagine this would be regarded as 'concentration camp chic.'"

Mim wanted to remind him that joking about concentration camps wasn't okay, but she couldn't have thought of a better description herself.

"Right. Let's do this thing."

They made their way gingerly to the hole.

"Ugh!" Mim's toe found a cold pool, her sock greedily drinking in the liquid. "Ew! Ew! Ew!"

Wiggy glanced at her soggy-socked foot. "Why are you not shod?"

She shot him a withering glare. "Right. Turn around." She shuddered, the cold tip of her sock repulsing her. Should she take it off? She wanted to vomit.

Wiggy turned slowly away.

Some pulpy toilet paper clung wetly to the side of the

lid and squatted around the area. Mim grimaced. *You wanted real travel*, she cursed herself. *Here it is.*

She placed one foot in a relatively mushy-paper free spot, wedging the other against the wall. There was nothing to hold on to, so she squeezed hard into the core muscles she hadn't been aware of until the agonising sit-up section at Boxercise and then tried to work out how to get her jogging bottoms and knickers to a suitable point to facilitate the weeing. She inched them as a pair over her bum and hips, stretching them to full capacity, before angling a hand through and bunching them together as safely as she could away from the stream. A gust of hot air blew onto her buttocks.

"Are you finished yet Miriam? I don't want to spend any more time in here than is strictly necessary. It smells like foreigners and poverty."

"Wiggy! You can't say that!"

"I just did."

Her wee started. She willed it swiftly on. Her angle was just about right to avoid spraying her trousers, though she was worried about the finish. She glanced at the wall where a thin sad toilet roll dangled from string. There was no way she would be able to reach it without adjusting her position.

"What is taking so long, Miriam?"

The train jolted.

"Wah!" Mim's foot slipped, taking with it her balance. Her head bounced off the wall, before sending her tumbling to the floor. Wiggy snapped down with her. The pair sprawled amidst sodden paper and strangers urine.

"I think I'm going to be sick!" Mim realised that her left foot was in the toilet hole. She heaved. Her bum was still out. She yanked her clothes back over it, wedging her knickers up way too far. "Ow."

"You utter moron." Wiggy pushed himself angrily to his feet. "I'm not sure I can forgive you for bringing me to this pit, Miriam. I am a gentleman of good standing."

She followed him up, peeling a wet square of paper from her leg. "You mean you were. You're not an anything anymore. Just a pain in my arse. You think I want you here? You think I wouldn't rather be doing this alone?" They eyeballed one another. Mim dropped her voice low. "You are dead Wiggy. I am living my life. If you don't like it, either figure out a way to piss off or shut the actual fuck up. I am covered in piss and not in the mood for listening to your shit. I neither want nor need your forgiveness. So shut that stupid toffish mouth of yours and keep it shut, got it?"

Wiggy bit his lip. He opened his mouth but closed it again almost immediately. His lip curled, but he gave a short nod.

Mim stalked back to her berth, a silent dead Wiggy in tow.

The family (apart from the gran who was snoring like an emphysemic walrus on the opposite top bunk) sniffed the air as she made a shameful arrival back into the berth. She smelled so bad, amplified by the small space and lack of air in the carriage. Her waterlogged socks squelched as she made her way up the ladder. The toddler, eyes warily regarding Mim, chattered to his mother. *Probably asking why they've let a piss-soaked hobo on the train in Vietnamese* she griped. Her face burned.

She wedged herself on the bunk, head twisted like a murder victim, Wiggy slumped sullenly by her side. She peeled off the socks and balled them up, fighting the bile rising in her throat. Mim looked at her possessions, wondering where she could put them. Obviously, she needed to bin them. Throw them in a bin, set fire to it then push it into a volcano. Perhaps then the searing horror of the pissiness might recede a little. But in the meantime - bin, fire-fodder and volcanoes currently unavailable - she needed to put the offending articles somewhere. *On Grandma's snoring pie-hole* probably was not an acceptable option.

There was a plastic bag containing a bread roll that she had intended to eat for breakfast. She could put the roll somewhere and use the bag.

A cockroach scuttling along a little shelf confirmed that there was nowhere she could leave the bread that he and his army of mean-looking critters wouldn't come along and eat it. Mim wondered briefly whether a cockroach-inflicted disease was worse than smelling like a urinary tract infection.

She frowned. If she wanted the bag, Mim was going to have to eat the bread. She did not really want to eat anything, covered as she was in wee, but she also didn't want her wee-covered clothes touching anything else she owned. She sighed. *Catch 22,* she mused, although she hadn't read the book so she wasn't sure if it really was or not.

Mim wiped her hands as best she could on the sheet. It was already tainted, she surmised: her trousers were touching it already. She held the bread between finger and thumb and nibbled it. It was pretty good bread, but generally, it can be hard to appreciate good bread when soaked in urine.

She left the bit that her fingers had touched. *Lucky Mr Cockroach will dine well tonight,* she thought, pushing it onto a shelf clearly designed for smaller bags than her massive backpack. She pushed her socks into the plastic bag before wriggling under the covers to remove the rest of her clothes.

Mim wedged her tracksuit bottoms, knickers, t-shirt and bra into the bag. It felt very wrong to be lying naked in a room with so many strangers. *What choice do I have?*

Wiggy pointedly ignored her, staring instead at the toddler on the floor.

She pulled her backpack under the cover with her, hoping to find some clothes without drawing too much attention to herself. One of the buckles was caught: a ropey bit who's purpose Mim hadn't been able to figure out had wrapped itself around the plastic fastener rendering it impossible to open. The weird angle she was coming at it from didn't help.

A tickle spread across her belly. It took her a moment to realise that her sheet had slid off.

"No!"

Mim looked to the floor. The toddler gripped her sheet in his fist. He said something and pointed at her. Snoring gran chose that moment to wake up. Only feet from Mim, her eyes flicked wide to regard the naked woman on the bunk opposite. She shrieked.

"No, don't shriek! It's fine."

Mim pulled her backpack on top of her.

Wiggy turned, shaking his head. "Oh Miriam," he tutted.

Gran covered her eyes as though protecting herself from Medusa's glare, the toddler waved Mim's sheet like a flag and the dad leapt up to see what was happening.

Copping an eyeful of Mim's naked side, he grinned. This prompted the mum to jump to her feet and administer a slap to his head. As they launched into a full scale argument in very rapid Vietnamese, Mim tussled with her bag. Finally liberating the buckle, she wriggled a hand in and found a pair of denim shorts and a vest. Using the backpack as a shield, she awkwardly managed to put her clothes on, threw the backpack to the floor and leapt after it.

The family ceased their goings on long enough to stare at Mim. She kept her eyes on the floor and beat a hasty retreat into the corridor, Wiggy trailing behind her.

They found a small enclave that smelled of old cigarettes where Mim threw down the backpack and sat on it.

"Do not even think about opening your pompous old mouth," she warned.

Wiggy shrugged. Glancing back along the train corridor, he stifled a snigger. *Only you, Miriam. Only you.*

19

THE BEST EXOTIC GREEN BANANA HOSTEL

They did not speak to one another for the remainder of the train journey. Stretching from the advertised seven hour trip to one that lasted closer to thirteen made this even more painful than it should have been. The train stopped repeatedly in the night. Mim fidgeted uncomfortably on her backpack, back against a wall, arms folded rigidly across her chest, while Wiggy hovered restlessly beside her. A yawning train guard tripped over her three times - each time just as she was drifting into an uncomfortable snooze - and yet he seemed just as surprised every time.

When they eventually rolled into Nha Trang, the day was already stickily under way. Having not slept in their bunk, they should have been first to disembark, but they had not reckoned on the scrum that formed about twenty minutes before their arrival. Mim found herself wedged amongst locals and a handful of remarkably fresh backpackers. She tried to catch an eye: to give a *oh, the travelling life!* conspiratorial nod, but they were all far too wrapped up in their general backpacking excellence to notice the slightly smelly older woman with the sleep-stolen red eyes.

They spewed out onto the platform. Mim followed the general flurry heading for the exit, Wiggy loping silently by her side. Only a few taxis hovered by the kerb, quickly commandeered by groups of backpackers.

"Taxi?" A grinning man with a bright green helmet pulled alongside her on a sputtering motorcycle.

"Erm…" Mim glanced hopefully up the street for signs of another taxi. She glanced back at the bike. "I don't know if I'll fit. Lots of stuff, see." She twisted so that he could see her large backpack.

"No problem. Why not?" The man laughed and clapped her on the backpack. "Come. Sit on."

Mim shrugged, casting a sidelong look at Wiggy. He was shaking his head, eyes wide, though maintaining his silence. She grinned. "Why not indeed?"

She swung a leg over and wiggled about, finding her centre of balance. The backpack was taking up what little space was left behind her on the seat and hanging slightly over the back.

"Good job there's only one of me," she called to the driver, who smiled, but evidently had no idea what she had just said. Mim looked back to Wiggy. "Well, well, well." He was shaking his head more quickly now. Actually, it was more of a pulsing twitch. Somebody was not excited about the trip.

"Where you go?"

"The Green Banana Hostel." Mim grinned. She was looking forward to this journey.

The driver revved the vehicle and Mim felt the thin bones of Wiggy's fingers curling around her shoulders.

They shot off. Mim had to grip the driver and squeeze the bike between her thighs. Wiggy's fingers dug. She turned around to see him billowing behind her like a spiky cape.

"Hahaha!" The breeze slapping her face was delightful. She stared at the buildings around her, the people milling around in the street and felt a surge of joy. *Who cares if a stuck dead man is annoying?* She mused, *I am free!*

The journey was shorter than she had hoped. She thanked her driver profusely, overtipping him and promising to see him soon. Wiggy looked pale, even for a dead chap.

"I enjoyed that," she told him unnecessarily. Wiggy grimaced. "Is that it? Do I actually get some time without you whinging at me?" Wiggy pressed his lips shut. "Great! Well, let's get checked in here at The Green Banana Hostel. Lonely Planet describes it as 'fun' and 'highly sociable'. Just what I need." Wiggy sighed audibly, but remained mute.

They stepped into a busy lobby. Young, spirited-looking people hovered about chattering. A few sat at computers doing whatever backpackers do at computers (surely postcards should suffice when there's an exciting world out there beyond the screen?) The reception desk featured a bored looking blonde woman with strawy hair pinned loosely to the top of her head. Mim pasted on her best smile, hoping there wasn't an age limit on this place like there had been on the one she and Stephen had embarrassingly been turfed away from in the Lake District that time.

"Hello." Mim waited. The blonde woman stared at her. "Oh, right. I'd like a dorm bed please."

"How many night?"

"Oh. Erm, I don't know. Maybe four. Or five?"

"You pay five. You tell me at eight ah em if you stay longer." Her accent was, Mim guessed, eastern European. Russian perhaps?

"Yes. Good. I will tell you." Mim fumbled some dong from her purse and deposited it on the counter.

"Name?"

"Yes. Miriam Angela Angus. Well, Webster. My passport says Webster, but I'm really Angus."

"I don't care." The reception woman pulled a lid from a chunky whiteboard marker and indicated a board behind her. There were numbers with names beside them and a few gaps. 'Henry', 'Ed', 'Jean' and disturbingly 'Tossa' were up there.

"Mim," she murmured. "M.I.M."

The receptionist scribbled 'MUM' next to number seventeen and shoved a key across the counter. Released from the burden of having to speak to Mim anymore, she took out her phone and began texting.

Mim turned away. There were three doors and a set of stairs. *Which way is seventeen?* she wondered. She turned back to ask, but thought better of it. She walked to the first door and pushed it.

"No!"

Mim unhanded the door. The receptionist was standing, pointing at her. The rest of the inhabitants of the lobby stopped their excellent backpacking conversations to stare at her.

"You go up the stair." The receptionist tutted loudly, shook her head at a random who nodded sympathetically and plonked back down to her seat.

Mim headed for the staircase, Wiggy glaring at the receptionist.

"The Lonely Planet failed to mention the most repellant receptionist on Earth," she mumbled to Wiggy.

"That woman," he declared, "is a snoutbanded smellfungus."

20

KITES ARE FUN

Bed seventeen was a top bunk in a pleasantly bright room of eight bunks which appeared to have been arranged haphazardly. It was also yet another bunk wherein, had Mim desired, she could have licked the ceiling without too much effort. She wedged her bag into a locker and lay on the bed with her Lonely Planet.

"Hi."

"Hi."

The top bunk running perpendicular to hers contained a friendly looking head topped with a shaggy mane of well-washed hair.

"I'm Eric."

"I'm Mim."

They grinned at one another.

"I'm from South Africa."

"I'm from England."

Mim glowed. This was backpacker conversation. Next, they'd talk about their adventures: where they had been, where they were going. She would learn things, make a lifelong friend who was different to her, and have a young, fun travelling companion to boot.

"So Mim. Do you read much erotic fiction?"

"What?"

"Erotic fiction. You know, *Fisty Shades* and the like?" She opened her mouth, then shut it again. "Only, women mostly consume erotic fiction, you know? So I've been thinking about doing some erotic fiction for men. What do you think?"

"Sounds great."

"Would you pay to shoot a buffalo?" He didn't wait for her answer. "And would it be just as bad to shoot a chicken?"

Mim looked at Wiggy. His eyebrows were pointing in a peculiar direction. So, she imagined, were hers. She had never had a conversation like this before. Briefly, she wondered what Steven would have thought of someone talking at him like this. *He would get angry*, she thought. *He'd think the guy was taking the piss out of him*. She turned back to Eric, determined to get something interesting out of this conversation.

"I wouldn't want to…"

"Or throw a hand grenade at a cow? Let's say it was fifty dollars to do any of those things. I mean, which is worse? Does the size of the animal matter? Or is it the method?"

"I'm not sure that…"

"Miriam, this man is insane. You can't possibly stay here."

"Listen to this song. It makes me happy."

He pressed a button on his phone and the room was filled with trilling seventies psychedelic pop-flute.

I think he's on drugs, thought Mim. She had never known

anyone on drugs before. Not proper drugs. Knew nobody who had tried anything more than a few spliffs at parties. She wondered if he would try to make her do drugs. She wondered if she might quite enjoy it. Eric seemed pretty happy after all.

"Ugh, you always with this song." Another man, who was a least two thirds beard strolled into the room and flung himself onto another bunk. His accent was sort of Frenchish.

Eric laughed and cranked up the volume.

The trilling escalated.

"Miriam, this music is killing me." Wiggy's eyes were screwed shut. Mim chanced a smirk.

"So," she hollered over the person wittering on about their green and white kite, "I'm Mim from England. Where are you from?" She was addressing the newcomer. It appeared that he hadn't heard her, and she was about to repeat her question when he swivelled his furry head to her.

"Mim from England, you may call me *Zhjon*," (at least that's what she thought he said), "but do not ask where I am from." Mim wondered if he had intended to rhyme and stifled a giggle. "I belong to no land. I am a citizen of the world."

Eric rolled his eyes in sync with Wiggy, although he obviously didn't realise that.

"Right." Mim dug around for another conversational topic to indulge in. "So, what is there to do around here?"

A guffaw from another new arrival meant that her question went unanswered. "No way man! Same bunk!" A tanned face grinned from beneath a mop of strawy hair. The man threw a bike helmet onto the bunk below Mim's. "G'day. Tom. I banged a chick on this bunk last time I was here." A happy sigh puffed out of him. "Ready to get on it?"

Eric leapt from his bunk, flicking the horrid music off (*"oh sweet relief, Miriam!"*) followed by a casual shift to upright from *Zhjon-don't-ask-where-I'm-from*. All eyes were on Mim.

"Miriam, you are at least fifteen years too old to even be sharing the same air as these children. Decline this 'invite' immediately."

Mim poked her tongue out at Wiggy (the rest of the company was clearly insane anyway) and slid down. "I am indeed ready to get on it (whatever 'it' may be)."

21

SHOES IN THE SHOWER

They bonded over a mutual avoidance of Chris. Or Fungal Foot Chris, as he came to be known. Chris was a member of The Brigade of the Perpetually Unfortunate, who further cemented his place with everything he said and everything he did.

Chris had been 'kidnapped' between the station and the hostel: his taxi driver had taken him deep into the jungle (according to Chris) and left him stranded there. He had used the sun to navigate and arrived at the hostel four hours later and burned to a crisp. As he lay in bed recovering the next day, the former occupant of Tom's bed had stolen his ipod. When he eventually ventured out to eat, he acquired some sort of gastro issue which left him spent and feeble in a sweaty pile on his bed for three days. Finally, in recovery, he'd discovered that he had a fungal foot infection.

"Erm, everyone," he'd muttered in a barely audible monotone, "just a heads up. I've got this fungus. On my feet. Looks pretty infectious."

Mim retched slightly, resolving to wear her shoes in the shower from that point onwards.

It did look infectious. But what seemed to be more infectious was his capacity for Unfortunatism. Eric, feeling sorry for him, had taken him for a coffee. Chris had vomited it back up all over Eric's foot.

"I'd offer to clean that for you, but I used my last tissue wiping pus off this sunburn blister."

Peter - a nine foot twelve (well, maybe not quite, but definitely the tallest man Mim had ever seen) Dutchman and Tom had gone to dinner with him, only for him to realise that he had a hole in his pocket and all of his money had fallen out.

Mim had been about to walk into the dorm when a hand grabbed her from the stairs.

"Oh!"

"Ssshhhh!" It was Peter, the giant Dutchman. "You can't go in there."

"Why not?"

"Because Fungal Foot Chris has just got news that his rabbit-pet was sent to bed."

Mim frowned. "Sent to bed?"

"Ya. For a forever sleep."

"Oh. Put to sleep."

"Ya. Put to sleep." Peter set his mouth into a grim line. "He is like a grey cloud."

Mim nodded. She did not want to be in the room with a grey cloud. "Is anyone else in there with him?"

Peter shook his head wildly. "No! I got them out. I felt the cloud and I got them out. I told Jean and Tom that they hadn't renewed their bed. And Eric walked in and remembered that he had to get tickets for a thing. I was just waiting for Ben and you."

"Aw, you waited for me?"

"Ya, and Ben."

"Ben?"

"Ya, *Canadian* Ben."

"Ah, Canadian *Ben*." Mim giggled. She liked the feeling. Someone waiting for her, wanting to shield her from miserable people. And the fuzzy niceness of being part of a group. "Right. So what now?"

"We eat a thing. Then we drink beer on the beach. And maybe he is sleeping when we get back."

"Like his rabbit," muttered Wiggy.

Mim was on excellent form. Just enough beer to make her fun and friendly, not enough to make her maudlin and unintelligibly Northern. Music was pumping from a nearby beach club that they were far too scruffy and backpackery to enter, and the water shimmered under the Edam-slice moon.

"So I'm looking for my bucket of cocktails and shouting at this German fella for stealing it, and I look down and I'm only sitting in my bloody bucket!"

Mim roared with the rest of them. They were a funny group. Jean was a bit quiet (not Zhjon, she'd discovered when he'd written it on a beer mat for her) but when he spoke, it was either deeply profound, or hilarious. Eric was delightfully insane. He reminded her of Schubert when he was a puppy. Tom was brash and adventurous - his stories mostly involving him being somewhere he shouldn't have been, doing things he definitely shouldn't have been doing with people he categorically shouldn't have been doing them with. She was in deep admiration of Ben. Travelling alone before his Muscular Dystrophy got the better of him, he was taking things slowly, but tackling as much of Asia as he could.

"It's no big deal," he shrugged when she spoke of her admiration for him. "But if you feel sorry for me, you could kiss me, and that'd make us both feel better." Mim nudged him, but suspected he was only half joking.

Peter was the one fanning some embers though. Just little ones. As the music from the bar took a turn for the mellower, they sat close together on the beach, their calves touching lightly.

"Say the name of it again."

"Oh-boh. Oboe." Mim grinned. "If you're talking to English people you have to say oh-boh, otherwise you'll get yourself into trouble."

"Oh-boh."

"That's it."

"In Dutch, it is hobo"

Mim laughed. "Yeah, but you don't want to go around telling people you've been blowing a hobo!"

Peter wrinkled his nose and grinned. "I'm going to go take a smash. When I get back, you can tell me more English instrument words." He patted her leg and headed for the water.

Mim rubbed the hairs on her arm that were standing to attention despite the heat.

"Miriam, do you have amorous leanings towards this stringbean?"

Her arm hairs wilted. "He's just nice, Wiggy. That's all." It was just about dark enough to mask the pinkness that skittered into her cheeks, but the heat was still there. "Why, do you have some form of prejudiced opinion on that?"

"Simply asking a question Miriam." He turned away from her. "You just seem…"

"Seem what?"

He faced her. "Happy." He stretched his head back to take in the canvas of pinprick stars.

Mim filled her lungs with the delicious night air. "I think I am."

22

BEN AND THE ART OF MOTORCYCLE MAINTENANCE

In Dong Hoi, they accidentally lost Peter. They lost him somewhere between the train station and the slightly run down hotel they were headed to; somewhere amidst a crowd of excitable children that took a shine to the giant man. Ben had been taking it slowly, as was necessary, and Mim felt obliged to stay with him, and though she had tried to keep her eyes on Peter, he'd become enveloped in the horde.

Mim surveyed the hotel. "It's not in the book," she offered.

"Dong Hoi isn't in the book."

Ben was correct. This whole expedition had been Peter's idea anyway. Mim wasn't that excited about caves and was downright terrified of motorbikes, but she wanted Peter to continue thinking that she was the intrepid feminine travelling goddess that she had sold herself as. And now they had lost him. Ben was okay, but - and she hated herself for thinking it - so slow.

"Where's the giant gone, Miriam?" Wiggy sniffed the air. "It's just you and the broken chap now."

Mim jabbed him with her elbow. Thankfully, Ben hadn't noticed.

"Come on Mim. I'll race ya!"

Mim swallowed a sigh and took off onto the first step slowly.

They booked a room with three beds in case Peter did show up, but later, over thin rice paper noodles wrapped around fat prawns, they decided that he had probably gone somewhere else.

"Probably run off with a Vietnamese woman," suggested Ben. "They're pretty attractive."

"Pretty devious, more like," muttered Wiggy. "That prawn looks good."

Mim hoped he hadn't run off with a Vietnamese woman. She hoped that, somehow, she would manage to tuck Wiggy into a box and try to get a bit romantic with Peter. *As long as they were sitting down,* she plotted. He really was extraordinarily tall.

"So Mim, will we still do this thing tomorrow?" Ben had a wisp of coriander hanging from his lip. Mim struggled not to stare at it. *Should she tell him?* she wondered.

She shrugged. "Of course. I'm excited."

"Miriam, he looks like the corpse of Davy Crockett with that hanging from his face. Tell him it's there for pity's sake."

"You've got a …" she paused.

He grinned. "Got a what?"

"Erm." She touched his lip with her finger, swiping the coriander pedicle from his mouth. She wiped it on her napkin.

Ben's grin widened, eyes softening. "Oh, Mim…" He licked his lips.

"No! You had a thing!" She pushed the napkin,

complete with green stalk at him. "There, see! I wasn't trying to…"

Ben cleared his throat, taking another bite of his roll, looking anywhere but Mim. Mim looked at the table.

"Hah! Miriam, that was painful." Wiggy chuckled. "How do you do it?" Mim flicked V shaped fingers at him.

"So Ben," Mim started. He pasted an overly bright grin on his mouth. "Where in Canada are you from?"

Ben glanced at his Canada sport team shirt. "I'm not." He swallowed the bit of food he was chewing. "Sshh. I'm American."

"Oh. You just like Canadian…" she fished for what the sport might be, "basketball teams?"

"No!" Ben swigged his beer. "I try to pass as Canadian because everybody hates Americans. Don't you hate Americans?"

Mim thought of Donald Trump and a ghastly woman who had been her team leader in the call centre for a few months. "A bit."

Ben nodded. "Me too." He finished the last bite of his roll. "Ready?"

Peter didn't appear that night. Mim was disappointed. She had left a message at reception, but in the morning, there was just her, Wiggy on the floor, Ben snoring into his pillow and a sad empty bed.

They trooped slowly to the garage next door where the receptionist had assured them they would get a good deal on the motorcycles. Mercifully, the motorcycles turned out to be mopeds - still terrifying, but marginally less so than a geary, growly death machine.

"You drive one before?"

Ben nodded confidently, Mim more slowly.

"You are a bona fide idiot, Miriam. You've already nearly killed me once on one of these things."

"Wiggy, you are already dead," she muttered. "It's me I need to worry about."

"It's easy," whispered Ben. "We'll get one each. I don't want to slow you down if you want to explore something that I can't do."

Without the bags, there was plenty of space for Wiggy and Mim did not need to wear him like a cloak. For this, they were both grateful.

Mim perched gingerly, barely touching the handles in case the scooter ran away.

"Come on Mim!"

She turned the key in the ignition and the machine jiggered into life. Ben was waiting for her on the garage forecourt. She flicked the foot stand up, as she had watched Ben do and gently turned the handle. The moped shot forward, scraping her toe on the gravel.

"Ow."

"Oh Miriam. Can we please just get off? Perhaps get a taxi there?"

"Mim!"

"I'm coming!"

She tried again, this time twisting the handle gently and lifting both feet to the foot rests. The moped started moving, slowly, but steadily.

"Yay!"

Mim copied Ben who was indicating left and they headed onto the road, immediately engulfed in traffic.

"It'll all end in tears, Miriam." Wiggy gripped her tightly about the waist. She didn't answer, focusing all of her energy into watching Ben and not getting flattened by a truck. They moved through the traffic.

Soon, they were out of the city. Mim picked up speed, keeping as close as she could to Ben.

"I feel like I'm flying!"

"I feel like I am dying."

"Oh Wiggy, stop being such a killjoy."

Lush green rice paddies made way to viney trees. Splashes of sunlight leapt through the leaves, dappling the road ahead of her. She wondered if Steven would be impressed. 'Boring' Mim racing through the jungle on a motorbike (well, sort of). She imagined him standing by the roadside (though why he'd be standing around in a jungle in Vietnam did cross her mind, but she was happy to dismiss it in favour of the fantasy), her whizzing by, her speeding tyre splattering him with jungley mud.

"Splat, you wanktard!"

"Pardon?"

"Nothing." She grinned and roared on.

At a crossroad, Ben had stopped and was consulting the map that the receptionist had given them. Mim slowed to his side.

"Which way?"

Ben turned the map around, then back. He handed it to Mim. She peered at it.

"I think we're here." She jabbed a spot on the map.

"No Miriam, we definitely are not."

"We are," she roared.

"I didn't say anything," laughed Ben. "I trust you. Do you want to lead."

"No Miriam. Do not lead. You will lead us into the abyss of monumental doom and perpetual lostness."

Mim scowled. "Okay. I'll lead." She thrust the map back to Ben. "I think I've got it."

She indicated left, lifting her feet and moving off slowly.

"No Miriam!" Wiggy shouted in her ear.

"What?" Mim shrieked and felt the moped swerve beneath her. The front wheel twisted and she felt them being carried downwards. "Aaaaaggh!"

Mim's face hit dirt.

"Mim, are you alright?"

Ben's engine stopped growling, and she could hear him limping towards her. Wiggy was squashing her.

"Get off me!" Mim wiggled, pushing Wiggy away. They were in a ditch. A shallow one, but a ditch nonetheless. She clambered out, dusting her knees, Wiggy scrabbling around behind her.

Ben frowned at the bike. "We've got to get that out."

Mim nodded. "Oh, right, yeah. Look, I'll do it." Her voice was shaky. Ben nodded and sat on a rock, taking a glug of water from his bottle.

"Well, that's torn it Miriam." Mim glared at Wiggy.

The ditch was approximately one moped deep by one moped wide. She had managed to successfully wedge the moped into a perfectly dug moped grave. Mim shook her head. There was no way she would be able to roll it anywhere: the only way out would be to actually lift the thing. *It didn't feel heavy when I was driving it,* she reasoned. *It shouldn't be that heavy to lift.* Besides, she had done a few more boxercise classes before she left, and, added to the fact that she had been lugging her backpack about, she was probably at her peak strength. She rolled her neck, cracked her fingers and slithered down into the ditch.

"Right." She grabbed it by the handlebars and tugged it upwards. It raised a little, but Mim realised that was not going to work. She would have to lift it over her head to get it out of the ditch and then she would be trapped under it. She put it back down and chewed a fingernail.

"Try the middle, Miriam," urged Wiggy, peering at her in the ditch.

Lost for other ideas, she straddled the seat and gripped it in a vehicular bear hug. With her chin resting on the saddle and arms gripping the footrest part, she couldn't really get purchase. Her arms weren't long enough and her fingers kept slipping off. She changed her grip so that she was clinging to the smooth side bit that she assumed housed the engine, owing to how hot it was.

"You could help," she muttered out of the side of her mouth to Wiggy.

"What?"

"Nothing Ben. I'm doing just fine." She muttered again. "Get down here."

Wiggy sighed. He placed a reluctant foot either side of the ditch over Mim and reached for her waist. "Three, two, one, heave."

They heaved. The moped lifted an inch from its tomb. "Again!" They heaved again. It travelled another inch closer to freedom. "And again!"

"Oof!"

They dropped it.

"It's no good Ben. It's too heavy." Ben buried his face in his hands. Wiggy shrugged. "Perhaps we can go get help?"

"Have you seen anyone else on this road?" Ben ran a

hand through his hair. "You're killing me here Mim. I'm disabled for Christ's sake."

Mim flashed a helpless squint at Wiggy, who shrugged.

Ben shambled to the ditch and surveyed it critically. He sighed and made a rolling up his sleeves gesture, despite wearing a short sleeved Canadian something else shirt. He shook his head.

He took a faltering limp into the hole and hooked his arms under the handlebars. Heaving, he managed to lift the front tyre so that it rested above the rim of the ditch. He inched round to the back, locking his fingers under the back seat and lifted. "Hup!" He pushed it forwards, gradually lifting the offending article out of the ditch.

"Bit of help would be nice, Mim."

"Right. Of course." She lolloped to the front of the bike and surveyed it for a moment, wondering where her fingers could go without getting them squashed. She eventually settled on the wheel itself. Ben pushed and Mim semi-rolled the bike, which eventually lurched free. It wobbled before flopping to one side in an exhausted heap. Mim dropped to the grass beside it.

Ben glared, dragging himself inelegantly out and joining them on the grass.

"Thanks." Mim blushed.

"Miriam, you are appalling. You just let a disabled chap fish your horrid vehicle out of a ditch." Wiggy guffawed. Mim stuck her elbow in his thigh.

23

CALL MY NAME AND CAVE ME FROM THE DARK

"Ah, Mim, Ben. You came!"

Mim almost wept at the sound of Peter's voice. Ben hadn't spoken to her since the bike incident, though she had caught him shaking his head a few times. She thought it would probably be a good thing to ditch him soon. Pun entirely intended.

"There's your giant Miriam. His friend is rather attractive."

Standing by Peter's side was a sinewy blonde girl whose deep tan screamed a lifetime of small-bikini beach trips. Her face was tilted curiously. Mim's belly flipped, a badly tossed pancake high in her innards.

Peter greeted Ben with a handshake, Mim with a slightly awkward hug which brought her face somewhere just north of his belly button.

"Did you get bikes?"

Ben nodded vigorously. "Yep. Yep we got bikes. Some of us managed to keep ours on the road too."

Mim's face burned hotly.

"This is Fleur." Peter slapped the girl's back, a little

hard, Mim noted with a small quiver of victory. Fleur half-smiled, half-scowled before flashing Peter with a dazzling grin. "Fleur. Mim. Ben."

"Peter, our boat goes in a few minutes." Her accent sounded like Peter's.

"Yeah guys. Get tickets for our boat."

Fleur fully scowled then.

"Ah, Miriam. I think you have acquired yourself a competitor!"

A little blue and yellow boat bobbed by a rustically constructed wooden jetty. Mim and Ben had successfully got tickets for the same boat as Peter and Fleur, much to Fleur's evident consternation. They climbed in and Mim found herself sitting next to Fleur.

"What age are you?" she asked Mim loudly.

"Erm. I'm thirty-five. Why?"

Fleur frowned in the way that most people do when they are trying to do difficult maths in their heads. "Peter and I are the same age." She twisted to look at him, but he was deep in conversation with Ben. "We are travelling. You know. For a long time. Are you on holiday?"

Mim shrugged. "What's the difference?"

"I think you are too old to be travelling. Only young people travel. Old people go on holiday."

"Ooh Miriam. You need to slap this sewer-mouthed harlot!"

Mim took a deep breath, and surveyed the scenery. Phong Nha cave yawned languorously in the midday heat. The gleaming turquoise water reminded her of a ring her mother had worn when she was young. It was gold, the bluey-green stone dappled with grey, small claws clutching it from both sides, holding it up like an offering. Mim had liked to run her fingertips over the cool stone when she sat on her mum's lap. She had lost the ring a few years earlier on a rainy moor walk with Steven. She blinked away a threatening tear, making sure her face was angled away from Fleur.

"Come on Miriam. Are you going to let her be rude to you like that?"

She had been about to move on, but a bubble of rage popped. "One day you'll be thirty-five, and you'll probably still have no manners."

"Is that it?" Wiggy shook his head sadly.

"You'll still be rude, and if you keep on sunbathing that much, you'll stop looking like a slab of caramel and instead resemble my nan's old leather suitcase. Good luck finding enough collagen cream to iron that out."

Mim grinned at Wiggy, who flashed her a thumbs up.

"Sorry Kim. Did you say a thing? I was asking a question of Peter."

Mim scowled. "Nope. Nothing."

The boat drifted slowly into the darkness of the cave. Mim trailed her hand through the cool water and admired the stalagmites and stalactites that made fibrous reaches to the ceiling and floor.

"I forget the names of these things." Peter indicated the calcious pillars.

Mim told him. "Tights go down!" Peter laughed. A good laugh, wide mouth, head thrown back. Fleur tossed her hair.

"You make funny jokes, Mim." He grinned at her. She shivered.

Further into the cave, they had a chance to climb out and walk around part of the cave. Fleur pushed past Mim and glued herself to Peter's side.

"Mim, can you help me?" Ben reached out his hand. "Struggling to get out of this boat."

Fleur and Peter disappeared around a corner. Mim reached her hand to Ben and heaved him out of the boat.

"What are you doing Miriam? Leave the hogtied Yank! The strumpet is trying to trap your giant!"

Mim shook her head lightly. She and Ben stepped onto the slippery walkway. Ben gripped her arm for support.

"Ben, I'm sorry. About the bike. I feel terrible."

Ben snorted. "Don't. You're a good chick. I know I'm a pain in the ass to be around, but you've hung out with me longer than most people do."

Mim cast a glance at Wiggy. *See*, it said. *I'm a good chick.* Wiggy shook his head, but Mim noted no real conviction in it.

"Hey, Ben. Why did Batman rush into the Batcave?" Ben stopped walking and shrugged. "He had to go to the bat room!"

He shook his head but gave a little laugh anyway.

"Hey Ben. I once drank tequila in a cave. It was a shot in the dark!"

"Mim, your jokes are so bad!" But Ben was laughing.

"What? What is funny?" Peter stopped walking so that Mim and Ben caught up. Fleur was still striding on, talking to a Peter who was no longer by her side.

"Mim. She's just funny."

"You're not funny Miriam. Your jokes are atrocious. These people are dimwits. That is the only reason that they are laughing."

Mim pulled a stupid face at Wiggy, which made both Peter and Ben laugh. It was her infamous rabbity one that she usually pulled when nervous, but in the cave, it was entirely intentional. Something about Fleur's attitude made her feel silly.

"Why are you all stopping in the cave?" Fleur was standing above them, fists pressed hard into hips. "I came to see the cave and you are all being slow."

"Well, I've got muscular dystrophy and these two are kind enough to wait for me. Please, be my guest. Walk on ahead."

She almost stamped her foot like a toddler having a tantrum. "Peter?"

He sighed audibly and followed her, a slight shrug in his shoulders.

"That girl's an ass."

Mim grinned. "She's clearly a bit insecure. I've met her type before." She pulled her camera out of her bag. "Now, stand next to this phallic rock formation and let me get a photo of you."

On the return journey, Fleur elbowed Mim aside to get a seat in the boat by Peter. His arms were draped over the back of the bench and Fleur nestled snugly in their width, looking to all intents and purposes as though his arm was deliberately around her.

"Is this your honey?" A small Vietnamese woman

wearing a large bow in her hair approached Peter, bobbing a nod at Fleur.

Peter laughed. "No." Fleur glowered.

The woman responded by flicking her hair and fluttering her lashes. Peter flushed and looked away.

"So," Peter said, "there's this other cave. Paradise Cave. It's like thirty kilometres away. We should go there. They say it's very good. They say that in my book."

"Isn't it like, a really big climb and a long walk?"

"Ya."

Ben shook his head. "Then I'll probably give that one a miss." He grinned at Mim. "Today's already been pretty physical. But you three should definitely go."

"I want to go," announced Fleur.

"Mim?" Peter poked her in the arm. "You will come?"

Mim looked at Fleur's sour expression and back to Peter's smile. He seemed to want her there. Maybe he liked her. Or maybe he was a raging narcissist who enjoyed having women fawn over him. Wiggy was being uncharacteristically quiet.

"Yeah. I'll go with you. Then maybe we can all have dinner together?" Peter and Ben grinned. Fleur frowned. "Unless you've got somewhere else you need to be Fleur?"

24

PARADISE BY THE CLASH CLAWED FIGHT

Fleur was not a happy bunny. Peter suggested that Fleur ride with Mim.

"It makes sense. You two are small, I am large." He shrugged. "Fleur knows the way. We came past that way already."

Mim grinned. She didn't want Fleur on her bike, but the woman's palpable objection made Mim want to demonstrate her 'better-personness.' Of course, it would make things uncomfortable for Wiggy, but that wasn't necessarily a bad thing.

"*I'm* happy to have you Fleur." She spread her arms wide, inviting Fleur to object.

Fleur tutted. "Fine. I will go with you." The *you* was accompanied by a dismissive wave. Mim beamed him her most angelic smile and clambered on the bike.

"Miriam, I object to having this fussock with us. I see why you did it, but really, it is going to be most dreadfully uncomfortable." Fleur looked both the bike and Mim up and down. "I wish I could do something horribly haunting to her." Mim gave a tiny shake of her head. "Aha! You have a revenge of your own planned. Are you going to drive her into a ditch?"

Fleur sighed as though she was doing everybody a favour at great personal sacrifice to her fabulous self. She lifted a brown leg gingerly over and parked her buttocks as close to the back as possible, far, far away from Mim. She hooked her fingers under the seat and sighed loudly again.

"This way Team Paradise!"

Mim whooped, following Peter's lead, Wiggy tucked between the women with room to spare. They roared through the jungle, Peter and Mim laughing and shrieking.

"I'm turning to face her Miriam." Mim waited. "My word, her visage is a picture! She looks like she's swallowed a mouthful of quinine." Mim had no idea what quinine was, but assumed that it was unpleasant.

It took them about forty minutes to get there. Mim was quite sweaty. When she got off the bike, her legs made a farty-suctioning noise against the seat. She hoped Peter hadn't heard. Also, the helmet had made her head hot. When she took a quick glance in the moped wing mirrors, her hair was stuck in a helmetty shape, making her look like a hairy bowling ball. She stuck out her tongue at her goblin-esque reflection and mussed her hair back into some sort of hair shape.

Fleur removed her helmet and shook her hair out slowly. There was no sweat glueing her hair anywhere untoward and it swayed from her follicles unencumbered. It was as though she was an advert, not for shampoo, but for hair in general. *See*, it mocked, *this is how hair should be.*

Mim spotted Peter watching Fleur and her hair. She couldn't actually read his expression, but Mim's hair had never been looked at like that before. Nor, she reckoned, pushing a cursory hand through it, would it ever be.

"Right. Well here we are. 'Welcome to Paradise,'" she sang. Peter frowned, Fleur rolled her eyes. "It's Green Day. Remember it?"

"No, because it is probably an old song," said Fleur at the same time as Peter yelled "yes! I remember it!"

Mim grinned. "It's all about…" she glanced at Wiggy, suddenly feeling shy. "Never mind that. Let's get in this cave."

It was quite a hike to the entrance. Peter's long legs carried him up easily. Athleticism was obviously one of Fleur's many physical attributes so she skipped by Peter effortlessly. Mim wasn't athletic and the heat was slowing her down, causing her to gasp for air. The millstone in the shape of a dead aristocrat hindered matters further. He kept stopping.

"I just don't understand the joy in this kind of endeavour Miriam. Transport exists for a reason you know."

About halfway to the entrance, Mim lost sight of Peter and Fleur. "Now look what you've done." She took a large swig of her water, spilling most of it down her chin. "She's probably seducing him right now with her hair and her suntan."

"And if he is so shallow that his desire is piqued by material things, then he is surely not worthy of ardent pursuit?"

"I don't know what ardent is. But I've never really done the pursuit thing before, you know. I was with Steven since we were at school."

"Nor should you, Miriam." He shook his head. "That is his role."

Mim rolled her eyes. "It's not the forties Wiggy." She wiped the errant water from her chin and sipped delicately this time. "People pursue. Male and female. That's just how it is now." She capped her bottle. "Hey, you've never told me about your love life."

"You've never asked."

"Well?" Mim wedged her hands to her hips waiting for answers.

"Well, what Miriam? What is it precisely that you want to know?"

"Were you married?"

"No."

"Why not?"

"What do you mean, 'why not?' It's not the law you know." He fiddled with his fingers.

"Right. But did you want to?"

"I…" he sucked his cheeks in. "Why are you suddenly interested in this? I've been stuck to you for months and you have asked me very little about my life."

"I'm asking you now." She took a few steps up. "Besides, you get a bit tetchy when I ask you things."

"About my death, Miriam. I get 'tetchy' when you rudely ask about my death."

"Right." She stopped again. "Well tell me now. Did you want to get married? Did you have someone in mind."

Wiggy stared out over the jungle forming a green blanket below as they climbed higher.

"Well?"

"Let's go rescue the giant from Mata Hari." He climbed. She had no choice but to follow.

"We waited for you!"

Peter patted her sweaty arm with an equally moist

palm. Fleur, arms wrapped across her body, looked neither delighted about waiting for Mim or, Mim noted with irritation, sweaty.

"Great! Well," Mim patted his arm back, "let's get in there."

"Miriam, patting his arm like an awkward father at the school gates is not terribly romantic. You may need to refine the wooing"

Mim pulled a face and they sank into the darkness of the cool cavern.

"Wow."

A yawning hole swallowed them, shrinking them into micro people. Mim had never felt so tiny or humble. Her breath faltered somewhere between her mouth and her chest and her lips stretched wide. Great leaden walls reached and curved: stone waves caught mid-roll. Protrusions rose like an enchanted city from the ground. Mim turned slowly, stretching her neck to take in everything in quiet reverence.

Walkways had been erected to stop tourists from breaking ankles and whatnot and the three stepped softly across them. Right then, Mim forgot. She forgot about Peter and Fleur, and she even forgot about Wiggy. She liked the cool, damp air on her skin, liked the rainy smell tinged with something slightly sour and she liked the way her shoes whispered on the wood. She trailed a finger across one of the stalagmites and shivered, delighting in the jewel of a water droplet that made its home on her fingertip.

"It is not so big as I had hoped."

Mim squashed the droplet between her finger and thumb. "What?"

Fleur shrugged. "I have seen better caves. And this

walking fence. It is silly." She slapped the rail with the heel of her hand. "No adventure here. Just tourist, tourist, tourist."

"I think it's magnificent." Mim said it quietly, but it had some force behind it.

"That's because you are a tourist. On holiday." She shrugged and folded her arms. "You are allowed to like the tourist things." She grinned slyly in Peter's direction. Mim felt her face grow warm.

Peter shuffled sideways to get around the two women. He nodded, stopped and then nodded again. "It's a big cave. Ya. Very big." He nodded for a third time, cleared his throat and continued following the walkway.

"Miriam, I hate this woman. And the giant is pretty pathetic too."

Fleur watched Peter go, flashed a mouth-only grin at Mim then continued after him.

"You do not have to stay with these people, Miriam. You can do this alone, or meet nicer people."

"I can't do it alone, can I Wiggy? I've got a dead fellow stuck to me." She snorted. "Now come on. Can you somehow haunt her? You know, just give her a little fright?" She threaded her arm through Wiggy's.

"Oh Miriam, I thought you'd never ask!"

Once again, they were waiting, Peter and his long limbs twitching, Fleur with her pointy little brown elbows poking out of a tight fold.

"You are very slow."

"And you are very impatient." Mim swigged her water. She felt an admiring pat on the back from Wiggy's thin fingers. "If you don't want to wait for me, don't." She strode towards the start of the descent that would lead them back to the car park.

"Wait Miriam."

Wiggy stopped dead at the top of the steps.

"I'm trying to stride purposefully," she hissed. "Come on. You're ruining my exit."

"I'm about to make it more impressive, Miriam." She followed his eyeline. A smallish grey macaque was peering from between some tree branches, surveying the passers by with a mixture of curiosity and longing. "What are you supposed to do in the presence of a monkey, Miriam?"

"Erm, stay calm, move slowly and not make direct eye contact, I think."

"Correct."

"Wiggy, no...please don't..."

Peter and Fleur reached Mim.

"Were you talking to yourself?"

"What are you looking at?" Peter peered where Mim was looking.

"Move her a bit closer, Miriam."

"No!"

"Oh, look at the monkey Peter! Isn't it..."

Wiggy angled himself directly behind Fleur. He stared directly at the monkey, challengingly. The monkey cocked his head to one side.

"Wiggy..." warned Mim.

Wiggy started dancing. Great, spasmodic flailing and waving bolted through his long arms right behind Fleur's pretty hair. His fingers waggled enticingly: they could have been a delicious spider or crab.

"Wiggy, no!"

The macaque stretched up. In one leap, he had swung from his spot in the tree.

Fleur screamed. The macaque, aiming for Wiggy, smacked into Fleur's head, gripping that shiny hair. Perched on her shoulder, he whipped his little clawish hands through the air at Wiggy's face, failing to meet anything solid. He swiped again. Fleur's cries pierced the air. The monkey grabbed her nose for further support which turned her shriek into a sort of honk. Peter waved his hands wildly, but backed away from Fleur and her face-monkey. Wiggy kept dancing, eyes wild and wired.

A crowd had stopped. "Macaque attack," someone muttered, but everyone kept a safe distance from the action.

Mim took a deep breath. She surveyed the scene for one more second before grabbing her water bottle. She felt like a Ghostbuster. Unscrewing the cap, she took aim. Lining the bottle up like a javelin, she leaned back. Another steadying breath, calm against the audio of screaming. Putting all of her force into the launch, she leaned her weight behind the bottle and forced it forwards.

The jet sprung from the vessel, hitting both the macaque and Fleur with gusto. The monkey stopped flailing at Wiggy and turned to face her. Mim kept her eyes away from the macaque's, staring instead at his hand curled around a chunk of Fleur's hair. He bared his daggery teeth at her, whistled out a hiss and then leapt from Fleur's shoulder into a nearby tree. His hand still gripped some strands of the shiny locks he had taken as a souvenir from his landing point's head.

Fleur quivered. Water dripped down her face and her hair resembled the remains of a mattress Schubert had eaten as a puppy. Her bottom lip hung down, trembling and her breath was ragged.

Mim took a deep breath. "Fleur, are you okay?"

Fleur shuddered in response, weeping. Peter swooped in, patting the soggy woman on the shoulder, all the while watching the monkey, now adorning himself with some of Fleur's hair.

Mim shook the last remaining droplets of water onto her tongue, recapped her bottle and walked shakily to the remaining steps, Wiggy by her side. The watchers parted; a red sea of tourists.

"Too far Wiggy. Too far." Mim's hand wobbled as she reached for a tree vine to secure her.

"Not far enough, Miriam. Still, at least you also got to be the hero."

She glanced back. Peter was patting Fleur on her wet head. He gave Mim a thumbs up and grinned, before pulling the shuddering woman behind him.

"If you ever do anything like that again, I'll…"

"You'll what Miriam? Send me to Coventry? There is nothing either of us can do about the other's behaviour, so perhaps we should just let one another get on with it."

Mim glared.

Wiggy chuckled. "Macaque attack. Brilliant."

25

ALL BY MYSELF

The group revealed their plans that evening over *bun bo nam bo*. Fleur sulked over the meal, but the boys were in good spirits. They washed their food down with Huda beer and toasted their onward journeys. Nobody mentioned the monkey.

Ben was heading straight to Halong Bay before flying back to America for college. It appeared that, either Peter and Fleur had made their plans together, or one had decided to glue themselves to the plans of the other. Mim suspected the latter, but couldn't be bothered to speculate. They were going to Hanoi for a few days before heading to Halong Bay, which had been Mim's intention too, until she heard that that was what they were doing. She had no intention of being a third wheel and so, after a quick glance at a map and a picture of a pretty structure dwarfed by a green-tufted rock wall, she decided to go to Thanh Hoa.

"Wow, Mim. That's a bit off the beaten track." Peter was impressed. "Maybe we should go there?" He raised an eyebrow at Fleur who muttered, "no." Peter shrugged.

"You see Miriam. He is pathetic."

Mim nodded, and glanced around seeking out Peter's backbone. She liked him, but the Peter-fantasies were being shut down quickly.

The four of them slept in the cramped room, the air growing fusty in the night, and in the morning, trooped off to the station. Mim played cards with Ben while Peter read a book and Fleur sulked by the window. Every now and then, Peter gazed longingly at the card game, but would glance back to Fleur and sigh.

Mim's stop arrived first. She gamely trotted off, nomadic turtle-like under her backpack and waved to the others from the platform. As the train pulled away, she deflated.

"Cheer up Miriam. It is just you and I now."

Mim deflated more.

Thahn Hoa was fine. Actually, after the loneliness had worn off, she quite enjoyed being by herself again. Well, as by yourself as you can be with a dead man on you. She walked, ate good food, slept really well and had lots of faltering conversations with friendly Vietnamese people. *A smile*, she mused, *goes a long way*. She liked the ache in her cheekbones and the dryness on her teeth after a good smiling session. She wondered when she had stopped smiling so much back home.

Wiggy too seemed more relaxed, content to just amble quietly by her side taking in the city. When they climbed on the train to Hanoi, it felt like being gently roused from sleep.

26

HOW VERY HANOI-ING

Hanoi was busy. And dusty and hot, but Mim loved it. Motorbikes, ten abreast, dominated the roads. Everybody seemed to have purpose; everybody was going somewhere, had somewhere to be, something to do. Mim didn't of course, and she was enjoying that too. By day, she ambled around, sometimes stumbling on tourist spots like Hoa Loa Prison (*"ugh. Too many mannequins, Miriam"*) or the mausoleum of Ho Chi Minh (*"So grim!"*), sometimes just enjoying getting lost in the labyrinthine streets. Once, she stumbled across a cock fight, another day, she watched water puppet theatre while sipping ca phe trung. Mim felt alive and in love and adored it.

Wiggy, on the other hand, hated it. He went back to the moaning about '*dirty foreigners*' and Mim yearned for the peace he had granted her in Than Hoa. His clipped, posh voice twittering in her ear all of the time was irritating, more so because she was enjoying it so much.

She liked the anonymity. Hanoians (*is that what you would call them?*) were used to tourists and cast barely a glance in her direction. Animals did though, because Wiggy would draw attention to himself whenever he saw one. The cock waiting in his cage to fight freaked out when Wiggy jabbed at him through his bamboo cage. A skinny cat objected to him stroking it by mewling with abandon. But she slipped by fairly unnoticed.

In her hometown, she had never been anonymous. Despite its expansion in the course of her lifetime, everybody knew everybody, and, worse still, everybody knew everything about everybody. How Geraldine had been unaware of her move back to her dad's was a mystery. And (Mim shuddered whenever she thought of it) how many people had known about Steven and Cheryl Tiplady?

At night, Mim sat on a small plastic stool on the pavement outside of some eatery and sampled things that made her taste buds dance. She drowned out Wiggy's offensive commentary and did some well-focused people watching. She imagined what type of music everybody would be. The shifty looking man on the corner was a slice of shadowy gangster rap. The woman serving her *pho* was a fluttering flute melody. And the studious teenager, face buried in a textbook, was some hardcore electronic dance music.

One observational evening, a whinging female European voice drifted into her consciousness. She wasn't sure about the language, but the content was all misery and entitlement. Mim was fairly sure she heard the word *McDonald's* in there. This person was a generic trashy pop song featuring that irritating whiney-buzz that sounds like an angry bee. Mim sniggered and looked up to see who owned the voice.

Fleur.

That was who owned the voice. They caught one another's eye at exactly the same moment and Fleur stopped talking. Behind her, Peter trailed. It took him a few seconds to notice Mim, but when he did, he pulled her from her seat, almost toppling her bowl and pulled her into a tight embrace. She smelled the tang of sweat through the cotton of his t-shirt, but found herself strangely unmoved.

"It's so good to see you Mim."

"Oh lawks! It's this pair of clog-loving, cheese-sniffers again, Miriam."

She pulled away and sat back to her noodles. "Good to see you, too." Peter sat. Fleur rolled her eyes and then joined them. "So, how come you're still here? I thought you would be in Halong Bay by now."

"Ah, yes, but Fleur got sick." Fleur shifted uncomfortably. "Yes, she got really sick with the shit. You know. The wet shit. What is the word for that?"

Mim dropped her spoon in her bowl. "I get the picture." She looked at Fleur, clammy now on closer inspection. "Peter, the word you are looking for is diarrhoea. Please, eat this pho, because it is delicious but you have just put me off wet food for a while."

Peter tucked greedily in, while Fleur tinged a little more greenly under the neon strip light strapped half-heartedly to a canopy spoke.

"She is better now," he patted her grimly on the shoulder, "aren't you Fleur? So tomorrow, we get on the boat."

Fleur's face was that of someone who should definitely not get on a boat, possibly ever. It was the face of a woman who needed soft cushions and someone stroking her hair back from a sticky forehead in a nice, dark, cool, land-based environment. Mim tipped her a sympathetic nod. Fleur scowled back.

"She's a cream-faced loon Miriam."

Peter dropped the spoon into the empty bowl. "You

should come, Mim! On this boat. We can ask the lady if there's space!"

Fleur froze. Her waxy face solidified in an expression of abject horror. Wiggy was violently shaking his head.

"No! Miriam, you cannot be in a confined area with this excrement-leaking strumpet!"

Mim opened her mouth to refuse the offer, but was at a loss for a suitable excuse not to. She had, after all, intended to go on a boat trip. It seemed petty to say no just because she didn't like Fleur and - more evidently - that Fleur didn't like her.

"Brilliant! We're in."

"We?" Peter grinned.

"Me. I. I, Mim. Am in."

Wiggy groaned.

27

HALONG HAS THIS BEEN GOING ON?

"And this your cabin. It's very nice for three persons."

Mim, Peter and Fleur were wedged in the doorway. Steven would have called it *bijou* (although he pronounced it *bidgoo* which always had Mim rolling her eyes behind his back), Trisha would have called it *fucking tiny*. Mim was going to call it Hell.

The majority of the cabin was made up of beds. Two beds to be precise, barely an inch apart. A double and a single snuggling side by side. A bathroom the size of a Polly Pocket case wedged itself behind the door.

Mim surveyed the beds and did some bed maths. There was really no way that the next three days could be anything other than intolerable. She ran the scenarios around in her head.

Scenario 1: Peter and Fleur would take the double leaving Mim out cold on the single. She shuddered. She categorically did not want to be in a room with two people who may possibly be getting it on. It was too hideous to contemplate.

Scenario 2: She and Peter could have the double while

Fleur had the single. That wasn't a bad option, certainly the best of the three, but she wasn't sure if she was in the market for three days of death glares from a Dutch ice maiden whilst snuggling into somebody she wasn't sure she even liked.

Scenario 3: She and Fleur would share the bed. Peter would have the single and she would have to spoon a woman who might have dysentery. Mim shuddered.

The boatman pushed past them leaving the decision firmly in their hands.

"Well, this is nice." Mim's voice was too bright and filled the small cabin.

"I cannot sleep in small beds." Fleur glared disdainfully at the single. " I sleep dramatically."

Both Mim and Peter frowned.

"Right." Peter clapped his hands. "Well, you girls take the big bed. I will have the small bed."

Fleur was on the brink of protesting, but changed her mind.

"You're sure you are well enough to share a bed Fleur? You know, with the bottom problems and all."

"Ah true! Perhaps Fleur you would have the small bed and Mim and I can have the big bed?"

"No!" Fleur roared so loudly that Peter dropped his backpack.

"Okay." He scooped it up and placed it on the single bed. "You and Mim can have the big bed."

Mim thrilled - just a tiny bit - that Peter would choose to share a bed with her over Fleur. Though, she reminded herself, that might simply have been on account of the 'wet shits'.

After lunch, they stopped at a cave. There were about forty other people there, seriously detracting from the echoing beauty that Mim wanted to revel in. She longed to linger alone, but a guide marched them through at speed, presumably so the next group nipping at their heels wouldn't catch up to them.

"Peter and I, we're the same."

Mim pursed her lips.

Fleur continued. "Ya, we're like on this journey, you know. Self discovery. You're old. You're just on holiday. So that's why there's nothing common." She shrugged.

Wiggy was ready to pounce. Mim held him back and took a deep breath.

"Fleur, shut up. I'm tired of your irrelevant opinions, and Peter doesn't need you as a spokesperson. You don't know me. Stop commentating my life! How about you and I don't talk for the rest of this trip?"

Fleur regarded her cooly. "You older ladies are very sensitive." She stalked away.

"Miriam…"

"No Wiggy, no revenge, nothing." She put up a hand to quash his protest, the beginnings of a tear threatening to escape. "I'm done with her. I wanted to come here so much and I'm going to bloody well enjoy it."

The evening's entertainment was offered to them. Karaoke or squid fishing.

Mim snorted. "Oh! I thought he said 'squid fisting'."

Sebastian, one of her new French buddies giggled. "You're funny Mim." He clinked her glass. "Sante!"

She sipped her cocktail that his friend Paul had mixed

for her and got on with enjoying the company of four Parisian mixologists travelling Asia for six months. Peter looked on, Fleur twittering in his ear. They told stories, sampled cocktails and when Mim's head started to whirl, Wiggy gently steered her out of a rooftop moonbathe with Cedric and back towards her cabin.

"He's nice!" She protested.

"Nice Miriam, yes. But French."

"You're so racist Wiggy."

"They have a reputation. Besides, sharing cabins is all very boarding school and deeply undignified. Hardly the most fertile ground for romance."

"A moonbathe on a boat rooftop surrounded by this?" she flung out her arms at the karsts rising like Loch Ness Monsters all around her, "with a charming and attractive Frenchman? Really, what could be more romantic?"

Wiggy mumbled something.

"What?"

"It's 'pardon' Miriam, not a fishwifey 'what'. And nothing. It does not matter." Mim turned to fumble with her cabin key. "You are worth more."

Peter groaned when he woke up. Then he groaned a bit more over breakfast.

"My stomach hurts."

Fleur stroked his arm. "Poor Peter. You are sick?"

"Gosh, I hope that he's not getting the trots too, Miriam. Stay away from these parasite-infested flapdoodles!" Wiggy puppeted Mim into wafting a used serviette at them.

"Stop it!" she hissed.

Peter shook his head forlornly. "I do not think that I can do the kayak today."

Fleur let out a little gasp that Mim found inappropriately dramatic. It would have been a shade too dramatic had he just announced that he'd murdered David Attenborough. She frowned, catching Cedric's eye who toasted her with his breakfast beer.

"You two girls must go on without me!"

Eyes drawn wide, Fleur shook her head frantically. Her hair was sticking sweatily to her neck. Mim wondered if she'd studied melodrama alongside cold glaring and acerbic putdowns.

"Yes, yes, you must."

Mim shrugged. "Fine by me."

"But Peter! I should tend you."

"That's what the Europeans call it these days." Wiggy chuckled, nudging Mim in the ribs.

"No." Peter shook his head firmly. "Or Mim will be alone. She cannot drive the boat alone."

Fleur's skin went the shade of Tangy Toms. Mim wasn't sure whether that meant devastation or fury. Either way, it definitely was not joyful.

"Miriam, please do not get on a private vessel with that thing." He shook his head. "It will definitely kill you."

Mim did get on a boat with that thing.

Fleur sat at the front, Mim providing the navigation from the back. Wiggy perched behind her nervously.

"Got on a little rowing boat with Diggers once. Dreadful experience, Miriam. Ghastly experience! Showing off, old Diggers. Trying to impress the girls."

He went silent. Mim twisted. He was staring wistfully into the horizon. She nodded to him to carry on.

"Oh! Sorry, went off somewhere. Yes, showing off. Dropped one of his oars in. Got me to lean out after it. Tipped me in!" He fell silent. Mim listened to the tinkle, the gentle pull of the water on her paddle. Wiggy coughed. "Anyway. That was a long time ago."

Mim looked back in time to see him fishing a droplet out of his eye. She patted his knee.

"Fleur, are you going to paddle?"

Fleur was leaning back her paddle resting across her middle like a fairground ride safety harness. She seemed lost in thought.

"Fleur?"

"Hmm?" Fleur shielded her eyes from the sun. "Oh. Yes. I can paddle."

They paddled on in silence, oars slicing the water.

"It's so beautiful, Miriam."

Mim stopped paddling and actually looked around properly.

"It is beautiful." She gazed around at the gleaming aquamarine surrounding her, grey and green humps rising like prehistoric creatures from the deep. She was in the picture. The picture that had taken her breath away all of those months ago in her sad kitchen stuffed with broken hope. The sun beamed on her skin, prickling with the kiss of the light breeze and the salty water. A small sob escaped her throat. She tried to swallow it before Fleur noticed.

But Fleur had stopped paddling too. She turned to Mim, caught her eye and gave a small smile. She nodded and turned away.

They sat like that until the guide told them that they were going back.

Mim found Fleur lying alone on the top deck staring up at the moon.

"She smiled at you once Miriam, and now you're taking her presents?" Wiggy indicated the two glasses of cucumber mint French gimlet that Cedric had mixed for her.

Mim ignored him and walked to where Fleur was.

"Thought you might like to try this." Fleur wriggled up to sit and took the glass. She glanced fleetingly at Mim.

"Thank you." She peered into it before taking a sip. "Oooh. It is very nice."

Mim sipped hers.

"You were quiet over dinner. I wondered if you were okay?"

Fleur looked back at the moon. For a moment, Mim wasn't sure whether she'd heard her or not.

"My father would take me to row sometimes, on weekends. I liked it." Fleur smiled. The moon shimmered on her face, reminding Mim of the piles of mother-of-pearl buttons she used to dig her fingers into at the market. "When he got sick, we did not go anymore. Then..." She did a little hiccup of a sob. "Today made me think about that."

Mim nodded. "How long's it been?"

"Five years. Eight since he was sick."

They sipped their drinks.

Mim swallowed, gazing into the water. "I was fifteen when my mum died." Fleur turned, surprised. Mim nodded again. "Just turned. Couple of weeks after my birthday. I've never felt pain like it."

Fleur bit her lip.

"One day she was there, the next, gone. I couldn't understand that she just wasn't anymore. I was horrible. Snapping at dad like it was his fault. And it wasn't, obviously. Faulty light at a crossing."

They both took a glug of their drinks.

"How long...until you were normal again?"

Mim shrugged. "I'm not sure what normal is. Or if it is even a thing. But this trip, being here, doing things on my own for the first time, that feels pretty good. I can maybe get used to this as normal."

Fleur smiled and a fat tear plopped out of her eye. "You and I, we're the same. I did not know, but we are."

Mim smiled back. "I guess we are. I stopped being horrible to my dad at some point, and we're closer now than ever."

"I'm sorry I was mean."

"I'm sorry a monkey jumped on your head."

Fleur scrunched up her face. "It smelled so bad!" She giggled then sighed. "My father always wanted to travel."

Mim patted her shoulder. "I bet he'd be really proud of you."

"And your mother proud of you."

They clinked their glasses.

Hi Trisha,

Halong Bay is so gorge Trish! Just like in the pictures. I've been eating fresh prawns and making loads of friends on a boat. May have buried the hatchet with my arch-nemesis! You always said I'd find another after Angie Moon moved to Grimsby!

I think you'd really like it here. Hope lambing season went well for Colin. Don't forget to drop in on dad and Schubes.

Love Mimintroll xxx

"You never told me about your mother."

Mim raised an eyebrow. "You never asked."

"It's a tricky subject, death, Miriam. Especially when you are actually deceased yourself."

"Yes. Tricky."

She leaned back and stared at the sky freckled with tiny stars. Fleur had gone to bed, wrapping Mim in a tight, unexpected hug before she went, but Mim was wide awake. She glanced at Wiggy who was studying his fingernails.

"Wiggy?" She stared into her glass at the soggy mint clinging to the side. She breathed deeply. "What...what does it feel like?"

"What does what feel like?"

She hesitated. "Dying."

Wiggy sighed, took a long blink and swivelled to face her. "Do you really want to know?"

Mim shivered before nodding. "Yes."

Wiggy studied her face. He licked his lips. "I can only speak for myself, you understand. I couldn't possibly speculate about what it was like for others. Or for her." He patted Mim's knee and looked over the guardrail around the deck.

"It's hard to describe. But it was like I was leaking. But instead of anything physical, it was thoughts, memories, feelings. A smell, a flavour, a recollection of something on my skin. It trickled at first, then gathered speed, things cascading out of me so fast until they were blurred. I couldn't grasp them or keep them inside. I tried, but then I just had to let them go."

He sniffed.

Mim filled her lungs. Pushed the air deep into her belly.

"Is that what you wanted to hear?"

She remained silent. Wiggy closed his eyes.

"Did she... do you think she would have thought of me?"

Wiggy wrapped his arm around her shoulders. "I'm certain you would have been what she grasped for the hardest."

28

BALI HAI

Mim stretched out on the sun lounger and sighed. She was in phase two of her new 'dip, dry, apply regime,' and feeling pretty happy with herself. She was surprised to have the pool mostly to herself, but delighted that she could explain her regime to Wiggy without being looked at like a crazy person.

"So you see, we dip in the water to cool off. We lie on the lounger to dry and then we apply the sunscreen."

She'd have to write that on a postcard to Trisha, but

she wasn't in any hurry to leave the poolside - complete with swim-up bar! - any time soon.

"Well Miriam, at least you've stopped living like a down-and-out in those ghastly hostels."

It was fair to say that Wiggy approved of the modest luxury she had booked for them in Bali. Actually, they'd been upgraded to a private villa on arrival, but she didn't feel the need to tell Wiggy that. Let him think that she'd chosen the pretty building with the decorated doors and the huge four poster bed.

The swim with Wiggy had been a delight. Or not. Mim had not fathomed how heavy it would be to swim with a dead man attached to you. Seconds after Wiggy's noisy protests had fallen on deaf ears, Mim had leapt into the sun-warmed blue water at the deep end. A spluttering Wiggy had dragged her down, and it had taken her strongest kicks to drag him to the shallow end where they could sit. After she had spat out the water, she'd had an almost-wee inducing giggling fit at the sight of him in his stupid suit, all disgruntled and spitty.

"I can't swim Miriam!"

"I noticed!"

"I was trying to tell you!"

Dips would take the form of a modest sit down in the shallow end, thereon in.

Mim poked her gently-browning skin and reached for her sunscreen. It felt slick on her skin, and a little throb found its way downstairs.

She was looking pretty good and she knew it. Less bony, softer than she had before she left. And browner, of course, which stopped her from looking like a nineteenth century scullery maid. And she was enjoying the freckles peppering her nose.

Steven had hated freckles, wrinkling his nose when she pointed out the absurdity of the tiny brown dots in her ears or straddling her cheeks. *Angel kisses*, her mum used to call them. *Then why do they only kiss me in summer?* she'd asked, and her mum had let out that throaty laugh that felt like Christmas and chocolate.

Mim wiped her hands on her towel and reached for her Strawberry Frozen Margarita. It tasted of summery joy.

"What are we going to do here Miriam?"

She licked a dash of salt from her lip. "I can see me spending a lot of time doing this." She grinned. "I might learn to surf."

Wiggy looked horrified.

"You know that there are creatures in the sea? Probably sharks and...and jelly stingers, out to kill you."

Mim laughed, although she wasn't sure whether there were sharks and crocodiles and jelly whatsits lurking beneath the glittering sea. And also, she thought, she might not learn to surf. She might just lie here on this sunlounger revelling in the joy of doing nothing for a while.

29

READY OR NOT

"I think I'm ready."

Mim announced this whilst wiping her fingers - slick with banana-pancake grease - on her denim shorts.

"Ready for what, Miriam? To wipe the butter from your chin? To stop dressing like a teenager? To go back to your hut to have airborne diseases wafted into you by a decrepit ceiling fan?" Wiggy folded his arms crossly.

"What's eating you today?" She drained the rest of her kopi luwak and sighed. Mim felt deeply content, and a geriatric ghost with the temperament of an angry wasp was not going to dent her content. "Wiggy, you're not going to dent my content!" She pushed her sunglasses onto her face and gazed out to sea, grinning. *God, she could be brilliant at times.*

"I am tired of being in the third world, Miriam. I am yearning for a good pavement and a light drizzle. When are we going back?"

Mim pulled off her glasses. "It's not 'third world', it's a developing country. I've told you this. And I love it. And I'm just growing so much..." she held a hand to his open mouth "...and don't even think about mentioning my expanding arse again. I'm healthy, happy and learning about the world, so there. Pineapple juice please, pak."

She glanced back out to sea. Mim could picture herself strolling along the shoreline, a warm hand cupping hers. She grinned. Yes, she was indeed ready. Wiggy throbbed with discontent by her side. A tiny gekko scuttled across the table, pausing to glance at the pair. He tilted his head curiously as Wiggy noticed him, scuttling away as the spirit bared his teeth and growled at it.

Mim slipped her phone out of her bag. She tapped on the icon that Trisha had recommended the last time they spoke. It leapt open, filling her screen.

She had fourteen matches. She basked in the thrill of being wanted and glanced back at the lapping surf, envisaging four tanned ankles being caressed by the water. *"Which one of you lucky buggers will it be?"* she wondered, eyes back on the screen.

The shortlisted fourteen, she noted vaguely, bore no passing resemblance to Steven. Not a thing. Not even as he was before his chin started being eaten by his neck or his hair started thinning. Steven wouldn't have made the cut. The realisation made her both thrilled and concerned. Why on earth had she wasted such a generous portion of her life on him?

Eight of the lucky winners had sent her messages. A thud in her chest told her that she was either excited or nervous. Or on the brink of a coronary.

Mim slid her eyes to Wiggy to check he wasn't looking. Mercifully, he was glaring at some form of beetle who was making a concerted effort to run away. She opened the first message.

hey lady you wan jiggy with me?

She deleted it immediately. It didn't matter who he was, she didn't want to jiggy with anyone who called it jiggy.

She tapped the second.

Are you new to Bali?

She typed back.

Yes! Arrived two days ago.

A message pinged back.

Travelling alone?

She grimaced.

It would appear so.

Want to see the most impressive thing in Bali?

Mim smiled. She pictured the shaggy haired chap taking her to a secret, jungle-swallowed waterfall. Perhaps bringing a picnic, or serenading her as they dried off after a cooling…

He replied before she had a chance to. She squinted at the image and then tapped to enlarge it.

"Oh no!"

A fleshy, veiny appendage assaulted her eyes.

"Miriam!" Wiggy glanced over her shoulder. He tutted, head shaking.

"It wasn't…"

"Just stop Miriam. You're embarrassing yourself."

Mim flushed. She hung her head, deleting the offending member and its owner quickly.

30

DO YA THINK I'M SEXY?

Adam seemed nice enough. He was tall, a tiny bit shabby looking, but with a good jawline and excellent hair. Much better hair than Steven's thinning pate. To boot, he was British too.

"You have come halfway around the world to go on a date with a man from Dorking?"

Mim waited until Adam went to fetch some water for them before hissing her reply. "He's nice, he was polite in his messages, and besides, he lives here. That's more interesting than just being from Dorking." Wiggy tutted.

Adam sat down, placing a large water, two Bintangs and two clear shots on the table.

"Shots?" Mim raised her eyebrows and smiled.

"Well, we may be seized by the urge to do something a little crazy later."

"Do not let this man see your underwear, Miriam. Who buys a lady shots?"

Mim shot Wiggy a withering glance. Adam giggled.

"What are you looking at Mim? Your face went all weird."

She smiled. "Just looking around. Enjoying this place." Music thumped in the background. "Do you come here often?"

Wiggy groaned. "Talk about cliche! Come on Miriam, you can do better than that."

"Oh, yeah. Loads. They know me here." To demonstrate how well known he was here, Adam called out "Wayan! My man!" A barman flashed a confused smile and scuttled away. Adam turned back to Mim. "See."

"This man is an ass, Miriam. Ask him something dark. Something a bit controversial."

Mim sighed. Wiggy would be obnoxious regardless of how the date went, but at least if she did ask some interesting questions, he may have a little more respect for her. She shook her head. When did she start caring about what Wiggy thought about her?

"So Adam. Do you believe in God?"

Wiggy patted her shoulder. "Better. Always open with politics or religion!"

Mim felt a rush of pride, then shooed it away.

"I don't believe in God, I believe in Rod!" He rolled up his sleeve to reveal a tattoo that covered his bicep. It was a portrait of Tina Turner regurgitating an ice cream cone and it looked - disturbingly - shiny and new.

"Good God Miriam! What has he done to his arm?"

Mim fixed a grin onto her face, but lost her battle with the brow furrow that revealed her confusion.

Adam laughed. "Don't you know who Rod Stewart is?"

"Oh! Rod Stewart. Right. I just didn't know he looked like that."

"Yeah, he's great. I've seen him in concert nine times. The first time was at Milton Keynes…"

"Miriam, this donkey is not worth your mop. I've never

valued fanaticism. Weird concept. Let's go. We can sit on the beach and laugh about this horncake."

Mim gave Wiggy a swift kick.

"...and I think my favourite is *First Cut is the Deepest*. Such a beautiful song. He wrote that from the heart. I think maybe it's the most beautiful song ever written."

Wiggy leaned in to Mim. "Rod Stewart didn't write that song. Cat Stevens did."

"Rod Stewart didn't write that song. Cat Stevens did." It was out of her mouth before she realised that she had parroted Wiggy.

Adam looked crestfallen. "Are you sure?"

Wiggy sighed. "Yes. Very."

"Yes. Very."

Adam drained his Bintang. Then he drained Mim's Bintang. Then he knocked both of the shots back. He tugged the sleeve of his t-shirt back down over the substandard etching, though the bottom lip and a flick of hair poked stubbornly from the end of the sleeve. He stared over Mim's left shoulder. For a moment, she wondered if he could see Wiggy, but then noticed that his eyes were glazed, watery and focusing on nothing in particular except his shattered ideas about his idol.

"Right. Shall I grab us some menus?"

"Menus?" Adam seemed confused.

"Yes. Menus. For choosing food."

"Oh, there are no menus here. This is just a bar."

Mim's stomach growled. "I haven't eaten anything. Can we go somewhere else?"

Adam reached for her hand. "Let's just stay here. Have a few more drinks. Get to know each other better."

Beside her, Wiggy stood. "Let's leave Miriam. This ninnyhammer doesn't even have the good grace to feed you. He's decorated himself with scribbles a child could have made more lifelike, knows less than nothing and has the audacity to still think he has some kind of ticket into your undergarments." He turned to leave, tugged back as Mim remained seated, hand still in Adam's. "He does not, does he? Have a chance with you?" He took hold of her other hand. "Look at me Miriam." She did. "You are better than this pointless oaf. You deserve more than a one night stand with a painted bobby-dangler."

Mim blinked, fighting a tear that threatened to fall. She stood, her hand sliding to her handbag. "It was interesting to meet you Adam. But I'm hungry and don't think this would go anywhere."

Adam looked momentarily devastated, then a flash of annoyance glittered in his eyes. "Go anywhere? What did you think this was? A proper date? No offence Mim, but that's not how it works here."

Mim turned away, Wiggy hot on her heels as Adam signalled poor confused Wayan again. She turned back.

"You could have Googled it. The song. Bit of an oversight perhaps. Good luck with the painful laser surgery removal of Tina Turner."

She strode out of the bar, Wiggy whooping at her side.

31

SURF'S UP, BABY!

"It is too hot Miriam."

Mim stretched out a gently roasting arm to collect the rays. "I thought that you couldn't feel the temperature?"

"That is true," grunted Wiggy. "It just looks too hot."

They had strolled from Seminyak all the way to Kuta beach. Hot tourists milled in the gentle surf, or lay on loungers ordering another Bintang from an agile attendant. Ample hipped women wove through the loungers, rainbows of sarongs piled high on their heads. A few feral-looking dogs sniffed at the sand.

"You want sunbed?"

"Hello ma'am. Foot massage?"

"Sarong?"

She had been tempted by a kite in the shape of a pirate ship that sailed across the dappled sky, but Wiggy stopped her after her first *berapa?* He wanted her to buy a crossbow instead.

Mim shuffled to the spot where Glenn had told her to meet. Brightly coloured surfboards stood sentry. One had fallen over, leaving a narrow hole, reminding Mim of the battered fences on the allotments they used to sometimes play hide and seek in when she was a kid.

"Mim?" A grinning man, browned to the colour of a coconut shell waved. A streak of blue zinc straddled his nose.

"Yes, I'm Mim." He shook her hand a little floppily, eyes scanning the water. Mim felt sand-crystals on his palm.

"I'm Glenn."

Glenn, it appeared, suffered from the inability to stay still. His bare feet padded the sand as he swayed back and forth; he licked his chapped lips repeatedly; his eyes swept the beach and the water and he cracked his fingers with bubble-wrap pops every couple of seconds. Mim was already exhausted.

"The others'll be here soon."

They waited silently, Mim still, not sure where to look, Glenn swaying and wriggling like a gecko.

"Aha!" Mim jumped as Glenn executed a lolloping gallop toward a man in a wetsuit, trailing three nervous young men behind him. "It's Maman! My-man! Maman, this is Mim!" He presented her with a sweeping arm and some dizzying bobbing. Mim found herself curtseying.

"Miriam, why are you curtseying?"

"I don't know," she hissed. "They were all looking at me! It just happened."

"Right!" Glenn clapped his hands and did a large and - Mim thought - rather over the top beckoning gesture. "Come, gather, gather." Mim and the three other wannabe surfers shuffled towards him and gathered, leaving just enough space between them so that they wouldn't actually touch. "Today, we learn to surf." He paused for emphasis, glancing at his congregation of novice surfers, before catapulting his eyeline back to the sea. Mim looked at the group and was surprised to note that she looked the most confident of them. They were all fairly similar looking. *Definitely English*, she concluded, noting their skin's resemblance to uncooked pastry. *I bet they're all called Ed.*

Glenn gave an impassioned speech about being at one with the ocean, to which Mim and the Eds nodded vaguely whenever he happened to look at one of them.

"Miriam, I beseech you to desist with this ludicrous endeavour."

"No!" she silenced him.

Glenn and the Eds stared at her.

"Erm, no...where could be better to surf, right?" She opened her arms, poking an Ed in the ribs.

Glenn laughed. "That's right." He slapped her on the back. "Now, go grab a board from Maman. My man!"

They trudged over to Maman, who pointed at them then indicated a board. The three Eds got the ones that were upright. Mim was allocated the one that had fallen over. She had to straddle it to pull it upright.

"Miriam, your buttocks are swinging loose."

"Oh shut up Wiggy."

She couldn't figure out how to carry it either. It wouldn't fit under her arm the way the Eds were carrying theirs. She had to grip it either side like the world's ungainliest dance partner, and then she couldn't walk properly. Waddling, and unable to see in front, she was feeling fairly sweaty. And she was concerned about the bikini bottoms that were wedged far enough up her bum to make a Bigg Market girl blush.

"Oh dear Miriam. Not going terribly well so far, is it?"

Mim glared.

She bumped into an Ed with her board and flopped it

down onto the sand next to theirs. She wondered how they made it look so effortless on Home and Away.

Maman demonstrated lying flat on his belly, paddling his arms from side to side. He then slapped his palms onto the middle of the board and sprung to his feet with the force of a Jack in the Box. Mim and the Eds applauded. Wiggy rolled his eyes.

"Now, your turn."

They lay on their fronts, Mim conscious of the rivulet of sweat dripping between her breasts and onto the sandy board.

"Come on Miriam, you look like a broken windmill." Wiggy sat on the back of her board.

Glenn groaned. Mim assumed that it was her awful arm motion that induced it, but when she glanced up, a stray-looking dog was squatting in the middle of their circle, defecating joyfully. Mim and the Eds sat up on their boards as the waft hit them.

"Ugh!"

Wiggy jumped from the board and ran at the dog. "Rah!" The dog yelped and skittered away, leaving its half-finished offering baking majestically in the sun. Maman kicked sand over the offending article, but Mim could still see the mound.

"A perfect metaphor for this activity Miriam." Wiggy curled his lip and snorted.

———

They finally got to the water after much beach paddling and poo-mound gazing.

"Erm, are there sharks here?" asked one of the Eds (who was actually called Brian and was Belgian).

"Yes," nodded Glenn, "yes there are. But they're little and don't care about you. So don't you care about them, Brian! Come on Mim."

She waded out to her board (which Glenn had to drag to the water for her) and pulled herself on to her belly.

"Take me back to land Miriam. I deplore this." Wiggy hopped gingerly onto the back of the board and wrapped his arms around his knees. Mim had to keep her legs apart to accommodate them both.

"Close your legs Mim." Glen was hollering over the splash from his own board.

"I can't," she replied, then added, "I'm not that type of girl." She cringed.

Mim paddled. It was much easier in the water than it had been on the beach with a pooping dog at eyeline. She smiled, a salty droplet trickling in from the corner of her mouth and paddled to where the rest of the group were.

"Right." Glenn gazed at the bumpy little waves rolling in behind them. They waited expectantly. Brian sniggered. "Right. So watch Maman, then, when I shout your name, it's your turn. Paddle in, get up, ride it."

Maman paddled off in the general direction of some incoming waves. In one swift move, he was on his feet, body twisting, arms extended. He looked like a kestrel. It was lovely to watch. Then he dropped into the water and bobbed up like a cork, grinning.

"Right go, Brian."

Brian went. He paddled, half stood and then flopped into the water.

"Good job Brian." Glenn applauded, straddling his board. "Okay, Keith, you go."

Apparently, one of the Eds was called Keith. Keith paddled, hit the wave, but instead of jumping up, he gripped his board tightly and howled as the small wave flipped him over.

"Next time Keith. You'll get it next time." Maman paddled over to rescue him. "Alright, Ed, go!"

Aha! Mim had got one right! Ed three was actually Ed, and he pushed his head down, exerting a manic splash that mostly went into his own face. He was ready to pounce up when the wave sneaked in and stole his board clean from under him.

"Ed, are you okay?" A soggy Ed surfaced and gave Glenn a thumbs up, bravado marred slightly by his wretched spluttering. "Okay Mim, you're up."

Mim put her head down and paddled hard. Her arms felt good. "Wiggy, are you okay?"

"Just fine Miriam. Now please, do a better job than those lubberworts."

The wave galloped towards her. It looked bigger close up than it had watching the others. She brought her hands to the middle of the board and jumped her feet in.

"Woah." She wobbled. Her legs were shaking. "I can't stand up, I...I..."

Two hands gripped her waist. "Come on Miriam, I've got you."

She pushed her weight down, letting Wiggy's hands pull her to a solid stand.

"Now lean forward, with me."

Mim leaned, feeling Wiggy lean with her. She extended her arms like Maman had done, and she was flying.

"Wiggy, we're doing it! Isn't it amazing!"

She flew almost all of the way back to the shore, Glenn cheering behind her, the Eds looking on enviously. She and Wiggy plopped into the water.

"Holy crap Wiggy! We just surfed!" She held up both

hands for a double high five. "Come on Wiggy. Give me five. Or ten or whatever."

He shook his head, conceding by flapping them in a half-surrender position. When she slapped his hands, a tiny grin tugged at the corner of his mouth.

"Thanks! Wiggy, your balance is amazing."

Wiggy shrugged. "My father made me do gymnastics for five years to correct a slightly abnormal gait. You should see me on a balance beam."

Mim laughed and threw a wet arm around his shoulders.

32

SHINE ON BABY

"So, there's this kind of beach-shacky place that we go to, if you want to join us?"

Glenn was towelling his hair. He shrugged, as though it didn't matter whether she joined them or not. Mim shrugged back, utterly delighted and still on a massive high.

"Okay!"

She had showered, thrown on a little t-shirt dress and was at the beach-shacky place before the others got there. She perched on a beanbag and ordered a Bintang.

"I just hate the sand Miriam. On the Riviera, it's all pebbles you know. Much more dignified."

Mim squinted at the dipping sun and gave a little smile. The moist bottle in her palm was so deliciously cool, the sand as warm as a freshly baked biscuit and the light breeze a feather-stroke on her skin. Something was coursing around her body and she had no idea what it was, but it felt lovely. A bit glowy and warm, but not in a sweaty way.

Glenn arrived with some of the other surfy teacher and

student types. Maman, a woman called Reba, Melky and Brian the Ed. Mim waved enthusiastically, and for once, didn't feel immediate shame after she had.

They clinked beer bottles, watched the sun bleed the sky to a vibrant violet and orange and chatted about the surf. Mim switched off a bit when they started to talk about tides, but quickly came back when Melky disappeared, coming back with a loose cigarette hanging from his mouth and a guitar.

"Oh Miriam no!" Wiggy shook his head forcefully. "I cannot abide an amateur musician. What fresh Hell is this?"

Melky strummed lightly and started playing a song Mim didn't know. She drummed her fingers on her thigh and ordered another beer. Deeply intoxicated by the sea air, the sunset and the metal-on-wood twang of the guitar, she found her eyes closing. Her mind was in their little garden on a Sunday, tucked between her mum and the guitar as she strummed and sang softly into Mim's hair. She sucked in some air as she felt her mum's breath tickling her ear and sat up abruptly.

Melky was just finishing something and Mim extended her hand before her mind had caught up with her.

"Oh no Miriam! Please don't embarrass yourself. This is not a colliery-town pub Friday karaoke you know!"

It was in her arms before she could question herself, nestled into her lap. Wiggy reached for her hand but she slapped it away.

She let her fingers cascade across the strings. They remembered.

"Hey baby, the snow is gently melting."

The words came right back to her. Her mum's favourite song. She closed her eyes.

"*Hey baby, it's been too long since we danced in the sun.*" The little wobble in her voice disappeared.

"*Shine down, beaming light, shine on, it'll be alright.*"

Her fingers kept dancing over the strings. She opened her eyes and surveyed the soft smiles on her companions' faces. She smiled back.

"*Hey baby, that little smile's there on your lips. Hey baby, take my hand and dance. Shine down, beaming light, shine on, it'll be alright.*"

Reba joined in on *shine, shine, shine, the sun is mine.* Mim was delighted.

When she finished, she passed the guitar back to Melky who took it from her wordlessly.

"Wow." Glenn nodded. "That was beautiful. God, you've got a beautiful voice Mim."

She laughed. "No I haven't! It's *bland.*" She borrowed Steven's favourite term for her voice.

A jumble of *stunning, gorgeous* and *breathtaking* came out of her companion's mouths.

"Really?" She screwed up her face in disbelief. "Who's next?"

Glenn reluctantly took the mantle, belting out an Oasis number. Mim turned to Wiggy. His mouth was hanging open. She raised an eyebrow at him.

"Why didn't you tell me you were really talented, Miriam?"

She flapped a scathing hand at him and joined in the chorus.

Am I? she wondered.

33

IT'S ALL COMING BACH TO ME NOW

Mim adjusted the straps on her sundress, grabbing Wiggy's arm as her ankle threatened to do her a mischief. Wiggy tutted.

"I haven't worn heels for ages. Forgotten how to walk on them."

Wiggy shook his head. "Somebody evidently did not go to finishing school."

Mim stroked her hair down, trying hard not to look sweaty as they entered the hotel.

"Oh my word. It's stunning!"

Even Wiggy, who'd had luxury stuffed into his hairy little nostrils for a lifetime, looked awed. The wide, airy vestibule carried the clack of her heels all the way up to the high ceiling, as white and gold clad staff nodded politely before bustling on their way.

"I feel like such an imposter," she hissed at Wiggy.

"Keep your head up and stride as though you own it, Miriam.

"I didn't think it would be this posh!"

The previous night, after Mim had played a few more

songs at the beach shack, a few of the surfy crew had asked her if she played anything else. She listed her instruments - "but piano's always been my top one" - and Glen told her of a beautiful piano bar at one of the swankiest hotels in Nusa Dua. They'd laughed when she suggested they go with her, but Wiggy had spurred her on to checking it out.

She half regretted it in the shimmering light of the marble floors and worried that someone would spot that thirty-something widows from County Durham definitely did not fit in a place like this.

A pudgy American was talking very slowly and very loudly to a receptionist whose smile remained fixed in place. "I know this is Bali, I'm asking you how I get to Indonesia!" Mim sniggered, wondering how the receptionist managed to maintain her poise.

The piano bar, when they found it, was as gorgeous as the rest of the hotel. Tall stools flanked the central bar while sumptuous velvet-clad chairs stood stiffly around squat teak tables. A terrace curved around the perimetre, presenting sweeping ocean views.

Mim let out a small squeak as her eyes settled on the piano: a dark elegant grand facing the room and the terrace.

"Is it a good one?"

Mim nodded.

"Madam, table for one?"

Mim was the only customer in the bar. The server bowed his head slightly as he waited for her response.

"Oh, yes please."

He took her to a table, presenting her with a leather-encased menu before discreetly hovering nearby.

"Look at these prices, Wiggy!"

"Just order a drink Miriam and stop being such a

goose. These prices are nothing compared to The Athenaeum."

She ordered a lychee martini. The waiter fussed around, depositing a small bowl of salty nuts in front of her.

"Ooh!" Wiggy slapped her hand as she reached for one.

"Never eat the nuts Miriam. Etiquette one oh one."

"But isn't that a waste?"

"No."

She shrugged and turned her attention back to the piano. It was a Bosendorfer Concert Grand, all dark and smooth and gleaming. Mim's fingers were itching to dance across its keys.

"What time is the music?"

The waiter furrowed his brow briefly as he neatly laid down a coaster and her beautifully presented beverage. Two fat lychees squatted at the base of the martini glass.

"The music starts at cocktail hour. Six o'clock."

Mim winced but thanked him for the drink. That was still three hours away. She wasn't sure she could justify the cost of three hours worth of cocktails and there was nothing else really around, certainly not within walking distance.

She sighed and sipped at the pale opaque liquid.

"Oh God Wiggy! This is gorgeous! I wish you could taste it!"

Wiggy tutted. "You could have ordered a soda, Miriam. Why are you always drinking in the daytime?"

"I'm not. And besides, why do you always get hung up around alcohol."

She flashed a grin at the waiter who was surveying her with puzzlement. He suddenly had urgent glasses to wipe.

"I'm not 'hung up around alcohol'. I'm just not a wine-soaked lush, which is more than I can say for many." Mim was about to interrupt. "Honestly, what it does to people: the bulbous red noses, the waxy pallor, the inability to hold a conversation without flying off the handle. Why would anyone bother?"

"Wiggy, did you…"

"And the shame, Miriam. The embarrassment they bestow on those around them. The excuses the others have to make! Mortifying. Absolutely mortifying."

She put her drink down.

"Wiggy. Is there something you want to get off your chest?" He shook his head. "Come on! You've known me, what, eight months? And you've confided nothing." She looked over her shoulder. The waiter was engrossed in cleaning the bottles of champagne on the shelf. She dropped her voice. "Come on Wiggy. Did you have a bad experience?"

Wiggy's face remained impassive. Mim looked back at the azure water beyond the goldy strip of sand underlining it. A sound like a coughing goat startled her. She turned to Wiggy, gulping down a sob.

"Come on Wiggy. Tell me what you're thinking about."

Wiggy's head dropped into his hand. Mim patted his arm. For a while, they sat in silence surveying the cottony tips on the water. Then Wiggy opened his mouth. Mim kept her eyes on the water.

"Daddy was what some might call an inebriate. But in our circle, they simply called him a 'good host'. You would not have known, but he was a quiet chap when he was sober. But at the parties, he was the gregarious fun one. 'Oh, we can always rely on old Heckles,' they would say. 'He is always the life and soul of the party.' He was too."

Wiggy smiled. "But after they had gone, after they had done the handshakes and the goodbyes, he was not so fun." He swiped something from his eye. "When they had gone, he was always angry. Always picking fault with something. Whether it was mother or me, or the staff. Something was never quite to his liking. And then he would drink more while he raged." Wiggy looked at Mim. "I idolised him, you know. I wanted to be just like him, even in his rages. I thought that he was commanding, strong."

"Did something happen?"

"One night, he shut himself in his study. Mother asked me to check on him. He was…"

Mim nodded gently. "No judgement here Wiggy. Promise."

"He was semi-conscious. Drooling down his face onto the desk. And he had…he had emptied his bladder in his trousers."

"He what?"

"He…he wet himself."

"Pissed his pants?"

He turned to her. "How could I respect a man who did that?"

Mim snorted. "Trisha peed herself trapped under a shopping trolley once." Wiggy's eyes popped. "Yeah. She was pulling me across the road in a Morrison's trolley. She'd put her Docs in there because her 'feet were hot'. We were singing American Pie. She went to pull me up a kerb and the wheels got stuck and she fell over backwards. One of her boots hit me in the face and knocked me unconscious and Trisha got trapped under me and the trolley. She was laughing so hard she needed a wee, but I was a dead weight and she was trapped! Nothing she could do.

Just had to pee right there! Hilarious! We still laugh about it today."

Steven hadn't laughed when a wee-covered Trish and half-concussed Mim had banged on the door at two thirty in the morning, but she and Trisha had sniggered over their Ricicles the next morning as Steven slammed the milk down telling them they were disgraceful.

She sighed.

"So your dad got smashed and peed himself once. Hardly the end of the world, is it? You said you idolised him. How would that be enough to stop you, if he truly was your idol?"

"Respect is everything, Miriam."

"No, Wiggy. Respect is one thing. There are other things" She sipped her drink. It really was delightful. "Like happiness. Fun. Joy." She sidled a look at him. "Love." Wiggy snorted. "Tell me Wiggy, was your father a happy man? Did he wake up every morning feeling joyful and loved?"

"How in Heaven would I know?"

"My dad wakes up feeling joyful and loved." She stared hard at Wiggy.

"How do you work out how somebody is feeling?"

Mim laughed. "You listen, look for signs and if all else fails, you ask them." Shook her head, digging out her wallet. She pulled out a bunch of tiny photos. The Angus family had always sent their photos to Tripleprint so they could all have a copy. She fanned them out on the table in front of Wiggy. Plucking one out, she brought it to her face before thrusting it at Wiggy. On it, a couple hugged, a small child in a flowered dress nestled between them. They were like a little triangle, all of their faces pointing to the centre of the picture, all of them smiling. "Look, what does that picture tell you about the people in it?"

Wiggy shook his head. "That they could not afford a portrait each?"

"No!" Mim scowled. "It's just love. Look, look at us grinning." She thrust it back in Wiggy's face.

She couldn't remember where it was taken, but the three are outdoors surrounded by greenery. Her dad's familiar eyes are crinkled, his mouth half open, as though he was mid-chortle. Her beautiful mum - Angie - has her eyes closed, soft eyelashes resting on her cheek and a smile that shows off her slightly-too-big teeth. And in the front, mini Mim, plump of cheek and a bowly of haircut tilts her chin upwards, gazing with adoration at her parents.

Mim knew this picture so well. She turned it over to glance at the looping blue biro strokes that had blurred, giving the words a feathery appearance.

Cup full

"What does that say, Miriam."

She placed a finger on the writing. The full sized copy of the picture lived on the fireplace at her dad's house. This one had lived in her mum's purse.

Mim sighed, gathering up the rest of the pictures and stuffing them back into her purse.

"I'm fairly certain my parents never looked at me like that."

Mim nodded and popped her empty glass down. "Different times, perhaps?"

"No." Wiggy shook his head. "Different people, Miriam. They were cold. Your parents were warm." He glanced at her. "You are lucky." He straightened his lapel. "Now, tell me more about this piano, Miriam."

She was taking it slowly, given the prices and all, but she was three cocktails in by the time the urge to examine the piano was threatening to overwhelm her.

"Are you any good?"

"What?" Mim looked at Wiggy.

"Are you any good? At the piano? Look at you! Your spindly little fingers are tapping out some odious little music hall ballad. Look at them."

Mim's fingers twitched.

"I was...okay I suppose."

"Well, get your fingers on that ivory, madam!"

"No! I can't! They pay a professional pianist. They don't want some amateur like me playing with their...dream of a piano."

Wiggy raised his eyebrows. "The waiter is gone."

Mim looked to the bar. It was empty, save for a tiny mustard-coloured bird with a disproportionately long beak pecking at a nut bowl.

"You know you want to, Miriam."

She did want to, she just didn't want to be unceremoniously hoisted out of the fanciest bar she had ever been in.

"Do it, Miriam. You might never get another chance to play such a lovely piano."

Perhaps it was that third lychee martini, or maybe Wiggy was very persuasive, but she found herself rising, stretching her fingers as she did so. She heard the click of her heels as they transported her to the Bosendorfer. And before she could give too much thought to what she was doing, she was tracing her fingertips over its perfectly polished lid.

She shivered.

"Play something Miriam."

Wiggy's eyes shone. She lowered herself onto the stool. Poking a finger out, she traced the swirling 'B' of the name before gently stroking a key. She brought her other hand up and rested them both on top of the keys.

Mim pressed lightly, no sound emerging, testing the weight of her fingers. She racked her brain for what she wanted to play. Something easy surely? It had been such a long time since she had played. On the other hand, if she was to play the loveliest piano in the world, she should choose something fitting. She let her fingers decide.

They started sombrely, pressing with the tenderness of a lover over the first movement of Schubert's number 21 in B flat major. Introspective and hair-raisingly haunting, her fingers remembered every note. Mim felt her body relax, while the energy flowed from somewhere in her chest all the way down her arms and into her fingers.

"You always feel the music Mim," Mrs Hunter, her old piano teacher used to say, "that's why you are such a joy to hear."

Moving on, her fingers picked up speed, tripping lightly over the scherzo, loosening her shoulders. She smiled. This was her favourite part. She knew it so well. All of the hours rehearsing with Mrs Hunter on her Fazioli and back home on her dad's plinky upright. All of that preparation for her audition.

Her head started moving, eyes half closed, drawn back into the beauty of the notes. And there she was. At the Royal College of Music audition. The life changer. The dream. What she had been striving for since her fingers first hit a key and she never wanted to do anything else.

The audition she had never attended.

She reached the dramatic lament of the piece.

Mim was there, in London. She had got the overnight

coach, freshened up at a leisure centre, her sheet music neatly tucked into the new folder her dad had bought from WH Smiths. She was early, having foregone breakfast: the nerves had trampled on her appetite like a little monster in wellington boots. Steven had called, her Nokia buzzing annoyingly in her bag. She ignored the first two, still smarting over their argument two days prior. The third time, she picked up.

"I just called to wish you good luck," he'd said. *"And to remind you not to let those snooty piano toffs make you feel bad."*

She had mumbled her thanks, but he carried on.

"Seriously Mim, do your best. But don't put too much pressure on, okay. You'll probably not get in anyway, and if you don't, we'll be together! We can go to Teesside and live together. A romantic little nest."

She had glanced up as two arty-types, swathed in scarves and self-confidence swooped up the steps past her.

"If you move to London...well, I'm just not sure we'll have a future together. Sad, but we've got to be realistic."

"No, Steven, don't say that!"

"Anyway," he continued brightly, *"best of luck."* And then he hung up.

Mim's fingers slowed, the tone returning to the measured, melancholy of the beginning, almost like a lullaby.

Waiting in an echoing room filled with the nervous chatter of people who actually want to get to know one another, Mim had replayed Steven's words. He had essentially stated that if she went, they were over. She sagged in the corner and stretched her fingers. They felt limp and clammy.

A girl with some kind of cape on had walked in and flicked it over her shoulder, the fabric swatting Mim in the

face. The girl hadn't even noticed, but a couple of audi-
tionees had and began to snigger. Mim felt their eyes roam
over her outfit: the black velvet dress she wore for perfor-
mances, the fifteen denier tights that made her legs look a
stormy shade of gray and her clunky formal shoes,
polished by her dad a few days before. The rest of them
had come casually dressed, but almost all of them were
pulling off creative and artsy. Scarves, capes, even a
turban. Mim felt frowsy.

A boy dressed in Santa Claus-red corduroys and a
floaty shirt called to her. *"Get lost on the way to a funeral, did
you?"* Some of the waiting musicians sniggered. A few
looked uncomfortable, but avoided eye contact. Mim could
still recall her face, flaming hot, her pulse jumping wildly in
her throat. *Steven had been right*, she had thought. *I don't belong
here with these people.* And she had turned and left, loitering
at Victoria until it was time to get her coach home.

She softly delivered the final notes and closed her eyes,
breathing in the silence.

The applause, when it came, was a surprise. Not simply
because she had been lost in her reverie, but because there
were numerous hands applauding. Wiggy applauded,
slowly, almost as though he was still half asleep. Three
waiters and a small crowd of well-heeled guests clustered
by the entrance, clapped appreciatively.

Mim laughed and jumped from the stool. The audience clapped harder. She took a tiny bow and stepped
away from the piano.

"No! Play some more!" Various shouts from the
onlookers requested another piece.

"Oh, I really couldn't."

But she could, and she did.

When the actual pianist - a rotund and angry little

German - arrived, she moved aside to polite, but clearly audible boos.

The waiter brought another lychee martini to her table. "On the house, madam." He bowed. "And the rest of your bill has been settled by the man over there." A moist looking man in a flamingo-printed shirt raised a tall beer to her and she blushed.

Wiggy glared at her.

"What?" She rolled her eyes. "Right. I get it. You're embarrassed. I'm sorry. But no-one can see you, so really, you've got nothing to be embarrassed about.

"I am not embarrassed, Miriam." His lips were squeezed together like the knot of a balloon. "I am angry." Mim was confused. "I am angry that you have squandered your talent."

Mim sighed. "Well, nothing I can do about it now."

"You are only forty Miriam!"

"I'm thirty-five."

"Years and years to do something with your talent."

She shook her head. "I blew my chance. I didn't go to college."

"Oh Miriam!" Wiggy drove his hands through his hair. "College isn't everything you know! It is all about who you know."

"I don't know anyone." Mim sipped her drink and tried to avoid looking at the keen beer man.

34

CHEER UP, SLOW DOWN, CHILL OUT

Byron Bay was everything *The Inbetweeners* promised it would be. Beautiful people glided artfully between backpackers and degenerates, everybody wearing a smile that suggested they knew far more than you could ever hope to.

Mim and Wiggy were staying out of the main town: an eye-wateringly expensive short taxi ride with Mim's bags. Still, she met her first zen master taxi driver, and that was novel.

"Actually," Dirk told her, warming to his theme, "I'm a

chemical engineer, but there's really not much call for that round here, ay."

"And taxi driving is better?"

"More time for meditation. For really enlivening my soul. I'm much poorer, but only financially."

The place she had rented - partly so Wiggy would stop moaning, but critically because she was ready for some bricks and mortar - was a little addition to a suburban house. It appeared to be a converted garage, but they'd done a nice job of creating a compact and airy studio which meant that she could probably argue with Wiggy in some degree of peace without anyone thinking her too mad.

Bryce, the owner had left her a friendly manual and a fixed gear bike. She flicked through the book.

"It says here that the most *Byrony* thing to do is the sunset drumming circle. What do you reckon?"

Wiggy shook his head. "We see sunsets every day. Why do we need to 'drum' about it? Sounds like New Age twaddle to me."

Mim grinned. "Excellent. We'll do that then."

"And you propose, I suppose Miriam, that we get there on that thing?" He flapped a hand at the pretty green vintage bike, a woven basket curving like a ship's bust at the helm.

"Yes. Yes I do." She shook her hair out of its ponytail, feeling lighter by the moment. "You know, I haven't ridden a bike for years."

Bryce's hand drawn map presented two routes into town, one along the road they had taxied in on and 'the scenic route'. He'd scrawled "cheer up, slow down, chill out" on the back of it.

"Scenic route it is."

Mim decided on the baggy pink trousers she had picked up in Ubud and one of her Saigon vests. It was winter in Australia, but the day had been beautiful with a cloudless blue sky and only a light breeze. She was sure she would be warm enough.

Wiggy frowned at the bike.

"It'll be fine. It's just like the motorbike."

"With considerably less room. Look at the tiny seat! It is for midget posteriors. Besides, we know how the motorbike turned out."

"It's going to be fine."

A woman walked out of the main house. She wrinkled her forehead quizzically, before smoothing it out and fixing a dazzling smile on her lips.

"How ya goin?"

Mim nodded hard, wondering how much of the one way conversation she had heard. "Yes, really good, um, all lovely, thank you. And yourself?"

"Sweet." She swung a stringy handbag over her shoulder. She wasn't dressed like Mim. She was dressed like she was born and raised ready for the beach; turned up striped trousers that were both casual and ridiculously stylish all at once, a tiny crop top and cascading salted hair. Mim felt sloppy and deeply parochial in her presence. The woman nodded brightly before striding past Mim, hips swinging with the confidence of one who capitulated to her own excellence many years ago.

"Might go shopping tomorrow."

"Yes Miriam. You really should. You look like a bag of stuff at a charity shop door." Mim ignored the insult and swung a leg over the bike, Wiggy regarding her critically.

"Pardon me for not leaping on with wild abandon: remember, I've been your passenger before."

Mim poked out her tongue and flicked up the kickstand. "Going, ready or not!"

Wiggy sighed and laced his fingers around her neck. She pushed off.

"Woah." She was quite wobbly. She hadn't ridden a bike since her cycling proficiency test at school where they had to cycle around cones spaced far apart and everyone passed, even Derek Sewell who only had one working arm and knocked over most of the cones. Even with Wiggy flapping around behind her, it came back pretty quick. "Just like riding a bike!" She chortled at her own mirth. "Did you hear that Wiggy?" She twisted to him. "I said just like riding a"

Smack.

Mim, Wiggy and bike were on the ground.

"Miriam! You are a liability."

Wiggy dusted himself off.

"Ugh. Why do I suck so much at transport?"

"It's because you're a…"

"Don't you dare say it's because I'm a woman!"

Wiggy tutted. "I was going to say that it is because you are a lummox, Miriam. A lummox."

She scowled, disentangling herself from the bike. "What did I crash into, anyway?"

"Just this signpost stating that we should be wary about brown snakes."

"Are they bad ones?"

"Only in the respect that their venom will destroy you."

"Right." She hopped back on the bike. "Hurry up, Wiggy. I don't want to die here."

Sunset was drawing in and a small crowd had gathered on the border between a car park and the beach. A handful of drummers were just warming up as Mim found a flatish-looking rock to perch on.

The rhythm was intoxicating, whirring somewhere between her chest and her belly. She drummed her fingers on her knees and noticed her head bobbing. More drummers arrived and joined the throng.

Mim looked at the sky. A vibrant pink stripe was bleeding into the block of blue on the horizon and a half moon began to subtly introduce itself. Ahead, the proud shape of a lighthouse offered directions to ships, whales and intrepid walkers.

The drummers picked up their tempo, an invitation to almost religious ecstasy. A barefoot girl in a Peruvian hat began to dance, jumping from foot to foot as though the ground was hot. Several others joined her. Mim wondered if, at some point in her stay, she might feel confident enough to join them.

"I think it may be a cult, Miriam. They all seem possessed."

Mim laughed. Wiggy was bobbing his head to the beat. "Then you are possessed too!"

He nodded, gravely, but rhythmically.

"Can I sit here?"

Mim looked up into a smiling face the colour of milky tea. A dimple in each cheek formed parenthesis around an open smile. A square jaw, bright green eyes and hair the colour of summer straw decorated the head. The excellent and very attractive face of a man about ten years her junior. A scratchy looking grey blanket was draped around his shoulders. He was also unshod.

"Yes! Please do."

The man sat. On Wiggy.

"Miriam! Get it off me!"

"I saw you talking, just now. Who were you communing with?"

Mim cringed. *Myself,* felt weird. She tried out a truth.

"My spirit."

The man nodded sagely. "Yeah, this is a great time to engage with your spirit."

"I engage with my spirit all of the time." *Fun!* she thought. *Telling the truth(ish) and getting away with it!* She caught sight of Wiggy, deeply uncomfortable under the man. "Actually, you're sitting on my spirit. Could you maybe move around this side?"

He threw his head back and laughed. "You are so funny." He adopted a formal accent. "Okay madam, I shall indeed move to the other side."

Clambering over her, Mim wondered if this man could possibly be attracted to her. He plopped onto the rock beside her.

"She speaks to her spirit. I love it!" He suddenly looked shocked. "That is your preferred pronoun, right?"

"What the blazes is he talking about Miriam?"

"Erm, yes. That one's my favourite." She couldn't really remember which one a pronoun was. She cleared her throat. "I'm Mim."

"Mim." He breathed her name as though she had just declared that she was made out of hand-chiselled diamond. "Griffin." He thrust a warm hand into her cold one. "Griffin Moonshine."

"Moonshine? That's not a name Miriam. It's a drink

designed to kill you." Wiggy shook his head. "Maybe his parents were drunk on it when they created it."

Mim shivered.

"Are you cold? Wanna get under my blanket?" Mim nodded and he draped it around her shoulders. Their arms were touching. The fine hairs on hers stood to attention.

"Miriam, you are under a blanket with a man you have only just met. A blanket! It is most indecorous!"

"So, Mim who speaks to her spirit, what sort of things do you talk about?"

"Oh, I spend a lot of time telling my spirit to be quiet and to lighten up." She flashed a grin at Wiggy.

"I see. A sacred being in control of her spirit. I like it." He dimpled at her. "But never forget how important it is to listen to your spirit sometimes."

"And on that," declared Wiggy, "we finally agree."

35

CHAKRA-KHAN!

Griffin arrived promptly at six, his new-breed turquoise Beetle purring in the driveway. He leaned out of the window looking at once dishevelled and clean, teeth gleaming out of his lopsided grin.

"There she is."

Mim bobbed a little curtsey as she pulled the door behind her. The extortionately priced 'boho smock gown' was pretty, but did look a tad like she had ripped down someone's nanna's curtains and pinned them on. *"Effortless,"* she had called it, when dressing for her date. *"Rag-and-bone-man's reject,"* Wiggy had retorted.

She hopped into the car, elbowing Wiggy into the back and grinned at Griffin.

"So, where are we going?" She rubbed her lips together. The Glam Shine was making its Australian debut appearance and a bit of her hair was stuck to it.

Griffin nodded slowly. "Just a little outing before dinner. Ah, you're going to be stoked."

The car plunged into the darkening night, the headlights making easy work of the road in front of them, but the velvety blackness crept in around, engulfing them from all angles.

"Australia is so dark."

"It's so we can see the beauty of the stars even more clearly." Griffin flashed her a smile, holding her eyes for just a fraction too long. Mim felt her pulse flitter around her neck.

Wiggy guffawed. "It's because you are a penal colony full of loafers and oafs who can't get your sullied little brains around the complexities of electricity."

Mim almost giggled. Almost. The flittering was still there and quite a novel and delicious sensation, much more enjoyable than Wiggy's Empirically-focused diatribe.

"There are those who say that night is just an invisible cloak between us and the other realms."

"Right." She nodded.

"Who said that precisely Miriam? Ask him. Ask him which kangaroo-straddling miscreant spouted that codswallop."

Griffin continued. "And you know Mim, you won't read about this in any book. It's spiritual folklore, passed on - verbally and through paintings, dance and music and such - from generation to generation." His eyes went all misty. "The land tells us stories. Our ancestors tell us stories. We just have to learn to listen."

A retching noise from Wiggy filled her ears. "What an absolute guff bucket. Stop listening to him immediately! Your brain will slide out of your ears, Miriam."

Mim sneaked sidelong glances at Griffin for most of the drive. He was better looking than Steven. For a start, his jaw hadn't started merging into his neck. It was very sharp, the slightest hint of stubble poking through curiously. She wanted to touch his pointy chin. She wedged her hands under her thighs, just in case she actually did.

Steven's chin had said goodbye sometime around the parting of the Spice Girls. He had carried it well though; she reassured him all of the time. Her suggestion that he cut back on the Monster Munch, however, was met with accusations of "fat shaming, and I'm not even fat!" Perhaps if he had worn his hair a bit more like Griffin's, it wouldn't have been quite so obvious. Mim sighed. She hadn't thought about Steven in ages.

Griffin indicated to turn off and smiled at her again. *I really want to have sex with him,* she thought. *But how?*

"Here we are." He licked his lips and Mim shivered. He parked up next to a large purple sign.

"The Crystal Castle and Shambhala Gardens," read Mim. "Wow, what is this place?"

"I'll bring you back in the day some time and show you around properly." He hopped out of the car. Mim joined him, thrilled at the prospect of a second date. "It's a temple dedicated to the healing power of crystals." Wiggy tutted. "They do aura readings too." He gazed at her. "I think that yours is probably a bright, vibrant red, but we can find out."

"Miriam, I think his 'aura' is the shade of cow excrement. Why have you let him bring you here? I bet it's a cult."

"Ssh," she hissed. Griffin looked at her quizzically. "Oh, I just thought I heard a ...kangaroo?"

Griffin nodded. "Perhaps you did. Sacred creatures, they are." He took her arm like an Edwardian gentleman from a book. "Let's get inside. You are going to love this."

Mim tried to love it. Really she did.

Chakra-balance kundalini sound healing.

That is what they were at.

In a Crystal Palace where they did aura readings.

Run by a person called Sage Loverose.

Mim sat on a mirrored cushion beside Griffin. She copied his cross-legged position, because that was what everyone else was doing and she didn't want to cause some weird, unknown offence by putting her legs elsewhere. She had a hole in her sock and it was trying to strangle her big toe. She pulled the sock over the offending toe and made sure that leg was underneath her dress.

She leaned over to Griffin, who had his eyes closed. "What do we do?"

He popped open his eyes. "Relax, Mim. I promise. You'll get so much out of this." He gave her shoulders a quick massagey-squeeze, before clamping his eyes closed again.

"Miriam, these people are deviants." Wiggy nudged her. "Look at that one." He pointed at a man in a purple hessian sack, white hair exploding around his ears, swaying softly on his cushion. Mim stifled a giggle. "And her over there." A ghostly slip of a girl wearing a mustard crocheted dress with tattoos twining her calves actually skipped to a cushion, underwear clearly on view as she plopped down. "And I think he's in the wrong place." An anxious middle aged man hopped from foot to foot, hands deep in his jeans pockets, darting glances at a floor cushion.

Sage Loverose, who had taken their fifteen dollars ("*fifteen dollars, Miriam. Criminal!*") at the door floated into the middle of the room. He was around forty five with tight curls swept up in a high bun. Linen trousers flapped loosely somewhere north of his ankles and a striped shirt was unbuttoned almost to the belly button.

"Namaste, brothers, sisters." His voice was so quiet, Mim could barely hear him. He spun in a circle, so that everybody could see what he looked like from the front then clasped his hands in front of his ribs. He had very rubbery lips, which he pursed in something between a smile and pout. "I," he paused for what seemed like a very long time, "am Sage. Sage Loverose." There were huge gaps between all of his words.

"This one's batteries are running low Miriam." She snorted, successfully disguising it as a cough. She mouthed *sorry* to Sage Loverose, who waited patiently for her to finish, then waited some more.

"To friends. Old. And new. Here to heal. Together. In this. This beautiful space." He swept his arms to the side, shirt wafting in his self-made breeze and executed another spin. His spin was only marginally faster than his speech. "I invite you. To make yourselves comfortable." Movement from all sides as people settled into their cushions. The old purple man lay on the floor. The middle aged uncomfortable man perched on a cushion, his jeans restricting any potential leg crossing. Griffin sort of slid down his cushion so that he was half-lying, half-reclining, legs sticking straight out in front of him. Mim copied, immediately regretting it as her toe escaped from its sock again.

Sage Loverose dimmed the lights.

"I invite you. To close. Your eyes. Should you wish. To do so." Mim wasn't sure she wished to do so, but didn't really know what else to do, so did so. She decided that it was probably best to follow the instructions. This sort of thing didn't really happen in County Durham. She couldn't imagine Trisha shutting her eyes for long. She didn't even properly close them when she slept. And someone like Mandy Horspool would never be able to get up off the floor. And Dennis, Dennis would find it silly. She brushed away thoughts of home and waited for Sage Loverose to speak again.

"I invite you." Mim wondered if he had ever just demanded that someone did something - *I command you to close your eyes* - but very much doubted it. She pictured him getting on a bus. *I invite you to take my money. I invite you to issue me a ticket.* She couldn't wait for the next thrilling invitation from him. "To look deep." Mim squinted one eye open to see what everyone else was doing. Griffin was softly exhaling, lashes resting against his skin. She glanced at Wiggy, staring with open hostility at the kundy-chakric apostles. Sage Loverose continued. "Deep. Inside of your beautiful. Beautiful self." Mim looked at some of the others. Even uncomfortable jeans man had his eyes screwed shut as though concentrating on some tricky puzzle. A hard sudoku, perhaps. "To find the source." She imagined glueing her eyelids together. "Of your pain."

"Miriam, he is the source of my pain."

She flapped a hand at Wiggy.

Mim rolled her shoulders and started to search inside for the source of her pain. Her hair was tickling her face. She brushed it aside. *Right. Back to the old pain.* Was it Wiggy? He was annoying, but sort of external. She didn't think that was exactly what Sage Loverose meant. She took a moment to reach down and pull her sock-hole back over her toe. Was it Steven? She squidged around her thoughts, trying to conjure Steven up, but found that she wasn't really feeling very much at all. *Damnit!* Her toe popped straight back out of her sock. Well, those stupid socks were going to find themselves living in a bin by the end of the night. She sighed and resigned herself to one cold toe. What then was the source of her pain? Did she even have any?

I am the source of my pain! The thought popped into her head like a balloon bursting at a children's party. She gasped.

"Miriam, are you dying?"

Mim swallowed hard and shook her head. What if she really was the source of all of her very own pain? What if the very thing she needed to escape was herself? Not Steven, not her crap job, not even Wiggy, but the downright agonising mundanity of being Mim. *Well,* she conceded, *at least I've got a bit of pain to concentrate on now. Sage Loverose would vomit himself into a mung-beany glob of joy if he could get his hands on my terrible thoughts.*

She scrunched her eyes up as hard as she could and focused on that. On herself. On all of the bad, terrible, miserable things about her. She concentrated on all of the opportunities she had passed up in favour of taking the easy option, like letting Steven get into her head about RCM. And the times she had taken her lovely mum for granted, shouting at her for some trivial slight that Mim blew up out of all proportion. Or the fact that she had been a selfish pain in the arse and not supported dad after mum had died. All the times she had got drunk in the park instead of helping out with the housework. The soul-sapping job that she had chosen to trudge into day in, day out for six years. That she hadn't stood up to Steven when everyone went to Lanzarote for Trisha's thirtieth. That she had been miserable with Steven for years and done nothing about it.

She let out a little sob. It was out there. She was to blame. She was the common denominator. She sank deep into the heady flap of bird's wings in her chest. A slimy tear slid down her cheek. She was ready. Ready to be healed.

Ting!

A fork on a glass. Someone about to make a toast at the world's weirdest wedding. It was followed by a high pitched thrum. She had seen street entertainers playing glasses filled with water when her parents had taken her into Newcastle for Christmas shopping. It was exactly like that, except the sound kept getting louder and quieter, as though Sage Loverose was...

"He is running round the room pinging a glass Miriam! This is bizarre! I think he might be an opium eater."

Mim squinted an eye open to discover that Sage Loverose was indeed running around the room pinging his glass at people. He stopped at Mim, straddling her in a way that his baggy trouser cuff tickled her ear. His genital region wasn't too far from her head. She bit her lip, stifling a very immature giggle.

"Miriam, he almost stroked your eyebrow with his bohemian nethers. It's obscene. That's why I've never trusted these dilettante ne'er-do-wells. Never know where they're going to want to put their privates."

Wiggy grabbed Mim's hand and wafted Sage Loverose's trousers. She snorted and pulled her hand away. Mercifully, he was so engrossed in his glass pinging, he didn't seem to notice. He moved on to Griffin who looked like a serene sleeping angel, a small smile playing at the corner of his lips.

After the glass pinging, Sage Lovejoy waved maracas over them while chanting something about 'setribules'. Mim wasn't sure what a setribule was, nor, after half an hour, did she care. Still, at least her pain seemed to be cured. She had stopped caring entirely about what a dreadful person she was. Instead, her attention was drifting between '*what is he going to wave at me next?*' and '*my left hip has fallen into a coma and I'm slightly jealous of it.*'

There was a great deal of metally banging, some buzzing noises which reminded Mim of an irritable bee and a lot of stamping. None of this made her feel relaxed. The bee noises were making her angry, the stamping and banging made her jumpy. She did try to think about what a terrible human she was, but small frights, sporadically dished out kept pulling her out of any reverie she was aiming for. She thought she'd started relaxing, but a jangling sleigh bell threw images of Santa into her head and her attention wandered off to what to get her dad for Christmas.

At least ten long and terrible years after the kindle-shafting noise balance session had started, Sage Loverose invited them to open their eyes. Mim sighed with relief and sat up. Wiggy was snoring softly by her side. She glanced at Griffin, blinking into the room like a vole surfacing. He wore a beaming tranquillity which seemed to glow from his innards all the way through to the golden wavy tips of his hair. Mim was fairly certain she didn't look like that. She wiped a crust of drool from the corner of her mouth and mined a lump of sleep-mascara from her eye.

Griffin blinked rapidly. "Ah," He said. Then he blinked a bit more. "Mmmm." Then he focused his eyes on Mim. "Ah. Mmmm. Yeah." He stroked her cheek. Mim liked it. "Wasn't that totally cosmic Mim? I mean, don't you feel so revitalised?"

Mim cleared her throat. "Yep. Yep, totally revitalised."

"I mean, Sage is one of the best, you know? He's like a total guru."

"Like a total guru, or is a total guru?" Wiggy was stretching beside her. "I tell you Miriam, the quality of education these days is woeful. I blame our American cousins for the bastardisation of our beautiful language."

"I can see it in you already, Mim. That glow. I can totally see it when people start vibrating on a higher level." Griffin grinned. "I mean, you were vibrating pretty highly anyway, but now, well, you're up there." He stretched a hand toward the ceiling, shaking his head in wonder.

"Oh, I'm right up there, vibrating and all."

Wiggy guffawed.

"Whatever was hanging heavy in here," he placed a hand on her collarbone, "you set it free tonight." He kept his hand there. A tremor wriggled through Mim's chest.

"That is some inappropriate touching Miriam. He did not ask your permission, did he? We have talked about this."

Mim took Griffin's hand from her chest and held it in hers. She stood. "Let's go."

36

A GOOD MAN SHARES HIS KNOWLEDGE SELFLESSLY WITH EVERYONE

Griffin was a 'pay it forward kind of guy.' Mim knew this, because Griffin told her he was a pay it forward kind of guy.

"I'm a pay it forward kind of guy Mim."

They were waiting in a queue for falafel.

"I'm not sure I know what you mean." Mim glanced at Wiggy sniffing a tray of food someone was holding by the counter. She was glad he wasn't listening.

"Well, I like to pay it forward. I'll pay for someone else's meal now and then the next person gets a free meal."

Mim wondered if he was planning to pay for her meal or whether she'd have to get her own. She didn't mind, really, she just wished she knew. She twisted to see who was behind them in line. A beefy man in a tight shirt and backwards cap didn't look like he really needed a free meal, but perhaps this was just some modern etiquette that hadn't really reached small rural ex-mining communities in England. She pictured Colin's bewildered expression as Kelly from the chippy told him he didn't need to pay for his battered sausage. She sniggered.

Griffin did pay for her falafel, and also for beefy hat man's falafel. Mim watched as the waitress told him he didn't need to pay. He whooped then swigged from a stout bottle of ginger beer, no apparent curiosity as to who had bought his dinner. She studied Griffin for signs that his actions had been validated.

He caught her looking. He grinned, flicked his eyes to Captain Beefhat then back to her. He nodded. "I know, right?"

Mim wasn't sure what he knew, or whether his question required an answer so she simply smiled in response.

"Miriam, this food looks very strange. What is it?"

"So, falafel is Middle Eastern. Have you been there Griffin?"

Griffin shook his head. "I don't travel to lands where oil is king Mim. What about you?"

"I went through Abu Dhabi airport. Does that count?"

Griffin laughed. "You're so funny."

"You are not funny," Wiggy countered. She flicked his arm.

"What's the gesture?" Griffin copied her flicking motion. "Is it a British thing?"

"Yeah, deep rooted Anglo Saxon paganism actually." Encouraged by Wiggy's amusement and Griffin's evident eagerness to learn something empyreal she continued. "Yes, in… um, setribulean Anglo Saxon paganism, it was believed that vexatious spirits could find their way into a, um, host - that's it - host, by ah, climbing through the skin of the arms." She repeated the flicking motion all around her arm, catching Wiggy every time.

"That was good Miriam. The flicking is annoying, but the story was good. Haha! Look at him!"

Griffin was flicking the area around his own arm. "Am I doing it right?"

Mim fixed a solemn expression on her face. "It depends on what you are…" she stole Sage Loverose's favourite word "inviting into your mind at the time. You can focus on the...uh, sacred canticles."

He nodded excitely.

"So think *Erlkönig* or *Winterreise*."

Griffin closed his eyes, still flicking his arm, lips moving over *Erlkönig* and *Winterreise*.

He looked ridiculous. Wiggy guffawed loudly. Mim felt bad. He seemed nice and she did want to do some high-quality sex with him, even though he was only…

"How old are you Griffin?"

He popped his eyes open and picked up a falafel. "Twenty-six."

Mim nodded. "I'm thirty-five."

"Age is but a number Mim." Griffin stroked the back of her hand. Mim thrilled.

"Oh come on Miriam. All heliacal guff aside, he is not much more than a child!" Wiggy shook his head. "And you are old."

Mim glared hard.

"Tell me about yourself, Griffin." She glanced point-edly at Wiggy. "I want to know everything about you. I want to listen to you talk for hours."

Griffin swallowed the bit of falafel he was chewing. "See, older chicks get it. So much more patient." Wiggy laughed. "Well, I grew up in a sort of community out in the hinterland."

"Cult, Miriam. Cult!"

"Loads of rainbow kids running wild. Beautiful times." Mim nodded, no clue what a rainbow child was, still smarting over the 'older chicks' comment. "My folks don't believe in societally constructed convention, so we've all - my brothers and my sister and me - got totally unique names."

"Like what?"

"So, I'm Griffin Moonshine. The Griffin is powerful and majestic. I was conceived under a full moon, so there's my name. One brother, he's Hurricane Pivot, because our parents just knew that he was here to cause riotous change to the world, my sister is Chimera Star and my other brother was Phoenix Dawn."

"Was?"

"Yeah, he goes by Bruce now."

Mim giggled. "Sorry."

"Me too. He works in a bank. Has a mortgage." He almost spat this. "But he's my bro. Gotta love him, right?"

Griffin parked up at her door.

"I won't come in." He tucked a strand of hair behind her ear.

Mim was glad. She hadn't invited him in anyway. Even though she wanted to have some sex with him, she needed a bit of time before she could. Needed to work through a couple of things first.

His hand was still on her ear. He pulled her towards him, their lips meeting softly. His mouth was moist and pillowy. Mim pressed herself harder against him. His lips parted and her tongue met his. A current raced through her body. She had to put a stop to this. It was delicious. She felt herself being pulled.

"Honestly Miriam, have you no decorum?"

She drew back from Griffin. His eyes were still closed.

"Mmmm. Mmmm, you kiss real good."

"Goodnight Griffin." She climbed from the Beetle, Wiggy at her heels.

"I'll come by tomorrow."

Mim waved without looking back. The car reversed slowly down the driveway. She kept her eyes on her keys, hands trembling, trying not to drop them.

"Miriam, that man, well, boy, is an idiot. You could do so much better, you know."

Mim let them in through the sliding door, locking it behind her and closing the curtain. She switched on the kettle to make herself a cup of tea.

"You know, you don't have to jump on the first man that comes along. You could wait, maybe. Maybe until you found true love."

"Tried that. Look where it got me. A broken heart and a bag load of regret." She glanced at Wiggy. "And a ghost glued to me."

"Not a ghost."

"Look, I appreciate you worrying about me." Wiggy snorted. "But it's really not your concern. I'm a grown woman with needs." She poked Wiggy's arm gently as he glared at the floor. "If my female needs make you uncomfortable, well, frankly, that's your problem to deal with. I'm not going to make apologies for that. You've been stuck to me for ten months now. Who knows how much longer you are going to be. I'm not going to never have sex again just because I've got a ghost stuck to me."

"I'm not 'uncomfortable' with your 'womanly needs'. You act like I'm some dreadful dinosaur. I saw Madonna videos in the eighties, you know."

Mim laughed. A picture of Wiggy pelvic thrusting in

the drawing room of some stately mansion, Madonna gyrating in a too-small television screen pinged into her head.

"Well, it's great that Madonna taught you to express yourself and that it's okay for women to have womanly needs. Cheers Madge! She wouldn't not have sex with a younger man, even if she had twenty ghosts stuck to her."

"I don't want to watch you fadoodling with a numbskull."

Mim arched an eyebrow. She had never actually heard Wiggy shout. Boom loudly, yes. That was his pompously go-to timbre. But shout? Never.

She nodded slowly and turned back to pour the water into her cup. Wiggy stood in the centre of the room, head down. This was all about Wiggy. His comfort over her needs. Mim unbuttoned the denim jacket, stepping around Wiggy to the wardrobe. He just did not want to be there. He was too English, too repressed to just close his eyes and let her get on with it. She could picture it: he'd make a fuss, make deeply inappropriate comments and totally ruin it for her. She fished a malformed hanger from the wardrobe and hung up her jacket. It was a pretty tall wardrobe.

"Wiggy?"

"Yes?"

"Come and look at this?"

"No."

"But it's a...oh my God! I can't believe it."

He was peering over her shoulder. She pointed.

"Right up there. In the top corner. See it?"

"Where? I don't see it." He stepped around her, one foot in the wardrobe."Where?"

"Right up there."

He followed the point of her finger into the dark top

corner of the wardrobe. He leaned right in, second foot following the first. "What is it?"

Mim slammed the door shut behind him.

"Agh! Let me out, Miriam. I despise the smell of cheap carpentry materials."

She danced around outside the wardrobe. Yes, that would probably do it.

37

IT'S GETTING HOT IN HERE

Mim checked herself out one more time in the bathroom mirror and smoothed her hair.

"You won't go back on the agreement now Wiggy? Will you? Will you?"

He raised a sardonic eyebrow at her. "I feel, Miriam, that you have left me no choice." He sighed dramatically and extended a hand. "Spend some time in a cupboard sniffing your desperate-need-of-a-wash jacket. Or," he extended the other hand, "listen to you playing nug-a-nug with the Dalai Banana." He tutted lightly. "It is a lose-lose. But, at least this way, you owe me that favour." He grinned suddenly. "That will be worth it!"

A faint crunch of tyres on gravel coughed through the air.

"Quick. Let's shake on it." Mim stretched a hand to Wiggy. "I promise that if you stay in the cupboard, I will take you to Hornbull…"

"Bullhorn!"

"…I will take you to Bullhorn and let you haunt him." She nodded frantically at her outstretched palm.

Wiggy tipped his head slowly from side to side, dusted his palms on one another and brought his hand to hers. "Agreed. I will stay in the cupboard."

"Hi!" Griffin poked his head around the curtain. "Permission to enter, goddess?"

A high pitched giggle fluted out of Mim's mouth. She coughed. "Yes, yes, come in, come in!"

Griffin stepped over the threshold, brandishing a bottle of something.

"Homemade Davidson plum wine."

"Gosh, that sounds lovely!" Mim realised that she sounded like a character from The Archers and made a mental note to speak as normally as possible for the remainder of the evening. Her face felt really hot, specifically around her neck and ears.

"Sounds like poison, Miriam."

Griffin hooked a hand around the back of her head and pulled her in for a hard, wet kiss. He put his bottle down and brought the other hand to her waist. Mim felt dizzy. It took her a moment to respond.

"Ahem."

Reluctantly, she pulled back and started hunting for glasses. Griffin grinned and threw himself into a heap on the sofa, feet on the coffee table.

"My nana would have had your guts for garters for that." She indicated his feet.

Griffin scrunched up his face. "I've no idea what you just said, but it sounded cute as, ay."

"So uncouth, Miriam. So very louche."

Mim poured the gloopy brown liquid into two tumblers, working hard to stop the quiver in her fingers. She turned, brightly.

"Here we go!"

They clinked glasses.

"Why don't you come and sit here with me, Mim?" Griffin patted the sofa beside him, then flung his arm around the back. It wasn't a large sofa and they sat close, legs pressing together, Mim nestled in the arc of Griffin's arm.

She raised the glass to her lips. It smelled like the sweet, rotten peach they had once found behind Trisha's sofa and a bitter tang of something nettley. Her sip was tiny. It tasted worse than it smelled. Like it might have just leaked out of a car. She coughed.

"Potent, right?" Griffin dimpled, swigging half the glass back in one. "Reminds me of my childhood."

Mim raised an eyebrow at Wiggy. He snorted. Mim bit her lip.

"What's that thing you do Mim?"

"What thing?"

"That thing where you look away and your face goes weird." He nudged her thigh with his. "Communing with your spirit again or something, eh?" He downed the rest of his plum brandy or whatever it was.

"I just…"

Griffin put his glass on the table and then covered her mouth with his.

"…talkmmmdnmsdn"

Her answer was lost in the kiss.

"Honestly Miriam. That's disgusting. He could at least let you finish your sentence."

Mim sank into his hot mouth. A magnificent blush started forging a path through her body, winding its way deliciously south. A surprise moan escaped her, momentarily sending the blush off track, but after a swift reminder that 'people moan', she got back into it.

Griffin's index finger tickled her spine. She shivered, pushing her face harder against him. How long had it been since she'd been kissed? She chanced a gentle nibble at Griffin's lip.

"Miriam, would this be a suitable juncture to put me in the cupboard?" Mim's eyes flicked open. Wiggy was staring longingly at the cupboard. "I'm happy to go in right now if you like."

Griffin's hand slid under her shirt, his warm palm sending little electrical pulses through her skin. She sat back and grinned at Griffin.

"This is nice. It's very…"

His hands were plucking the buttons at the front of her shirt. When the first few were unleashed, Griffin looked down at her now visible breasts, slung as they were in a sensible bra.

"Oh please put your wallopies away until I am in the cupboard Miriam! I beseech you!"

"These are really something, Mim." Griffin was studying them intently.

"Good something, or bad something?" She hadn't thought about whether they were good, bad or weird since she was about fourteen.

"A good something. A great something. May I?" He held his palms towards her.

Mim laughed. "Yes. Get in there!"

Griffin squeezed one breast, gently at first, then a little more firmly. It reminded Mim of the way Steven had tested avocados in Morrisons. She'd never been entirely convinced that he knew what he was testing for, but his face always showed deep contemplation of the squeeziness of the avocado.

"Miriam stop! This is as romantic as a jumble sale. You can back out now. There's still time."

Mim gave a tiny shake of her head. Griffin had a breast in each hand now and was squeezing and rotating them in opposite directions. Her blush had dissipated somewhat, but she was determined to carry on. What had it been? A year? Two? She gasped. Three!

"Yeah, you like that, don't you?"

She smiled politely. "Oh, yes, it's very nice." Wiggy grimaced. Mim sighed. "Actually Griffin. It's not really working for me." She stood and pulled him to his feet. "I hope you'll forgive me for being both unladylike and un-British here, but I haven't had sex for three years and what I want is for you to rip off my clothes, throw me up against that cupboard and bang me til I scream. Think you can manage that?"

Griffin gulped.

Mim marched to the cupboard and pulled it open. "In."

"Who, me?"

Wiggy stepped gratefully inside. "You are quite scary when you get assertive, Miriam."

She slammed the cupboard door. "Good." She raised her eyebrows at Griffin. "Well?"

Griffin's eyes shone. With a hushed reverence he stepped lightly towards her. "You're amazing," he glowed.

She laughed. "Just get on with it."

He nodded, swallowed and then tore her shirt apart. "Yeah?"

"Like that. Exactly like that."

He pulled the shirt from her and pushed her against the cupboard. Her back met the door with a faint thud. "Ooh, was that a bit too hard?"

"Just get on with it!"

She was throbbing now, adrenaline coursing through her veins. Griffin leaned her forward to unhook her bra. His fingers were shaking. He fumbled with the catch. She slipped her hands round and had it unhooked before Griffin even realised he was struggling. She pulled down her skirt and her knickers, feeling resplendent in her nakedness. Everything in her was pulsating. She pulled Griffin close, biting his ear, pulling his hair. With her other hand, she yanked down his shorts, which puddled around his ankles. He was panting hard and ready.

"Is this good? I'm pretty excited right now Mim."

She looked him straight in the eye. "Do it."

Mim felt their bodies merge, her back being thrust and slammed against the wardrobe, the sweat dripping between them, making their bodies slide against one another so that they had to grip harder. The delicious novelty of using muscles she had forgotten about as she curled a leg snake-like around Griffin's hips. It was raw, but it was more than that. There was something cracking inside, breaking open.

As she reached her climax, the something shattered, bursting out of her. She got there before him and pushed him away. He finished, bewildered in the middle of the room.

Mim took a deep, deep breath and grinned. Griffin, still glowing golden in the eyes, cupped her cheek.

"You're magnificent," he whispered. The reverence of his awed whisper was marred slightly by Wiggy whistling. She recognised it as the tune from the Great Escape. She was about to join in, when she remembered that she had just had sex for the first time in three years and it was considerably better than any sex she had ever had with Steven.

She felt magnificent. Sated and like a thrumming goddess.

"Can I come out now please Miriam? Are you done?" Wiggy sounded slightly pathetic.

Mim sighed and rolled her eyes. She hastily threw her clothes back on. "Thanks Griffin. That was lovely. You'll have to go now though."

He ran a hand through his hair. He looked faintly ridiculous, shorts shackling his ankles, socks and trainers still on. Slowly, he pulled up his shorts. Mim leaned back against the cupboard to help her still trembling legs to hold up her body.

"Do you really want me to go?"

Mim faked a yawn. "Ooh, yes. I'm just really tired, you see."

"Can't I stay?"

"Erm, no. Not tonight Griffin. Another night, maybe."

He nodded, leaned forward and kissed her. He was shaking. "I've never met anyone like you before. You're just, like, wow."

"Yes, I'm a bit wow. Goodnight now. Drive safe."

She stayed leaning against the cupboard until his golden head retreated into the darkness. Mim sighed and opened the cupboard.

Wiggy looked a little crumpled. "Perhaps next time you could put some music on. Whistling the Colonel Bogey March while you have your sordid little dalliances did little for my spirits." He shook his head sadly. "Is it going to happen again?"

"Definitely!"

38

IF WISHES WERE FISHES, WE'D ALL CAST NETS

Griffin dropped them off at the library.

"I'll catch some waves and pick you up later." He kissed her hard with cappuccino lips and hopped back in his car, oblivious to the angry motorists he was holding up.

"Miriam, I still fail to see what attraction this holds."

"Well, it's a library. I need to sort out my tickets on the internet."

Wiggy muttered. "I meant your man-child lover who just suctioned your face in public."

Mim giggled.

The most cheerful librarian in the world, resplendent in big hair, big teeth and a voice way too big for a library showed her to a vacant computer.

"You've got an hour there, dal." She extended a quivering jazz hand to the printer. "Print what ya like."

Mim nodded and took a seat, Wiggy fidgeting by her and logged on.

"You know, this is like something from a science fiction film, Miriam. All of this technology." She raised her eyebrows. "Well, it makes a change from those tiny phone-computer contraptions you people are always staring at. Honestly, I have no idea how they can captivate you people for extended periods of time."

Mim sniggered and typed in her email password. It was probably time for a change, she decided. Mimsandsteve1 really held nothing for her anymore. She selected the option to change it. Adventuremim123 seemed like a better fit. She grinned. *Begone Steven*, she murmured.

It had been a while since she had checked her email. The last few weeks had mostly been occupied by Griffin. He had taken her 'everywhere a woman like you should see' in the area: beaches, secret waterfalls, cute little hillside villages with boutique shops where she had picked up a couple of presents for Trisha and her dad. And of course, doing all the sex. She blushed a little, thinking about the way his fingers felt on her skin.

Everything was good for her flight and she pressed print on her tickets. Gold Coast to Singapore, then Singapore to Heathrow. Just three more days before she was due to fly, leaving behind this adventure, Griffin and Traveller Mim. She smiled and replied to an email from her dad.

Hey Dad,

Great to hear about the apple tree. Hope Schubes isn't weeing on it! Still landing in Heathrow as planned, but got to take a little detour via Hertfordshire. Call it a travel-related reunion of sorts. I'll be home for Sandra's birthday though. Can't wait.

Love Mimosa xxxxx

The little timer at the bottom of the screen told her that she still had forty-six minutes and twenty three seconds remaining. She typed Griffin's name into the search bar.

"Miriam, what are you doing there?"

"A gentle spot of cyber stalking," she whispered. "Look, there's Griffin at the 'Mardi Grass Weed Festival'." Griffin was wearing a grass skirt like a hula girl and a lazy smile, a drooping joint hanging from the corner of his mouth. "And look, here's him being interviewed at a 5G protest!" She sniggered. He didn't come off particularly intelligently, but he looked quite sexy in the photo in his lumberjack shirt cut off at the sleeve.

"You found all of that just by typing in his name?" Wiggy leaned over her shoulder.

"Yes. It's very simple." Wiggy's mouth was twitching. "Is there...is there something, perhaps someone that you'd like me to search for?"

"No!" Wiggy crossed his arms and shook his head hard. "No. No, definitely not. No. No, there's no-one, really. No. Unless...No."

"Come on Wiggy. Give me a name. I won't judge, I promise." She arranged her face into neutral. "We've got forty-one minutes and seventeen seconds we need to waste."

"No, it is really not appropriate Miriam. It is like bad espionage without the cocktails."

Mim laughed, met by a glare from her neighbour who was looking at videos of tractors. "Just a name Wiggy. You don't have to look if you don't want to."

"El…" he muttered.

"What?"

"Pardon, Miriam. Manners, please. Elspeth."

"I'm going to need a surname, Wiggles!"

He coughed. "Well, I suppose Montjoy."

Mim typed it into Google and then clicked onto images. A petite little woman appeared in a few grainy old photos. Saucer eyes framed with black hair and a tiny mouth gave her a pixie-like quality that couldn't be hidden by the severe suits and dresses in sombre colours.

She clicked on the first of the pictures and brought it up to a full screen. A small gasp fell out of Wiggy. He leaned in close to the monitor, shoulder nudging her sideways.

"That's the person you were looking for?"

His answer was a tiny breath carrying a barely perceptible *yes* on it. Wiggy extended a quivering finger towards the screen, stopping just before it. He snatched his hand back and stood abruptly. "Does it...say anything?"

"Give me a sec." Mim clicked the link. It took her to a newspaper website. *The Riddlington Courier* displayed its banner proudly, boasting about serving the 'Riddlington and Surrounds with all of the local news for 170 years.' She scrolled down to the article.

Octavia Veronesi-Bullhorn to Wed!

"What does it say Miriam?"

"I'll tell you when I've had a chance to read it." Her eyes scanned the words. "Okay, so this Octavia woman is getting married to some doctor chap at Candleford House." There was a shiny new picture of this Octavia, who looked to be about twenty-five and almost facially identical to the Elspeth woman they'd just looked at. She was beautiful with the same elfin face and impish grin playing at the corners of her little mouth.

"It goes on to say that she's the daughter of blagh blagh and unpronounceable toff and the only granddaughter of Major Digby Heckles Bullhorn the third who did blagh blagh in some conflict somewhere and Elspeth Octavia Bullhorn (nee Montjoy), Countess of somewhere stupidly named."

"And this… when is this wedding?"

"Soon. Couple of months." Wiggy began to pace as though electrically charged, juddering occasionally, elbows spasming. Mim had never seen him in a state of such weird excitement.

"Who is she anyway?"

"Oh, just a…friend. A woman I used to know. Years ago now." He continued with his strange, jittery movement.

"And the guy is your arch nemesis, right?" Wiggy glared. He turned away from her, fidgeting more.

Mim turned back to the screen and continued reading silently.

Miss Veronesi-Bullhorn will be given away by her grandfather, Major Bullhorn. Her parents were tragically killed when she was an infant and she was raised by her grandparents at Candleford House. Major Bullhorn is her only surviving relative, having lost her grandmother Elspeth only three years ago.

Mim shut down the website and leaned on the desk. She glanced at Wiggy who was now nodding and clapping his hands together, his back still to her. Tractor man beside her was chortling at a tractor stuck in a deep mud channel.

She sighed and logged off.

39

I'M COMING HOME

Griffin cried into his cardboard coffee cup. Mim shifted, checking to see if anyone was watching him.

"But God, Mim. I didn't think it would be this hard!"

He had driven her and her bags to the airport. She was all checked in and ready to go when he gripped her hand and suggested a final drink together.

She patted his hand. "Yes, it's very hard."

"But you'll message me, right? And I'll come visit."

She smiled. "Of course." She couldn't picture Griffin in the Three Horseshoes sipping a pint of John Smiths with her dad. He would just look so...*Australian.* She almost sniggered, but the poor guy genuinely seemed bereft.

"Mim, this last month has been incredible, and I think I'm..."

Wiggy punched her cup from underneath, sending her tea splashing all over her.

"Ow, that's really hot," she growled through her teeth.

"I'll get you a thing." Griffin almost fell over a chair in his haste to fetch her a cloth.

"What did you do that for?" she hissed.

"He was about to tell you he loved you, Miriam."

"And?"

"And, that would be a dreadful thing. You'd be all moony and weird on the plane and start wondering whether you loved him too and have this gigantic crisis as women are inclined to do in these situations."

Mim snorted. "How little you think of me." She shook her head. "I am perfectly capable of dealing with this. And you know what? My feelings are very clear. I don't need you stepping in and dealing with stuff for me." Wiggy sulked. Mim softened. "I know it's because you care. And I appreciate it, you know. I really do. But please, let me handle this."

Griffin returned with a stack of napkins and a concerned expression. He patted her down with some of them before handing the rest to her to finish off. She smiled and took his hand.

"Come on Griffin. You can walk me to the departure gate."

Just before they reached the screening area, Griffin stopped, pulling her towards him, kissing her hard. She melted into it, rather enjoying the romantic vision of herself being kissed hard as a bottleneck formed behind her. In reality, people were able to get around them quite easily, except for a short-sighted looking woman who rammed Mim's ankle with a trolley.

She pulled back from the kiss. "If this was a film, there'd be a romantic montage sequence now of us curled up in bed and feeding each other strawberries, sappy music in the background. Maybe a bit of Celine Dion."

Griffin laughed. "You're so funny Mim. And that's why I love you."

"And that's a beautiful thing." She gently kissed a tear

from each of his cheeks, brushed her thumb across his lips and smiled. "I will never forget you Griffin Moonshine."

His hands hung limply at his sides as she took a breath and walked away.

"Well, Miriam, I will hand it to you. That was quite good."

She grinned at Wiggy and linked her arm through his.

Wiggy found it funny to antagonise a sniffer dog lurking in the screening area. He managed to get the dog chasing his tail, much to the confusion of his handler who bustled it away to whatever 'backstage' area was hidden behind the body scanners and conveyor belts.

"Stop it Wiggy!"

She gulped as a uniformed stern chap asked her where she had been and where she was going.

"Well, I'm going to Singapore then on to Heathrow."

He rooted through her handbag.

"Hmm." Then he tutted. "I'm afraid there is a banned substance in here."

Mim's hands fluttered to her neck and she swallowed. "What? What banned substance?"

She briefly wondered if Griffin had completely taken her for a ride and planted drugs in her bag like in Bridget Jones. The Mardi Grass picture popped into her head and her neck went all hot.

"This." He drew out the small portion of cream cheese that she hadn't used on her breakfast bagel.

"Oh!" About three gallons of air expunged itself from her body and she almost folded in half with relief. "Sorry. I didn't need it. Thought I might use it later."

"You may not use it later," he declared flintily before throwing it in a bin. "Move on."

———————

Mim ordered a glass of champagne in the departure lounge. Actually, it was prosecco. They didn't have any champagne, but it was close enough and she was ready to celebrate. Wiggy shuddered as she took a sip.

"Wiggy, please tell me about Elspeth." Wiggy stared at the table. "You've been stuck to me for nearly a year, you know everything about me, and, well, I'd like to know. About you. About Elspeth."

"Maybe it is a long-haul flight kind of story Miriam. Maybe I will tell you, but I'll have to start at the end."

40

WIGGY'S DEATH

Stradgrave Abbey
  July 1992

The *Jaguar's* tires prowled crisply across the gravel. Stradgrave Abbey looked just as impressive as it had when he had last been here. It had been eight years ago, almost to the day. Wiggy counted how long it had been every time he glanced at a calendar. He had been right here for Rupert Hipworth-Stanley's last wedding.

Rupes was so unimaginative. This was his fourth (or possibly fifth - no-one was entirely sure what had happened when he disappeared for six days from the Positano jaunt) wedding, and at least his third at Stradgrave Abbey. Luckily, his subsequent wives spoke less and less English, so he probably had not needed to communicate this.

Wiggy wondered who this poor sap could be. The last one was Filipino. Maya? Malaya? Something beginning with an M. She had seemed nice enough. Apparently, she was now living in blissful sin with a plumber closer to her own age in Loughborough. Good on her, thought Wiggy. Who would want to wake up with that lardy cumberwold every morning? Smell his chicken liver pate breath and watch his nasal hair quivering on every exhalation?

Wiggy had not been invited to this wedding. Not after the last one. Not after they'd all closed ranks and cast him out of the circle. He had always floated on the periphery of it anyway. Never been one of the special ones. After the last wedding, he had decided that he hated these people with a passion. But he had to be here. There was someone he needed to see. Knew that this was the place.

Bouquets of delicate pink and white roses were tethered to every fencepost. A decadent flowered arch straddled the end of the driveway. Wiggy wondered if the same florist had been employed at all of Rupert's weddings. She could probably retire on the Hipworth-Stanley's flower bill alone.

He swung the car into a parking bay tucked away behind a heavily thatched elm. There were not many people about: in his dotage, Rupert must have decided to move his weddings into the afternoon.

Wiggy slipped from the car and straightened his jacket. Even though he was most definitely a pariah, he wanted to ensure that he looked as well as he felt.

A delivery truck pulled up to the entrance. The driver hopped down from his cab and swung open the back doors. Crate upon crate of Dom Perignon were piled up to the ceiling. The driver flicked his eyes across them, shook his head and scooted through the open front doors of the Abbey. Wiggy smiled. *Rupes is not downgrading the cost of his weddings then!*

He glanced towards the door. He would pop inside, find a

comfortable lurking spot and choose his moment to say hello wisely. He closed his eyes for a second, savouring that last time, that day eight long years ago. Despite all of the backlash, it had been the finest day of his life. Wiggy would have done anything to be back there, back then. Nothing, but nothing would he change if he could just have that time again.

Wiggy sighed and took a gravelly crunch to the entrance.

"Not so fast, Wiggleton!"

Wiggy stopped. "We meet again, Digby."

"What the bally-heck do you think you are doing here? You do realise that you are cordially not invited, do you not?"

Wiggy took a small step towards his old friend and adversary. "Now Diggers. Can we please try to be civilised about this?"

"Civilised?" Digby Bullhorn blustered like a man twenty years his senior. His hair had turned a crisp grey, jowls quivered on his tomatoey visage. "Civilised? You do have a nerve, Arthur."

Wiggy sighed. This was not how he had pictured this. In fact, he had hoped to avoid Digby entirely, which was ludicrous, because Digby had been best man at all of Rupert's weddings (except the dubious Italian one), and their old Head Boy clearly hated to break with tradition. *Still, faint hearts never won fair maidens*, he reminded himself.

"Diggers." Wiggy took a step towards him. "I know that there was that terrible upset last time. I just wanted to see if I could make amends." He proffered a hand. "For old time's sake?"

Digby shuffled to him. For a moment, Wiggy thought that Digby was actually about to shake his hand and let eight years of ferocious animosity disintegrate between their sweaty palms. But he did not.

Instead, Digby Heckles Bullhorn did take him, Arthur Patrick Wallop Wiggleton by the shoulders, to have and to hold in as forceful a grip as his sausagey gout-riddled fingers could manage and did shove him with great venom against the truck.

"Steady on old chap!" Wiggy's smaller frame held him at a disadvantage. If there had been a fight, Wiggy could have deftly avoided his blows, but this was a bulk-led, hate-fuelled propellation into a solid stationary vehicle. Wiggy felt his spine slam into the truck, air rushing out of his lungs in protest. "Stop that at once," he commanded, but his lack of breath spewed only about half of the letters out, and in no particular order.

Digby pulled a floppy Wiggy to him. Wiggy thought for an awful moment that Digby was about to hug him - most certainly a worse prospect than being hurled at the vehicle again - and tried to duck from his grasp. The lumpen fingers held him in a vice as he was slammed into the truck. Two, three, four more times he was slammed, Digby's spittle-flecked mouth looming and receding in his vision, before he was unceremoniously released. Wiggy sagged to the ground like a limp ragdoll, back against the dusty tyre.

Digby stepped back panting and sweating. "Stay away Wiggleton. Nobody wants you here. Nobody!" He flicked a shiny-toed shoe at Wiggy's leg, landing a pitiful kick to the side of his shin. With one last glare, he turned on his heel and titubated through the Abbey doors.

Wiggy sighed and pushed himself to standing. He dusted the gravel from his trousers and straightened his hair. *What to do?* he wondered. To have come all this way and to not even get to say hello was tragic. But he was certain that by this point, all of the old boys had been roused and would be ready to pummel him to a watery pulp if he so much as set foot inside the Abbey.

He would leave, he decided. He stepped around the back of the truck, wincing at the pain in his spine. It wasn't easy to recover from a pummelling when your sixties had come for you.

Wiggy felt eyes upon him. He could just walk away, he thought. Didn't have to look back at the accusatory eyes of his former 'friends'. But he did. He turned back.

Nobody stood outside the building. Nobody, it seemed, was watching him. He glanced up to an open upstairs window. His heart trembled in his chest, breath leaving him for a second time that day.

She was there. Elspeth Montjoy. The woman who stole his heart forty years ago and had yet to give it back. Elspeth Bullhorn, he corrected himself.

Age had not withered her. Her eyes danced, lips parted as though to speak. As though eight years had not passed since he finally confessed his undying love to her and she responded with the tenderest flutter of a kiss. As though she wanted to speak of what had passed between them: the lightning jolt that surged through them both and threatened to rip them apart.

Elspeth smiled, extending elegant fingers towards him. He returned the smile, stretching his hand towards hers. His heart hammered, eyes filling with crystalline water. He blinked them onto his face, not wanting this moment to be obscured by his tears. It had been worth it, the long drive, the painful encounter, to hold this woman in his vision, that smile on her lips, the crackling static fizzing between them.

Her eyes darkened, her mouth formed a tiny little 'o'. Six cases of Dom Perignon teetered, before launching themselves from the truck. Six cases of Dom Perignon made a gravity laden topple for freedom, hurtling to the ground with unstoppable speed. Elspeth's face twisted as six cases of Dom Perignon rained upon Wiggy's body, crushing every bone, including those in his well-coiffed skull. Six cases of Dom Perignon came to rest on the gravel, pinning the body of one Arthur Patrick Wallop Wiggleton to the driveway.

She loves me, he smiled as his spirit ebbed out of his destroyed body.

PART III

41

TAKE ME HOME

Heathrow delivered exactly what they both expected: a thick blanket of grey cloud to cushion their return to home soil, the crisp sting of September air on their cheeks and delightfully rude airport staff in varying shades of dissatisfaction. Wiggy was delighted, though Mim found herself yearning for a shiny-toothed hello.

"What is your purpose for visiting the United Kingdom, madam?"

"I live here!" The immigration officer shot her a piercing stare. "Look, it says so right there on my passport."

The piercing stare morphed into a hostile glare. "Immigration is a serious business, madam. I'll thank you to treat the situation accordingly."

Mim frowned. "I am. I just said…"

"I heard what you just said, and I'll request that you keep your tongue."

An indignant 'huh' started to form in her mouth, but she gulped it down. The officer stared at her passport, flicking through the pages with something that might have been seething resentment. She took a deep breath, which awarded her with a tut from the officer.

"What a jobsworth, Miriam! Evidently he has not seen sunlight in a while." It did seem to be taking him an awful long time to look at her passport. "I think it might be your clothes. You still look like a geography teacher's sofa."

Mim elbowed Wiggy in the side. "Is there a problem officer? Is there anything you would like to ask me?" The desk lord raised an eyebrow. "Only, I have been away a long time and have important things to be getting on with." She didn't add that the important things included having a packet of cheesy Wotsits and watching a rerun of *Mock the Week* on *Dave*.

"Oh. Sorry." He pushed the passport across the counter, but kept his fingers on it. He glanced at the next desk. His neighbour was engrossed in interrogating a pensioner. "You're just really pretty. And your passport photo isn't." He grinned.

"Oh. Um, thanks? Maybe I'll get a new one."

"You should. That one's horrible."

"I was dep…" Mim started. "Right, well thank you for your time and your entirely unwanted opinion. Have a lovely day, here at your desk."

Wiggy guffawed as they headed to baggage collection. They quietly watched the rotation of bags that weren't hers.

"You do look different, Miriam."

"Do I?"

"Yes. Your face was dreadfully pasty and pinched when I met you. And you had those dark circles under your eyes."

"You mean bags?"

"Yes. Or in your case, shipping containers. Dreadful, you looked. Absolutely ghastly." Wiggy shook his head.

"I had just been widowed by a man who was cheating on me! Looking after my eye bags wasn't top of my concern list."

"I am trying to compliment you, Miriam. But as usual, you accept it entirely without grace."

Her backpack came into view on the belt. It looked like a giant upturned cockroach, limbs quivering in its final death throes. She slipped effortlessly into the strap and hoisted it onto her back.

"Come on Wiggy. I need pie, mash and gravy."

———

The hotel was basic, though Mim baulked at the cost. One night was equivalent to what she'd incurred in a ten day stay at the Green Banana Hostel. As her hands fumbled with the oversized banknotes, she wondered if she would compare every hotel she ever stayed in with the places she had laid her head during her travels.

It was clean, and somehow that made her feel a little bit depressed. The window offered a portrait of some neatly lined up wheelie bins and a bald, sweaty-looking man smoking on a doorstep. The sun was out, but it only served to enhance the greyness of the gunmetal sky.

"Sit down and get that timetable out, Miriam. We need to organise our visit to Candleford."

Mim sighed and sank to the plastic chair. She jabbed the timetable. "There. We'll get that train so I can have a lie in. I imagine the jetlag's going to get me."

"It's a myth, Miriam. Everyone knows that." He

tapped his lip with a finger. "Now, this afternoon, we ought to get you something to wear tomorrow."

"Why?"

"Why? Why? Well Miriam, one simply does not stroll casually into Candleford Hall! We need a plan. And you need a disguise."

"What's wrong with my clothes?"

Wiggy puffed out his cheeks. "Where to begin with such a question? But we don't have all day. Now listen, I have a cunning plan."

"Fire away Baldrick!"

Mim found herself being bustled into a ridiculous little South Kensington establishment called *Tiggy Burrell*. The name made her think of Mrs Tiggywinkle from the Beatrix Potter books she'd loved as a kid, and the shop was just as tiny and twee as the books were. Mim jumped as a heavy bell signalled her entrance. The air inside the shop was dusty and still, as though the modern London beyond its yellow-tinted windows was a silly futuristic fantasy. Blank-faced mannequins sagged under the weight of too much tweed and brown, most perched ridiculous feathered hats on their bald heads. *They've not heard of wigs then*, mused Mim.

"Hello?" A tinny voice floated from somewhere behind a rack of blazers.

Mim cleared her throat. "Um, yes, hello. I'm just browsing."

Silence. Mim frowned at Wiggy. He nodded and beamed.

"There is nothing here that I'd be caught dead wearing Wiggy," she hissed.

"Oh, you can speak up, Miriam. Old Tiggy's been deaf forever."

"I can't wear these clothes," she stated, her voice sounding extra loud over the thick silent air. Some motes danced up her nose and she sneezed.

"Of course you can." Wiggy picked up Mim's hand and stroked a mossy-green velvet lapel with it. "It's very simple. You just put them on." He wrapped Mim's hand around a hanger and pulled it from the rail. "Here, try this one."

"This is like a horror version of *Pretty Woman*, Wiggy."

"I have no idea what you are talking about Miriam." He tucked the ugly jacket under her arm and made her hand pull an array of awful heavy garments from the rail. "Ooh, my mother wore one just like this!"

"Oh great. What every girl hopes to look like. A dead aristocrat's mother!"

———

Wiggy oohed and ahhed over high necked blouses, tweed jackets and calf-length pleated skirts in fabrics that could treble a person's weight in a light shower. Mim tried them on with resignation, stomping out from behind the changing curtain with a scowl. She finally conceded to a houndstooth jacket and a plain white blouse that only made her look about twenty years older than she was, as opposed to fifty like everything else did.

"But I'm wearing it with my jeans," she insisted.

Tiggy Burrell, who was somewhere in the region of a hundred and three years old, painstakingly wrapped each item in brown paper, tying intricate little knots in string with her knobbly fingers.

"I've thrown in this beautiful brooch for you too, dear. I do know how you young ones love to sparkle."

The brooch was huge, designed to look like a basket of flowers with brightly hued gemstones inlaid all over it. Mim had never had a brooch before. Mim didn't know anyone who had ever owned a brooch and was almost overcome by the giggles. Well, that was Trisha's Christmas present sorted!

42

THE RAIN IN SPAIN

Mim sipped her too-hot tea and stared out of the window. The green and grey fine English countryside blurred like a watercolour beyond the rain-streaked window.

"Miriam, you are not listening. Now could you please try it again?"

Mim sighed and put down her cup. "Okay." She straightened her back and pursed her lips primly. "Gosh, I don't think I have seen old Cressida Pilkington-Ward since Henley last year!"

"No, no, no!" Wiggy ran a hand through his hair. "You need to say 'oh-le-duh' not 'owld'! They will hear straight through that. It was just so...Northern!"

"I am Northern!"

"As I am constantly reminded, Miriam. Is there a vowel you people have not dulled?" Mim nibbled at the edge of the styrofoam cup. "What is it that you are contemplating? Your forehead is wrinkled."

Mim shifted in her seat. "I'm just not sure this is a good idea." Wiggy opened his mouth to protest. "I know! I said I'd do it, and I will." She grinned for a moment, remembering exactly what she got out of the agreement. "But, you're just going to give him a quick haunting and we can be on our way, right?"

"Indubitably Miriam."

"Okay. And it's him you're going to see, Hornbull?"

"Bullhorn!"

"Bullhorn. Not Elspeth?"

"Of course not!" Wiggy rubbed his hands together. "Just want to give old Digby a fright and we will be out of there in a jiffy."

Mim picked up her cup and rested it against her mouth, enjoying the heat on her lip.

"Right, try the other one again. Repeat after me: terrible ballyhoo on the Amalfi coast this season, what what!"

Mim snorted.

43

SWEET LITTLE LIES

Gravel crunched beneath the taxi wheels. Mim gasped as Candleford Hall came into view. It was huge and dignified. Standing three stories high and with long sash windows peppering its expansive width, the blushing brick glowed against a yellowing sky. A portico straddled the wide front door, and high, gabled roofs reached heavenwards.

"It's so big," she whispered.

Wiggy shrugged. "It's reasonably sized. You don't get lost in it like we used to at old Rupes place! Gosh! I got locked in the priest hole there once!" He chuckled. He was in fine spirits, if a little jumpy.

The taxi stopped at the front of the house, the driver demanding an exorbitant amount of cash. He grunted at her small tip and pulled away before she had time to shut the door properly.

"Ah, I spent many a holiday here at Candleford. Whatever is wrong, Miriam? You appear to be on edge." Mim pulled on the stupid jacket, adjusted the horrid brooch that Wiggy insisted she wore and gripped her handbag in front of her body. "Confidence, Miriam. Confidence will get you inside. Then you just need to take my lead."

She nodded, drew in a big breath and crunched to the front door. She pressed the brassy bell button, hearing a clanging somewhere deep inside the house.

They waited. Mim bit her lip and checked her reflection in the glass of the door. Her hair was wrapped at the back of her head in a neat but dated chignon that Wiggy had directed her to do; two ugly oversized pearl earrings clung to her lobes and the top half of her looked like the receptionist at her dad's doctors surgery.

"Yes?"

The door was opened by a smartly clad, ridiculously attractive young man.

"The butler," murmured Wiggy. She had been told to expect a butler, but what she expected was a paunchy old chap with bushy eyebrows, like the bloke from Downton Abbey. Since when were butlers young and attractive?

"Um, I…"

"Confidence, Miriam!"

She straightened up to her full height and tilted her head skywards, peering down her nose at the butler and trying really hard to ignore his well-crafted jaw.

"You are expecting me." The butler stared at her blankly. She sighed and folded her arms across her torso. "I telephoned from the airport! Was it you that I spoke to?"

"I'm Redford, miss." He executed a small bow.

Mim tapped a finger on her lower lip. "No, no, I do not think it was you. I spoke to someone this morning."

"Perhaps Mr Carrahar?"

"Carrahar! That's the chap!" Mim thought that her clipped voice was going splendidly. "Yes. You see, it's very important that I speak to Major Ho..Bullhorn at once. I explained this all to Carrahar."

The butler smiled slightly. "My apologies madam. Mr Carrahar is...well, he is getting on a little. Sometimes he forgets."

"Yes. Quite."

"You're doing well Miriam. Now, you need to get into the house."

"Well?" She tapped her foot.

"Of course, madam." The butler opened the door. Mim and Wiggy stepped over the threshold. Wiggy shuddered a little by her side. "What shall I say it is in regards to?"

Mim made a show of rolling her eyes. "I went over this with Carrahar. It is a matter of a delicate nature. Regarding Octavia's wedding."

The butler straightened up. "Of course. I will fetch Major Bullhorn right away. And, I am dreadfully sorry madam, but who should I say is calling?"

"Lady Miriam Angus-Frankworth of course." She opened her hands, as if she had just pronounced that the Earth was round. "Of the Durham Angus-Frankworths, naturally."

Wiggy applauded. "Fantastic! Now tell him you will wait in the Morning Room, and ask him to bring you tea!"

"I'll see the Major in the Morning Room, Redford. And I'll take an Earl Grey. Twist of lemon and honey on the side, there's a good fellow."

Redford bowed again. "Shall I show you to the…"

"No need. I know the way."

Redford closed the front door and headed to the staircase which swept grandly up the centre of the hallway. Mim could barely breathe. She had been in some stately homes - her mum used to love them - but never ones that people actually lived in.

"Take the hallway on the right, Miriam." Her heels clacked on the mosaic tiles. She marvelled at the wood panelling and the portraits of cloudy-haired ancestors. "Yes, fourth door on the right. Here we are."

Mim turned the handle and stepped inside. Her feet sank into a deep plush carpet. Cornices clung to the high ceilings and a laden chandelier glimmered. Heavy drapes hung at the windows. A huge fireplace graced one of the walls, two straight backed armchairs gathering politely around it. A painting of some bloody hunting scene squatted above. Mim turned away.

She gasped when she saw it: a huge grand piano dominated part of the room. "Oh Wiggy, that's a…"

"Steinway. Yes, I know." He grinned. "It casts a little shade over that instrument you were playing in Bali, does it not?"

Mim couldn't speak. She wondered briefly if she was still even breathing. "Is that why…? This room…? Is…?"

Wiggy patted her on the arm. "You ought to look at it. It really is a beautiful specimen."

She practically ran across the room. "Oh, my," she breathed. "It's gorgeous."

Wiggy licked his lips. "You could, ahem…have a turn." Mim shook her head. "It will take lardy old Diggers an eternity to get here." Mim frowned. "Imagine your fingers running over that? Dancing across the ivories? You would really enjoy that, Miriam, would you not?"

Mim sagged. "You know I would, but I just can't go playing someone else's piano."

"Of course you can! You're Lady Miriam Angus-Frankworth, of the Durham Angus-Frankworths! She was born entitled to do exactly as she pleased. You know you want to."

Mim hesitated, then sat down. Tenderly, she lifted the lid, brushing the keys lightly with her fingertips. "Wow."

"I have a request. Do you know that lovely little tune *Clair de lune*?"

Mim smiled. "Of course. It was one of Mrs Hunter's favourites."

"Mine too. Please, Lady Miriam Angus-Frankworth, play me *Clair de lune*." He fluttered his eyelids and clasped his hands in a mock-begging motion.

She cracked her fingers, rubbed her hands together and let them rest on the keys. Her feet found the pedals and she began.

The familiar piece took hold of her fingers and carried them over the keys. She cast a glance at Wiggy, who's eyes were closed. He was swaying lightly. She closed hers too, savouring how smooth and effortless the notes sounded on this beautiful instrument. Mim felt her shoulders relax - the world was butter-soft and for a moment, she quite forgot who she was, or where or why.

Her fingers meandered softly over the piece and Mrs Hunter's voice sang through her memory. *"You are the breeze rocking the pale waterlilies Mim!"* The corner of her lips curled upwards. She turned slightly and fluttered her eyes open, maintaining the delicious softness of hazy focus. Wiggy's eyes were still closed. A hand rested on his chest, and, was that a tear in his eye? She sighed back into the music, closing out the rest of the world.

Her fingers tickled the rolling chords. Wiggy gasped.

"What?" she asked, her fingers continuing without her attention. He was staring at the door. Mim craned her neck around. "Oh!" She lifted her hands from the keys as though she had been scorched.

A small, dark haired woman clutched the doorknob, her mouth frozen in a tiny 'o'. She looked about twenty and was dressed in the sort of pyjamas Mim would never buy: they were far too fancy just to be worn as pyjamas. All flowery with kimono sleeves. They were most definitely pyjamas that matched this house, though.

Mim jumped to her feet. "I'm so sorry, I just…" Wiggy elbowed her in the ribs as her Northern accent floated self-consciously around the room. She coughed. "I am dreadfully sorry to have disturbed you. And…" she gestured to the piano. "Well, this is just such a beautiful instrument, I…"

The woman closed her mouth and swallowed. "Granny's."

"Oh?"

She cleared her throat. "Granny's tune." She closed her eyes. "I love it. Please continue."

"Um, okay." Mim sat back down, swivelling away from the door but conscious of the woman looking at her back. She flicked a glance to Wiggy, but he was gawping at the new arrival, transfixed.

Her hands seemed to remember where she was up to and tiptoed gently over the floaty arpeggios. *"Always a light touch for this part, Mim,"* Mrs Hunter reminded her, *"so that you have something to build from."* And build she did. Despite the oddness of the situation, her slightly uncomfortable jacket and the fact that she had not played this for years, she was playing with confidence. Her fingers felt at home, there on the keys and the strange, pleasant swirl that used to gently rotate in her belly was present again.

Mim moved through the piece, succumbing to the urge

to let her head sway softly. The young woman padded silently across the carpet and folded herself into an armchair, fingers knitted together, Wiggy watching her.

She trilled the final notes and placed her hands primly in her lap. Both the woman and Wiggy were statue-still, Wiggy staring at the woman, the woman staring at Mim. She shifted slightly, then got up. "I…" Mim had no idea what to say. She looked to Wiggy for assistance, but he was like a petrified rabbit. *Bugger,* she thought.

A gentle clink roused the strange spell. An angular looking woman bustled in with a tray. "Oh!" she remarked.

The young woman unfolded herself from the armchair and stood. "Ah, Millicent. You brought tea!"

"Yes," nodded Millicent. "I'm sorry Miss Octavia. I didn't realise you were here. I'll have your coffee brought up right away."

Ah, this is Octavia! Mim briefly wondered why she hadn't realised that immediately. She had seen pictures of her, though she looked oddly doll-like and young in her pyjamas with her hair scraped from her face.

Octavia switched on a dazzling smile. "Oh, tea is fine, Millicent. Thank you." Millicent placed the tray neatly on a low coffee table and hovered. "I'll pour. That will be all." Millicent bobbed and scuttled pointily away, closing the door behind her. "Won't you join me?" Octavia gestured to a creamy-fabric chaise.

Mim and Wiggy sank into the sofa, and Mim had to resist the urge to run her hands over the silky textile. Wiggy still looked as though he'd seen a ghost, which suddenly struck Mim as absurdly funny. An odd giggle leaked out of her mouth. Octavia tilted her head to one side.

Mim licked her lips and ran the sentence around in her

head to make sure she had the accent right first. "I suppose you are wondering who I am?"

"I suppose I am!" Octavia poured the tea, though still seemed oddly incurious as to who the strange woman playing the piano in her house was. She handed a delicate china cup and saucer to Mim.

"I am Miriam Frangus-Ankworst." She cursed herself. Wiggy would be furious that she had just messed up her own name! She dipped her head slightly to catch his expression.

He was asleep! His chin lolled on his chest, his bottom lip protruding like a petulant toddler's. *Oh crap!* She thought. *How do I muddle my way through this without him?* She smiled at Octavia and sipped the tea. *Some haunting this is going to be!*

"Hello Miriam. Please excuse the pyjamas. I am somewhat jetlagged."

"Me too!"

"Oh!" Octavia seemed a little surprised that anyone else could possibly be jetlagged. "And where is it you have travelled from?"

Mim put on her best voice. "I returned from Australia yesterday. Jolly long way, down under!" Octavia offered a tinkly little laugh. "And yourself?"

"Malawi."

"Wow!" Mim had expected a glamorous answer like Martinique or Bora Bora, not Malawi.

"Yes. Taxing on the system, travel."

"Quite." Mim couldn't even begin to fathom what a woman like Octavia was doing in Malawi. She didn't really know much about Malawi, but she was suddenly desperate to find out.

They sipped their tea companionably. "Oh, there's

shortbread here! Dear Millicent. She does know how I miss it when I'm abroad. Shortbread Miriam?"

Mim nodded a little too eagerly. She hadn't had shortbread for ages either. It reminded her of days out with her parents and her nana. They'd go to Alnwick or Richmond and immediately have to find a tea room to have tea and shortbread. Her dad would jokingly grumble that they could have had tea and shortbread at home, but he always dipped his moistened finger in the crumbs when they had finished.

"So I assume that you are here about the music at the wedding?" Octavia held the shortbread in her fingers, but was yet to take a bite. Mim had taken a large, buttery crumbly bite and was currently deeply involved in loving it.

"Yes?" She had tried to sound confident, but the question mark had crept in of its own accord. Also, it can be difficult to sound confident whilst spraying shortbread crumbs all over a deep-pile cream carpet.

"Oh good! And you can play Clair de Lune! It was Granny's favourite and mine too." Octavia nibbled her shortbread then wiped her chin with a napkin. "I believe Grampy has had the most terrible trouble with the musicians. The harpist got arrested for smuggling cocaine and the other pianist broke both of his arms in a luging accident. Dreadful luck!" She shook her head. "But you're here and what beautiful fate smiled upon us that you were playing Granny's favourite piece!" Mim glanced at Wiggy, snoring softly by her side.

"I've heard wonderful things about her. About Elspeth."

Octavia lit up like a Christmas tree. "Oh gosh, she was just so wonderful! You know, you remind me a little of her."

"Really?"

"Yes. Oh, not in looks so much, but you dress like her and...and you play like her too."

"Elspeth played piano?" Octavia nodded. Mim's eyes slid to her sleeping Wiggy, then to a portrait of Elspeth that she hadn't seen when she came in. The portrait was rough, but delicately rendered. Elspeth was grinning at the artist, elbows resting on the top of the piano. Her hair was in a chignon, but a few dark strands had worked themselves loose, giving her a carefree air. Her eyes gleamed with wicked humour and mischief which had been absent from the photos Mim had found on Google. "She's beautiful."

"Yes." Octavia beamed proudly.

"You look just like her." Octavia blushed, but carried on grinning. "It must have been hard for you when…" she checked Wiggy "...when she passed." Octavia's grin remained, but her eyes shone with a watery film. "I lost my mum when I was fifteen."

"I'm so sorry." A tear rolled down Octavia's cheek. "Getting married without her will be…". Mim put down her teacup. "Tell me Miriam, do you believe in the afterlife?"

Mim laughed. "Yes! I *know* there's an afterlife."

Octavia smiled. "Me too."

Octavia insisted that she stay the night and not make the "ghastly" journey back to London. Apparently, even First Class had gone to the dogs these days. And besides, two jetlagged women would make for the best late night companions!

A year ago, Mim would have refused with a clawing

desperation not to be forced into intimacy with a stranger. But she had shared a dorm with Fungal Foot Chris. She was a different person now

As Octavia went to make arrangements with the staff, Mim stayed in the Morning Room feasting on shortbread. Wiggy was still entirely comatose.

"Jetlag is a myth, Miriam," she mimicked to his sleeping form. She really wanted to play the piano again, but wouldn't have been able to stretch that far with the deadweight of Wiggy attached to her. She stood and stretched, twisting her body from side to side. It really was a lovely portrait of Elspeth. Mim was certain that she would have liked her.

She moved towards the portrait, her heels sinking into the soft carpet. Damnit! She was just too far to reach it, Wiggy anchoring her heavily back towards the sofa. She really wanted to get a closer look. She wondered what was making Elspeth smile that way.

Mim poked Wiggy in the arm, gently at first, but then with a harder stabbing motion. Nothing. He was snoring, so he definitely wasn't dead. Well, obviously he was dead, but not dead dead. Not properly dead. She shoved him hard causing him to whinny like an indignant pony. She sniggered. Hooking a finger in each corner of his mouth, she pulled his lips into a joker smile.

"Ew!" She squished his cheeks up and wiggled them around, a wet slurping noise making her laugh again. He looked like a pickled walnut. *This is fun! Wiggy is never asleep while I'm awake.*

She got bored fairly quickly and found herself searching Elspeth's portrait once more. Placing one hand on Wiggy's thigh and another on his shoulder, she pushed him along towards the end of the sofa. It was easier than she thought it would be given the lovely shininess of the fabric. She wondered briefly if she should buy a silky sofa then dismissed it on account of the fact that she was essentially homeless and jobless. Wiggy mumbled something inaudible.

With Wiggy firmly ensconced at the far end of the sofa, Mim was able to get close enough to look at the portrait in more detail; tiny pearl studs dotted each of Elspeth's earlobes and the artist had perfectly captured their opalescent sheen; she wore a crisp white blouse, but on one side, the material had slipped, revealing a hint of a bra strap; her fingers clasped just below her chin and Mim observed that she wasn't wearing a wedding ring. She looked as though she was in her early forties in this picture, probably married at that time. Mim shrugged. Maybe she didn't like wearing it. Mim hadn't liked wearing her wedding ring either - it made her feel itchy and like part of her finger was withering away - but Steven had been the insistent type. Maybe Elspeth had been ahead of her time in the feminist stakes.

Mim noticed that the portrait had been signed by the artist in a curling script. It was in the bottom right-hand corner and hard to make out against the dark outline of the piano. She squinted, vowing to get her eyes checked at some point soon.

It came into focus.

Arthur Patrick Wallop Wiggleton

44

THIS OLD AND EMPTY HOUSE

Octavia led her to a large room. A huge canopied bed dominated, laden with heavy-looking blankets. This was pushed firmly against the mossy-green wallpaper, adorned with swirls and flowers. *William Morris?* She knew nothing about luxury wallpapers, but Sandra was a big home renovation enthusiast when it came to her television choices. She'd get all excited if someone uncovered some old William Morris wallpaper lurking somewhere below a nasty woodchip and headache-inducing psychedelic fleck. The room was spotlessly clean, and Mim wondered how futile the staff felt cleaning a room that may, on the off chance, be used once every seven years.

"It's lovely, thank you Octavia."

Wiggy rubbed his eyes sleepily by her side. They had trudged slowly up the stairs, Mim feigning heaviness in her own limbs to compensate for Wiggy's inability to walk like a normal, well-behaved ghost.

Octavia beamed. "It is so nice to have you here, Miriam. I feel that we're going to get along splendidly!" She held both of Mim's arms and examined her. "I will bring you some pyjamas and something nice to wear for dinner."

Mim watched her go, closing the heavy oak door behind her.

"I do not understand Miriam." He blinked rapidly, shaking his head.

"Well, Wiggy. You appear to be jet lagged. I was left to navigate your difficult social situation alone and now I'm too tired to battle the crowds of London. Besides, I really like Octavia." She cocked her head. "Surely your haunting of Bullhorn will be easier if we stay the night? Don't all good hauntings happen at night?"

Wiggy stretched. "I suppose they might. Now please navigate me to the bed Miriam, I can barely stand."

"So, how are you going to haunt him?"

Wiggy brightened up. "Ah! Well, you'll be having dinner with him I assume?" Mim nodded. "Well, you can push a chair over!"

Mim frowned. "That's just me pushing a chair over. He won't feel haunted by me pushing a chair over. He'll just think, why is this reprobate pushing my Chippendales over?" Wiggy tapped his chin. "You haven't thought this through at all, have you?"

"I spent my time playing Professor Higgins to get you in here, Miriam."

"I know! And it's wonderful!" She sat on the bed and took off a boot. "Octavia asked me to play piano at her wedding."

"She did?"

"Yes!" She unfastened the buckle on her other boot. "So thank you for bringing me here. And also, she's lovely! I might even have a new friend." Wiggy raised an eyebrow.

"Oh stop it! Octavia can be friends with a commoner if she wants."

Mim lay back on the pillow, her head suddenly feeling sludgey.

"So, Miriam. What are your thoughts on the haunting."

"Leave it. Move on." She yawned. "Life's too short."

"But death is not!" He shook her gently. "Miriam, you promised."

She sighed and pulled herself up to sit. "Okay. Well, there's always the animal thing."

"Miriam, you are brilliant!" He hopped to his feet, all traces of sleepiness ebbing away. "Old Diggers loves a blood-hound. There is bound to be at least one of those wrinkly old saliva-vessels lurching about the place. Did you smell dog?"

"No. But I've still got aeroplane nose." She sniffed to prove her point.

"He has them go everywhere with him. Even in the bedroom. It drives Elspeth to distraction!" Mim stiffened at the mention of her name. "*She* will know that it is me. I told her that if I died before him, I would come back and haunt him. She will know!" He clapped his hands joyfully. "Whatever is the matter, Miriam? You have turned all rigid and uptight governess-esque."

Mim crossed her legs. "Sit down Wiggy." He didn't.

"What is it, Miriam? Did you see her? Has she suffered a stroke or something equally disfiguring?"

"Wiggy...." Mim pushed all of the remaining air out of her lungs. "I don't...well...you see…"

"Come along Miriam. Sally forth!"

She reached for his hands. "Elspeth is dead." She said it slowly, her eyes unwavering from his. She was conscious of the heavy ticking from a moon-faced wall clock. "I'm sorry."

Wiggy's chin dropped to his chest. Mim stared at the top of his head. She could see his pinky scalp through his hair and it made her want to cry. She placed a hand on it and gently rubbed. His shoulders were shuddering.

The clock counted down seconds, then minutes. They stayed as they were. "I just wanted to see her," Mim thought she heard him breathe, but it was so faint, it could have been the wind whispering at the sash.

Eventually, he raised his head. "I think I have the aeroplane nose affliction that you are suffering from." He snuffled.

"Probably." She patted the bed beside her. He eased himself down. "Do you want to talk? About Elspeth?"

"No." He examined his fingernails. "It's just a shock. We were friends."

"I saw your portrait. You never told me you were an artist!"

He shrugged. "You never asked."

"Did you tell her? That you loved her?"

Wiggy froze, then sagged. "Yes."

"And she loved you too?"

He gasped slightly. "I think so."

Mim recalled the intensity in the eyes of the portrait, that mischievous grin and the flushed cheeks. The image was a far cry from the polite, detached smile Elspeth wore on the photographs alongside her husband that Mim had observed on Google.

"It was too late by the time it all came out." Wiggy sighed. "She had a family and a reputation to consider." He grinned ruefully. "I always was the black sheep of the group."

"Wow." Mim picked at a thread on her blouse. Sure-footed, outspoken, boorish Wiggy had been too afraid to tell the woman he loved that his heart was hers until it was too late. How many of his sixty-two living years had been wasted on 'what-ifs'? Living a half-formed life because of fear. Mim's chest ached.

She had done exactly the same thing. Granted, she had been spared early, but still!

She glanced at Wiggy, eyes glazed in some reverie. He looked old. Older than when she had first met him, if that was possible. She gently squeezed his fingers resting limply by his side and silently promised him that she would never waste a moment of her own life again.

45

GHOSTBUSTERS!

"The Durham Angus-Frankworths you say?"

Mim nodded. She couldn't answer as she had a large boiled potato in her mouth. Major Bullhorn's cheek pockets wobbled with the effort of cutting a brussel sprout in half. He seemed torn between wanting to cross-examine Mim and the achievement of sprout-slicing accuracy. It was not possible to focus one's attention on both matters simultaneously, it would appear.

Mim swallowed the floury potato. The major had definitely been too sprout-focused to see her nod. She clarified. "Yes. Durham."

The major furrowed his brow. His whole head creased in response, which made him look like an old crumpled blanket. "What is your grandfather's name?" He jabbed his knife in her general direction. A small blizzard of dandruff rained to his shoulder and settled on his navy blazer. A mustard yellow cravat, slightly skewed at his neck, picked up a couple of flakes too.

"Maurice," she answered, trying hard not to focus on the dandruff. "Alas, my dear grandfather is no longer with us." She heard her voice and cringed at how Pride and Prejudice she had become in the presence of Wiggy's arch nemesis.

He would have been a formidable adversary once, Mim could see that. Although the wheelchair robbed him of his stature, his shoulders were still broad, a thick neck protruding like a tree stump from them. He had rather a large head, and his whiskery moustache dipped floorwards, dragging his mouth and his jowls into a permanent frown. The moustache was in need of a trim, catching globs of potato as he ate. He reminded Mim of a big, blubbery walrus. His lips were slick with gravy as though he had just swallowed a slippery fish down whole.

"Maurice Angus-Frankworth." He rolled his sprout around his mouth. "Textiles?" Mim nodded, not entirely sure what relevance textiles had to her granddad. "Was he the chap that was importing all of that Thai silk back in the day?"

"Um…" Wiggy nudged her. "Yes! Grandpapa is, was, the chap to whom you refer."

"Thought as much." He took a large gulp of his wine and gestured with a flabby hand for a hovering person to refill it. Mim didn't know what to call them. Waiters? Servants? Did people still have servants in 2019? "I'm never wrong, you know. Never. I remember everybody and everything." He jabbed his temple with a fat sausage of a finger. "Sharp as a tack I am. Nothing gets past me." He smacked his tongue across his lips. "Who knew silk could be so popular? Think I met him once at a Rotary dinner. Bally fine chap."

"So Grampy, Miriam is going to play at the wedding." Octavia clapped her hands, splashing gravy onto her dress.

"Terrible problems with these musicians. You see, the

problem with musicians is that they are all so bloody bohemian. Who was that first one? The filly who looked like a shot putter."

"Alina."

"Something like that. What went on there?"

"She was arrested for drug smuggling, Grampy."

The major let out a guffaw like a donkey sneezing. "Drug smuggling! Had half an opium farm lodged up her bottom." He leaned towards Mim. "I don't mind telling you that she was big enough to have lodged twenty or so kilograms up there. Pah! Bloody Russians! Can't trust a single one of them."

Mim shifted uncomfortably in her chair.

"Alina is Ukrainian, Grampy. And she was trying to raise the money to buy her father out of jail." Octavia addressed Mim. "Political prisoner, Miriam. Poor Alina."

The major chewed noisily, eyes scouring his plate for the next hapless vegetable he could conquer. Mim took a sip of her wine and tried to focus her attention on anything but the sound of a distinctly average roast dinner being masticated roughly. The major swallowed, thick neck convulsing with the effort.

"A lump, she was. A veritable lump. What happened to the last one, Occy? The ugly chap"

"Do you mean Leon? He had a luging accident, Grampy."

"Luging accident! Have you ever heard such nonsense?"

Mim smiled politely.

Wiggy nudged her. "He would not be able to fit his planet-sized posterior in a luge Miriam!" Mim snorted, then had to pretend that she was choking on a carrot.

"Of course," the major continued, "those Germans are

all the same. Lurking around doing…" he waved his fork searching for the words, a wet leaf of cabbage propelling itself straight through Wiggy. "…unsavoury activities."

Wiggy's disdain was plastered all over his face. Despite his own pomposity at times, Mim could not envisage these two as ever having been friends. Bullhorn was simply…unpleasant. She wondered what the petite, mischievous woman from the portrait had seen in him. Her dishevelled hair and musical heart couldn't have fitted too well with the man across the dinner table demolishing half a chicken.

She sighed. Who was she to criticise? She'd married Steven.

"So, Octavia. Please tell me about your fiancé. He is a doctor, is he not?"

Octavia beamed, while the major appeared to have the sudden need to clear a Goliath frog from his throat. Octavia shot him a disapproving glare, but halfheartedly, as though this was something they had disagreed on many times before.

"Theo is a doctor and he's wonderful." Octavia folded her fingers under her chin. "We met in Malawi, when I first went to see the proposed site for the hospital."

The major had gone an interesting shade of puce. Mim tipped her head. She had no idea what Octavia did and was fascinated.

As though reading her mind, Octavia went on. "I project manage for an Aids charity and we are currently building specialised hospitals in some of the worst hit countries. Theo is the lead Doctor at our new Zomba facility. We met to go through the plans and it was love at first sight!" The major spluttered. "Grampy doesn't like that Theo isn't white. But Grampy also knows that I love Theo, cannot wait to be his wife and there is nothing on the planet that Grampy can do to stop it!"

Mim smiled. Octavia's eyes were shiny as baubles, and her cheeks had a rose-gold hue in the candlelit dining room. Mim wondered if she would ever talk about anyone with her face all luminescent with joy like that.

"Ah, Jasper!" The major seemed delighted by the distraction from his undefended dislike of non-white people, as a tall, wrinkly dog with sagging eyes stalked into the room. It cast a dubious glance at the diners, before settling by the major's wheelchair, head planted in his blanket covered lap. "This is Jasper. He is a wonderful dog." The major pulled a strip of chicken from the bone and let Jasper devour it wetly from his fingers.

"Oh good lord, he is even worse than he used to be, Miriam!" Mim wasn't a fan of feeding dogs at the table either. Schubert always had to wait until everyone had finished and the plates had been carried away and washed. "Of course, his table manners have always been dreadful. The result of never having a nanny strong enough to actually beat some discipline into him."

"Jasper is the best." The major peeled another lump of chicken from the bone with fingers still slick from Jasper's tongue. He ripped it in half, thrusting some at the dog and cramming the rest into his mouth. He then picked up the bone with both hands and began slurping and chewing the meat from it. Mim's stomach lurched. Octavia did not appear to have noticed.

"Right, that is it Miriam! I cannot sit here and watch this disgusting man eat like a savage."

Wiggy strode to Jasper who was still eyeballing the bone in his master's grease-slicked mouth. He leaned in close to one of the dogs floppy ears and growled. The dog looked quizzically to the side, but Wiggy had already bounced across to his other ear and emitted another low growl. The dog seemed to crease his unironed forehead before seeking the source of the growl. Catching sight of Wiggy, he let out a grumble a bit like an old motorbike starting up. Wiggy gnashed his teeth, whipping from ear to ear, increasing speed and intensifying the growls as he did. The dog's head went back and forth like a tennis spectator.

Wiggy leapt to the other side of Bullhorn, facing off against the dog over the major's tartan blanket-swathed legs. Jasper glared at Wiggy.

"Jasper? Whatever is the matter, old boy?" the major asked. Octavia looked nervously at Mim, who shrugged. Jasper continued his rumble, curling back his lip to show a glimpse of teeth. "Jasper?"

Wiggy slapped both hands on his chest and roared, maintaining eye contact with the antagonised dog. Jasper let out a bark, which had a fair bit of welly behind it, observed Mim, for such a languorous looking beast. Wiggy jabbed his fists at Bullhorn's head and Jasper snarled.

"Come on," yelled Wiggy. Jasper sprung towards Wiggy's throat using Bullhorn's useless legs as a spring-board. His thick tail swiped across the major's plate, flinging vegetables and chicken carcass everywhere. The impact of the dog's legs in his groin propelled the major forwards, his face landing squarely on his gravy drenched plate.

The dog sailed through Wiggy, directly into the staff member holding the wine. The Chateau Latour Pauillac that Bullhorn had boasted about cascaded from the bottle in an arc, fountainously pooling around the major's head.

"Goodness!" exclaimed Octavia hopping to her feet. She looked around at the mess, opting to help the wine waiter out of a crumpled heap on the floor. Mim wondered if she should help Bullhorn out of his gravy.

"Major? Are you all right?"

He sat up slowly. Bordeaux trickled out of his hairy left ear and his face was smudged with vegetables. He spluttered something, splashing a glob of gravy onto the dress Mim had borrowed from Octavia. His eyes were wide, and he blinked a few times, raining flecks of dinner from his eyelashes onto his jacket. A blob of chicken grease perched on the end of his nose and Mim remembered the globule of chicken goo that stuck to Steven the night he had told her he wanted a divorce.

"Redford! Get in here." She was delighted by the commanding tone she managed to produce while still sounding posh. The handsome Redford scuttled into the dining room. He must have been lurking around outside. Mim admired his slightly olivey skin, before she realised that he was awaiting an instruction from her. "Yes. As you can see, there has been a bit of a to-do over dinner." If Redford was shocked by the chaos, he was doing an excellent job of hiding it. "Perhaps you could be so kind as to arrange to have the place cleaned. And of course, someone will need to clean the gravy off the major."

"Of course madam." Was that a smirk playing on his lips? Mim felt a tiny one tug at hers.

"This poor...wine chap…"

"Sommelier!" Called Wiggy.

"This poor sommelier will need to be cleaned up too." Mim strolled over to Jasper and stroked his ears. "And Jasper seems to have had a funny turn, so perhaps somebody could take him for a refreshing stroll around the grounds."

"Right away madam."

"I say," Mim pondered, looking as dramatically deep in thought as she could muster. "You don't have a resident ghost, do you?"

Wiggy let out a most impressive ghostly 'whooooooooooooooo!' and winked at Mim.

46

WHO SAYS YOU CAN'T GO HOME

Mim heard them before she saw them.

A shriek echoed from behind a twenty-headed, six-legged, foil balloon monster blocking valuable commuter space on the platform. Trisha's squeal was piercing, threatening to shatter the glass of the canopy overhead. Her dad's shout was deep and sonorous and just so familiar that Mim felt tears prick her eyes. Sandra's was modest, but enthusiastic nonetheless. The balloon-monster barrelled towards her, Trisha and her dad breaking away to leap into a rugby-tackle of a hug. Mim, not quite braced for the onslaught, fell over her backpack, dragging Wiggy down on top of her.

"Oh Miriam! You have failed to become any more sophisticated for all of my teachings." He shook his head, but there was a weird little spark in his eyes that Mim couldn't quite decipher.

"Sorry! Mimzo, I am so sorry." Trisha was an interesting shade of pink. " I'm just so fucking excited to see you." She glanced at Sandra. "Soz, Sandra. Terry. Mouth like a sewer. I'm just so fucking excited though!" She picked Mim up and jiggled her about like a ragdoll. "God Mimmel! You look incredible."

"Oh Trish! I've got so much to tell you!"

Wiggy tutted. "I had mercifully forgotten about this majestically uncouth flap-dragon you insist on acquainting with."

Mim hugged Trisha hard.

"Is he still with you?" Trisha whispered. Mim nodded.

Trisha released her and she stepped into her dad's patiently outstretched arms.

"Mimsy."

"Dad."

His jumper smelled of toast and tea and Sunday mornings. She breathed him in as he patted her hair.

"Mim, you look so well." He bit his lip. "You're all brown and sunny."

Mim laughed and indicated the balloon-forest. "Are these for me?"

Sandra peeked out from amongst the bobbing silver and gold foil bubbles, grinning a little shyly. She looked tiny, and Mim decided that her dad and Trisha were being hugely irresponsible, leaving a diminutive woman at the mercy of so much helium. She batted them out of the way to wrap an arm around Sandra.

"Miriam, you will suffocate me in this balloon hell!"

"I brought you some mints." Sandra started digging around in her handbag. Mim had to grab the bundle of strings to stop the enthusiastic balloons from escaping. "Oops! Sorry. I brought you hankies as well. Trains don't half give me the sniffles."

Mim popped a mint in her mouth while her dad attempted to manoeuvre the heavy backpack onto his shoulder.

"Eh pet! What'ya got in here? The Sydney Opera House."

"I'll get that Terry." Trisha tried to wrestle it from him.

Mim watched her dad and best friend since the dawn of time tussle over her backpack, the small woman she viewed as her stepmum trying to untangle herself from the ribbon prison she had become entangled in and it all felt mildly surreal. It was too familiar, but too alien at the same time. A gasp escaped, but went unnoticed by her nearest and dearest.

"Miriam, are you quite well?" Wiggy touched her arm gently. She nodded. "You have been alone for so long. This must feel rather strange."

"I haven't been alone, have I Wiggy? I've had you." She slipped her arm through his.

Trisha, it would appear, had won custody of the back-pack which she hoisted triumphantly on her back. Her green-clad legs sticking out of the bottom and the back-pack curving up to her shoulders gave her the appearance of a displaced turtle. Mim smiled. She loved this funny little group of people.

"Come on Mimmage!" Her dad wrapped his arm around her shoulder, sandwiching her between himself and Wiggy. "Jimmy MacBeth loaned us his range rover in case you had loads of stuff."

She was home.

47

IT'S PARTY TIME!

Wiggy frowned over the nibbles.

"Miriam, what kind of celebratory feast is that supposed to resemble?"

He wrinkled his nose at the spread, to which Mim was putting the final touches. They'd covered her dad's decorating table with a shimmery cloth that may or may not have been some form of Christmas decoration. Bowls of the kind of crisps Mim had missed on her travels squatted in the corners of the buffet, fencing in the rest of the fayre. Mim sneaked a Walker's Salt and Vinegar into her mouth, sucking every tangy drop of flavour from her fingertips. Sausage rolls, vol-au-vents stuffed with egg mayonnaise, crumbed chicken, bread sticks, creamy coleslaw, cheese-pineapple-hotdogs on sticks, carrot and celery, a four pack of dips and a huge plate of Party Rings ("*Sandra's favourites*") waited patiently for the guests to arrive. Mim had convinced her dad to add some chicken satay skewers and some spring rolls into the mix to spice things up a little.

"Well, you ate some fancy stuff on your travels!" Her dad grinned at her proudly.

She and Trisha had spent the afternoon baking a chocolate cake which had turned out surprisingly well, considering their history of failed dual-baking attempts. It boasted proudly from its centre spot on the table.

Happy birthday Sandro it read. Trisha had messed up the icing, but Mim could not, hand on heart, have said she could have done a better job with her spidery handwriting.

She licked a rogue salty crystal from her lip and smoothed down her dress. It was one that she'd picked up in Byron Bay and had seen a couple of pretty impressive sunsets, as well as having been indelicately manhandled by an enthusiastic Griffin. Mim blushed. He had been emailing daily, enthusing about her beauty and 'pulsating vibes'. The dress looked weird in her dad's living room, but it made her feel like a lovely thing, so she brushed the weirdness aside.

"Please be on your best behaviour tonight Wiggy. I'm planning a nice surprise for them."

Wiggy raised his eyebrows and folded his arms. "I shall be pretending that I am not here." He glanced back at the party tea laid out. "As indeed, I wish I were not."

Schubert nudged her hand with his big wet nose. She stroked his head, delighted to feel his coarse shaggy fur on her fingers once more. Wiggy stepped closer to Mim and Schubert let out a low growl, but it was half hearted.

"I think he's getting used to you, Wiggy." Wiggy shrugged, but grinned at the dog when Mim looked away.

The guests arrived in a steady stream: a mixture of local people Mim had known forever and Sandra's work friends. Mrs Dibley was there, sporting a mossy green velour tracksuit.

"I've taken up jogging," she told Mim over her Bucks Fizz. "Been the absolute making of me!"

People were curious about her trip, and asked her questions, but each of them were followed up with an uneventful story highlighting exactly how little had occurred in her absence. Had it always been this sedentary?

Mrs Jain told a riveting yarn about her son-in-law's investment in a bread making machine. Gladys Horspool had a great one about Mandy losing ten pounds after a nasty bout of gastroenteritis, only to put it back on again at an all-inclusive in Calella. Oddly, the mundanity thrilled her more than sharing any of her stories.

She was opening the second pot of dips that were two-for-one in Tesco when Colin sidled over.

"These spring roll things? Are they Chinese?"

"Um, I think they eat them in China. They eat them in Vietnam too. That's why I got them."

He nodded. "Right. Did you like China?"

"I didn't go to China."

"Of course." He let his eyes wander the room.

Mim had known Colin for years, but had only ever spent time with him in Trisha's presence. On the rare occasions they found themselves alone, they had close to nothing to say to one another. There was always palpable relief when Trisha returned from wherever they both wished she hadn't been. Mim had no idea what Trisha saw in him, but when her best friend talked about him doing something mundane and dull, she glimmered.

"Well, isn't this one a rare gem of a human, Miriam! Quite the debonair conversationalist!" Wiggy leaned in close to Colin's ruddy face and blew. Colin wrinkled his nose, like he had just smelled something bad. He shook his

head and took a bite of his spring roll. He chewed it
thoughtfully. Mim was about to find something else to be
doing when he looked at her with a directness she hadn't
seen in him before. "I'm glad you're back Mim."

"Oh?"

Colin nodded, a fleck of pastry clinging to his lower lip.
"Yeah. I…" He glanced from side to side like a bad
comedic spy. "You can't say, right?"

"Say what, Colin?"

"Like, because I'm going to ask Trish. But I know she'd
want to tell you first and stuff. So I thought I'd wait until
you were back. And you are!"

"Ask Trish…?"

"You know. Like, wife stuff."

Mim's mouth fell open. "You're going to… propose."

Colin shrugged. "Well yeah. I'll ask."

"Oh Colin! That's…what a…she's going to be so
happy!" Mim stretched out her arms to hug him, but he
clutched his can of Boddington's tightly to his chest, so she
patted his arms instead. "Do you know how you're going
to do it?"

He shrugged again. "I just will." He registered the
disappointment on Mim's face. "I just will. I know how to
say things to her."

She nodded. "I'm really happy for you. And I won't say
a word." He checked his watch and then picked up
another spring roll. He pointed it towards Trisha, a doughy
smile playing at the corner of his lips when she caught his
eye, and headed towards her.

"Gosh, Lord Byron must be terrified, Miriam. A
contender to his romantic throne!"

"I think it's sweet." She sipped her Bacardi and coke
and put it down on the table. "Right. I'm going to do this."

She clapped her hands. Everyone turned to look, apart from Mr Bindle from number 22 who was deaf as a squid and talking about the giant marrow he'd grown. Someone nudged him and he turned. Trisha switched the hi-fi down.

"Erm, I just want to say happy birthday to Sandra." Someone whooped. "And, er, well, this is for her."

Mim sat down at the dusty upright piano wedged in the corner. There were a few mumbles behind her. She zoned them out, lifting the lid and finding her place on the keys. She had called a tuner round a few days earlier, who had teased the ageing thing into the best sound it could muster.

"Plenty of life left in her yet," he'd exclaimed, patting her like an old donkey.

Mim cleared her throat and pressed the keys. The old instrument trilled lightly, and Mim gathered speed over the carnival toned notes. Sandra gasped.

"My song!"

Mim sang. "*Everything she touches bursts to life.*" Her hands skipped across the sweet tune. "*A rainbow and colours every-where.*" Her voice spun mellifluously, the room warming to its sound. "*Blues and greens, so debonair. My rainbow girl.*"

She glanced over her shoulder. Sandra was dancing with a woman in a fat crocheted shawl, jiggling in a way that only sixty-somethings can. Schubert was lacing himself hairily around their legs. Mrs Dibley was tapping her feet. Someone was explaining to Mr Bindle what was going on. Colin had Trisha wrapped in his meaty arms and she was laughing. Mim played on.

"*Have you seen her in that coat of red?*"

Wiggy stood by her side, eyes closed, head swaying. He looked peaceful. Mim wondered if he was thinking about Elspeth.

Mim glanced at her dad. He was perfectly still, smiling lightly, the rough beer mug her mother had made him in a pottery class clutched in his hand. Mim grinned. He bobbed his head in time with the music.

"Did you see her in that golden dress?" Mim took a few liberties, put her own stamp on it, but her audience were delighted. She felt as though she was inside a happy, psychedelic music box. They danced on, most of the guests now moving in some way on her dad's worn out carpet. *"My rainbow girl, la la la la!"* She finished with a flourish.

"Oh Mim! That was wonderful!" Sandra hugged her tight.

"Glad you enjoyed it. Oh, look! Someone's got a present for you over there."

Sandra skittered away, beaming.

Mim felt a hand on her shoulder. Her dad didn't look at her, his eyes on Sandra, unwrapping a big, green, bobbly cardigan.

"It's great to hear you playing again, Mim. It's been too long." Mim nodded. "You get more like her every day, you know?" He turned to her. "I'm so proud of you. She would have been too."

Mim took hold of his hands. "Well, I'm going to do something with my life now, you know? Really, really live it."

He smiled. "I know."

"Terry! What do you think?" Sandra was rotating in the lumpy knitwear. She looked like an avocado.

"Ravishing!"

Mim watched him go. "Come on Wiggy. Let's get a bit of fresh air."

WE'RE ALL FULL OF CAKE AND
WISHING THERE WAS MORE

Mim was getting into the flow. Lilting, classical notes cascaded from her fingertips across the ivory keys as the early guests spilled elegantly into the ballroom. The Steinway was set up in the corner. Large French windows allowed the incongruous November sun to warm the room, affording Mim unbroken views of the guests arriving at Candleford Hall.

The first of the throng were milling about, kitten heels clacking discreetly on the parquet floor. It was so shiny, Mim had slipped twice on her way in. The early arrivals were neatly dressed, though there were a few vaguely outlandish hats on view, including one that looked like a pretzel. She hoped to get a photo of that one to show Trisha later.

The music was flowing out, as though her fingers were quite separate to the rest of her.

She had never been in a place like this before: even the rest of Candleford Hall paled into mundanity in comparison to the ballroom. It was like something out of a fairy story. Gleaming chandeliers hung from the gilt ceilings, classical paintings faded into the recesses between the cornices. Mim wanted to lie on the floor to look at them properly. The walls were adorned with a thick brocade wallpaper in a coppery-golden hue. Elegant chairs sat soldier-like in rows, ready to gently caress the buttocks of the English aristocracy, while ensuring that they maintained finishing-school posture. Peachy-pink tea roses nestled between their white counterparts perched on stands around the room, and the table that would serve as an altar was strewn with more roses and dark green foliage.

Mim's wedding had been nothing like Octavia's: she and Steven had got married in a hotel, in a room that was technically a 'medium sized conference room' and Mim's walk up the aisle had been short. Not that she minded. She had been a bit embarrassed about all of those people staring at her, but the long, thick, cream carpet that would mark Octavia's journey into married life was oddly inviting.

"This must be the husband, Miriam." Wiggy nudged her as a tall, willow thin man shook hands with some of the guests. He was breathtaking, skin like a polished stone and a smile that ended in neat dimples. His manner was easy, confident and very attractive. Wiggy guffawed. "Old Diggers must hate him! Brilliant!"

The groom waved to Mim and she felt colour rush to her cheeks. She took a deep breath and settled back into the notes.

"So many familiar, ghastly faces," murmured Wiggy as the rest of the congregation filed into their seats. "Oh look, the butler is signalling you."

Mim slowed the piece she was playing to a gentle halt, paused momentarily, then softly launched into the *Clair de Lune* opening. The groom moved into position with his best man. The guests rose from their seats, arcing necks to be the first to glimpse the bride.

Over the standing crowd, Mim could not see the bride's entrance, but Wiggy gasped, bracing himself on her shoulder.

"She's here," he breathed.

"I know, that's why I'm playing this," she whispered back.

"No. *She's* here!"

Mim played on, as Octavia reached the front of the ballroom. Instead of carrying a bouquet, the bride had chosen to push her grandfather's wheelchair and she leaned to kiss him tenderly on the cheek. Digby Bullhorn looked momentarily flushed, though a quick glance at Theo reinduced his customary scowl.

Theo took Octavia's hand, and they glimmered in a square of early afternoon sunlight slipping through the window. Mim softened the music, letting it discreetly trickle away like Mrs Hunter had taught her.

"She is here, Miriam!" Wiggy was gripping the flesh on her shoulder tightly. She slid a hand up to remove it, but Wiggy clung on. "Can't you see her?" His eyes were wild.

Mim shrugged. Everyone could see Octavia: she was the bride in an explosion of lace.

"Elspeth." He whispered it at first. "Elspeth. Oh Elspeth."

"Where?" The registrar, bride, groom and entire front row of assorted bridesmaids and ushers glared at her. She coughed, grinned apologetically and looked at the ceiling.

"Behind Octavia. She has her hand on her back, and she's still so beautiful and graceful and, oh God, Miriam! She is looking directly at me. Can you see her? Why can you not see her?"

Mim couldn't see anything behind Octavia except the quivering wattle bunching up around the major's chin.

"This place, in which we gather, has been sanctioned by law to permit the celebration of marriages." The registrar was a nasal man with a bald, bumpy head. "We are gathered here today to witness the matrimony of Theodore Mwangi to Octavia Millicent Elspeth Veronesi-Bullhorn, and I am sure that they are all delighted that you could all join them here to celebrate their special day."

Bullhorn didn't look delighted. He looked like he might pop, which Mim found vaguely amusing. Wiggy did look delighted. In fact, he looked rapturous. His hand still pressed hard on her collarbone, a minor tremor shuddering through it, but his face was soft. Lips parted, the slight clench that he always carried in his jaw was gone. His eyes were bright. Mim had never seen him look like that before. He was younger, nicer looking, less grey.

The nasal registrar went on for quite some time, broken up by Theo and Octavia's nervous giggles as they stumbled their way sweetly through their self-penned, slightly cryptic vows. Wiggy quivered throughout, eyes not wavering from the spot directly behind Octavia. Mim squinted, but couldn't see anything, apart from the watery silver wiggles that appeared when she looked into the sun for too long.

"It gives me great pleasure to declare that you are now legally married."

Mim took her cue to launch into the second part of *Clair de lune*, her favourite part to play. The guests applauded politely as Octavia and Theo made their way back down the aisle as a pair. They giggled and grinned at one another, waving at friends, Octavia flashing her ring with a gorgeously dorky smile. The guests filed out after them, chatting cheerily. Wiggy remained still, gazing at the spot where Octavia had stood just a few moments earlier.

Mim played until the last guests filed out, circling through the most romantic pieces she knew until the staff came in to set the room for the reception. She lifted her hands from the keys and folded them in her lap.

Wiggy clapped his hands together and nodded. "Of course! I will be waiting for you."

Mim raised her eyebrows, awaiting an explanation, but Wiggy's eyes were moving slowly up the aisle and towards the door. He pressed his fingers to his lips, fluttering them away in the tiniest of waves.

"Well?"

He wrapped both of her hands in his. His cheeks were the colour of uncooked salmon. "Oh Miriam! She is here." He sighed. "She will meet us in the rose garden. She has something to do first. We should go there now."

She squeezed his hands. "Let's."

49

THE ROSE

Mim shivered under a trellis arch hugging her Marks and Spencer's pashmina around her. Although the sky was still bright, the naked rose bushes snuggling into shadows were jacketed in a layer of glinting frost.

She and Wiggy had just arrived in the walled rose garden. Wiggy jiggled antsily. His eyes did not waver from the tall hedge pillars that, in the summer, would be festooned with roses, cocooning them from the watchful gaze of Candleford Hall. The bareness of the shrubberies afforded Mim a tantalising view of the house, pumpkin-spiced light spilling from every window.

Mim glanced at Wiggy. His lips moved slightly, as though murmuring a prayer. "Wiggy..." she began, but trailed off. A light flush spreading up to his temples and into his thin, grey hair suggested that she leave him to his thoughts. She pulled her shoulders up to trap some hair-warmth around her ears.

"Oh!" Wiggy's lips parted, eyes flashing. "Elspeth!"

Mim took a side step, but Wiggy's fingers gripped hers. Gently, he pulled her back towards him.

"You're really here." Wiggy's voice was a whisper, no more than a warm breath in the crisp air.

Mim studied her shoes, a puddly patch creeping up the side. She held her breath.

"You look…" His voice was oddly formal and stiff. Mim studied him. His brow was folded like an envelope. "…nice."

Mim rolled her eyes. Nice? A lifetime of unuttered passion and the best Wiggy could muster was 'nice'? She plucked a ball of fluff from her pashmina and watched it tumble to the mud.

"Lovely wedding," she heard Wiggy say. "Awfully long time." His trembling fingers were still gripping Mim's. "Octavia has turned out terribly well."

Mim gave his fingers a sharp tug.

"Yes, Miriam?"

Mim sighed. "Say what you mean Wiggy."

He coughed. "Right. Yes. Well, what I mean is, erm,…jolly mild winter we are having, would you say?"

"Wiggy!"

"Right." He licked his lips a few times, but no amount of lubrication seemed to help any words to form.

Mim pulled her hand from his and took him by the shoulders. "I don't want to embarrass you Wiggy, but you wasted your life not telling her how you felt when you were alive. Stop wasting time now! You have nothing to lose."

"Miriam I…oh, you think this is amusing too?" He turned his head. "Well, you know what? I…I…" He harrumphed like an obstinate donkey. "Yes, all right. I am useless at this. Miriam, Elspeth says that you are right. She too wishes I would get on and tell her what it is I need to tell her."

Mim grinned. He grinned back. "Well get on with it,

Wiggy!" She waved her arm at the sludgey puddle where
Elspeth stood, apparently oblivious or unaffected by under-
foot sogginess. She moved aside and he let her go this time.
She dusted a lone leaf from a bench and sat, feeling a cold
bite sneaking through her dress.

Wiggy held his hands in front of him, fingers curled
lightly like a scroll. Mim wondered how Elspeth was feeling
about the inevitable declaration of love. Was it welcome?
Would she nod politely and pat his hand? Or were these
the words she had died longing to hear?

Mim tried to tune out, to give Wiggy his privacy as he
had not-so-graciously done for her, but his soft laugh
floated on the breeze. His voice sounded young, and that
edge of vague disdain had disappeared entirely. Snatches
of their conversation reached her ears. She heard him say
"it was always you," followed by a deep sigh. She also
heard him say "never loved anyone else." Mim felt her
ventricles straining, and something close to either grief or
elation.

After a while, an odd, gasping whimper scurried
through the air. Mim looked sharply at Wiggy, his face
buried in his hands. "Please don't go." He whispered.
"Don't leave me!" Mim leapt from the bench and started
towards him.

Let him have this, Mim.

She stopped. Was that her voice? Or someone else's?

He needs this.

Mim moved back to the bench and sat stiffly, ready to
wait for as long as it took.

50

YOU BELONG AMONG THE
WILDFLOWERS

Mim pulled the covers up to her armpits and settled back against the slightly lumpy cushions. Wiggy sat at her side, staring vacantly into the lamplit room. She patted his hand that was lying languidly beside her.

"If you want to talk, I'm all ears."

The wedding party was still going on, sounds of general merriment dancing up the stairs, but Mim had made her excuses soon after they returned from the rose garden and headed up to bed. Not before her diary had become stuffed with bookings to play at though: another wedding, a bar mitzvah and a 'debutante event' whatever that may be.

Wiggy flashed her a small smile, but it didn't reach all of the way to his eyes. Mim remembered something Griffin had told her about 'holding space', which seemed like the right thing to do in a slightly uncomfortable situation. She wasn't sure how to go about holding space so she made her head repeat the sentence 'I am holding space for you,' over and over again.

"Miriam, what in Pete's name are you doing?"

She opened her eyes and uncreased her face. She had been concentrating really hard. "I'm holding space for you."

"Lawks! Did you learn this from the rainbow-vomiting scarecrow? What utter codswallop is 'holding space'?"

Mim shrugged, but smiled. "I don't know. You looked like you needed me to...hold...space."

They both snorted.

"Miriam, I may be a little pensive, but I am absolutely fine and dandy." He shifted his body so that he was facing her. "Actually, I am more than well. I did something I should have done a very long time ago. And I can lament my foolishness all through the afterlife, or I can celebrate that I finally did it. I choose the latter."

Mim hugged Wiggy tightly.

"Steady on Miriam!"

When she pulled away from him, her eyes were damp. "I'm proud of you."

"I am proud of us both." He moved over to the other side of the bed. "Now, switch off that lamp Miriam. Tomorrow is a brand new day, and it ought to be seized after much rest."

Mim stretched over and flicked the switch on the heavy brass lamp. The room was plunged into darkness. She settled back, suddenly exhausted.

"Miriam?"

"Yes?"

Beyond the silence of the room was the faintest trickle of jazz. She could hear Wiggy's soft breath. She wondered if he had fallen asleep.

"What a grand adventure we have had."

Mim laughed. "Yep. It's been epic so far." Wiggy didn't reply. "Goodnight Wiggy."

"Goodnight Mim."

And Mim drifted off to sleep thinking: *he's never called me Mim before.*

51

ALL BY MYSELF

Mim stretched. A band of weak morning light had found its way through a chink in the heavy velvet curtains and lay in propriety across her eyes like a superhero mask. She blinked, then, putting off waking for a little longer, scrunched her lids together. She shifted, shrugging off the light-mask and letting her eyes soften into the darkness once again.

Her mouth felt a little sandpapery. "Wiggy," she croaked. "Is there water by the bed?"

Thick silence yawned back at her. She snuggled deeper under the covers. Water could wait. Her sleep was heavy, warm and delicious. She sank in, but a tickly little cough rattled her out of it. She dragged herself to sitting and stretched blindly for the glass. The water felt tepid, but she slugged it down, quashing the cough before it had time to shake through her throat again. She sighed.

"Wiggy? Did my cough wake you?"

Evidently not, she thought at the gaping quiet. She flicked on the bedside lamp, checking to see whether the light had woken him.

The space beside her was empty.

"Wiggy?"

She scrambled to the other side of the bed, leaning to see if he had fallen on the floor.

"Wiggy?"

Mim peered under the looming frame. A couple of dust bunnies blinked back at her, but the space was distinctly Wiggy-free.

She jumped out of the bed and stood in the middle of the room, arms extended to her sides like an aeroplane. She rotated slowly, pyjama sleeves billowing. Feeling nothing, she dropped her arms to her side.

"Wiggy?"

She stared at the bed, wondering if her eyes weren't working properly, or if she was still asleep. How was this possible? She flung the curtains open, whipping round, getting tangled in the thick yield of them.

The bed stared back at her, still empty. The crumpled covers dipped towards the floor like icicles on a frozen waterfall: something interrupted.

"Wiggy! If you're hiding, this isn't funny. Come out!"

Her own voice echoed back to her. It sounded frightened and young.

"Wiggy!" It came out as a sob. She crumpled into a heap on the floor - a small island in a thickly carpeted sea.

By ten am, Mim was dressed, packed and thrumming as though filled with a thousand locusts.

Wiggy was gone.

It seemed that was true.

She repeated his name under her breath while dressing.

Her eyes flitted hopefully as she packed. She revisited the rose garden, calling his name under the suspicious gaze of a muddy gardener.

There was no sign - no sight, no sound. She even stood by the trellis arch, whispering Elspeth's name into the wind. Only some mournful pigeons replied.

Mim breakfasted with the other guests, but she was too confused to eat any of the shiny pastries laid out on the dining table. Instead, she swallowed some bitter coffee, which made her even more jittery.

Victor, Theo's best man and colleague from the hospital chatted amiably, marvelling over the architecture of the house. Mim grinned politely, but her eyes continued to scan the room for Wiggy. She felt like she had an arm missing.

"So you see, it really would be a most splendid opportunity for them."

"Mmm, yes."

"And if you could do, say a month, they would have some confidence before striking out on their own." Victor bit into a flaking pastry, custard oozing from its centre.

"Mmhmm. Mmhmm." Mim nodded. She jumped as a waiter caught her arm with the edge of a silver tray.

"Are you quite well, Mim?" He tilted a concerned head. "Only, you seem a little agitated."

She forced out a long breath. "I'm fine, Victor." She smiled too widely.

He regarded her carefully, then, evidently deciding that she was fine enough to continue speaking to, went on. "So, when will you come?"

"Oh!" Mim had no idea what he was talking about. "Erm, I suppose...I, I don't know."

"Of course, of course. I understand. You're a busy woman. Check your diary and let Occy know."

"Right. I will."

Octavia hugged Mim as she left.

"I'm so excited, Mim!"

"Of course you are. You just got married!"

Octavia bounced on the balls of her toes. "No, silly goose! About you coming to Malawi for the music workshops. Victor said that you were keen to come for a full month."

"He did?'

"Come in May when it's drier. You can stay with Theo and I. My *husband* and I!" She clapped her hands together and giggled.

"Right." Mim supposed she could go to Malawi for a month. There was nothing stopping her, now she was a seasoned traveller. But she couldn't imagine travelling anywhere without Wiggy.

Mim's eyes swept the hallway, seeking him out once more. They settled on a formal looking portrait of Bullhorn, Elspeth and an apple-cheeked Octavia.

The blushing bride's eyes clouded for a moment when she saw what Mim was looking at. "Yes. I wish Grandmama could have seen me."

"Oh, but she did."

"What do you mean?"

"She walked down the aisle with you. Had her hand on your back all through the ceremony."

"Did you…" Octavia glanced around her "…see her?"

"No." Mim shook her head. "But she was there.

Trust me."

Octavia gripped Mim's hand. "I felt it. A warm patch just here." She laid Mim's hand at the bottom of her spine. "Is she still here?"

Mim took another sweep around the hallway. "I think she's gone, Octavia."

Octavia nodded, a jewel of a tear glimmering in the corner of her eye. She pulled Mim in for a final hug, holding her for a bit too long. "See you in Malawi."

———

Mim's eyes barely registered the streaky grey landscape beyond the train window. It had started to rain torrentially when she boarded, and although the carriage was warm, she shivered in her houndstooth blazer.

The seat beside her was vacant and she kept turning to it expectantly. *Surprise!* she kept hoping Wiggy would holler, *I figured out invisibility!* At one point she fell asleep, rocked into a sad slumber by the train, declaring on waking "have we missed Durham?" to a confused stranger. The man wedged headphones in his ears and held up his newspaper like a shield against her. She seethed with resentment. *That's Wiggy's seat.* She felt as though someone had taken an ice cream scoop to her innards. *Why did he leave her?*

Trisha's fishwife logic hammered in her head. *Well, at least you can shower without some posh git there! Poo in peace! Get your jollies with a hottie!* She smiled in spite of herself. It didn't feel like liberation though. Not yet.

She stretched and plucked the stiff triangular sandwich packet she had picked up at Kings Cross from her bag. Starving to death wouldn't help. Though, she surmised, it might let her actually see Wiggy again.

52

NOTHING COMPARES

The early morning dew clung delicately to blades of grass like shy crystals. The sun was just beginning to poke his head out from under the covers and Mim found herself standing still to watch the coral light bleed into the grey.

Something wet touched her finger and she rubbed Schubert's big head. He gazed up at her with adoration before snuffling a confused snail by the path.

Mim had been living in Newcastle for a couple of months and was loving the fresh air and green spaces that the city was so proud of. Jesmond Dene was her favourite, with its pixie-bridges and stepping stones, and Schubert seemed pretty delighted with the arrangements too.

She checked her watch. She had got back late last night after playing at a fancy company dinner at the Thistle Hotel, but thankfully, her new flat was only a few minutes stroll from there. She yawned, looking forward to a cup of tea and a biscuit before filling out the forms for her Malawi visitor visa.

"Come on Schubes." She tripped across the stepping stones that made her feel like a hobbit. Schubert usually just bounded straight through the stream, but today, he was standing on the bank. Mim fake-sighed and jumped back across the stepping stones to retrieve him. A faint grumble vibrated in his throat, his head stretching forwards. "Schubes?" She looked at the ivy-clothed wall Schubert was staring at. "See, nothing there." She rubbed his head and hooked his leash back onto his collar. "Let's go."

Back at her flat, she set the kettle straight to boil. She opened her notebook and scanned the list of documents that she needed for the application. Everything was there in a nice folder on her laptop, including the invitation letter from her hosts. The formality of Octavia's letter was in contrast with her giddy emails, but she had added a cheeky little line in there about Mim as an archetypal 'English rose', which would apparently go down very well with the visa officials.

She poured water onto the Tetley tea bag and leaned back against the kitchen counter. She sighed into the space that she had fallen in love with at first sight. The living and kitchen area had windows on two sides, one of which framed the majestic St Nicholas' Cathedral like a picture in a gallery. A small curved window nestled into the corner between them where Mim had chosen to place a pretty antique chair she had found at a flea market. It was her favourite place to sit. The morning light seeped through the windows, carpeting the oak floorboards in a buttercup glow. Her small bedroom was equally light-drenched, and a neat modern bathroom finished the place off. True, it was tiny, but it was all hers and she had decorated it with souvenirs from her travels.

If a place could be a person, she thought, *this place was definitely her.*

She poured the milk into her tea and waggled the bag around for a bit before dunking it in the bin. She put a few Crunch Creams on a plate and stepped over a slumbering Schubert, dreaming with his big head resting on his paws. Settling into her chair, she flopped open her laptop and clicked on the bookmarked page. She just had to upload all of the documents and then this was done. In just over a month, she would be on her way to Malawi to run music workshops for patients at Octavia and Theo's hospital.

Schubert barked. Mim giggled, as she often did when he sleepbarked. He leapt unsteadily to his feet and galumphed to the front door.

"What's up Schubes?" He pushed his nose up to the frame and emitted a low growl. "It's probably just the neighbours. Come here."

He didn't come here. He stayed there and the growl became a snarl. Mim put down her laptop, wondering whether or not to get up. Trisha was always telling her terrible stories about the crime rates in Newcastle and city girls being attacked. Not that Trisha ever objected to a night out in the city with free accommodation. Mim shook her head. She wasn't fearful Mim: she was brave Mim who travelled the world and bluffed her way into stately homes and ran music workshops in Malawi.

She pushed herself up from her chair and went to Schubert. Gripping his collar in case he decided to jump on a pensioner, she eased the door open a crack. She couldn't see anyone. She pulled it fully open and stepped into the hall. It was still and very definitely empty.

"See Schubes, no one here." He gave her a suspicious frown, glanced up and down the hallway then stomped noisily inside. A breeze snaked in from somewhere, tickling Mim's neck. She shivered into her cardigan and stepped back inside.

Closing the door, something on the floor caught her eye. It hadn't been there before, she was certain. She picked it up. It was a postcard showing a black and white photograph of two old people laughing uproariously in the rain. Mim frowned, casting a suspicious look at the door.

She turned the postcard over to see a faint line of looping handwriting on the back. Squinting, she drew it to her face.

To grand adventures.

W x

She reached for the door handle, then stopped. She closed her eyes, fighting a small sob.

"Goodbye Wiggy," she whispered. "And thank you."

She tacked the postcard to her corkboard covered in pictures of her trip and went back to her chair. In the softly unfurling light of the morning, she began to prepare for Mim's Grand Adventure.

ABOUT THE AUTHOR

Jay lives on the Gold Coast with her fiancé, daughter and a dog called Duck. She is a prize winning short story writer whose micro, flash and short stories have been published in numerous publications and anthologies, including Unleash Lit Magazine, Cerasus Magazine, Leicester Writes and Fabula Nivalis. She won the 2022 Exeter Short Story Prize, Fabula Aestas 2023, the fifth Writers Playground challenge and is a two time winner of AWC's Furious Fiction. She was shortlisted for the 2022 Exeter Novel Prize and the 2023 Commonwealth Short Story Prize. Mim and Wiggy's Grand Adventure is her first novel.

www.jaymckenzieauthor.com

ACKNOWLEDGMENTS

Writing a book is hard. You immerse yourself in the world of your characters, grow with them, love them. Then the time comes to fling them out into the world, and, like a neurotic parent, you panic about your little darlings. When the first rejections come in, you take it personally, feel devastated for your baby, angry at the world for not loving it as hard as you do. Then, you find someone like Sarah Williams. I will forever be indebted to Sarah for seeing potential in my little darlings and loving them with me. Thank you, Sarah, for taking a chance on a little unknown like me and my merry band of fictional weirdigans.

When I started writing this novel (well, this version of it anyway), the Binklings had already nurtured its shy older sibling into existence (though she needs a complete makeover before she's ready to meet the world). Lynton Burger, Susan Perrow, Jenni Cargill-Strong, Vicky King, Ana Davies and Mitchell Kelly are the most wonderful writers group I could ever have hoped to be part of. Your encouragement, intelligence, wit and love have made this novel what it is, and it most definitely wouldn't exist without you. I used to boast about you in my dreams - now I get to do it in print.

To the wonderful staff at Ballina library, where a huge chunk of this was written. Thank you for your lovely writing space, kindness and patience, especially when, after being a member for years, I still couldn't figure out the printing process.

This book is also a lovesong to the joys (and trials) of travelling, which I have been lucky enough to do plenty of. Massive thanks to my various travel companions, many of whom have inspired stories that make an appearance in this novel. Helen Telford, Deborah Laverick, Wendy Tuck, Claire Hamilton, Laura Leeks, Katie Evans, Larissa Green, Adri Valkering, Kristin Sakuth, Liam Brennan, Joe Gimblett, Sara Melville, Veena Mistry and Charlotte Freeland are just some of my fellow travellers whose company has been inspiring.

A big thanks to Dawn Morris and Phil Shayer for their excellent advice on pianos.

Behind every writer is someone who made them believe it was possible. My high school English teacher Malcolm Davison went the extra mile to make me feel seen, and it will never be forgotten. I have spent much of my adulthood dreaming of publishing a novel so that I can thank him in the most meaningful way possible. Sadly, Malcolm passed away a few years before I got this chance. I hope that his wife Wendy and daughter Joanne see this and understand what an impact he had on me.

Every writer needs someone to champion them, and I am beyond lucky to have a group of people who have given me unwavering support and encouragement. Many thanks to Anne and Les Kranicz and Lucy Hughes for always celebrating and sharing my little wins. Your encouragement means the world to me.

I am privileged to have wonderful parents Tom and Carol McKenzie. You instilled in me a love of reading, encouraged my writing at every turn and have celebrated my every little accomplishment as though I have won the Booker Prize. I love you so much. Thank you.

Finally, biggest thanks to my incredible fiancé Michael Kranicz and our beautiful daughter Abigail Kranicz. You are my everything. I love you both more than words can say. Go Team Awesome! You are my world.

MORE FROM SERENADE PUBLISHING

Brigadier Station Series

By Sarah Williams:

The Brothers of Brigadier Station

The Sky over Brigadier Station

The Legacies of Brigadier Station

Christmas at Brigadier Station (An Outback Christmas Novella)

The Outback Governess (A Sweet Outback Novella)

Heart of the Hinterland Series

By Sarah Williams:

The Dairy Farmer's Daughter

Their Perfect Blend

Beyond the Barre

A Dying Second Sun

by Peter A. Dowse

Winner Winner Chicken Dinner

by Sarah Jackson

A New Page

by Aimee MacRae

Middle Women

By Jack Garrety

For more information visit:

www.serenadepublishing.com

Printed in Great Britain
by Amazon

27745301R00205